BEHOLD!

ODDITIES, CURIOSITIES AND UNDEFINABLE WONDERS

EDITED BY DOUG MURANO

Let the world know:
#IGotMyCLPBook!

Crystal Lake Publishing
www.CrystalLakePub.com

Other Anthologies by Crystal Lake Publishing

COPYRIGHT ACKNOWLEDGEMENTS

CONTENTS

Undefinable Wonders

For Franny, who showed me that true miracles and real magic exist.

FOREWORD

WANNA SEE SOMETHING WEIRD?
Come on. This way . . .
Turn a page. Turn another.
Something weird. See?

We've got extraordinary. Touching. Devastating. Even profound.

Come on.

That's what you want, yeah? It's what I want pretty much all the time and it's definitely what I was hoping for when I saw the cover for this beauty of a book. Inspires something in you, doesn't it? Yeah. Almost like it activates the village of imps within, the unseen governors that direct you one way or another, that help you decide things. Like picking up this book. That cover. That title. And, if you'll follow me, the stories most of all.

Doug Murano is on a roll and for an editor to be rolling, it means he's got an eye. It's an eye for what he's looking for, yeah, and an eye for what he thinks is good, yes, but it's really an eye for *putting stories together*. That's the best part of *Behold! Oddities, Curiosities and Undefinable Wonders*. I'll tell you straight up that's the best part because by the end of this book, you'll find yourself reaching for a quilt that isn't actually in the room. Nope, it's not a physical quilt, but a woven thing nonetheless, a thing that's kept you warm for the

I

duration. If you're anything like me, you'll reach for it, and if you're a lot like me you'll still cover yourself up with it, long after you realize it's unseen, unreal, and that it was the stories, after all, that warmed up the room all along. Lovers of short stories, and, specifically, those of us who devour horror shorts, we know the power, the promise, of any anthology we pick up.

Will this be the sort of book that grips you by the shirt and tosses you into the fray, ready-or-not-here-I-come? Yes. This *is* that kind of book. And yet, the images you'll find within are much more tangible than the animatronic beasts and witches that wait for you in a traveling house of horrors. There's no crappy lighting in here to make you squint your eyes, no track-car moving too fast, no loud music to distract you.

That leaves you and your mind, you know. Nothing between. Just you, the writers, and your mind.

Come on.

This way.

We've got curiosities. We've got wonders, too.

And that's how you like it. That's how we all like it.

Did you know a man with tentacles wanders these pages? And so does a woman who discovers she's able to crush powerful men with her imagination? Wanna meet them? Yeah, sure you do. Hell, I'd like to get coffee with them in an all-night diner and talk about oddities. Talk about wonders. About desire.

There's a lot of desire in this book, these pages, a lot of *want*. Erinn Kemper's brilliant "In Amelia's Wake" gives us a boy who wants to marry a girl who seeks adventure in her life, not unlike Amelia Earhart herself, whose fateful plane the boy and his brothers stand guard over and who wanted quite a bit of adventure herself. John F.D. Taff's "A Ware That Will Not Keep" stars a young man who wants to destroy the evil in his way. And yet, sometimes that's a dangerous idea, isn't it: exacting revenge? For, as in the beloved film "Pumpkinhead," sometimes the beast to whom you say "sick 'em" doesn't know when to stop sicking 'em.

Yes, there's a lot of *want* in this book. A lot of craving. A lot of appetite. And yet, no vampires. No. In fact, the second half of this book's title sums up the lot you're about to encounter rather well: *Oddities, Curiosities, and Undefinable Wonders.* How else to describe the Kindred in Sarah Read's subterranean "Through Gravel"? Edith in Kristi DeMeester's "The Wakeful"? The titular Jacqueline Ess in Clive Barker's classic story "Jacqueline Ess: Her Will and Testament"? These may sound like mere titles to you now, but soon you will know them. You will know them well.

Come on.

This way.

Let's go look at something haunting.

The train-hopping duo of Brian Hodge's masterful "The Shiny Fruit of Our Tomorrows" sure as shit wants something. They want something big, and they're willing to travel across the country to see if it's still there for the having. The knight in Neil Gaiman's superb "Chivalry" is after the biggest score of all. And Patrick Freivald's Jamie wants and then gets "Earl Pruitt's Smoker." Oh, the places she goes.

But this book isn't about being "careful what you wish for." This book is about being drawn to the implied, unspoken, second half of that statement: The writers in *Behold!* seem to start when things have already been twisted.

Come on.

You'll see what I mean.

The book's cover may inspire images of men and women entering curio marts, underhanded deals with shadowy pawn brokers, people purchasing things they shouldn't have. And yet, aside from John Langan's "Madame Painte: For Sale" (scary, this one), the sought-after emporiums in *Behold!* cannot be found at First and Main; here, the pawn shop packed with mystifying matter is the *world*. And isn't that just the truth?

Don't we all want oddities?

Curiosities?

Undefinable wonders?

Hell, I do. You do, too.

Behold.

Follow me.

This way.

Maybe the cover and title have you thinking of sideshows instead. You pick up the book and it feels something like buying a ticket to the kind of show that includes parting curtains and feelings of guilt for having contributed to the caging of aberrations. And yet, aside from Lisa Morton's stirring "LaRue's Dime Museum," the stories herein aren't so much sideshow as they are front and center.

Wanna know a secret? The freaks you'll find in here are the *writers* themselves. The guys and girls bold enough and enthusiastic enough to put pen to paper, to write, as Brian Kirk did with the heartbreaking "Wildflower, Cactus, Rose," the best pocket-symphonies they could. It might not take a freak to spot a freak, but it sure as hell takes one to make these ideas accessible. It's the fantastical writer-mind that can see both things happening at once: the undefinable . . . defined. The two poems by Stephanie Wytovich encapsulate this idea perfectly and add pepper to, say, Hal Bodner's "The Baker of Millepoix," perhaps giving Bodner's pastries just what they needed to procure miracles indeed.

Behold.

Richard Thomas's parable-pastoral "Hiraeth" reminds us that there's good reason Mom and Dad say don't stick your hand in every cookie jar you come across and Ramsey Campbell's "Fully Boarded" makes you wanna reach into that cookie jar of a story and assist Warden yourself.

So much to see here. So much to *be* here.

Let's go.

Where Murano really excels is in his ability to juggle light and dark, the track-listing, so to speak, of this album. Take Lucy Snyder's "Hazelnuts and Yummy Mummies," a story written for writers and deviants alike (I am both. You might be both, too.); Snyder makes you laugh, hard, then gently turns you around, shows you the heart of the matter, and by the end of her tale your chuckles have molted into sobs. Christopher Coake pulls off a similar sleight-of-hand with "Knitter" (scary as hell, this one), wherein his delightful village is inhabited by something unfair enough to drive you mad.

If you think about it too much.

Which I am. Which you will do, too.

There's a line in Coake's story that serves as an anthem for the book as a whole: "You will turn a page; you will fold another world across this one . . . "

And so you will, as the unseen quilt of this collection is woven, you will turn the pages and behold . . .

JOSH MALERMAN
Michigan, May 2017

ODDITIES

LaRue's Dime Museum

LISA MORTON

LIVE ON STAGE
THE HUMAN SQUID

THE FIRST THING in the old photo that caught Julia's eye was the banner strung across the rear wall of a small stage. It took her a few seconds to realize that the tall man standing in front of the banner had appendages that looked like tentacles pushing up around the sides of his 1940s-style shirt and double-breasted jacket.

There were more banners, all sporting whimsical lettering in a curving style long obsolete.

MR. INSIDE–OUT
APPEARING DAILY

Next to the man with tentacles was a smaller performer whose skin glistened darkly, highlighting the whites of his eyes and his bared teeth. Although the glossy photograph was in black and white, Julia guessed the dark color was a deep crimson red . . . like blood.

SEE CONUNDRA
WORLD'S GREATEST CONTORTIONIST

The woman to the far right of the stage stood with her back to the audience, hands on her hips, and her head, smiling, sitting between her shoulder blades facing the camera.

LARUE'S DIME MUSEUM

Between Conundra and Mr. Inside-Out stood a small, dapper African American man, grinning proudly, one arm around the contortionist. The stage the quartet stood on was raised perhaps three feet, lit by bare overhead bulbs dangling at the end of wires, surrounded by banners proclaiming their unusual attributes.

Julia felt one brief stab of guilt at being so fascinated by the image. It was no longer politically correct to gawk at . . . what had they called them back them?

Human oddities?

Sideshow attractions?

Freaks?

But she couldn't deny that the photo exerted a pull on her. It wasn't just the performers, nor even the quaint banners and the cheap stage, but also the composition and lighting of the photo. It was brilliant, bringing the subjects to life with rare skill. She turned the eight-by-ten over, saw a name written on the back—*Greta*. No last name, not enough to go on. Was that the photographer, the woman in the photo, or someone who had previously owned the photo?

She set the photo down on an old scuffed teak end

table with inlaid glass and thumbed through the rest of the photos and clippings in the handwoven basket. One more gem emerged: another large still obviously by the same photographer, showing the box office/entrance to "LaRue's Dime Museum." Inside a glass-and-wood cubicle papered with notices ("Dr. Mostel's World Famous Flea Circus!"), a bored clerk who couldn't have been more than twenty didn't even muster a hint of smile.

Once again, Julia was taken by the photographer's obvious gifts. She felt as if she knew that clerk, as if they'd often gone out for coffee, chatted about boys and college classes. Even though the photos dated back probably seven decades, Julia had *seen* this young woman's expression in the faces of baristas and social media junkies.

Julia picked up the two photos and turned to find the store's checkout counter. She hadn't really expected to buy anything when she'd come into Round Again Antiques; she'd only wanted to visit the new business in the neighborhood (even though they'd been open for two months now). She found the rest of the store unremarkable—a typical collection of termite-ridden cast-off furniture, American primitive art and hip reproduction tin signs—but she at least wanted to know more about these photos.

She spotted a thirtysomething with purple hair behind a wood-paneled desk and approached. "Excuse me," she said, holding the two stills out, "but I was wondering if you could tell me anything about these?"

The clerk examined the photos. "Oh, those! Yes, believe it or not, we're pretty sure that place used to be *this* place. We found those in an old file cabinet in the back when we took over this spot, and a maintenance guy who's worked here forever said he remembered LaRue's. He thinks it closed sometime in the '60s."

"Do you know the person whose name is written on the back?"

Shaking her head, the clerk answered, "Sorry, I don't. If you want those, I'll let them go for five each."

As the clerk rung up the purchase, she glanced at the photos again and laughed. "Wow, look at the guy with the tentacles. You don't think those could be real, do you?"

Julia shrugged.

That was the first time Julia saw the man with the tentacles.

Julia's shift at Java Jane's started every morning at 5 a.m., preparing the shop for a 6 a.m. opening and soon-after influx of downtown's government workers and bankers heading into their offices and cubicles. Julia didn't mind the time; in fact, she enjoyed the commute, driving through L.A.'s quiet pre-dawn streets, a world of shadowed doorways and sodium lights that reminded her of the film noir movies she loved.

She felt more comfortable in the black-and-white world of men in wide hats and black, wet pavement than she did in her own time. She'd been born and raised into a Southern California that gave success to the beautiful and the ambitious, and she was neither. When she'd seen the two photos in that basket at Round Again Antiques, what she'd immediately felt was a sense of *belonging*.

She'd Googled LaRue's Dime Museum, but there wasn't much to find. She learned that dime museums had once been popular attractions across the country, offering "lowbrow" audiences a mix of displays, freak shows, magicians, and even music. They'd largely died out by the mid-Twentieth-Century, undoubtedly replaced by a combination of changing morality, rising real estate values, and ubiquitous television.

LaRue's had started in 1888 as a series of tents on the outskirts of downtown. A year later, Walter LaRue moved his displays into a building at Eighth and Temple. The museum had apparently been popular clear into the '50s, long after the LaRues had died and sold it to "Slick" Charlie Johnson (who Julia guessed was the well-dressed man onstage with the performers). Slick Charlie had converted most of it into a game arcade by 1960, but it died with the rest of old L.A.'s glamour in the following decade, about the same time that once-elegant Bunker Hill had seen the last of its old Victorian mansions vanish. There was no mention in any of the articles on LaRue's of a "Greta."

Downtown L.A.—or DTLA, as some hipsters insisted on referring to it—was now one part faceless bureaucracy in shining towers, one part trendy artists' lofts, and one part Skid Row, where the discarded slept in cardboard boxes and rat-chewed blankets. Julia passed them all on her way into work. She felt sorry for the junkies, the handicapped, the vets, the unlucky, but at the same time she was thankful that Java Jane's was many blocks removed from the alleys and crumbling warehouses that formed the bulk of the homeless encampments. Java Jane's covered her monthly parking fees, in a structure across the street, so she didn't have to walk far to reach the shop.

This morning, she parked and hurried to the nearest crosswalk; she'd slept badly, had finally dozed off and then overslept, so she was a few minutes late. She didn't see any sign of her usual work partner Gabriel, though, so she decided to wait for the light to change rather than risk (as she often did) dodging across the wide street illegally.

As she stood on the corner, she noticed a man standing in the doorway of the office building next to Java Jane's. The man was backlit by a single overhead light in the entryway, so it was difficult to make out details, but he seemed to be wearing a long coat. A trench coat, in fact, like the ones in old movies. His head was bare, but something about his neck—was he wearing a bulky scarf? Did he have something draped around his neck?

As she stared, he stepped forward, into the dull overhead light of a sodium lamp, and Julia saw what wound around his neck: tentacles. Or at least they were tentacle-like, long fleshy appendages about as thick as two of her fingers. And they were moving slightly, as if caught in a breeze, except they all moved independently of each other. There seemed to be six, or—no, eight.

He was the man in the photo. The Human Squid.

No, Julia thought, her heart picking up speed, *that's not possible. He'd be a hundred years old. This man isn't even bent.*

His head swiveled slightly, gazing up and down the street—and then his eyes fixed on her.

Julia's pounding heart froze. She locked eyes with him—*The Human Squid*—as a rush of emotions coursed through her. Fear, yes, and dread, of what might happen next . . . what if he stepped into the street, came toward her? She imagined him pulling her roughly into an embrace, those writhing lengths of flesh against her neck, her face—

Her paralysis broke when the rumbling of a bus sounded. It crossed between them, an early morning Metro already packed with riders, cutting off her view of the man. The bus slowed, only for a second, surely not long enough to let anyone off or on, but when it moved on down the street the man was gone. Julia let out a shaky breath and gulped in air, her eyes still on the bus as it headed into the heart of the city. Where would he go? How could he take public transportation? Had those really been tentacles, or had she been deceived by light and shadow, like any sucker who ever bought a ticket for the sideshow and soon realized the mermaid was nothing but a mummified dolphin?

When her heart slowed again, the bus gone from view, she walked across the street and entered Java Jane's, almost relieved to be back among the mundane concerns of obligation.

When Julia returned home that afternoon, she tried to look up more information about LaRue's Dime Museum, but her phone had stopped functioning. She'd recently replaced the battery and knew it was fully charged, so the only other alternative was to take it in for repairs. Irritated, she tried to turn on her laptop, but it also failed.

What are the chances?

Instead, she pulled out the two photographs, examining them closely for clues. There was the Human Squid, gawky and angular except for the mass around his neck.

Julia was certain it was the same man she'd seen in the pre-dawn morning.

Had she misinterpreted the age of the photos? Could they have been recent, perhaps even staged? A play, a piece of performance art, a Halloween attraction?

No, she was sure they were authentic and decades old. They possessed the startling, harsh quality that cameras (and their flash bulbs) from the '40s had. The prices on the ticket booth ("Only 50¢!") were obviously obsolete.

In the photo, the Human Squid looked thirty years old. That would mean the man she'd seen earlier would have been a century.

Julia didn't sleep much that night.

She awoke at her usual time of four a.m. As always, she showered, dressed, had a piece of fruit as she stood before her second-floor living room window, looking out on Wilcox Avenue.

Julia was about to leave when two figures ambling along the sidewalk caught her attention. They were on her side of the street, moving toward her apartment building.

One was tall, with something massed around his neck.

The other man, smaller, wore a driver's cap, a dark jacket, light shirt, and chinos. The two seemed to be chatting, leaning toward each other as they walked.

When they reached Julia's building, they stopped.

She pulled back from the window, but not away. Moving to the side, she peeked around the vertical blinds.

They'd stopped beneath a street light that painted them in yellowish hues. The tall man had a circle of narrow, fleshy appendages around his neck. The other had dark red skin above his white shirt. After a few seconds, Julia realized it wasn't a shirt at all but bandages, wound horizontally around his torso. His wrists and fingers were similarly bound.

They didn't look up toward her. The one in the bandages was patting the pockets of his jacket. He found what he wanted, pulled out a package of cigarettes, shook one out, returned the rest to the pocket, and lit up. He sucked the smoke in, tilting his head up.

His face gleamed, as if moist. It was a deep crimson color.

The Inside-Out Man.

When he exhaled, his companion coughed in disapproval. The tentacles around his neck rose to wave the smoke away. The Inside-Out Man laughed and blew out more smoke.

He waved the cigarette in Julia's direction. Then both the Inside-Out Man and the Human Squid turned and looked up.

Julia had to stifle a scream. She stumbled back, certain they'd seen her. She started to move toward her phone, thinking to call the police, *anyone*, but remembered the phone didn't work. Should she rush to a neighbor's, ask for help? She realized that she didn't know any of her neighbors, only the manager, who was rarely around. And what would she say? That two human oddities from eighty years ago were looking up at her as they smoked in the street?

She waited for several minutes, willing her pulse to slow. At last she crept, slowly, back to the window and risked a look out.

The crimson man was just stubbing out the cigarette with a foot. He and his friend turned and walked away down the street, nonchalant, as if they were completely at home in a world where they shouldn't exist.

Before heading down to the parking garage, Julia walked to the front of the building, where the two men had just been standing. If she'd needed proof that what she'd just seen hadn't been a dream or hallucination, there was the lingering scent of tobacco in the air. She looked down and saw something on the sidewalk. She knelt to see what it was, and only the short, tan end showed it to be a cigarette butt, flattened into the concrete—and covered in blood. Julia poked it with a finger and immediately regretted the act—the blood was warm and sticky. She wiped her finger tip on her pants leg, and, resisting an urge to rush back to her apartment, lock the door, and spend the next hour scrubbing her hands, she headed for her car in the building's parking garage. When she pulled out onto the street she looked for them, but they were gone.

She knew she'd see them again.

That afternoon she drove to the phone store, located in a strip mall, where she'd bought her phone.

Every space in the strip mall was vacant. It looked new, as if it had just been renovated. There was a liquor store next to the mall that Julia remembered going into for a bottle of water. She went in, picked out a cheap bottle of wine, and asked the clerk when the phone store had moved out.

"I don't know anything about a phone store," he said in a thick Middle Eastern accent.

Julia didn't pursue it. The only person who ever called her, aside from robot salesmen, was her mother, who wasted the data charges complaining about her life or Julia's. Julia decided she could live without that for a few more days.

She spent that evening with the wine, gazing at the photos. The photographer's skill at capturing the scenes captivated her, caused her to fall into the world of LaRue's Dime Museum all over again. It was a world she felt comfortable and happy in.

By the end of the evening she'd decided (albeit drunkenly) that the photographer was the key. But how could she find out more? Was it "Greta"?

In college, Julia had been on exactly two dates (neither had led to a second). One had been with a young man named Ivan who had been obsessed with photography. He'd taken her to an exhibit at the Mulholland Museum that she'd found thoroughly boring, but which he found so fascinating that Julia began to suspect there might be something wrong with him.

The next day was her day off. By 11 a.m. she was waiting in an office at the Mulholland Museum, a chic modern structure located in the hills above Westwood, to speak to the museum's associate director of collections.

Catherine Deane turned out to be an affable fortysomething whose natural elegance was so unattainable to Julia that she couldn't even feel envious. Catherine (and Julia knew instinctively that no one *ever* called this woman "Kate" or "Kathy") met her in the museum's lobby and led her to an office cluttered with bookcases and photos spread out across a long work table.

"I understand you have some interesting material," she said, after they were seated.

Julia handed her a manila folder with the photos. "I hope so."

Catherine opened the envelope, withdrew the photos, eyed them critically for a few seconds, turned them over— and gaped. "Oh my God," she said, softly.

"What?"

"I'm sure these are Greta Hoffman's work."

"I'm sorry, I don't know her."

Catherine rose, scanned her bookcases, and plucked out a hefty coffee table book she handed to Julia. The book was labeled *Greta Hoffman: 1943-1956*. The cover showed a photo of old downtown L.A., when the theaters were vital and hadn't yet become flophouses or abandoned curiosities, when men wore fedoras and women stylish dresses. The image centered on a little girl, eating a chocolate ice cream cone, her chin and cheeks smeared, while her mother stood over her, looking down with a mixture of disapproval and amusement; behind and around them was Broadway Avenue, packed with pedestrians and old cars, the whole scene bursting with life.

Even though the subject matter was completely different, Julia recognized the similarity to her photos immediately. The slightly off-kilter framing, the contrast between the little girl's pale face and the chocolate, the excitement and glamour of the city . . .

Julia flipped through the book, seeing page after page of extraordinary shots, many of L.A. in the '40s and '50s, but nothing else showing LaRue's. As she scanned the book, Catherine moved up behind her. "Greta Hoffman is one of photography's great unsung heroes, or I guess we should say unsung heroines. We don't really know much about her: she was born in Germany, left when Hitler rose to power and found her way to New York, where she got work as a nanny. She'd only been there for a few months when the couple she was working for relocated to Los Angeles. She came with them and ended up spending the rest of her life here. When she died in 1962, they cleared out her apartment and found thousands of photos; it turned out that Greta, who never married, had a secret passion for photography. The photos were boxed and stuck away for fifty years, but found in an attic a few years ago and brought to us. Now Greta's a *cause célèbre* more than half a century after her death."

Julia flipped the book to the back. On the rear dust jacket flap was a grainy photo of a plain-looking woman dressed in a severe black dress and matching hat. The photo was captioned *Greta Hoffman in 1952.*

Catherine leaned over her desk, picked up Julia's photos—almost tenderly—and examined them again. "I know Greta's work very well and I've never seen these before. Where did you find them?"

"I bought them in an antiques store downtown. They said they'd found them in a box when they took over the space."

Squinting at the photos, Catherine shook her head. "Extraordinary. Greta almost never even showed her photos to anyone, let alone gave them away." Looking up at Julia, she added, "I don't suppose you'd be interested in selling these? I'll make you an offer right now, if you're interested. Five thousand."

Julia blurted out in surprise, "Five *thousand*?"

"That's for each photograph, of course." When Julia didn't answer, Catherine added, "I'll be frank with you: you could probably get more if you go to auction—a *lot* more. But I would love to have these as part of our collection, and I can write you a check right now."

Julia sat back, trying to wrap her thoughts around what she'd just been offered. Ten thousand dollars? More if she went elsewhere? Why? Did other people experience the same thing she did when she looked at the photos— the sense of being drawn into another world?

She didn't want to live without that.

Reaching for the photos, Julia said, "Can I think about it?"

Catherine nodded, but not without a hint of resignation. "Of course."

Julia left with a business card, an astonishing offer, the photographer's name, and a renewed sense of the power of Greta Hoffman's art.

When she got home, she idly turned on the television, but none of her favorite channels was working. Only a few of the local channels came in, showing images blurred with lines of static. She'd have to remember to call her cable company from work tomorrow.

The next day at Java Jane's, she asked her co-worker Gabriel if she could borrow his phone. He gave her an odd look before passing her the handset from an old black dial phone mounted to the wall. Its presence didn't surprise her; it gave her only a moment of panic before she accepted it as the real, natural order of things.

Looking up from the phone, she glanced out the shop's front window and saw a woman waiting on the sidewalk, her back to the store. Something about her was familiar. Julia stepped from behind the front counter, curious. She ignored Gabriel when he asked, "Where you going?"

She stopped just past the counter. The woman was moving—or at least her head was, turning to look back into the store . . . and *turning* . . .

Her head turned all the way until it was aligned between her shoulders. She was blandly pretty, like a forgotten film ingénue. She saw Julia, smiled, and winked.

Julia stumbled back. As she turned, clumsy from shock, to move behind the counter, she barreled into her co-worker, who reached out to steady her. "Whoa, you okay?"

She looked up at Gabriel, a dark-skinned young man with a face that betrayed a losing battle with acne—and saw that her co-worker was now completely covered with tattoos. Every square inch, including his throat and the back of his hands, demanded attention with swirling, colorful designs. As she staggered back, he asked, "What's wrong with you?"

She fled the store, using the back door to avoid Conundra, the World's Greatest Contortionist.

On her drive home, she sensed that something was missing. Looking around the landscape of downtown Los Angeles, she finally pinpointed it:

The new skyscrapers—the bank buildings, all gleaming metal and glass—were gone. City Hall's iconic spire now loomed above everything. She saw nothing but old-model cars, men and women in out-of-style suits and dresses. She drove past the longstanding Clifton's Cafeteria, but it was Polynesian-themed.

She pulled up to a stoplight at the intersection of Seventh and Figueroa. The light was a strange design, with a sign that read "STOP." As it moved from red to green, the sign slid down while one reading "GO" slid up. When a car behind Julia honked, she hit the gas too sharply and her car lurched forward, slamming her back into the seat. She nearly rear-ended a 1943 Packard in front of her before braking, throwing her forward.

A few seconds later the car's engine died.

Julia coasted to the side of the street, pulling into a red zone. She tried turning the key three times while hitting the gas, but the car didn't even grind or click. It was simply incapable of functioning, like her phone or television.

She sat in the driver seat, gripping the wheel tightly while anxiety held her in a strangling grip.

What's going on? Am I crazy? What do I do now?

Looking around, she saw that the car had stopped almost in front of the Pantry, a restaurant she'd eaten in many times. The historic eatery was the one thing in the street completely recognizable, a rock standing against the river of time. Julia went to it, a desperate traveler seeking an oasis.

Inside, she was seated and handed a menu. The items listed were what she was used to—but they were offered at a fraction of the price.

When the waiter returned, Julia ordered coffee. Maybe it would help her sort things out, decide on a plan.

The coffee arrived—strong, black, reassuring. Julia wrapped both hands around the sturdy cup and stared down into the contents, as if she'd find an answer there.

"Excuse me . . . " A feminine voice with a slight accent interrupted. She looked up.

A woman with a black coat and hat stood over her, holding an old-fashioned, bulky camera, the kind with a fat glass lens and no LCD screen on the back. She spoke again, gesturing with the camera. " . . . would you mind if I took your picture?"

Julia set the coffee down and said, "You're Greta Hoffman."

The woman blinked in surprise. "I'm sorry, have we met?"

"No, but . . . I'm a fan of your work."

Greta frowned. "My work? How do you know my work?"

"I own two of your photos. In fact, someone just offered me a lot of money for them."

Emotions flickered across Greta's features—skepticism, hope, pleasure—and after a second she motioned at a chair across from Julia. "May I sit here?"

Julia nodded. Greta took the chair, placing the old-fashioned camera to one side of the table. Up close, without the confines of a blurry photograph, Julia saw that she'd been wrong to judge Greta Hoffman as plain-looking; her eyes in particular were extraordinary, creased lightly with humor and worry, the pupils ringed with rich hazel irises.

Greta cleared her throat, trying to speak, and Julia wondered if the other woman shared her astonishment at this meeting. "What is your name?"

"Julia—Julia Chandler." Julia almost extended a hand, but something told her not to, that Greta would frown on physical contact with someone she'd just met. "Your photographs are very special to me," Julia said, barely looking up. "They take me places."

"As all art should."

Now Julia did look up, and Greta was smiling at her. It was a smile of shared understanding, of secrets exchanged. Julia was about to say something when the waiter returned. "Can I get you something?"

Julia looked up—and couldn't stifle a gasp when she saw the waiter was tall, with a ring of tentacles surrounding his neck, poking out from over his waiter's apron. She must have gone pale because he asked, concerned, "Hey, doll—you okay?"

When she couldn't answer, Greta said, "Give us a minute."

"Sure thing." The waiter moved off.

Greta said, "That's Stanley. He's a nice man—works hard at two jobs."

Her voice barely a whisper, Julia said, "The other is at a museum."

"Yes, LaRue's. Have you seen him perform there? He's very gifted."

Julia looked up, surprised. "Gifted?"

"Yes. He's an extraordinary pianist. They call him 'The Human Squid' because of how he can seemingly reach eight octaves at once."

"But I thought . . . " Julia glanced over at the waiter, now leaning over the grill to retrieve plates of food. " . . . I thought . . . "

"They called him that because of what grows from his neck?" Greta's face twisted slightly in disapproval.

"Yes."

Greta hesitated before picking up her camera. "Miss Chandler, do you know why I wanted to take your picture?"

"No."

"Because you seem out of place. It's not just your clothes, although they are strange, or your hair, but . . . *you*. I think maybe you are still trying to find your place in the world, yes?"

Julia nodded, uncomfortable, as if she'd been caught doing something illicit. "I don't know why I'm here, but I think . . . I think it has something to do with your photos."

"Did you know," Greta said, pausing to smile up at Stanley as he set a steaming cup before her, "that some tribes of primitive people believe that cameras capture the soul?"

Julia glanced up as two people sat down in the booth behind Greta. The man was wrapped in bandages, the exposed skin of his face glistening red. The woman was slender, pretty but forgettable—until she yawned, stretched, and rotated one arm all the way back until it was behind her head. They laughed together over some small joke, grinned at Stanley when he approached to take their order. Julia envied their ease with each other,

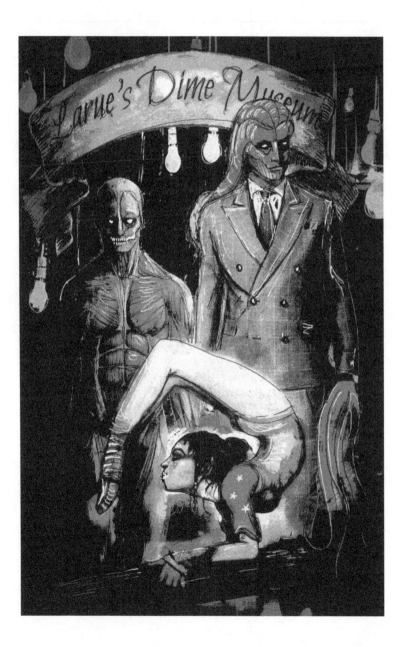

their camaraderie; she wanted to be with them, in their world.

Greta asked, "May I take your picture?"

"Yes," Julia said, composing herself.

Greta raised the camera's viewfinder to her eye.

LIVE ON STAGE
THE HUMAN BLANK

The first thing that caught Stanley's eye in the old photo was the banner strung across the rear wall of a small stage. It took him a few seconds to realize that the woman standing in front of the banner had absolutely nothing special whatsoever to offer. He pitied her dull, symmetrical form, her unmarred skin, her unmemorable features.

Stanley's tentacles writhed in irritation—it was warm in the antiques store, and he was getting uncomfortable. But something about the photograph drew him in, caused him to examine it with more care—

There. He had it: the girl's face, while neither beautiful nor ugly, nevertheless possessed one special quality that struck him the more he looked at it.

He'd never before seen someone so completely at peace, so centered in their surroundings.

I'd like to meet you someday, he thought, as he took the photo to the small shop's front counter.

(For Diane Arbus and Vivian Maier)

WILDFLOWER, CACTUS, ROSE

BRIAN KIRK

SEE HER IN silhouette and you'd think you're looking at a starfish. Or Lisa Simpson from behind. The dorsal fins, as she calls them, are triangular polyethylene implants. BPA-free, of course. She used to have voluminous, glossy red hair—mine is more strawberry blond—but she shaves it in the spots where the fins break through and keeps the rest cropped close to her skull. Her skin has been scalloped into wedges. Pale stitches form the crevices beside each ridge. Her face is punctured with steel tread holes where the two-inch spines screw in. She was beautiful once. Then she was ugly. Now she's a cactus.

Here's a trick she taught me. Stand at the corner of some bustling street—say Fifth Avenue and Broadway or Haight and Asbury or Hollywood and Vine—and pick a mood: happy, angry, horny, scared. Set your face to epitomize said mood, then walk and watch the world transform. A smile will get you a smile. People light up like Christmas bulbs as you stroll along. Same with a scowl; it's like lowering a dimmer switch. Turn off too many people and you can trigger a mob. I liked to act frightened as it attracted the most attention. Plus, I didn't really have to pretend that hard. I met Clegg that way. And Clegg inspired Mom—Samantha is her name—to visit Dr. Xavier. And Dr. Xavier turned her into a cactus. She's transcended this trick she taught me. Now when she walks down the street people go into a state of shock no matter what expression she wears.

That kind of power frightens me. Everything frightens me.

I was huddled against the brick wall of Saks Fifth Avenue, looking lost and scared, like I'd just narrowly escaped a serial killer's trunk. Basically, my default setting. We'd passed a homeless man begging for change and Mom had whispered, "Free Range Human." That's another one of her tricks. Use perspective to shift reality. It all comes down to the words we use, which is why I prefer words that are literal descriptions of the objects they define. Like, Toothbrush. That's a good word. Or Washing Machine. Spoons should be Food Scoopers. Shoes should be Foot Cushions. Lady Bugs should be Flying Polka Dots. Actually, Lady Bug is pretty good.

I was crying. Always crying. My eyes—I call them Looking Balls—had sprung a leak early in life and never been repaired. Must have happened when my dad left and began his great migration out west. New York > Chicago > Denver > Flagstaff > San Diego. The calls coming less frequently as the long-distance rates climbed. Now it seems like the only time he calls is to tell me I have a new step-mom. My real mom—my cactus mom—dubbed the castaways Dad's Alum. We read their old birthday cards whenever we need a good laugh. *To The Daughter I Always Wanted*. And had for like eleven days. Signed with the least sincere "Love You" ever written. XOXO, my Seat Cushion. AKA, my Ass.

Some men see a beautiful girl—my dad's words, not

mine—looking scared and crying and it's like a vulture spying road kill. Three other guys came over to rescue me before Clegg, each with their own brand of bullshit. This was before Mom's surgery. Maybe even the day before. She had visited every accredited plastic surgeon in Manhattan to confirm the initial prognosis. Obstructive sleep apnea, potentially fatal if not corrected. My poor mom was at risk of snoring to death.

Clegg looked like a skeleton in skin-tone latex. Spiky hair, blurry tattoos covering his arms, ribbed chest, and neck. More steel in his face than a studded coat. My dad would have hated Clegg, even though they had much in common. I fucked him later that day and made the mistake of giving him my number. I figured Mom would sleep most of the afternoon following her surgery. But neither of us could have predicted the aftermath. I'm not sure what went wrong in the operating room, but she went in with a face that could cover Vogue magazine and came out with a malpractice suit.

"Please Doc, don't fuck up my face," she had said, and we had all laughed while in the bland comfort of the prep room. The one adjacent to the operating room, where blood gets shed.

"Relax, Mom. You've got beauty to spare."

"Yeah, well." Her hands began trembling despite the two milligrams of Klonopin she'd taken before leaving home, and that made me more scared than usual. "If this goes badly, I may be taking back some of yours."

The doctor motioned for the anesthesiologist, who wheeled her equipment over to my mom's cushioned reclining chair. "You won't feel a thing," he said as she lost consciousness, which was the one thing he got right.

She was supposed to keep the bandages on for twenty-four hours, but couldn't resist the urge to look, guiding me to the powder room with its large vanity mirror as soon as we got home. I watched with escalating dread as she unwrapped the dressing—the curse of the mummy coming to life. Blood stained the inner layers and we both gasped as it unwound and fell to the floor.

Forget the mummy. She was a werewolf caught mid-transformation.

"It's not that bad," I said as tears began to drip from my leaky faucet. "Dr. Lask said there would be bruising."

Mom took a step forward, angling her face, which only made things worse. "Bruising? He butchered me." *Ruined* was the word her boss at Darkstar Energy would later use. "I'm fucking disfigured!" Which was the only way to describe the rodent-like protrusion of her nose and upper mouth creating an overbite that made eating seem impossible. "My face is everything!" Or had been. I'd seen childhood pictures of her at Nana's house, back when we were still allowed to visit, and she was less a child than some miniaturized adult. Wielding her beauty like a weapon the moment she broke free of the womb.

The front door opened and slammed closed as we stood there in shock. Heavy footsteps thundered up the stairs. "Hey, T, where you at?"

T is for Tyler. This was Clegg who had been drawn in by my not-so-pretend fear.

Mom was searching for a place to hide her face—the toilet bowl a potential option. "Who is that?"

"Yo, T!"

All I could do was cringe.

Clegg gave a cursory knock before barging into the bathroom. Mom could have been sitting on the toilet and it wouldn't have slowed him down. He started laughing when he saw her reflection in the mirror. "Holy botch job, Batman!" he said. "You've got a malpractice suit for days!"

The most horrifying moment of my life was the most momentous of hers. "His tattoos were like tiger stripes," she later told me. "His face so deliberately ugly it's become impervious to further insult." In many ways, my mom became a cactus because of Clegg.

He called her a "wererat" that night in my room and I started laughing. Then I started crying. Then I slapped him and he slapped me back, just like I knew he would. I pushed him and he pushed me so hard I fell. I said mean things about his manhood and he choked me until I saw black dots and then we had sex one more time and he left and I never saw him again. That's pretty much how most of my relationships go. Or went. I'm expecting this to change.

After much trial and error, I found that Kat Von D concealer is the best cosmetic for covering bruises. Or, as I like to call them, Blood Shadows. I applied it liberally until Clegg's fingerprints faded from my neck. Mom had asked for a week off from work, but something terrible had happened that required her immediate attention. Unfortunately, I knew of no cosmetic able to conceal her newfound snout or camouflage the purple and yellow patches underneath her eyes. No utensil to thin her bulbous nose. She wore a turtleneck, and a scarf. And a hat. And wide-rimmed sunglasses. The forecast called for a balmy 92 degrees. At least her hair looked good. Thick, flowing red locks curling down from underneath her felt cap. This was before she shaved it for the dorsal fins and dyed the rest green.

She returned two hours later. Mark, her boss, had sent her home. One look and he had fallen into a coughing fit that lasted long enough to attract an audience of stunned onlookers. "What the hell happened to you?" he had said when he finally regained his voice.

"I thought you were having minor surgery, not going twelve rounds with Mike Tyson."

Beauty had been my mother's greatest asset, and it was being repossessed.

They sent a computer guy to our house a day later. Programmers are the punk rockers of the corporate world. Shaved head, long sleeves to hide the ink, plugs in the stretched ear holes that held spacers on the weekends. This was Clegg, just with better clothes. He was there to install a new video conferencing app on Mom's laptop for an important call with one of their major clients. He at least had the decency to blush when the app loaded. I started crying, of course. It was difficult to discern Mom's expression through the misalignment of parts.

On the screen was a cartoon replica of Mom pre-surgery. An illustrated caricature where every feature was exaggerated: the cascading red hair, the wide, green eyes, even her cartoon boobs were a cup size larger. Some asshole had drawn that garish thing. It had probably been approved by a committee.

"It's, um, voice activated," the computer guy said, and the cartoon avatar began moving its lips in a crude mimicry of speech.

I leaned closer, and said the first thing that came to mind. "I like big butts and I cannot lie." A beat passed, and I began crying even harder—squirting Salt Liquid out my Looking Balls. "I'm sorry, Mom," I said.

She turned and was eye level with my ravaged neck. Kat Von D can only do so much, and I could tell she saw the marks Clegg's fingers had made. Saw it in the crinkle between her eyebrows. That wrinkle of concern.

I showed the computer guy out. He asked for my number and I gave it to him. We went out a couple of times, and it ended poorly. I've got the Blood Shadows to prove it.

I knew my mom was in public relations, and that she worked closely with the media. And I knew that Darkstar Energy was a major oil company. But I never really considered what it was she did for them. I hid in the hallway as she made the call. She was still dressed in her robe with her disheveled hair and her mangled face. At least the avatar was wearing a chic business suit.

Here's what I heard.

"Leaks occur all the time," Mom said. "It's an expected cost of business. The cleanup is already underway, so our attention should be focused on how best to capitalize on the event."

Some man spoke. He sounded like a toad. "Our money is washing down the river as we speak! Unless you plan to refund us, I don't see any silver lining here."

I imagined the avatar miming this next part as I heard my mom say, "The government will subsidize the spill, so you will indeed be refunded. In fact, this spill will only drive up the cost of oil, improving your returns. The cleanup effort creates jobs, which the state loves. And Trump has rekindled his feud with Rosie O'Donnell, calling her, quote, 'Blubber Brains,' which will dominate network news. This whole incident will be swept under the rug, and will result in greater overall profits for your stake in the project. That, sir, is your silver lining."

Wait a minute. This was that oil pipeline in North Dakota that I'd protested against. I'd fucking checked into the location on Facebook to confuse the local law enforcement, or something.

"Didn't I tell you not to worry," I heard her boss say.

Without realizing it, I had been sucked in by the call and was now peering around the corner at my mom. She looked up and saw me then. Saw whatever ugly expression was stamped on my face.

"This will not impact your investment negatively in any way," her boss was saying. The man who had kicked her out of the office and forced her to hide behind a cartoon drawing. "In fact, in many ways it's a win."

My mom's transformation started at that very moment. I could see something shift in her swollen and bloodshot eyes.

"Actually, there is one negative to this," she said, and silence fell. Toad-man cleared his throat. I watched as she hit the command to cancel the avatar so that her face was broadcast to the room.

Chairs screeched. "Jesus!" was screamed in mortal fear.

"Despite the cleanup," she said, her voice turned oafish from the overbite. "We will all have to live with the truth of what we've done. We promised these people this wouldn't happen. And we lied. And while we benefit financially, the locals are forced to feed their children toxic water and poisoned fish. So, there is a downside. The downside is that we could have prevented this, and didn't."

"Turn her off!" her boss was saying. "Get that thing off the screen. The doctor ruined more than your face, Samantha!"

"No," she said. We didn't know at the time the call was being recorded through the conference app. "He fixed me."

My mom once said she thought grooves would form on my cheeks through erosion. She made sure I drank saline water to sustain my constant flow of tears. These, at least, were happy ones. I think. Life is so confusing.

Now my mom was plaintiff in two court cases. Malpractice and wrongful termination. It was during this downtime that she got Clegg's number from my phone.

He gave her the name of someone who gave her the name of someone who sent her to Dr. Xavier. "Peace out, Minnie Mouse," he told her. Which I guess is an upgrade from wererat.

Dr. Xavier's office—Doctor? I assume he was a doctor—was down a dark alley underneath a place for prenatal yoga that looked like it could maybe accommodate three or four clients at a time—depending on the trimester. Twins? Forget about it.

Opening the door triggered the sound of a Tibetan singing bowl—a resonant gong that gently faded. Dr. Xavier was there to greet us. It didn't appear as though he employed a receptionist. Or an assistant. Or a suit. He was wearing a black button-down shirt with a cactus embroidered on the back and camouflage cargo shorts. He had the face of a lizard—an appearance so shocking I actually squealed. His brow had pronounced ridges, his nose had been reduced to slits, lines had been tattooed on coarsened skin to create scales. When he smiled, I saw that his teeth had been filed to points and his tongue forked down the middle. His voice hissed during his introduction, pleasantly.

"That is so cool," I said.

He basked in our wonder like a reptile under the sun. "Let's talk about you," he said to my mother. "What brings you here?"

"Isn't it obvious?" she said, and the hurt in her voice— yep, you guessed it—moved me to tears.

Dr. Xavier's head ticked to one side, then the other. "No," he said. He motioned for her to sit in a plush corduroy chair, and she did. I smooshed in beside her. The walls were adorned with pictures of people you see in National Geographic magazines. Women with rings that elongated their necks. Men with large plates through their lower lips. A child with a wood skewer impaled through both cheeks, like some human kabob.

"My doctor fucked up my operation and left me disfigured."

"Disfigured?" Dr. Xavier said. "According to who?"

If life is theater, I was sitting front row.

"To me," Mom said. "I mean, look at me."

"I am," he said, offering his sharp-toothed smile. "Look at *me*."

"Yeah. But you choose to look that way."

"Sure, but did you choose to look the way you did before?"

My mom looked down at her hands, and I looked at them, as well. Saw the deepening wrinkles despite the small fortune she spent on lotions.

"What bothers you most about your new appearance?" Dr. Xavier said.

Her breathing was shallow and raspy. Everything inside me was breaking.

"Is it how people look at you?"

She nodded. My shirt top was soggy with tears.

Dr. Xavier stood and retrieved something from a display table near the back of the room. I heard the flick of a lighter and looked up. It was a wide cylindrical candle encased in glass with a network of intricate lines curlicued down its side and traced with what looked like glitter. He lit the wick, and the flame sparkled before taking hold.

"Close your eyes," he said, and we both did. "Go back in time to before your operation. Picture yourself in a room full of people. Friends, strangers, colleagues. Lovers. You are standing on a pedestal before them—all eyes are on you. What do you see?"

It takes a moment for these faces to form in my mind.

It's like they're all gradations of the same person. A crescent of open space separates me from them like a moat protecting a castle. I want them to look at me kindly, but they don't. I see fear in their eyes. A hint of loathing, jealousy. They are shuffling forward now. Crowding my space. Reaching toward me with greed and lust—it's all I ever see. Hands grab to rip me down. Off my pedestal. Wanting to lower me to their level or below.

We both gasped as our eyes sprang open. The candle flame touched the top of the glittering trench etched in wax and began to burn with purple phosphorescence.

Dr. Xavier had pulled a sketchpad onto his lap and was drawing, his forked tongue curled up in concentration. "The world is a mirror," he said. "What we see is a reflection of who we are." He looked up. "So, the question is, what kind of world do you want to see?"

"It sounds like you're describing my job," Mom said. "That's what I do, alter the way people view the world. I guess I want to see the truth."

He began to sketch some more—quick, jagged strokes—then squinting as he shaded. The pencil made a soft scratching sound that mixed with the crackle of the candle as it burned down that phosphorescent line. "Truth, like what? Like, nature? Tell me, what do you feel when you see a flower?" he said. "Not from a florist. Just a plain wildflower, like the ones growing along the side of a road."

"I love those," I said. Mom turned to me and nodded. I saw her eyes flicker to the heavy coating of concealer underneath my jaw.

"Love them enough to pull over your car and take a closer look?"

She grabbed my hand and squeezed. Shook her head, no.

"How about a rose, then? Imagine the biggest, most beautiful rose you've ever seen. What does it make you want to do?"

"Stop and look?" Mom said.

"More than that. Do you feel the urge to take it home and put it in a vase?"

We both nodded. Nothing existed beyond this room.

"To possess it."

We nodded again.

"And we do so without caring what the rose desires. Have you ever wondered why nature created the cactus?" Dr. Xavier said, and we both shook our heads. The candle smelled like autumn spices. "I like to think it's to grow and protect a flower no one can possess."

Dr. Xavier added some final detail to his drawing, then ripped the page from his sketchpad and stuffed it in an envelope he pulled from his desk. Handed it to Mom. I tried to picture what he looked like before he became a lizard and came up blank.

"Your decision, then. The wildflower, the rose, or the cactus."

"Can't you just fix my overbite?" Mom said, using her hand to cover her crooked smile.

"Any doctor can do that." He walked us to the door, and reached for the handle. "Become something more."

I hesitated at the threshold. It felt like I'd smoked the world's largest joint. "What's with the candle?" I asked.

Dr. Xavier narrowed his elliptical eyes. "That is an enchantment," he said, sniffing the air with his two slits. "The markings describe a spell that has been etched into the wax and is cast as it burns."

"No way! What kind of spell?"

"An incantation of transformation," he said. "Don't worry, I only conjure positive change."

The Tibetan singing bowl chimed as we exited onto the dark alley. A streetwalker glanced at my mom and scurried away.

We didn't talk much for a while. Our world had changed and we needed time to acclimate. Mom spent much of this time in her room, contemplating. I spent much of this time going on Tinder dates. Bringing home boys that reeked of bar scum and Axe body spray. I get loud, even with Mom at home. So loud it embarrasses the boys, which is partly why I do it. I want them to feel the shame I think I should feel, but don't. I just feel frightened, and alone. When they hit me I feel less afraid because the worst is happening and I handle it. With no one to defend me, I survive.

Mom used a teeny tiny fraction of the large settlement we received from Darkstar Energy to pay for her first surgery. The defense team was quick to offer terms when they heard the call recording. Somehow it still got leaked to CNN. Oops! I hadn't seen the sketch Dr. Xavier provided, so I had no idea what aesthetic she was going for.

"The face I was given is gone," she told me. "Now I want to design my own."

Designer face! My mom is rad.

That doesn't mean I wasn't scared. Watching my mom mutilate herself in this way. Wondering if she had lost her mind. The dorsal fins came first and I thought she was trying to become the Statue of Liberty. A woman of justice, or something. Then we had the talk.

She asked me to wash my make up off. I guess the Kat Von D concealer wasn't as effective as I'd thought. I'd pushed one of my Tinder dates too far and he'd blackened my eye and bloodied my nose. Men are so easily upset. It's no sport at all.

Mom winced when she saw the extent of my injuries. "What happened, sweetie?"

"It's nothing. Honestly, Mom. You know how easily I bruise." She wasn't the only one skilled at sculpting the truth.

Her eyes lingered. "You deserve someone who will treat you with respect."

"What, like Dad?"

"Wait a minute. Your father . . . " had ditched soon after I was born for the next pretty face. Called me his beautiful angel from afar.

Here came the tears, right on time. "They're all the same," I said.

I heard Dr. Xavier's pleasant hiss: *The world is a mirror.*

"Or you keep attracting the same kind of guy."

"I don't want to talk about this."

Mom waited, silently. I never could endure the quiet for long.

"Nobody gives a shit about who I am," I said. Where this was coming from, I didn't know. I wasn't even sure I felt this way. "They just like the way I look. And when they can't have that, it's like they want to destroy it." But it was more like I hated the way *they* looked *at me*. That ravenous desire. Just cut my neck like the stem of a rose and mount the head in a trophy room, already.

Mom traced the outline of my Blood Shadow with a finger that's become tenderer with age. "They hurt you because they feel like you could hurt them, and they're too weak to take it," she said. "You're beautiful. It's a blessing and a curse. Like the most powerful magnet and the most destructive bomb."

Stock in Kleenex must be skyrocketing. "I just wish people were different."

What kind of world do you want to see?

"Sorry, sweetheart. The only person you can change is yourself."

She got the spine holes inserted three weeks later. My mom is a cactus and I'm her desert flower.

I hit the streets. Walking with a rage I didn't feel. Pinballing off shoulders and getting shoved against walls. I don't have friends. I make fun of everyone. Have a reputation for being both stuck-up and a slut. I reached the end of the block and turned around. Composed myself, fluffed my hair, smiled. Sunspots flared off ivory teeth. A lane opened down the middle of the sidewalk. I could have powered streetlamps with the wattage of goodwill. This was all too exhausting, too confusing. I veered down a dark alley. Smeared road grime onto my face and into my hair. I don't want to have to act. I just want to be.

At first, Mom forgot about the spines and kept pricking her hands when she went to touch her face. Kissing is out of the question. She takes the thorns out at night, but not always. Wakes up with feathers strewn about the room. Now she goes to hospitals and parks and stands or sits in silence as people gaze upon her with hushed reverence. She's not just my guardian. She's a breathing work of art.

I don't think she knows I saw Dr. Xavier's sketch. She kept it in her safe, but the combination is my birthdate. He didn't just draw Mom. He drew me, too. And I traced that drawing onto another sheet of paper I keep in my room. Pull it out and study it while I contemplate his words: *The world is a mirror. What do you want to see?*

I wonder if imagining it is enough to effect the transformation. The intricate grooves running down from my eyes, curlicued across my cheeks. The tears glistening as they flow through the channels, like the glittering trenches in Dr. Xavier's candle, or the spark of a fuse. If beauty is a weapon, like Mom says, should I detonate or disarm?

THE BAKER OF MILLEPOIX

HAL BODNER

"**THE CHATEAU IS** very beautiful," Henri said.

"You mean that it *was* beautiful," Marc laughed. "The Marron family lived here for generations. When my father succumbed to his affection for dark-eyed women and roulette, the government took it away. Now, like so many things the government puts its hand to, it has fallen into ruin."

Henri's eyes roved over the gorse and bramble choked gardens, and the clinging vines patching the walls where the masonry had long ago crumbled away. He rolled over and fetched the second bottle of Merlot to refill their glasses. Though the lawn upon which they had decided to hold their picnic was badly neglected, patches of intrepid wildflowers still managed to poke their faces above the weeds and flaunt their vibrancy in contrast to the muted eiderdowns and taupes that colored most of the shops and houses in the picturesque village of Millepoix below.

"Still," Marc added, with melancholy, "my fondest memories are of growing up in this place. One day, I think I should like to be buried here."

Three years, seven months and four days later, he was.

"What a blessing that it was over so quickly," Louise said. "How fortunate that he did not suffer."

As the unchallenged diva of *L'opéra Palais de Grandier*, Louise Semillion was not expected to remove her attention from such vital matters as selecting her costumes for Strauss' *Elektra*. That she devoted herself to the bereavement of Henri, who was not merely her dear friend but her favorite conductor as well, was a mark of her affection for the couple and showed how truly desolated she was by Marc's death.

Though Henri knew her words were meant to offer him comfort, they gave him little peace. What difference did it make whether Marc had perished slowly or had been taken *tout de suite* by a crash of the afternoon train? What matter if his liver had failed him gradually, or if he had succumbed to the poison of a treacherous mushroom? The strike of a serpent. A bolt of lightning from the heavens. A sudden fever, or a thief in the night with a blade. In the end, it amounted to the same thing. Marc was gone; and Henri was alone.

He took leave from the opéra so he could accompany Marc's body to the funeral. He remembered the first time they had come to Millepoix, and had stayed for several weeks during the opéra's summer hiatus. Marc's excitement at returning to his childhood home had been so infectious that Henri had crept back into the village within the month to surreptitiously take out a mortgage on a small, two-story cottage. It was located just off the Avenue des Grandes Idées which, in reality, was not much grander of an idée than a cobblestone lane lined with a few quaint, tawny-colored shops and cafes. It was full of charm, the cottage was, with poured glass mullions and eaves draped in purple wisteria. The estate agent optimistically described the large puddle on the property as a "pond." Nonetheless, it was sufficient to support a single family of ducks and Henri was quite taken with it. There was also a hulking vegetable patch that had shamefully been allowed to go fallow, and a cunning little well in the side yard from which, at any moment, a horde of pixies or elves might emerge.

By the time Henri was ready to hang up his conductor's baton and retire, the cottage would be paid for. He eagerly anticipated the look of delight on Marc's face when the surprise was finally revealed but first, there were many repairs and improvements to be made. Before his husband first laid eyes upon it, the cottage must be *absolument parfait*, just perfect! But he had not reckoned on the age of the place, or the state of its disrepair. Each time he snuck away to check on the progress, the workmen had found something new that must be attended to: a leak in the roof, a small termite infestation, an omission relating to a *permis de construire* which Henri had overlooked when he decided to have the kitchen updated.

All of these things conspired against him and time continued to plod along. And now, he would never see the light in his beloved's eyes when he handed him the key and, for the first time, ushered him across the threshold.

Once the townspeople discovered that he had married into La Famille Marron, their innate aversion to strangers departed and they went out of their way to be pleasant to him whenever he was in town to argue with the carpenters or to pay the gardeners. After all, for centuries the Marrons had lived in the chateau and provided the village with both protection and profitable custom. This did not, of course, prevent Madam Duran from overcharging when Henri breakfasted at Le Coq Calicot, nor did it stop Monsieur Bouvard from leaving a heavy finger on the scale when he weighed out Henri's cutlets. But that was simply good business. At least, they assured themselves, they smiled warmly and engaged Henri in conversation while they collected their extra francs and centimes, so that he would feel welcome among them.

Even when they realized that Henri's relationship was with *Marc* Marron, and not *la Marron filles*, their cordiality did not diminish. Marc's sister had been known to put on airs, even before she moved away to Roubaix where, it was generally assumed, she sold her favors to unemployed textile workers; the townspeople of Millepoix did not miss *her* presence at all! Besides, according to Pierre Roubeau, who had in his youth once given up reading law for Lent and never resumed it, the unusual marriage had occurred in England. It had been validated in the eyes of the Church and before God, both of whom apparently looked at things quite differently on the other side of the Channel. The people of Millepoix simply shrugged. After all, they reasoned that no one was truly free of idiosyncrasies—just look at Mademoiselle Cachouète and her cats! Besides, as the local old saying went, "A chestnut is a chestnut is a chestnut" and the Marron family had always been held in high regard in spite of their hereditary eccentricities.

As a result, Marc's funeral was widely attended, not just by friends and colleagues from the opéra, but by the citizens of Millepoix themselves. Even Étienne the Drunkard was there, clutching a bottle of inexpensive *vin ordinaire* given to him by Father Phillipe in return for digging the grave and looking forward to a second bottle promised to him if he would forgo relieving his bladder upon the tombstones within sight of the mourners until the eulogy was complete. So many people, in fact, crowded into the churchyard that, but for the somber tones of their costumes and the propensity among the distaff of a certain age for black veils, a passer-by might have mistaken the occasion for a festival.

For Henri, it was anything but. His heart broke just a little more when the pallbearers lowered the casket into the ground, and the force of his weeping unsettled the sparrows where they nested in the trees above the marble monuments. Afterward, the entire company returned to the cottage. The city folk came to help ease Henri through his grief; the locals brought their curiosity to see what the conductor had done to the interior of the place.

Most of the changes were met with grudging approval; the modernized loo in the downstairs powder room was particularly admired. The people of Millepoix were even more impressed that Henri—who was after all a relative stranger to the town—had not scrimped on the wake. Though some of the local shopkeepers felt it was a trifle self-centered, perhaps even pretentious, for Henri to have hired a caterer from Paris, no one could complain about the quality of the victuals. Moreover, unlike the parties held by Madam Pamplemousse of the ambitiously named Hôtel Superbe, the food tables were kept piled high and the liquor never ran dry—not that anyone expected generosity from Madam who, it was rumored, was secretly a Protestant.

For days, the lavishness of the buffet was the talk of the village. Every hors d'oeuvre was reviewed and analyzed. The seasoning of the casseroles was the subject of intense discussion. The tenderness of the roast and the succulence of the fowl were debated with the gravity of Descartes until, by the end of the following week, it was generally acknowledged that Marc Marron's funeral had been a resounding success, both respectful and generous.

By the end of that same week, the villagers were

surprised to find that Henri Marron (though he was not technically a Marron, they found it easier to refer to him that way) was still in residence.

The morning after the funeral, Henri had awakened in the largest of the cottage's three bedrooms. Unlike many of the guests at the wake, Henri had remained stone cold sober; the pain he felt had nothing to do with an overindulgence in cognac or the local red.

"Henri, my poor tragic darling!"

Louise had somehow managed to boil a pot of coffee. A fresh cup sat, with a tiny raft of scorched grounds floating on top, upon the table. Henri, still dulled with grief, noticed only a slight graininess to the brew which, in a way, was a kind of blessing in itself.

"We'll leave this mess." Louise threw her arms wide with a gesture she'd used to great effect when she'd played Tosca, to indicate the ravaged buffet table, the soiled plates, crumpled napkins and empty glasses and bottles. "We'll leave it for the hired people to clean up. Later this afternoon, we'll visit the agent to list the cottage and, tonight, we shall return to Paris." Her gesture was from *Aida* this time, a filling of her lungs with air and a thrusting forward of her chest to demonstrate that, though she was perhaps not as young as she appeared to be on stage, she could still hold her own against those willowy infants who called themselves sopranos but who were hardly old enough to show any bust. Henri did not, of course, appreciate such charms but still, she liked to keep in practice.

"No."

The word slipped out before he was quite conscious of having said it. He realized with a sudden shock that, more than anything else, he dreaded returning to his empty apartment in the city.

"I think I'll stay," he continued with a tinge of wonder at his own boldness, both at his whimsy at altering his life so drastically and at his bravery for contradicting Louise who was, after all, a diva.

"Don't be silly, *ma cher*. Marc's death has hit you harder than you know. Tragedy has muddled your thinking. You cannot seriously consider keeping this . . . shack." Her mouth formed a small moue of distaste as she looked upon surroundings which she would have called charming a scant moment ago. However, once she risked being seen in the company of anyone who actually lived in such a place, those same surroundings revealed themselves to be an anathema, not to be flaunted in polite society.

"Don't you think it's terribly primitive?" she finally ventured. "And a trifle small?"

"Nevertheless," Henri said with newly found purpose, "that is exactly what I intend to do."

"But . . . *why*?" The soprano seemed on the verge of tears on behalf of the irresponsible decisions about to be made by her dearest friend. Or, perhaps, she had merely taken a sip from her own cup of coffee. "You have a perfectly lovely home in the city," she cried with dismay, "with a *patio*!"

"I shall sell it. And I shall live here where I can be . . . " Emotion caused his voice to catch within his throat for a moment. " . . . where I can be close to Marc. Besides," he added when he saw Louise's expression of horror, "what need have I of a patio? Here, I have an entire garden. With ducks."

Try as she might, Louise could not convince him of his folly. His colleagues from the opéra added their voices to hers, including an extraordinarily handsome flautist with whom he had dallied some years ago, well before he had met Marc. But as tempting as revisiting that *liaison* might have once been, Henri was adamant.

His swan song was a triumph. Never had *Carmen* been conducted with such passion. Debussy's Pelléas and Mélisande had never before been so in love. A braver and more noble Turandot never trod the opéra stage. When the season ended, he laid down his baton for the last time. Within six months after Marc's death he had sold the Paris apartment and moved to the cottage in Millepoix. Within six more, Henri was bored stiff.

That is not to say that those early months were not filled with a frenzy of activity. Once he had skimmed the scum from the pond, the ducks gave voice to their gratitude with effusive quacks each morning, just after dawn. Not only would he soon be feasting upon the bounty of the vegetables he had planted in the garden, but his laboring with hoe and rake while stripped to the waist under the country sun, had rendered his body lean and his skin brown.

In time, Henri got to know his neighbors and developed a warm affection for them. In return, the residents of Millepoix began to look upon Henri not as *the* Marron, but rather as *our* Marron. Monsieur Bouvard's fingers pressed a little more lightly upon the scales and the waitress at Le Coq Calicot began replenishing his Café Americain without being asked, and without the usual extra charges. When he grew tired of the incessant local chat about the weather, and the griping about the tourists who sometimes stopped in Millepoix on their way to visit the wineries farther north, he had only to spend some time at the flower shop of old Monsieur Seldemer who, it turned out, was surprisingly knowledgeable about French opéra. Henri even found himself engaging in a mild flirtation with Laurent of the well-muscled arms and winning grin who worked part-time at the garage of M. Grandevere. Though the youth was far too young for him, Henri warmed to the attention. While the sting of Marc's passing was still tender, interest from a handsome lad was always a welcome palliative.

Despite the excitement of growing vegetables, making a pleasant home for the ducks, and dreaming of a young man's smile, Henry longed for more. Then, for no particular reason other than that it caught his fancy and the Widow Lavoisier was interested in selling, Henri bought a bakery.

"But you know nothing about baking!" Louise cried when Henri told her what he had done.

The diva was a frequent house guest, ostensibly to recover from her love affair with a dashing Czech tenor who, it turned out, was primarily interested in getting her out of her gowns so that he could try them on himself. Henri suspected that the truth was that Louise was getting older, though she'd never admit to it. There were times when she was no longer offered the best roles, and the languid lifestyle and country air appealed to her when the bustle of Paris and the intrigues of the younger singers proved taxing to her stamina.

"Remember that we are French. We can survive anything, even the Germans. But in the matter of bread, we are unforgiving."

"I'll learn," Henri said.

And he did.

In the beginning, he churned out trays of misbegotten baguettes and leaden croissants of bilious brown that the Good Lord, in His infinite wisdom, had never intended be a proper color for a baked good. But perhaps to compensate him for taking Marc, God had bestowed a gift upon Henri and, within a very short time, he discovered he had a true talent for baking. In the mean-time, his business thrived nonetheless when the villagers discovered that Mademoiselle Cachouète's cats had an aversion to Henri's eclairs. There was nothing more effective for keeping the wretched beasts from shitting among the aubergines and in the marigold beds and, soon, every garden in town had a border of strategically placed pastries.

By the time Henri grew confident enough in his abilities to try his hand at the legendary *Gateau St. Honoré*, the legendary dessert which requires a mastery of every known baking technique, the villagers of Millepoix were already boasting of the skill of their new baker, though they never did it within Henri's hearing lest his head should swell with the sin of vanity. Business improved, and when Henri found he needed an extra pair of hands in the bakery, Laurent from the garage was happy to relinquish his grease-smeared overalls in favor of a flour-daubed smock.

Louise expressed suitable shock when she found Henri working along such an attractive and much younger man. But he almost convinced her that his need for an apprentice was greater than his need for a lover and she eventually ceased her objections. Besides, when Laurent moved the bread from oven to cooling rack, her breath caught at the sight of his bulging arms and the strong column of his throat as he strained to lift the heavy pans. Since *le Bon Dieu* had seen fit to create such beauty on earth, she reasoned, she would be committing a minor sin if she were not to be suitably admiring of it. In time, the village tongues ceased wagging and, should anyone witness a certain kind of glance or the exchange of a tender gesture between the two men, they simply shrugged. After all, Henri had come to them from Paris and, as everyone knew, the habits of Parisians were often exceedingly strange.

As for the event which so drastically changed things in Millepoix, it was, as such events often are, rather minor in and of itself. While Henri was certainly a talented baker, he was by no means a formally trained one. As a result, his technique was often improvisational and accidents, as accidents are wont to do, happened. In this case it was a momentary inattention while cutting dough for the almond pastries. The bell above the front door of the shop tinkled at an inopportune moment and, in the instant of distraction, the knife sliced several layers of skin from the tip of Henri's finger. Bright droplets of blood decorated the dough, incarnadine against the creamy beige.

Henri quickly wrapped his finger in a cloth, called for Laurent to discard the ruined tray of pastry and put the other into the oven, and went to fetch Madam Lescailles a boulle of whole wheat and two plum tarts. When he returned to the kitchen a few moments later, he did not realize that Laurent had mistakenly prepared the pastries with the spoiled dough.

The tainted tarts were not out of the oven five minutes when Madam Auberge entered the shop with a tearful little Marie-Claire in tow.

"Her new puppy has escaped," Madam explained. She lowered her voice so that the child could not hear. "We tracked it to the Avenue de Parc, where the tourists drive past at great speed and we fear . . . " She shrugged and ventured a wan smile in typical Gallic acceptance of God's will when disaster strikes. "We are hoping that perhaps one of your almond croissants might ease the sting."

While the little girl was indeed grateful for the pastry, it was clear that the loss of her beloved pet would not be ameliorated by mere almonds and sugar paste. Still, it was something and, when Madame Auberge and her daughter left the bakery, the child's tears seemed to be flowing a trifle less freely.

Henri put the incident from his mind and busied himself with bandaging his hand. But when Mademoiselle Cachouète of the many cats crossed the threshold a few moments later, a second helping of tragedy flavored the afternoon.

"Alas, it is the cancer," the spinster confided. "It is not for myself that I sorrow. I am an old woman and if le Bon Dieu sees fit to call me to his breast, who am I to object? But *mes bébés. Mes petits choux.* It is for them that I weep." As if to confirm her words, a single tear made its way down one leathery cheek. "Who will care for my dear cats when I am gone? *Eh bien,*" She squared her shoulders so that they could endure the burdens they could not avoid carrying. "I think I shall have a sweet croissant." She grinned ruefully and patted her ample stomach. "After all, it is not as if I must worry about my weight for much longer."

Custom was brisk all afternoon and, finally, just before Henri was about to shutter the bakery for the evening, Yvette and Claude Poinard entered the shop. The domestic situation *chez Poinard* was well known to be an unpleasant one and their visit to Henri's bakery certainly did not contradict their reputation for bickering. Today, the subject of their disagreement was either the excessive attention which Claude had paid to the new barmaid at Le Chevalier Bleu, or the excessive price paid by Madam Poinard for a new hat. It was hard to tell which.

"Do you see what I must endure while married to this beast?" Madam implored Henri.

"And I, what I must endure from this shrew?" her husband made sure to interject, simply to make sure the baker was privy to both positions in the argument.

"Perhaps some almond pastry might help you to find the sweetness that first led you to each other?" Henri suggested.

Though the couple scoffed at the foolishness of the idea, they nonetheless purchased several of the pastries and departed in an uninterrupted cacophony of insults and vituperation.

The following day, Henri was delighted to hear that Marie-Claire's puppy had returned, lively and un-squashed by the automobiles of the tourists. Even more delightful was the news that Mademoiselle Cachouète's doctor had made a mistake. The old woman was not only not dying of cancer, but she interpreted the reprieve as a sign that God approved of her charity, and wished her to add several more homeless felines to her household. Perhaps most remarkable was the change that came across the Poinards. The couple, who had been at each other's throats for almost two decades, were behaving like newlyweds smitten with love for one another. Claude, who had never before gifted his wife with so much as a single chocolate, showered her with elaborate bouquets. And, since the weather had grown warmer and the Poinards had taken to keeping their windows open, their closest neighbors could swear to the enthusiasm with which Yvette thanked her husband for the flowers.

All over the village, miracles began to happen, both large and small.

On the east side of town, Pierre Roubeau found a long-lost pocket watch which had belonged to his father. A plantar wart, which sorely vexed Madam Durand, vanished overnight, evidently having gone the way of

Monsieur Grandevere's chronic lower back pain. Young Faustine Arnaud astonished her teachers by proving she could effortlessly add sums in her head, when only the days before she had been the worst student in her class.

On the west side of Millepoix, the discovery of a bank error saved the La Fuete family from eviction. Madam Prevaine appeared in public in a dress she had not been able to fit into since her wedding forty-six years ago. And the large strawberry birthmark on Richard Navarre's left cheek faded into invisibility.

Tongues wagged about the remarkable good fortune that had blessed so many. Slowly, as the villagers gossiped and compared notes, an astonishing theme developed. It was discovered that all of those who had received blessings had one thing in common: they had partaken of one of Henri's luscious almond croissants. What's more, they had all purchased the pastries on the same day. As for those who had not, the trials and tribulations of their lives remained unaffected and unchanged.

When the rumor first crossed his ears, Henri laughed. While he had no argument with the increased business it fostered, he found it quaintly rural and a trifle foolish until he realized that the day in question was the very day he had bled into the dough. As a good French Catholic, Henri was well acquainted with miraculous healing brought about by the blood and other body parts of the saints. His own parents had ascribed to two foolproof ways of dealing with sickness and injury, whether it be as mild as a hangnail or as severe as bubonic plague. In either case, the cure was the same: aspirin from the doctor and, if that failed, kissing the relic at the local church, a brittle scrap of bone which once purportedly resided in the shoulder of Our Savior's great aunt. If neither course of treatment worked, it was obviously God's will that the victim continue to suffer.

He questioned Laurent about the tray of adulterated dough and, after much scratching at his chest and armpits while he thought, and prolonged furrowing of his handsome brow, Laurent allowed that it was indeed possible that he had confused the two trays and baked the wrong one. Perplexed, for he did not consider himself particularly saint-like, but unable to deny the manifestations of his neighbors' fortuity, Henri decided to try an experiment. He prepared two portions of dough. Into one, he pricked his finger and dribbled a small measure of blood. The other, he left unadulterated. He baked *brioche* and kept the batches carefully separated. When he offered the finished breads for sale, he kept careful note of which of his neighbors selected from which tray.

The results astonished him.

Eighteen-year-old Michel Crevaine received an unexpected inheritance, almost precisely enough to purchase the forest green roadster he'd been lusting for. Elaine Gougeon's beau finally set a wedding date after six years of engagement. Old Philemon's bowels began to operate like those of a man half his age. Each of them, along with others who experienced similar good fortune, had eaten the brioche made with Henri's blood.

As for those who had purchased from the other tray, no similar blessings accrued. Madam Harmon's canaries were attacked in their cage by a raven and perished. Capitaine Racine still suffered from excruciating gout. And Felix Valery struggled to find employment that would allow him to support his wife and five young children.

And yet when Henri prepared a special batch of *pain*

ordinaire, and made certain that the three customers each had a loaf of it, within a day, Felix had found a well-paying job, the Capitaine tossed away his cane, and Madam Harmon found an injured lark in her garden that sang with an angel's sweetness and was tame enough to eat breadcrumbs of the tainted brioche from her hand. Even more astonishing, the lark's wing healed overnight with nary a trace that it had ever been broken!

"You are suffering from delusion," Louise proclaimed when Henri told her of his suspicions, "brought on by too much country air. We must spend a weekend in Paris immediately."

In the coming months, much to Louise's disgust, Henri continued to experiment. He found that, while his blood alone effectively overcame most mundane problems, more severe troubles required a measure of flesh, as well. When Madame Cachouète's cancer returned, Henri lined the puff pastry of a special Napoleon with thin slices of skin from his hip. When the Poinard's relationship exploded into physical violence, he sacrificed the first joint of the little toe on his left foot, and baked a tourtière du veaux to their continued happiness.

"You must stop," Louise told him. "There is something unholy in this gift of yours. It cannot but end badly."

"Did not Our Savior provide His blood and His body to the faithful in Holy Communion?"

The singer pressed her lips tightly together. To accuse a good friend of blasphemy, or even sacrilege is not something one embarks upon lightly and so, she refrained from arguing her point as vociferously as she would otherwise have done.

It wasn't long before word of the Miracle Bakery

spread beyond Millepoix. Madam Grandevere mentioned it to a cousin who lived near Rheims, who gossiped with the ladies in her sewing circle who, naturally, passed the news on to their husbands. In Aix-en-Provence, the halls of the university echoed with tales that grew more fantastic as they spread from classroom to classroom. Eventually, a whisper from his valet to the Bishop of Avignon served to involve the Church, at which point, efforts to stop the tale from spreading would have been like asking the cheeses not to ripen or the vintners not to harvest their grapes.

As time passed, all sorts of poor souls found their way to the bakery: a woman stricken with paralysis; spinsters who despaired of finding husbands; a young man who yearned to emulate Brando; young women who longed to dance at the Théâtre National; soldiers who had lost limbs; businessmen who had lost fortunes. By the time the morning sun crested the horizon, the desperate and unhappy were already assembled into a queue which stretched down the avenue.

"This is getting out of control," Louise proclaimed.

But Henri remembered the pain of Marc's death and it was unbearable to him that anyone else should similarly suffer, not when he had been blessed with the power to remove their sorrows and grant them a better life. He and Laurent toiled at the ovens from dawn until dusk. And when Laurent realized that Henri's recipes contained ingredients other than butter, flour and eggs, he said not a word. That the young man was beautiful of both face and body did not necessarily mean that le Bon Dieu had balanced the scale by depriving him between the ears. Laurent had wisely claimed a profiterole or two for himself and had both a midnight blue Vespa and an extra inch of manhood to show for it. And when Henri had reached the limits of both what he could do without his wounds protruding past what his clothing covered, Laurent took up the knife without comment and assisted his employer in using parts of his body that were beyond Henri's reach.

"You must rest yourself." Louise said while she helped Henri change the bandages on his chest, arms and legs. "You are going too far and will soon be used up."

"Nonsense," Henri said.

While it was true that the loss of blood had made him weak and the loss of his toes had made him wobbly, he had not sacrificed so much as a millimeter of skin from his hands, absent a few fingernail clippings with which he spiked the clafoutis. He could still use them to bake and, after all, was that not the most important thing?

"I have a gift. It would be sinful *not* to use it."

So Louise clucked her tongue but held her peace until, one day, there came a knock at the cottage door from Laurent.

"You must come at once," he said.

With uneasiness growing in her heart, she wrapped a shawl around her shoulders for, since she had left the opéra, she'd become sensitive to the slightest chill. As she hurried toward the bakery, she noticed the first traces of grey at Laurent's temples and reflected that he was no longer a boy. Nevertheless, he still had the finest buttocks of any man she had known so she was content to allow him to lead the way.

A deep sorrow enfolded her heart when she saw Henri on the floor, his lifeless hand clutching an empty tray from which a scattering of as-yet unfrosted *mignardises* had fallen and formed a rough halo of sweet pastry around his head and shoulders.

"He was taking the petits fours from the oven," Laurent explained with a shrug. "*Et voila*, he was gone."

The singer knelt upon the floor and pressed closed the staring eyes of the reluctant saint.

"You must tell those outside that their wait has been in vain," she said.

Laurent's eyes widened. "I cannot do that, Madam. I am a simple baker's apprentice. They would tear me apart. Perhaps if the news came from someone who was once famous at l'opéra . . . "

He interrupted himself as the thought occurred to him, "Besides, Monsieur Henri would never have turned away so much business. You should tell them only that he is gone and that, after today, the miracles must cease."

"It is many hours until closing," she pointed out. "What will we do . . . ?"

"I have *une petite idée* and a sharp knife," Laurent said. "To refuse the francs they offer, that would indeed be ungracious."

"You cannot possibly . . . !"

"Attend to the crowd. I shall attend to the rest."

Louise squared her shoulders, adjusted her shawl so that it seemed more of a statement *en vogue* and less of a *nécessité*, and made sure that enough of her ample bosoms were displayed to impress, but not so much as to distract.

"I am Louise Semillion," she announced to the line of hopefuls, "You will remember me as *La diva de L'opéra Palais de Grandier*."

A respectful hush fell over everyone. Though some few of them were from the cities, most were from the countryside and were cowed by the presence of such an august *personnage*.

"Our beloved baker has been unexpectedly called to God . . . "

A murmur of understanding rippled throughout the

crowd. When it came to miracles, it was not unknown for le Bon Dieu to intervene lest mere mortals develop unreasonable demands upon His time. However, as Louise continued to assure them that the bakery would remain open for the day at least, they were content to pass, one by one, through the door to purchase their pastries and their dreams.

"Voila!" Laurent told her, once the windows were shuttered and even the crumbs from the last baguette had been sold. "We have made of this day a success, even if only by the hair of our beards. Toward the end, I was worried that I would have to employ the grinder that we use for the venison pies."

"Poor Henri." Louise gazed upon the sheet-covered remains of the baker, her eyes glistening. "He seems so small and sad."

Laurent paused his counting of the coins in the till. "There is, indeed, less of him then there was this morning. Fortunately, the Good Lord despises waste."

"I always knew country life would be the death of him. It is times like this when I most wish I was younger, still strong of voice, and could return to the opéra."

Laurent flashed her the same winning smile that, so many years before, had first intrigued the late baker.

"I thought you might feel that way some day." He pushed a single *macaron* across the counter toward her. "I saved this for you. After all you were his closest friend."

"I could never . . . !" Louise, said aghast.

Laurent simply shrugged and, with his index finger, pushed the pastry a little closer.

Distant echoes of applause seemed to echo in the shop. Louise inhaled sharply and, for an instant, her bosoms felt high and firm once again. When she exhaled, she resisted the urge to give voice to a note or two,

perhaps even a scale, for fear the tones would be harsh or shrill.

"*Bon appetit*," Laurent said.

Louise reached for the pastry. Hesitated. Glanced nervously at Henri's body.

She reached again.

Jacqueline Ess: Her Will and Testament

CLIVE BARKER

MY GOD, she thought, this can't be living. Day in, day out: the boredom, the drudgery, the frustration.

My Christ, she prayed, let me out, set me free, crucify me if you must, but put me out of my misery.

In lieu of his euthanasian benediction, she took a blade from Ben's razor, one dull day in late March, locked herself in the bathroom, and slit her wrists.

Through the throbbing in her ears, she faintly heard Ben outside the bathroom door.

"Are you in there, darling?"

"Go away," she thought she said.

"I'm back early, sweetheart. The traffic was light."

"Please go away."

The effort of trying to speak slid her off the toilet seat and on to the white-tiled floor, where pools of her blood were already cooling.

"Darling?"

"Go."

"Darling."

"Away."

"Are you all right?"

Now he was rattling at the door, the rat. Didn't he realize she couldn't open it, wouldn't open it?

"Answer me, Jackie."

She groaned. She couldn't stop herself. The pain wasn't as terrible as she'd expected, but there was an ugly feeling, as though she'd been kicked in the head. Still, he couldn't catch her in time, not now. Not even if he broke the door down.

He broke the door down.

She looked up at him through an air grown so thick with death you could have sliced it.

"Too late," she thought she said. But it wasn't.

My God, she thought, this can't be suicide. I haven't died.

The doctor Ben had hired for her was too perfectly benign. Only the best, he'd promised, only the very best for my Jackie.

"It's nothing," the doctor reassured her, "that we can't put right with a little tinkering."

Why doesn't he just come out with it? she thought. He doesn't give a damn. He doesn't know what it's like.

"I deal with a lot of these women's problems," he confided, fairly oozing a practiced compassion. "It's got to epidemic proportions among a certain age bracket."

She was barely thirty. What was he telling her? That she was prematurely menopausal?

"Depression, partial or total withdrawal, neuroses of every shape and size. You're not alone, believe me."

Oh yes I am, she thought. I'm here in my head, on my own, and you can't know what it's like.

"We'll have you right in two shakes of a lamb's tail."

I'm a lamb, am I? Does he think I'm a lamb?

Musing, he glanced up at his framed qualifications, then at his manicured nails, then at the pens on his desk and notepad. But he didn't look at Jacqueline. Anywhere but at Jacqueline.

"I know," he was saying now, "what you've been through, and it's been traumatic. Women have certain needs. If they go unanswered—"

What would he know about women's needs? You're not a woman, she thought she thought. "What?" he said.

Had she spoken? She shook her head: denying speech. He went on; finding his rhythm once more: "I'm not going to put you through interminable therapy sessions. You don't want that, do you? You want a little reassurance, and you want something to help you sleep at nights." He was irritating her badly now. His condescension was so profound it had no bottom. All-knowing, all-seeing Father; that was his performance. As if he were blessed with some miraculous insight into the nature of a woman's soul.

"Of course, I've tried therapy courses with patients in the past.

But between you and me—"

He lightly patted her hand. Father's palm on the back of her hand.

She was supposed to be flattered, reassured, maybe even seduced. "—between you and me it's so much talk. Endless talk. Frankly, what good does it do? We've all got problems. You can't talk them away, can you?"

You're not a woman. You don't look like a woman, you don't feel like a woman—

"Did you say something?" She shook her head.

"I thought you said something. Please feel free to be honest with me."

She didn't reply, and he seemed to tire of pretending intimacy. He stood up and went to the window.

"I think the best thing for you—"

He stood against the light: darkening the room, obscuring the view of the cherry trees on the lawn through the window. She stared at his wide shoulders, at his narrow hips. A fine figure of a man, as Ben would have called him. No child-bearer he. Made to remake the world, a body like that. If not the world, remaking minds would have to do.

"I think the best thing for you—"

What did he know, with his hips, with his shoulders? He was too much a man to understand anything of her.

"I think the best thing for you would be a course of sedatives—" Now her eyes were on his waist.

"—and a holiday."

Her mind had focused now on the body beneath the veneer of his clothes. The muscle, bone and blood beneath the elastic skin. She pictured it from all sides, sizing it up, judging its powers of resistance, then closing on it. She thought:

Be a woman.

Simply, as she thought that preposterous idea, it began to take shape. Not a fairy-tale transformation, unfortunately, his flesh resisted such magic. She willed his manly chest into making breasts of itself and it began to swell most fetchingly, until the skin burst and his sternum flew apart. His pelvis, teased to breaking point, fractured at its center; unbalanced, he toppled over onto his desk and from there stared up at her, his face yellow with shock. He licked his lips, over and over again, to find some wetness to talk with. His mouth was dry: his words were stillborn. It was from between his legs that all the noise was coming; the splashing of his blood; the thud of his bowel on the carpet.

She screamed at the absurd monstrosity she had made, and withdrew to the far corner of the room, where she was sick in the pot of the rubber plant.

My God, she thought, this can't be murder. I didn't so much as touch him.

What Jacqueline had done that afternoon, she kept to herself. No sense in giving people sleepless nights, thinking about such peculiar talent.

The police were very kind. They produced any number of explanations for the sudden departure of Dr. Blandish, though none quite described how his chest had erupted in that extraordinary fashion, making two handsome (if hairy) domes of his pectorals.

It was assumed that some unknown psychotic, strong in his insanity, had broken in, done the deed with hands, hammers and saws, and exited, locking the innocent Jacqueline Ess in an appalled silence no interrogation could hope to penetrate.

Person or persons unknown had clearly dispatched the doctor to where neither sedatives nor therapy could help him.

She almost forgot for a while. But as the months passed it came back to her by degrees, like a memory of a secret adultery. It teased her with its forbidden delights. She forgot the nausea, and remembered the power. She forgot sordidity, and remembered strength. She forgot the guilt that had seized her afterward and longed, longed to do it again.

Only better.

"Jacqueline."

Is this my husband, she thought, actually calling me by my name?

Usually it was Jackie, or Jack, or nothing at all. "Jacqueline."

He was looking at her with those big baby blues of his, like the college boy she'd loved at first sight. But his mouth was harder now, and his kisses tasted like stale bread.

"Jacqueline." "Yes."

"I've got something I want to speak to you about."

A conversation? she thought, it must be a public holiday. "I don't know how to tell you this."

"Try me," she suggested.

She knew that she could think his tongue into speaking if it pleased her. Make him tell her what she wanted to hear. Words of love, maybe, if she could remember what they sounded like. But what was the use of that? Better the truth.

"Darling, I've gone off the rails a bit."

"What do you mean?" she said.

Have you, you bastard, she thought.

"It was while you weren't quite yourself. You know, when things had more or less stopped between us. Separate rooms . . . you wanted separate rooms . . . and I just went bananas with frustration. I didn't want to upset you, so I didn't say anything. But it's no use me trying to live two lives."

"You can have an affair if you want to, Ben."

"It's not an affair, Jackie. I love her—"

He was preparing one of his speeches, she could see

it gathering momentum behind his teeth. The justifications that became accusations, those excuses that always turned into assaults on her character. Once he got into full flow there'd be no stopping him. She didn't want to hear.

"—she's not like you at all, Jackie. She's frivolous in her way. I suppose you'd call her shallow."

It might be worth interrupting here, she thought, before he ties himself in his usual knots.

"She's not moody like you. You know, she's just a normal woman. I don't mean to say you're not normal: you can't help having depressions. But she's not so sensitive."

"There's no need, Ben—"

"No, damn it, I want it all off my chest."

On to me, she thought.

"You've never let me explain," he was saying. "You've always given me one of those damn looks of yours, as if you wished I'd—"

Die.

"—wished I'd shut up." Shut up.

"You don't care how I feel!" He was shouting now. "Always in your own little world."

Shut up, she thought.

His mouth was open. She seemed to wish it closed, and with the thought his jaws snapped together, severing the very tip of his pink tongue. It fell from between his lips and lodged in a fold of his shirt.

Shut up, she thought again.

The two perfect regiments of his teeth ground down into each other; cracking and splitting, nerve, calcium and spit making a pinkish foam on his chin as his mouth collapsed inward.

Shut up, she was still thinking as his startled baby

blues sank back into his skull and his nose wormed its way into his brain.

He was not Ben any longer, he was a man with a red lizard's head, flattening, battening down upon itself, and, thank God, he was past speech-making once and for all.

Now she had the knack of it, she began to take pleasure in the changes she was willing upon him.

She flipped him head over heels on to the floor and began to compress his arms and legs, telescoping flesh and resistant bone into a smaller and yet smaller space. His clothes were folded inward, and the tissue of his stomach was plucked from his neatly packaged entrails and stretched around his body to wrap him up. His fingers were poking from his shoulder blades now, and his feet, still thrashing with fury, were tipped up in his gut. She turned him over one final time to pressure his spine into a foot-long column of muck, and that was about the end of it.

As she came out of her ecstasy she saw Ben sitting on the floor, shut up into a space about the size of one of his fine leather suitcases, while blood, bile and lymphatic fluid pulsed weakly from his hushed body.

My God, she thought, this can't be my husband. He's never been as tidy as that.

This time she didn't wait for help. This time she knew what she'd done (guessed, even, how she'd done it) and she accepted her crime for the too-rough justice it was. She packed her bags and left the home.

I'm alive, she thought. For the first time in my whole, wretched life, I'm alive.

VASSI'S TESTIMONY (PART ONE)

To you who dream of sweet, strong women I leave this

story. It is a promise, as surely as it is a confession, as surely as it's the last words of a lost man who wanted nothing but to love and be loved. I sit here trembling, waiting for the night, waiting for that whining pimp Koos to come to my door again, and take everything I own from me in exchange for the key to her room.

I am not a courageous man, and I never have been: so I'm afraid of what may happen to me tonight. But I cannot go through life dreaming all the time, existing through the darkness on only a glimpse of heaven. Sooner or later, one has to gird one's loins (that's appropriate) and get up and find it. Even if it means giving away the world in exchange.

I probably make no sense. You're thinking, you who chanced on this testimony, you're thinking, who was he, this imbecile?

My name was Oliver Vassi. I am now thirty-eight years old. I was a lawyer, until a year or more ago, when I began the search that ends tonight with that pimp and that key and that holy of holies.

But the story begins more than a year ago. It is many years since Jacqueline Ess first came to me.

She arrived out of the blue at my offices, claiming to be the widow of a friend of mine from law school, one Benjamin Ess, and when I thought back, I remembered the face. A mutual friend who'd been at the wedding had shown me a photograph of Ben and his blushing bride. And here she was, every bit as elusive a beauty as her photograph promised.

I remember being acutely embarrassed at that first interview. She'd arrived at a busy time, and I was up to my neck in work. But I was so enthralled by her, I let all the day's interviews fall by the wayside, and when my secretary came in she gave me one of her steely glances as if to throw a bucket of cold water over me. I suppose I was enamored from the start, and she sensed the electric atmosphere in my office. Me, I pretended I was merely being polite to the widow of an old friend. I didn't like to think about passion: it wasn't a part of my nature, or so I thought. How little we know—I mean really know—about our capabilities.

Jacqueline told me lies at that first meeting. About how Ben had died of cancer, of how often he had spoken of me, and how fondly. I suppose she could have told me the truth then and there, and I would have lapped it up— I believe I was utterly devoted from the beginning. But it's difficult to remember quite how and when interest in another human being flares into something more committed, more passionate. It may be that I am inventing the impact she had on me at that first meeting, simply reinventing history to justify my later excesses. I'm not sure. Anyway, wherever and whenever it happened, however quickly or slowly, I succumbed to her, and the affair began. I'm not a particularly inquisitive man where my friends, or my bed-partners, are concerned. As a lawyer one spends one's time going through the dirt of other people's lives, and frankly, eight hours a day of that is quite enough for me. When I'm out of the office my pleasure is in letting people be. I don't pry. I don't dig, I just take them on face value.

Jacqueline was no exception to this rule. She was a woman I was glad to have in my life whatever the truth of her past. She possessed a marvelous sang-froid, she was witty, bawdy, oblique. I had never met a more enchanting woman. It was none of my business how she'd lived with Ben, what the marriage had been like, etc., etc. That was her history. I was happy to live in the present, and let the past die its own death. I think I even flattered myself that whatever pain she had experienced, I could help her forget it.

Certainly her stories had holes in them. As a lawyer, I was trained to be eagle-eyed where fabrications were concerned, and however much I tried to put my perceptions aside I sensed that she wasn't quite coming clean with me. But everyone has secrets: I knew that. Let her have hers, I thought.

Only once did I challenge her on a detail of her pretended life story. In talking about Ben's death, she let slip that he had got what he deserved. I asked her what she meant. She smiled, that Gioconda smile of hers, and told me that she felt there was a balance to be redressed between men and women. I let the observation pass. After all, I was obsessed by that time, past all hope of salvation; whatever argument she was putting, I was happy to concede it.

She was so beautiful, you see. Not in any two-dimensional sense: she wasn't young, she wasn't innocent, she didn't have that pristine symmetry so favored by ad-men and photographers. Her face was plainly that of a woman in her early forties: it had been used to laugh and cry, and usage leaves its marks. But she had a power to transform herself, in the subtlest way, making that face as various as the sky. Early on, I thought it was a make-up trick. But as we slept together more and more, and I watched her in the mornings, sleep in her eyes, and in the evenings, heavy with fatigue, I soon realized she wore nothing on her skull but flesh and blood. What transformed her was internal: it was a trick of the will.

And, you know, that made me love her all the more.

Then one night I woke with her sleeping beside me. We slept often on the floor, which she preferred to the bed. Beds, she said, reminded her of marriage. Anyway, that night she was lying under a quilt on the carpet of my room, and I, simply out of adoration, was watching her face in sleep.

If one has given oneself utterly, watching the beloved sleep can be a vile experience. Perhaps some of you have known that paralysis, staring down at features closed to your inquiry, locked away from you where you can never, ever go, into the other's mind. As I say, for us who have given ourselves, that is a horror. One knows, in those moments, that one does not exist, except in relation to that face, that personality. Therefore, when that face is closed down, that personality is lost in its own unknowable world, one feels completely without purpose. A planet without a sun, revolving in darkness.

That's how I felt that night, looking down at her extraordinary features, and as I chewed on my soullessness, her face began to alter. She was clearly dreaming; but what dreams must she have been having. Her very fabric was on the move, her muscle, her hair, the down on her cheek moving to the dictates of some internal tide. Her lips bloomed from her bone, boiling up into a slavering tower of skin; her hair swirled around her head as though she were lying in water; the substance of her cheeks formed furrows and ridges like the ritual scars on a warrior; inflamed and throbbing patterns of tissue, swelling up and changing again even as a pattern formed. This fluxion was a terror to me, and I must have made some noise. She didn't wake, but came a little closer to the surface of sleep, leaving the deeper waters where these powers were sourced. The patterns sank away in an instant, and her face was again that of a gently sleeping woman.

That was, you can understand, a pivotal experience,

even though I spent the next few days trying to convince myself that I hadn't seen it.

The effort was useless. I knew there was something wrong with her; and at that time I was certain she knew nothing about it. I was convinced that something in her system was awry, and that I was best to investigate her history before I told her what I had seen.

On reflection, of course, that seems laughably naïve. To think she wouldn't have known that she contained such a power. But it was easier for me to picture her as prey to such skill, than mistress of it. That's a man speaking of a woman; not just me, Oliver Vassi, of her, Jacqueline Ess. We cannot believe, we men, that power will ever reside happily in the body of a woman, unless that power is a male child. Not true power. The power must be in male hands, God-given. That's what our fathers tell us, idiots that they are.

Anyway, I investigated Jacqueline, as surreptitiously as I could. I had a contact in York where the couple had lived, and it wasn't difficult to get some inquiries moving. It took a week for my contact to get back to me, because he'd had to cut through a good deal of shit from the police to get a hint of the truth, but the news came, and it was bad. Ben was dead, that much was true. But there was no way he had died of cancer. My contact had only got the vaguest clues as to the condition of Ben's corpse, but he gathered it had been spectacularly mutilated. And the prime suspect? My beloved Jacqueline Ess. The same innocent woman who was occupying my flat, sleeping by my side every night.

So I put it to her that she was hiding something from me. I don't know what I was expecting in return. What I got was a demonstration of her power. She gave it freely, without malice, but I would have been a fool not to have read a warning into it. She told me first how she had discovered her unique control over the sum and substance of human beings. In her despair, she said, when she was on the verge of killing herself, she had found, in the very deep-water trenches of her nature, faculties she had never known existed. Powers which came up out of those regions as she recovered, like fish to the light.

Then she showed me the smallest measure of these powers, plucking hairs from my head, one by one. Only a dozen; just to demonstrate her formidable skills. I felt them going. She just said: one from behind your ear, and I'd feel my skin creep and then jump as fingers of her volition snatched a hair out. Then another, and another. It was an incredible display; she had this power down to a fine art, locating and withdrawing single hairs from my scalp with the precision of tweezers. Frankly, I was sitting there rigid with fear, knowing that she was just toying with me. Sooner or later, I was certain the time would be right for her to silence me permanently.

But she had doubts about herself. She told me how the skill, though she had honed it, scared her. She needed, she said, someone to teach her how to use it best. And I was not that somebody. I was just a man who loved her, who had loved her before this revelation, and would love her still, in spite of it.

In fact, after that display I quickly came to accommodate a new vision of Jacqueline. Instead of fearing her, I became more devoted to this woman who tolerated my possession of her body.

My work became an irritation, a distraction that came between me and thinking of my beloved. What reputation I had began to deteriorate; I lost briefs, I lost credibility. In the space of two or three months my professional life dwindled away to almost nothing. Friends despaired of me, colleagues avoided me.

It wasn't that she was feeding on me. I want to be clear about that. She was no lamia, no succubus. What happened to me, my fall from grace with ordinary life if you like, was of my own making. She didn't bewitch me; that's a romantic lie to excuse rape. She was a sea: and I had to swim in her. Does that make any sense? I'd lived my life on the shore, in the solid world of law, and I was tired of it. She was liquid; a boundless sea in a single body, a deluge in a small room, and I will gladly drown in her, if she grants me the chance. But that was my decision. Understand that. This has always been my decision. I have decided to go to the room tonight, and be with her one final time. That is of my own free will.

And what man would not? She was (is) sublime.

For a month after that demonstration of power I lived in a permanent ecstasy of her. When I was with her she showed me ways to love beyond the limits of any other creature on God's earth. I say beyond the limits: with her there were no limits. And when I was away from her the reverie continued: because she seemed to have changed my world.

Then she left me.

I knew why: she'd gone to find someone to teach her how to use strength. But understanding her reasons made it no easier.

I broke down: lost my job, lost my identity, lost the few friends I had left in the world. I scarcely noticed. They were minor losses, beside the loss of Jacqueline . . .

"Jacqueline."

My God, she thought, can this really be the most

influential man in the country? He looked so unprepossessing, so very unspectacular. His chin wasn't even strong.

But Titus Pettifer was power.

He ran more monopolies than he could count; his word in the financial world could break companies like sticks, destroying the ambitions of hundreds, the careers of thousands. Fortunes were made overnight in his shadow, entire corporations fell when he blew on them, casualties of his whim. This man knew power if any man knew it. He had to be learned from.

"You wouldn't mind if I called you J., would you?"

"No."

"Have you been waiting long?"

"Long enough."

"I don't normally leave beautiful women waiting."

"Yes you do."

She knew him already: two minutes in his presence was enough to find his measure. He would come quickest to her if she was quietly insolent.

"Do you always call women you've never met before by their initials?"

"It's convenient for filing; do you mind?"

"It depends."

"On what?"

"What I get in return for giving you the privilege."

"It's a privilege, is it, to know your name?"

"Yes."

"Well . . . I'm flattered. Unless of course you grant that privilege widely?"

She shook her head. No, he could see she wasn't profligate with her affections.

"Why have you waited so long to see me?" he said. "Why have I had reports of your wearing my secretaries down with your constant demands to meet with me? Do you want money? Because if you do you'll go away empty-handed. I became rich by being mean, and the richer I get, the meaner I become."

The remark was truth; he spoke it plainly.

"I don't want money," she said, equally plainly.

"That's refreshing."

"There's richer than you."

He raised his eyebrows in surprise. She could bite, this beauty. "True," he said. There were at least half a dozen richer men in the hemisphere.

"I'm not an adoring little nobody. I haven't come here to screw a name. I've come here because we can be together. We have a great deal to offer each other."

"Such as?" he said.

"I have my body."

He smiled. It was the straightest offer he'd heard in years. "And what do I offer you in return for such largesse?"

"I want to learn—"

"Learn?"

"—how to use power."

She was stranger and stranger, this one.

"What do you mean?" he replied, playing for time. He hadn't got the measure of her; she vexed him, confounded him.

"Shall I recite it for you again, in bourgeois?" she said, playing insolence with such a smile he almost felt attractive again.

"No need. You want to learn to use power. I suppose I could teach you—"

"I know you can."

"You realize I'm a married man. Virginia and I have been together eighteen years."

"You have three sons, four houses, a maid-servant called Mirabelle. You loathe New York, and you love Bangkok; your shirt collar is 16½, your favorite color green."

"Turquoise."

"You're getting subtler in your old age."

"I'm not old."

"Eighteen years a married man. It ages you prematurely."

"Not me."

"Prove it."

"How?"

"Take me."

"What?"

"Take me."

"Here?"

"Draw the blinds, lock the door, turn off the computer terminus, and take me. I dare you."

"Dare?"

How long was it since anyone had dared him to do anything?

"Dare?"

He was excited. He hadn't been so excited in a dozen years. He drew the blinds, locked the door, turned off the video display of his fortunes.

My God, she thought, I've got him.

It wasn't an easy passion, not like that with Vassi. For one thing, Pettifer was a clumsy, uncultured lover. For another, he was too nervous of his wife to be a wholly successful adulterer. He thought he saw Virginia everywhere: in the lobbies of the hotels they took a room in for the afternoon, in cabs cruising the street outside their rendezvous, once even (he swore the likeness was exact) dressed as a waitress, and swabbing down a table in a restaurant. All fictional fears, but they dampened the spontaneity of the romance somewhat.

Still, she was learning from him. He was as brilliant a potentate as he was inept a lover. She learned how to be powerful without exercising power, how to keep one's self uncontaminated by the foulness all charisma stirs up in the uncharismatic; how to make the plain decisions plainly; how to be merciless. Not that she needed much education in that particular quarter. Perhaps it was more truthful to say he taught her never to regret her absence of instinctive compassion, but to judge with her intellect alone who deserved extinction and who might be numbered amongst the righteous.

Not once did she show herself to him, though she used her skills in the most secret of ways to tease pleasure out of his stale nerves.

In the fourth week of their affair they were lying side by side in a lilac room, while the mid-afternoon traffic growled in the street below. It had been a bad bout of sex; he was nervous, and no tricks would coax him out of himself.

It was over quickly, almost without heat.

He was going to tell her something. She knew it: it was waiting, this revelation, somewhere at the back of his throat. Turning to him she massaged his temples with her mind, and soothed him into speech.

He was about to spoil the day. He was about to spoil his career.

He was about, God help him, to spoil his life. "I have to stop seeing you," he said.

He wouldn't dare, she thought.

"I'm not sure what I know about you, or rather, what

I think I know about you, but it makes me . . . cautious of you, J. Do you understand?"

"No."

"I'm afraid I suspect you of . . . crimes."

"Crimes?"

"You have a history."

"Who's been rooting?" she asked. "Surely not Virginia?"

"No, not Virginia, she's beyond curiosity."

"Who then?"

"It's not your business."

"Who?"

She pressed lightly on his temples. It hurt him and he winced.

"What's wrong?" she asked.

"My head's aching."

"Tension, that's all, just tension. I can take it away, Titus." She touched her finger to his forehead, relaxing her hold on him. He sighed as relief came.

"Is that better?"

"Yes."

"Who's been snooping, Titus?"

"I have a personal secretary. Lyndon. You've heard me speak of him. He knew about our relationship from the beginning. Indeed, he books the hotels, arranges my cover stories for Virginia."

There was a sort of boyishness in this speech that was rather touching. As though he was embarrassed to leave her, rather than heartbroken. "Lyndon's quite a miracle worker. He's maneuvered a lot of things to make it easier between us. So he's got nothing against you. It's just that he happened to see one of the photographs I took of you. I gave them to him to shred."

"Why?"

"I shouldn't have taken them; it was a mistake.

Virginia might have . . . " He paused, began again. "Anyhow, he recognized you, although he couldn't remember where he'd seen you before."

"But he remembered eventually."

"He used to work for one of my newspapers, as a gossip columnist. That's how he came to be my personal assistant. He remembered you from your previous incarnation, as it were. Jacqueline Ess, the wife of Benjamin Ess, deceased."

"Deceased."

"He brought me some other photographs, not as pretty as the ones of you."

"Photographs of what?"

"Your home. And the body of your husband. They said it was a body, though in God's name there was precious little human being left in it."

"There was precious little to start with," she said simply, thinking of Ben's cold eyes, and colder hands. Fit only to be shut up, and forgotten.

"What happened?"

"To Ben? He was killed."

"How?" Did his voice waver a little?

"Very easily." She had risen from the bed, and was standing by the window. Strong summer light carved its way through the slats of the blind, ridges of shadow and sunlight charting the contours of her face.

"You did it."

"Yes." He had taught her to be plain. "Yes, I did it."

He had taught her an economy of threat too. "Leave me, and I'll do the same again."

He shook his head. "Never. You wouldn't dare." He was standing in front of her now.

"We must understand each other, J. I am powerful and I am pure. Do you see? My public face isn't even touched by a glimmer of scandal. I could afford a mistress, a dozen mistresses, to be revealed. But a murderess? No, that would spoil my life."

"Is he blackmailing you? This Lyndon?"

He stared at the day through the blinds, with a crippled look on his face. There was a twitch in the nerves of his cheek, under his left eye.

"Yes, if you must know," he said in a dead voice. "The bastard has me for all I'm worth."

"I see."

"And if he can guess, so can others. You understand?"

"I'm strong: you're strong. We can twist them around our little fingers."

"No."

"Yes! I have skills, Titus."

"I don't want to know."

"You will know," she said.

She looked at him, taking hold of his hands without touching him. He watched, all astonished eyes, as his unwilling hands were raised to touch her face, to stroke her hair with the fondest of gestures. She made him run his trembling fingers across her breasts, taking them with more ardor than he could summon on his own initiative.

"You are always too tentative, Titus," she said, making him paw her almost to the point of bruising. "This is how I like it." Now his hands were lower, fetching out a different look from her face. Tides were moving over it, she was all alive—

"Deeper—"

His finger intruded, his thumb stroked.

"I like that, Titus. Why can't you do that to me without me demanding?"

He blushed. He didn't like to talk about what they did together.

She coaxed him deeper, whispering.

"I won't break, you know. Virginia may be Dresden china, I'm not. I want feeling; I want something that I can remember you by when I'm not with you. Nothing is everlasting, is it? But I want something to keep me warm through the night."

He was sinking to his knees, his hands kept, by her design, on her and in her, still roving like two lustful crabs. His body was awash with sweat. It was, she thought, the first time she'd ever seen him sweat.

"Don't kill me," he whimpered.

"I could wipe you out." Wipe, she thought, then put the image out of her mind before she did him some harm.

"I know. I know," he said. "You can kill me easily."

He was crying. My God, she thought, the great man is at my feet, sobbing like a baby. What can I learn of power from this puerile performance? She plucked the tears off his cheeks, using rather more strength than the task required. His skin reddened under her gaze.

"Let me be, J. I can't help you. I'm useless to you."

It was true. He was absolutely useless. Contemptuously, she let his hands go. They fell limply by his sides.

"Don't ever try and find me, Titus. You understand? Don't ever send your minions after me to preserve your reputation, because I will be more merciless than you've ever been."

He said nothing; just knelt there, facing the window, while she washed her face, drank the coffee they'd ordered, and left.

Lyndon was surprised to find the door of his office ajar. It was only seven-thirty-six. None of the secretaries would be in for another hour. Clearly one of the cleaners had been remiss, leaving the door unlocked. He'd find out who: sack her.

He pushed the door open.

Jacqueline was sitting with her back to the door. He recognized the back of her head, that fall of auburn hair. A sluttish display; too teased, too wild. His office, an annex to Mr. Pettifer's, was kept meticulously ordered. He glanced over it: everything seemed to be in place.

"What are you doing here?"

She took a little breath, preparing herself.

This was the first time she had planned to do it. Before it had been a spur-of-the-moment decision.

He was approaching the desk, and putting down his briefcase and his neatly folded copy of the Financial Times.

"You have no right to come in here without my permission," he said. She turned on the lazy swivel of his chair; the way he did when he had people in to discipline.

"Lyndon," she said.

"Nothing you can say or do will change the facts, Mrs. Ess," he said, saving her the trouble of introducing the subject, "you are a cold-blooded killer. It was my bounden duty to inform Mr. Pettifer of the situation."

"You did it for the good of Titus?"

"Of course."

"And the blackmail, that was also for the good of Titus, was it?" "Get out of my office—"

"Was it, Lyndon?"

"You're a whore! Whores know nothing: they are ignorant, diseased animals," he spat. "Oh, you're cunning, I grant you that—but then so's any slut with a living to make."

She stood up. He expected a riposte. He got none; at

least not verbally. But he felt a tautness across his face: as though someone was pressing on it.

"What . . . are . . . you . . . doing?" he asked. "Doing?"

His eyes were being forced into slits like a child imitating a monstrous Oriental, his mouth was hauled wide and tight, his smile brilliant. The words were difficult to say—

"Stop . . . it . . . "

She shook her head.

"Whore . . . " he said again, still defying her.

She just stared at him. His face was beginning to jerk and twitch under the pressure, the muscles going into spasm.

"The police . . . " he tried to say, "if you lay a finger on me . . . "

"I won't," she said, and pressed home her advantage.

Beneath his clothes he felt the same tension all over his body, pulling his skin, drawing him tighter and tighter. Something was going to give; he knew it. Some part of him would be weak, and tear under this relentless assault. And if he once began to break open, nothing would prevent her ripping him apart. He worked all this out quite coolly, while his body twitched and he swore at her through his enforced grin.

"Cunt," he said. "Syphilitic cunt."

He didn't seem to be afraid, she thought.

In extremis he just unleashed so much hatred of her, the fear was entirely eclipsed. Now he was calling her a whore again; though his face was distorted almost beyond recognition.

And then he began to split.

The tear began at the bridge of his nose and ran up, across his brow, and down, bisecting his lips and his chin, then his neck and chest. In a matter of seconds his shirt was dyed red, his dark suit darkening further, his cuffs and trouser-legs pouring blood. The skin flew off his hands like gloves off a surgeon, and two rings of scarlet tissue lolled down to either side of his flayed face like the ears of an elephant.

His name-calling had stopped.

He had been dead of shock now for ten seconds, though she was still working him over vengefully, tugging his skin off his body and flinging the scraps around the room, until at last he stood, steaming, in his red suit, and his red shirt, and his shiny red shoes, and looked, to her eyes, a little more like a sensitive man. Content with the effect, she released him. He lay down quietly in a blood puddle and slept.

My God, she thought, as she calmly took the stairs out the back way, that was murder in the first degree.

She saw no reports of the death in any of the papers, and nothing on the news bulletins. Lyndon had apparently died as he had lived, hidden from public view.

But she knew wheels, so big their hubs could not be seen by insignificant individuals like herself, would be moving. What they would do, how they would change her life, she could only guess at. But the murder of Lyndon had not simply been spite, though that had been a part of it. No, she'd also wanted to stir them up, her enemies in the world, and bring them after her. Let them show their hands: let them show their contempt, their terror. She'd gone through her life, it seemed, looking for a sign of herself, only able to define her nature by the look in others' eyes. Now she wanted an end to that. It was time to deal with her pursuers.

Surely now everyone who had seen her, Pettifer first,

then Vassi, would come after her, and she would close their eyes permanently: make them forgetful of her. Only then, the witnesses destroyed, would she be free.

Pettifer didn't come, of course, not in person. It was easy for him to find agents, men without scruple or compassion, but with a nose for pursuit that would shame a bloodhound.

A trap was being laid for her, though she couldn't yet see its jaws. There were signs of it everywhere. An eruption of birds from behind a wall, a peculiar light from a distant window, footsteps, whistles, dark-suited men reading the news at the limit of her vision. As the weeks passed they didn't come any closer to her, but then neither did they go away. They waited, like cats in a tree, their tails twitching, their eyes lazy.

But the pursuit had Pettifer's mark. She'd learned enough from him to recognize his circumspection and his guile. They would come for her eventually, not in her time, but in theirs. Perhaps not even in theirs: in his. And though she never saw his face, it was as though Titus was on her heels personally.

My God, she thought, I'm in danger of my life and I don't care.

It was useless, this power over flesh, if it had no direction behind it. She had used it for her own petty reasons, for the gratification of nervous pleasure and sheer anger. But these displays hadn't brought her any closer to other people: they just made her a freak in their eyes. Sometimes she thought of Vassi, and wondered where he was, what he was doing. He hadn't been a strong man, but he'd had a little passion in his soul. More than Ben, more than Pettifer, certainly more than Lyndon. And, she remembered, fondly, he was the only man she'd ever known who called her Jacqueline. All the rest had manufactured unendearing corruptions of her name: Jackie, or J., or, in Ben's more irritating moods, Ju-ju. Only Vassi had called her Jacqueline, plain and simple, accepting, in his formal way, the completeness of her, the totality of her. And when she thought of him, tried to picture how he might return to her, she feared for him.

VASSI'S TESTIMONY (PART TWO)

Of course I searched for her. It's only when you've lost someone, you realize the nonsense of that phrase "it's a small world." It isn't. It's a vast, devouring world, especially if you're alone.

When I was a lawyer, locked in that incestuous coterie, I used to see the same faces day after day. Some I'd exchange words with, some smiles, some nods. We belonged, even if we were enemies at the Bar, to the same complacent circle. We ate at the same tables, we drank elbow to elbow. We even shared mistresses, though we didn't always know it at the time. In such circumstances, it's easy to believe the world means you no harm. Certainly you grow older, but then so does everyone else. You even believe, in your self-satisfied way, that the passage of years makes you a little wiser. Life is bearable; even the 3:00 A.M. sweats come more infrequently as the bank balance swells.

But to think that the world is harmless is to lie to yourself, to believe in so-called certainties that are, in fact, simply shared delusions.

When she left, all the delusions fell away, and all the lies I had assiduously lived by became strikingly apparent.

It's not a small world, when there's only one face in it you can bear to look upon, and that face is lost somewhere in a maelstrom. It's not a small world when the few, vital memories of your object of affection are in danger of being trampled out by the thousands of moments that assail you every day, like children tugging at you, demanding your sole attention.

I was a broken man,

I would find myself (there's an apt phrase) sleeping in tiny bedrooms in forlorn hotels, drinking more often than eating, and writing her name, like a classic obsessive, over and over again. On the walls, on the pillow, on the palm of my hand. I broke the skin of my palm with my pen, and the ink infected it. The mark's still there, I'm looking at it now. Jacqueline, it says. Jacqueline.

Then one day, entirely by chance, I saw her. It sounds melodramatic, but I thought I was going to die at that moment. I'd imagined her for so long, keyed myself up for seeing her again, that when it happened I felt my limbs weaken, and I was sick in the middle of the street. Not a classic reunion. The lover, on seeing his beloved, throws up down his shirt. But then, nothing that happened between Jacqueline and myself was ever quite normal. Or natural.

I followed her, which was difficult. There were crowds, and she was walking fast. I didn't know whether to call out her name or not. I decided not. What would she have done anyway, seeing this unshaven lunatic shambling toward her, calling her name? She would have run probably. Or worse, she would have reached into my chest, seizing my heart in her will, and put me out of my misery before I could reveal her to the world.

So I was silent, and simply followed her, doggedly, to what I assumed was her apartment. And I stayed there, or in the vicinity, for the next two and a half days, not quite knowing what to do. It was a ridiculous dilemma. After all this time of watching for her, now that she was within speaking distance, touching distance, I didn't dare approach.

Maybe I feared death. But then, here I am, in this stinking room in Amsterdam, setting my testimony down and waiting for Koos to bring me her key, and I don't fear death now. Probably it was my vanity that prevented me from approaching her. I didn't want her to see me cracked and desolate; I wanted to come to her clean, her dream lover.

While I waited, they came for her.

I don't know who they were. Two men, plainly dressed. I don't think policemen: too smooth. Cultured even. And she didn't resist. She went smilingly, as if to the opera.

At the first opportunity I returned to the building a little better dressed, located her apartment from the porter, and broke in. She had been living plainly. In one corner of the room she had set up a table, and had been writing her memoirs. I sat down and read, and eventually took the pages away with me. She had got no further than the first seven years of her life. I wondered, again in my vanity, if I would have been chronicled in the book. Probably not.

I took some of her clothes too; only items she had worn when I had known her. And nothing intimate: I'm not a fetishist. I wasn't going to go home and bury my face in the smell of her underwear. But I wanted something to remember her by; to picture her in. Though on reflection I never met a human being more fitted to dress purely in her skin.

So I lost her a second time, more the fault of my own cowardice than circumstance.

Pettifer didn't come near the house they were keeping Mrs. Ess in for four weeks. She was given more or less everything she asked for, except her freedom, and she only asked for that in the most abstracted fashion. She wasn't interested in escape: though it would have been easy to achieve. Once or twice she wondered if Titus had told the two men and the woman who were keeping her a prisoner in the house exactly what she was capable of: she guessed not. They treated her as though she were simply a woman Titus had set eyes on and desired. They had procured her for his bed, simple as that.

With a room to herself, and an endless supply of paper, she began to write her memoirs again, from the beginning.

It was late summer, and the nights were getting chilly. Sometimes, to warm herself, she would lie on the floor (she'd asked them to remove the bed) and will her body to ripple like the surface of a lake. Her body, without sex, became a mystery to her again; and she realized for the first time that physical love had been an exploration of that most intimate, and yet most unknown region of her being: her flesh. She had understood herself best embracing someone else: seen her own substance clearly only when another's lips were laid on it, adoring and gentle. She thought of Vassi again; and the lake, at the thought of him, was roused as if by a tempest. Her breasts shook into curling mountains, her belly ran with extraordinary tides, currents crossed and recrossed her flickering face, lapping at her mouth and leaving their mark like waves on sand. As she was fluid in his memory, so as she remembered him, she liquified.

She thought of the few times she had been at peace in her life; and physical love, discharging ambition and vanity, had always preceded those fragile moments. There were other ways presumably; but her experience had been limited. Her mother had always said that women, being more at peace with themselves than men, needed fewer distractions from their hurts. But she'd not found it like that at all. She'd found her life full of hurts, but almost empty of ways to salve them.

She left off writing her memoirs when she reached her ninth year. She despaired of telling her story from that point on, with the first realization of oncoming puberty. She burned the papers on a bonfire she lit in the middle of her room the day that Pettifer arrived.

My God, she thought, this can't be power.

Pettifer looked sick; as physically changed as a friend she'd lost to cancer. One month seemingly healthy, the next sucked up from the inside, self-devoured. He looked like a husk of a man: his skin gray and mottled. Only his eyes glittered, and those like the eyes of a mad dog.

He was dressed immaculately, as though for a wedding.

"J."

"Titus."

He looked her up and down. "Are you well?"

"Thank you, yes."

"They give you everything you ask for?"

"Perfect hosts."

"You haven't resisted."

"Resisted?"

"Being here. Locked up. I was prepared, after Lyndon, for another slaughter of the innocents."

"Lyndon was not innocent, Titus. These people are. You didn't tell them."

"I didn't deem it necessary. May I close the door?"

He was her captor: but he came like an emissary to the camp of a greater power. She liked the way he was with her, cowed but elated. He closed the door, and locked it.

"I love you, J. And I fear you. In fact, I think I love you because I fear you. Is that a sickness?"

"I would have thought so."

"Yes, so would I."

"Why did you take such a time to come?"

"I had to put my affairs in order. Otherwise there would have been chaos. When I was gone."

"You're leaving?"

He looked into her, the muscles of his face ruffled by anticipation. "I hope so."

"Where to?"

Still she didn't guess what had brought him to the house, his affairs neatened, his wife unknowingly asked forgiveness of as she slept, all channels of escape closed, all contradictions laid to rest.

Still she didn't guess he'd come to die.

"I'm reduced by you, J. Reduced to nothing. And there is nowhere for me to go. Do you follow?"

"No."

"I cannot live without you," he said. The cliché was unpardonable. Could he not have found a better way to say it? She almost laughed, it was so trite.

But he hadn't finished.

"—and I certainly can't live with you." Abruptly, the tone changed. "Because you revolt me, woman, your whole being disgusts me."

"So?" she asked, softly.

"So . . . " He was tender again and she began to understand. " . . . kill me."

It was grotesque. The glittering eyes were steady on her.

"It's what I want," he said. "Believe me, it's all I want in the world. Kill me, however you please. I'll go without resistance, without complaint."

She remembered the old joke. Masochist to Sadist: Hurt me! For God's sake, hurt me! Sadist to Masochist: No.

"And if I refuse?" she said.

"You can't refuse. I'm loathsome."

"But I don't hate you, Titus."

"You should. I'm weak. I'm useless to you. I taught you nothing."

"You taught me a great deal. I can control myself now."

"Lyndon's death was controlled, was it?"

"Certainly."

"It looked a little excessive to me."

"He got everything he deserved."

"Give me what I deserve, then, in my turn. I've locked you up.

I've rejected you when you needed me. Punish me for it."

"I survived."

"J.!"

Even in this extremity he couldn't call her by her full name.

"Please to God. Please to God. I need only this one thing from you. Do it out of whatever motive you have in you. Compassion, or contempt, or love. But do it, please do it."

"No," she said.

He crossed the room suddenly, and slapped her, very hard. "Lyndon said you were a whore. He was right; you are. Gutter slut, nothing better."

He walked away, turned, walked back, hit her again, faster, harder, and again, six or seven times, backward and forward.

Then he stopped, panting.

"You want money?" Bargains now. Blows, then bargains.

She was seeing him twisted through tears of shock, which she was unable to prevent.

"Do you want money?" he said again.

"What do you think?"

He didn't hear her sarcasm, and began to scatter notes around her feet, dozens and dozens of them, like offerings around the Statue of the Virgin.

"Anything you want," he said, "Jacqueline."

In her belly she felt something close to pain as the urge to kill him found birth, but she resisted it. It was playing into his hands, becoming the instrument of his will: powerless. Usage again; that's all she ever got. She had been bred like a cow, to give a certain supply. Of care to husbands, of milk to babies, of death to old men. And, like a cow, she was expected to be compliant with every demand made of her, whenever the call came. Well, not this time.

She went to the door. "Where are you going?" She reached for the key.

"Your death is your own business, not mine," she said.

He ran at her before she could unlock the door, and the blow—in its force, in its malice—was totally unexpected.

"Bitch!" he shrieked, a hail of blows coming fast upon the first. In her stomach, the thing that wanted to kill grew a little larger.

He had his fingers tangled in her hair, and pulled her back into the room, shouting obscenities at her, an endless stream of them, as though he'd opened a dam full of sewer-water on her. This was just another way for him to get what he wanted, she told herself, if you succumb to this you've lost: he's just manipulating you. Still the words came: the same dirty words that had been thrown at generations of unsubmissive women. Whore; heretic; cunt; bitch; monster.

Yes, she was that.

Yes, she thought: monster I am.

The thought made it easy. She turned. He knew what she intended even before she looked at him. He dropped his hands from her head. Her anger was already in her throat coming out of her—crossing the air between them.

Monster he calls me: monster I am.

I do this for myself, not for him. Never for him. For myself!

He gasped as her will touched him, and the glittering eyes stopped glittering for a moment, the will to die became the will to survive, all too late of course, and he roared. She heard answering shouts, steps, threats on the stairs. They would be in the room in a matter of moments.

"You are an animal," she said.

"No," he said, certain even now that his place was in command.

"You don't exist," she said, advancing on him. "They'll never find the part that was Titus. Titus is gone. The rest is just—"

The pain was terrible. It stopped even a voice coming out from him. Or was that her again, changing his throat, his palate, his very head? She was unlocking the plates of his skull, and reorganizing him. No, he wanted to say, this isn't the subtle ritual I had planned. I wanted to die folded into you, I wanted to go with my mouth clamped to yours, cooling in you as I died. This is not the way I want it.

No. No. No.

They were at the door, the men who'd kept her here, beating on it. She had no fear of them, of course, except that they might spoil her handiwork before the final touches were added to it.

Someone was hurling himself at the door now. Wood splintered: the door was flung open. The two men were both armed. They pointed their weapons at her, steady-handed.

"Mr. Pettifer?" said the younger man. In the corner of the room, under the table, Pettifer's eyes shone.

"Mr. Pettifer?" he said again, forgetting the woman.

Pettifer shook his snouted head. Don't come any closer, please, he thought.

The man crouched down and stared under the table at the disgusting beast that was squatting there; bloody from its transformation, but alive. She had killed his nerves: he felt no pain. He just survived, his hands knotted into paws, his legs scooped up around his back, knees broken so he had the look of a four-legged crab, his brain exposed, his eyes lidless, lower jaw broken and swept up over his top jaw like a bulldog, ears torn off, spine snapped, humanity bewitched into another state

"You are an animal," she'd said. It wasn't a bad facsimile of beasthood. The man with the gun gagged as he recognized fragments of his master. He stood up, greasy-chinned, and glanced around at the woman.

Jacqueline shrugged.

"You did this?" Awe mingled with the revulsion. She nodded.

"Come, Titus," she said, clicking her fingers. The beast shook its head, sobbing.

"Come, Titus," she said more forcefully, and Titus Pettifer waddled out of his hiding place, leaving a trail

like a punctured meat-sack. The man fired [
remains out of sheer instinct. Anything, anything at all to
prevent this disgusting creature from approaching him.

Titus stumbled two steps back on his bloody paws,
shook himself as if to dislodge the death in him, and
failing, died.

"Content?" she asked.

The gunman looked up from the execution. Was the
power talking to him? No; Jacqueline was staring at
Pettifer's corpse, asking the question of him.

Content?

The gunman dropped his weapon. The other man did
the same. "How did this happen?" asked the man at the
door. A simple question: a child's question.

"He asked," said Jacqueline. "It was all I could give
him." The gunman nodded, and fell to his knees.

VASSI'S TESTIMONY (FINAL PART)

Chance has played a worryingly large part in my romance
with Jacqueline Ess. Sometimes it's seemed I've been
subject to every tide that passes through the world, spun
around by the merest flick of accident's wrist. Other times
I've had the suspicion that she was masterminding my
life, as she was the lives of a hundred others, a thousand
others, arranging every fluke meeting, choreographing
my victories and my defeats, escorting me, blindly,
toward this last encounter.

I found her without knowing I'd found her, that was
the irony of it. I'd traced her first to a house in Surrey, a
house that had a year previous seen the murder of one
Titus Pettifer, a billionaire shot by one of his own
bodyguards. In the upstairs room, where the murder had
taken place, all was serenity. If she had been there, they

97

had removed any sign. But the house, now in virtual ruin, was prey to all manner of graffiti; and on the stained plaster wall of that room someone had scrawled a woman. She was obscenely over-endowed, her gaping sex blazing with what looked like lightning. And at her feet there was a creature of indeterminate species. Perhaps a crab, perhaps a dog, perhaps even a man. Whatever it was it had no power over itself. It sat in the light of her agonizing presence and counted itself amongst the fortunate. Looking at that wizened creature, with its eyes turned up to gaze on the burning Madonna, I knew the picture was a portrait of Jacqueline.

I don't know how long I stood looking at the graffiti, but I was interrupted by a man who looked to be in a worse condition than me. A beard that had never been trimmed or washed, a frame so wasted I wondered how he managed to stand upright, and a smell that would not have shamed a skunk.

I never knew his name: but he was, he told me, the maker of the picture on the wall. It was easy to believe that. His desperation, his hunger, his confusion were all marks of a man who had seen Jacqueline.

If I was rough in my interrogation of him I'm sure he forgave me. It was an unburdening for him, to tell everything he'd seen the day that Pettifer had been killed, and know that I believed it all. He told me his fellow bodyguard, the man who had fired the shots that had killed Pettifer, had committed suicide in prison.

His life, he said, was meaningless. She had destroyed it. I gave him what reassurances I could; that she meant no harm, and that he needn't fear that she would come for him. When I told him that, he cried, more, I think, out of loss than relief.

Finally I asked him if he knew where Jacqueline was

now. I'd left that question to the end, though it had been the most pressing inquiry, because I suppose I didn't dare hope he'd know. But my God, he did. She had not left the house immediately after the shooting of Pettifer. She had sat down with this man, and talked to him quietly about his children, his tailor, his car. She'd asked him what his mother had been like, and he'd told her his mother had been a prostitute. Had she been happy? Jacqueline had asked. He'd said he didn't know. Did she ever cry, she'd asked. He'd said he never saw her laugh or cry in his life. And she'd nodded, and thanked him.

Later, before his suicide, the other gunman had told him Jacqueline had gone to Amsterdam. This he knew for a fact, from a man called Koos. And so the circle begins to close, yes?

I was in Amsterdam seven weeks, without finding a single clue to her whereabouts, until yesterday evening. Seven weeks of celibacy, which is unusual for me. Listless with frustration I went down to the red-light district, to find a woman. They sit there you know, in the windows, like mannequins, beside pink-fringed lamps. Some have miniature dogs on their laps; some read. Most just stare out at the street, as if mesmerized.

There were no faces there that interested me. They all seemed joyless, lightless, too much unlike her. Yet I couldn't leave. I was like a fat boy in a sweet shop, too nauseated to buy, too gluttonous to go.

Toward the middle of the night, I was spoken to out of the crowd by a young man who, on closer inspection, was not young at all, but heavily made up. He had no eyebrows, just pencil marks drawn onto his shiny skin. A cluster of gold earrings in his left ear, a half-eaten peach in his white-gloved hand, open sandals, lacquered toenails. He took hold of my sleeve, proprietorially.

I must have sneered at his sickening appearance, but he didn't seem at all upset by my contempt. You look like a man of discernment, he said. I looked nothing of the kind: you must be mistaken, I said. No, he replied, I am not mistaken. You are Oliver Vassi.

My first thought, absurdly, was that he intended to kill me. I tried to pull away; his grip on my cuff was relentless.

You want a woman, he said. Did I hesitate enough for him to know I meant yes, though I said no? I have a woman like no other, he went on, she's a miracle. I know you'll want to meet her in the flesh. What made me know it was Jacqueline he was talking about?

Perhaps the fact that he had known me from out of the crowd, as though she was up at a window somewhere, ordering her admirers to be brought to her like a diner ordering lobster from a tank. Perhaps too the way his eyes shone at me, meeting mine without fear because fear, like rapture, he felt only in the presence of one creature on God's cruel earth. Could I not also see myself reflected in his perilous look? He knew Jacqueline, I had no doubt of it.

He knew I was hooked, because once I hesitated he turned away from me with a mincing shrug, as if to say: you missed your chance. Where is she? I said, seizing his twig-thin arm. He cocked his head down the street and I followed him, suddenly as witless as an idiot, out of the throng. The road emptied as we walked; the red lights gave way to gloom, and then to darkness. If I asked him where we were going once I asked him a dozen times; he chose not to answer, until we reached a narrow door in a narrow house down some razor-thin street. We're here, he announced, as though the hovel were the Palace of Versailles.

Up two flights in the otherwise empty house there was a room with a black door. He pressed me to it. It was locked.

"See," he invited, "she's inside."

"It's locked," I replied. My heart was fit to burst: she was near, for certain, I knew she was near.

"See," he said again, and pointed to a tiny hole in the panel of the door. I devoured the light through it, pushing my eye toward her through the tiny hole.

The squalid interior was empty, except for a mattress and Jacqueline. She lay spread-eagled, her wrists and ankles bound to rough posts set in the bare floor at the four corners of the mattress.

"Who did this?" I demanded, not taking my eye from her nakedness.

"She asks," he replied. "It is her desire. She asks."

She had heard my voice; she cranked up her head with some difficulty and stared directly at the door. When she looked at me all the hairs rose on my head, I swear it, in welcome, and swayed at her command.

"Oliver," she said.

"Jacqueline." I pressed the word to the wood with a kiss.

Her body was seething, her shaved sex opening and closing like some exquisite plant, purple and lilac and rose.

"Let me in," I said to Koos.

"You will not survive one night with her."

"Let me in."

"She is expensive," he warned. "How much do you want?"

"Everything you have. The shirt off your back, your money, your jewelry; then she is yours."

I wanted to beat the door down, or break his nicotine-stained fingers one by one until he gave me the key. He knew what I was thinking. "The key is hidden," he said, "and the door is strong. You must pay, Mr. Vassi. You want to pay." It was true. I wanted to pay.

"You want to give me all you have ever owned, all you have ever been. You want to go to her with nothing to claim you back. I know this. It's how they all go to her."

"All? Are there many?"

"She is insatiable," he said, without relish. It wasn't a pimp's boast: it was his pain, I saw that clearly. "I am always finding more for her, and burying them."

Burying them.

That, I suppose, is Koos's function; he disposes of the dead. And he will get his lacquered hands on me after tonight; he will fetch me off her when I am dry and useless to her, and find some pit, some canal, some furnace to lose me in. The thought isn't particularly attractive.

Yet here I am with all the money I could raise from selling my few remaining possessions on the table in front of me, my dignity gone, my life hanging on a thread, waiting for a pimp and a key.

It's well dark now, and he's late. But I think he is obliged to come. Not for the money; he probably has few requirements beyond his heroin and his mascara. He will come to do business with me because she demands it and he is in thrall to her, every bit as much as I am. Oh, he will come. Of course he will come.

Well, I think that is sufficient.

This is my testimony. I have no time to reread it now. His footsteps are on the stairs (he limps) and I must go with him. This I leave to whoever finds it, to use as they think fit. By morning I shall be dead, and happy. Believe it.

My God, she thought, Koos has cheated me.

Vassi had been outside the door, she'd felt his flesh with her mind and she'd embraced it. But Koos hadn't let him in, despite her explicit orders. Of all men, Vassi was to be allowed free access, Koos knew that. But he'd cheated her, the way they'd all cheated her except Vassi. With him (perhaps) it had been love.

She lay on the bed through the night, never sleeping. She seldom slept now for more than a few minutes: and only then with Koos watching her. She'd done herself harm in her sleep, mutilating herself without knowing it, waking up bleeding and screaming with every limb sprouting needles she'd made out of her own skin and muscle, like a flesh cactus.

It was dark again, she guessed, but it was difficult to be sure. In this heavily curtained, bare-bulb-lit room, it was a perpetual day to the senses, perpetual night to the soul. She would lie, bed-sores on her back, on her buttocks, listening to the far sounds of the street, sometimes dozing for a while, sometimes eating from Koos's hand, being washed, being toileted, being used.

A key turned in the lock. She strained from the mattress to see who it was. The door was opening . . . opening . . . opened.

Vassi. Oh God, it was Vassi at last, she could see him crossing the room toward her.

Let this not be another memory, she prayed, please let it be him this time: true and real.

"Jacqueline."

He said the name of her flesh, the whole name. "Jacqueline." It was him.

Behind him, Koos stared between her legs, fascinated by the dance of her labia.

"Koo . . . " she said, trying to smile.

"I brought him." He grinned at her, not looking away from her sex.

"A day," she whispered. "I waited a day, Koos. You made me wait—"

"What's a day to you?" he said, still grinning.

She didn't need the pimp any longer, not that he knew that. In his innocence he thought Vassi was just another man she'd seduced along the way; to be drained and discarded like the others. Koos believed he would be needed tomorrow; that's why he played this fatal game so artlessly.

"Lock the door," she suggested to him. "Stay if you like."

"Stay?" he said, leering. "You mean, and watch?"

He watched anyway. She knew he watched through that hole he had bored in the door; she could hear him pant sometimes. But this time, let him stay forever.

Carefully, he took the key from the outside of the door, closed it, slipped the key into the inside and locked it. Even as the lock clicked she killed him, before he could even turn round and look at her again. Nothing spectacular in the execution; she just reached into his pigeon chest and crushed his lungs. He slumped against the door and slid down, smearing his face across the wood.

Vassi didn't even turn round to see him die; she was all he ever wanted to look at again.

He approached the mattress, crouched, and began to untie her ankles. The skin was chafed, the rope scabby with old blood. He worked at the knots systematically, finding a calm he thought he'd lost, a simple contentment in being here at the end, unable to go back, and knowing that the path ahead was deep in her.

When her ankles were free, he began on her wrists, interrupting her view of the ceiling as he bent over her. His voice was soft.

"Why did you let him do this to you?"

"I was afraid."

"Of what?"

"To move; even to live. Every day, agony."

"Yes."

He understood so well that total incapacity to exist.

She felt him at her side, undressing, then laying a kiss on the sallow skin of the stomach of the body she occupied. It was marked with her workings; the skin had been stretched beyond its tolerance and was permanently crisscrossed.

He lay down beside her, and the feel of his body against hers was not unpleasant.

She touched his head. Her joints were stiff, the movements painful, but she wanted to draw his face up to hers. He came, smiling, into her sight, and they exchanged kisses.

My God, she thought, we are together.

And thinking they were together, her will was made flesh. Under his lips her features dissolved, becoming the red sea he'd dreamed of, and washing up over his face, that was itself dissolving: common waters made of thought and bone.

Her keen breasts pricked him like arrows; his erection, sharpened by her thought, killed her in return with his only thrust. Tangled in a wash of love they thought themselves extinguished, and were.

Outside, the hard world mourned on, the chatter of buyers and sellers continuing through the night.

Eventually indifference and fatigue claimed even the eagerest merchant. Inside and out there was a healing silence: an end to losses and to gains.

An Exhibition of Mother and Monster

STEPHANIE M. WYTOVICH

Inside the teratology room sleeps the fate of monsters, a resting place for the deformities whose faces line these walls the rejects of Mother Nature, her prodigious anomalies spat out and left to die.

These oddities, stagnant in century-old formaldehyde, relax in public tombs available for viewing at $18.00 a day, a wholesome fee for the Devil's smile, this collection of curiosities: beware the wickedness of spiral beggars, look upon the whispers that went against God's plan, these mutilated baby boys, these fractured femme fatales, opened and stretched, split-lipped and broken, we showcase their corpses in air-tight jars their mouths, yawning graveyards of abandonment, their eyes, a reflection of consent forms and sins.

Stand before them, read their stories, their dissected diaries of splintered bone, of engorged muscles, webbed and bulbous, they wrote with lobster claws, breathed with gills, their heart-beats preserved in an exhibition to the

evils who bore them: of mother and monster, of doctor and demon, these be the rotted seeds, the archetypes of luciferous defect conserved as warnings to the loose, to the imaginative and wicked, the small-womb'd and the back-wood witch.

Come close, now, listen to them breathe: them, the disfigured vibrations, the warped frequencies of our fetishes and kinks, these fallen seraphs, these nightmare machines. Look, but don't touch, memorize and never forget, the half-baked children, the angel-food warriors their clocks may have broken, but their spirits still tick so take your pictures, claim your keepsakes, remember this history of beatific pain,
Bless yourselves before you leave, and may God have mercy on your curious, curious souls.

CURIOSITIES

Madame Painte: For Sale

JOHN LANGAN

"**T**HIS?" **THE MAN** behind the counter says. "Why, this is Madame Painte."

The figure is short, a foot and a half tall, and squat, about the same dimensions across, composed of what might be porcelain. The face is round, the eyes squeezed shut by the wide smile lifting the cheeks. A pointed hat fails to conceal the pointed tips of the figure's ears. It wears a long apron dress over a peasant blouse. A typical garden gnome, you think, except for the colors, from which it obviously derives its name. It's been painted without regard for the margins of clothing and skin. Black, green, and orange slash down the figure from right to left. The face is mostly dark green, the hat orange mixed with black. A splash of white paint traverses the closed eyes; the effect is less a mask and more a piece of webbing. You saw the figure sitting to the left of the door to the antiques shop as you walked up the path to it and were so struck by its remarkable grotesquerie that you lifted and carried it inside, setting it on the front counter. On the way, you read the notecard strung to the top of the hat: MUST BE KEPT OUTSIDE.

"I didn't mean its name," you start.

"Of course not," the man says. He's on the small side, more wiry than slender. Based on the ratio of salt to pepper in his mustache and hair, he's somewhere in the deep middle of middle age. He says, "You meant the warning."

"*Must* be kept outside," you read. "Why must?"

"The official reason is, she's covered in lead paint."

You step back from the counter, wipe your hands on your jeans. "There's an unofficial reason?"

"There's a story," the man says. "Would you like to hear it? It's brief."

"Um. Sure," you say, but do not move any closer.

"Madame Painte," the man says, "hails from Holland by way of Guam by way of Australia. She was part of a line of garden ornaments manufactured by a factory outside of Amsterdam in the 1980s. I'm not sure how she traveled to the western Pacific, possibly via cargo ship. I know she was decorating the front lawn of a house in Yigo by 1995. This was the residence of a colonel stationed at the U.S. Air Force base there. She was already sporting her distinctive paint job, though I'm unclear who gave it to her. It may have been the colonel's wife, whose name was Priscilla. As I understand it, she was an artist—bit of an amateur anthropologist, too. She's the first person I'm aware of who insisted the figure be kept outside. This was when she sold it to a young Australian couple, Trudi and Lenard Niles, visiting the island. The Colonel had been transferred back stateside, and he and his wife had decided to take the opportunity to thin their possessions. The Nileses—well, mostly Trudi—were quite infatuated with the Madame. Priscilla was reluctant to part with her, said she couldn't let her go with just anyone. The Nileses thought she was trying to up the price, but that wasn't it. She'd give the figure away for free to the exactly right person. I guess the young couple wasn't quite perfect, because she took their money, but they were good enough for her to part with Madame Painte. Only after they'd sworn to keep her outside their home, though.

"This was how the figure made her way from Guam to Canberra."

"Let me guess," you say, "the couple brought her inside their house."

"Not at first, no," the man says, "but eventually, yes. Initially, they placed her in their back garden, next to a tall Claret Ash. The Nileses had a small metal table and pair of chairs near that spot. When the weather was warm, they would bring their morning coffee there. Trudi was a writer, a travel writer; Lenard was high up in an electronics company. After he went off to the office, she would carry her notebook, and later her laptop, to the table and work on whatever article was due that month. Actually, she wrote an article about the trip to Guam, which is how I know as much as I do about Priscilla and the promise she extracted."

"What changed?" you say. "I mean, what made the couple break their promise?"

The man shrugs. "I don't know. I'm not certain anything did change, which is to say, I'm not sure there was a moment when one of them looked at the other and said, 'The time has come for us to forsake our vow.' I suspect their promise wasn't that much to begin with, just words said to get what they wanted. Then one day, years later, they decided to redecorate, and thought their garden ornament would look better in a corner of the living room. If they recalled their conversation with the colonel's wife, their pledge to her, it was in a bemused, hey-do-you-remember way. They cleaned the dirt and insects off Madame Painte, and brought her inside."

"And?"

"At first, nothing. As I said, they were redecorating, painting walls, replacing furniture, putting in a new kitchen. For a time, the interior of their house was fairly chaotic. Madame Painte sat in her corner and waited."

"Waited for what?"

"The right moment. Months had passed. Everything had calmed; the house was in its new configuration. One night, Lenard woke up to use the toilet. On his way back to bed, he saw something on the wall outside the room. It was a splash of white, as if someone had swiped a paintbrush across that spot, or as if moonlight were reflecting off a mirrored surface in the living room. He waved his hand in front of it, which had no effect. He placed his palm against it, but could feel no difference in texture. To the best of my knowledge, he did not notice a resemblance between the white streak on the wall and the white mask Madame Painte wore.

"Next morning, after her coffee and writing, Trudi saw that a patch of the wall beside the bedroom door was discolored, faded the way paint gets after years of direct sunlight. She touched the spot, and it crumbled under her fingertips. She found it strange, especially since the surface had been painted so recently, but she decided it must be some form of dry rot. When she discussed it with Lenard over dinner, he mentioned his late-night vision, but neither drew any conclusions from it. They made plans to call a contractor.

"A couple of days later, Trudi saw the white streak. Once again, it was late at night, the house dark. She had stayed up finishing an article whose deadline she had let draw too near. Walking into the bedroom, she glimpsed something white draped over the hindquarters of Toro, the Niles's cat, who was asleep at the foot of the bed. So tired was she that she took the white streak for moonlight shining through the venetian blinds; only later would she realize it had been a new moon that night.

"In the morning, Toro was gone from the bed, which was not unusual, and he didn't come for his breakfast, which was. Trudi found him in the garden, when she brought her coffee out there (Lenard had left for an early meeting). The minute she sat, she heard a low moan from somewhere nearby. She recognized it as the cat, but it was a sound he'd never made before, halfway between a complaint and a warning. It raised the hairs on the back of her neck. She stood, called the cat's name. He uttered that weird groan again. She looked around the garden. He wasn't hard to find: what remained of him lay under a bush—some variety of hakea, I think it was."

"What do you mean, 'what remained'?"

"From a little below his midsection, the cat had shriveled, the fur gone, the skin blackened and shrunken against the bone. It was what you might have expected to find had the cat been dead for years. He was panting, obviously in pain, unable to understand what had happened to him. Trudi's first impulse was to take him to the veterinarian, but Toro wouldn't let her near him, hissing and clawing at her as she reached for him. She had to settle for calling the vet, who promised to stop by after her office was closed. By then, it was too late. Toro had bared his fangs at some unseen foe, and breathed his last. The vet was puzzled, to say the least. This degree of atrophy suggested some type of venom, but the speed with which it had acted was, in her experience, unprecedented. She asked to take Toro's remains to her office for an autopsy, which Trudi consented to. As the vet lifted him, though, the cat . . . came apart. His lower portion crumbled and his insides slid out onto the ground. The vet removed what she could, but it was a messy business."

"Did she find anything?" you say.

"Not exactly," the man says. "She phoned Trudi a day or two later. From what she'd been able to see under the microscope, the cat's cells had collapsed, lost their integrity and dissolved into one another. It's the kind of effect certain kinds of spider venom have on their victim's tissues. There was more. The worst affected portions of Toro were completely dry, every last drop of moisture drained from them. Of course, Trudi wanted to know what spider or other creature had done this to her cat. The vet didn't know. It was a familiar joke that Australia was full to the brim with deadly wildlife, but nothing she was acquainted with operated in this fashion on mammals of any size. Possibly, they were dealing with an invasive species. She was going to make some calls, ask if anything new had snuck into people's back gardens. In the meantime, Trudi should be careful, and should tell her husband to be careful, as well.

"During the following day, there was a moment Trudi looked at Madame Painte, at the white swath across the figure's smiling face, and was struck by the resemblance between the decoration and the white stripe she had seen on Toro. Hadn't Lenard mentioned a white mark on the wall outside their bedroom? She remembered the promise she'd made to Priscilla. For an instant, the details threatened to cohere into a bizarre and awful whole. As quickly as the thought occurred to her, however, she rejected it. It was ridiculous, absurd, like something from an old horror story. Over dinner that night, she shared the idea with Lenard. He nodded at the coincidence, but dismissed it, as well.

"Do I have to tell you what happened, next? Sometime

late in the night, Trudi dreamed she sat up in bed, looked at Lenard asleep beside her, and saw the splash of white traversing his face, from just above his right eyebrow down to the left corner of his mouth. In her dream, she wasn't afraid as much as curious. With the index and middle fingers of her right hand, she touched the white streak where it crossed Lenard's nose. It was like brushing her fingers against a spider web. She lowered her head onto her pillow, and was instantly asleep."

"It wasn't a dream, was it?"

The man shakes his head. "It was not. You can imagine the sight that greeted Trudi when she woke that morning. She ran screaming into the street, and who can blame her? Eventually, the police were called, and the emergency services, but it was all over. The best anyone could do for poor Lenard was opine that at least he hadn't suffered, and how could they be sure? Initially, there was some suspicion of foul play. The idea was that Trudi had murdered Lenard by pouring acid on him while he slept. There were too many problems with the theory for it to hold up very long, not least of which was the coroner's report. This showed that Lenard had died from something that had liquefied a portion of his face, skull, and brain, then drained the liquid, all without spilling a drop on the pillow. The closest analogue the M.E. could suggest was a spider melting its victim's insides with its venom and slurping them out. But like Trudi's veterinarian before him, he couldn't name an arachnid capable of dissolving and consuming this amount of tissue. Eventually, the cause of death was settled on as a previously unknown strain of MRSA.

"Which was bullshit, but more acceptable than the explanation Trudi was giving."

"Madame Painte."

"To anyone who would listen, she repeated the story that had become overwhelmingly, hideously obvious to her. She refused to re-enter the house, and it wasn't long until she was taken to the hospital, where she was given a bed in the psychiatric ward. No doubt, she was prescribed a sedative, at minimum. When all was said and done, she agreed to return home, but she insisted that the figure be removed from the living room, first. Her doctor decided it was easier to comply with this request than continue to go back and forth with her. Someone—it might have been the psychiatrist, herself—entered the house, located Madame Painte, and brought her to a local charity shop. She went so far as to follow Trudi's instructions and stipulated that the figure must be sold with a warning to keep her outside.

"This was how I found her. The charity shop listed some of its merchandise online. I subscribe to a couple of groups that keep an eye out for unusual pieces. The instant Madame Painte popped up on my screen, I clicked the purchase button."

"Weren't you, I don't know, nervous?"

"No—although that was because I didn't know the full story behind her. Not that I do, now: let's say I didn't know Trudi and Lenard's portion of it. I assumed the instruction to keep the figure outside had to do with the paint that had been used on her. I went so far as to e-mail the charity shop, but they weren't much help. What I've told you I learned from Trudi, who sent me a long e-mail a few months after I set Madame Painte outside my front door. For weeks, Trudi had been plagued by a combination of guilt and anxiety at passing on the Madame without disclosing her history, until she decided the only thing for her to do was contact whoever had purchased the figure. The charity shop supplied my e-mail, and she wrote me the whole strange, sad story."

"And you believed her?"

"I didn't not believe her. Before I opened this place, I was a cop in Albany for twenty years, and as the saying goes, I've seen some things. Business was slow, which let me do a little digging online. Lenard's death had made national news, briefly, and had sparked a series of articles about the dangers of drug-resistant super-bacteria. Based on the information included in the initial report, I was able to track down the veterinarian, who confirmed the details of Toro's death. In the end, I decided there was nothing wrong with leaving Madame Painte where she was. She seems happy enough watching the front door, and I've noticed a decrease in the local rodent population." The man smiles thinly.

"What do you think, I mean, what is she?"

"Aside from the focal point for a woman who suffered an excruciating loss? I don't know. My father was a big fan of Kipling, Stevenson, and this sounds like the kind of story one of them would have written. White people encounter a cursed object in the mysterious East—which, my older daughter would say, is pretty racist (she's working on her Ph.D. over at Amherst). I suppose it is. I wonder if there mightn't have been something wrong with the figure early on, right after she emerged from the factory. Maybe something attached to her, or was attached to her, whatever the white mask is. Maybe a version of what happened to the Nileses took place in a pretty house beside a canal, and the decision was made to send her far away, to the other side of the earth, where she wouldn't harm any more Dutch folks. Like dumping your supernatural toxic waste in a place whose inhabitants you don't give a rat's ass about."

"Why not just smash her, then, solve the problem that way?"

"What if I let loose whatever's in or on her?"

"Sounds like that's happening already."

"Only if she's kept inside," the man says. "Apparently, Priscilla, the colonel's wife, had her in their garden for years without any problems. There are fewer mice, chipmunks, around, but I can tolerate that"

"You sound like her caretaker."

"I suppose. That's one way of looking at it."

"Then why have her for sale?"

"Because it's a big responsibility. One I'm not certain I completely believe in, but I feel better erring on the side of caution. I would be happy to pass the care of Madame Painte onto someone I could be satisfied would maintain it with due diligence.

"Now that you've heard the story, the question is, is that someone you?"

There is a moment, which is not that long but which will lengthen in your memory, when you think it might be. Not for any good or noble reason, but due to the cause that chased you out of your house this morning, sent you driving east on the thruway until you took the first exit for Albany and wound up here: your grandfather, ninety-two, who lives in the basement apartment under you and your spouse's home. His brain clotted by dementia, but his body strong from a lifetime of construction work, he has been expelled from the last three nursing homes to which you've brought him. He can live on his own, he insists. Surrendering to necessity, you and your spouse have refurbished the basement to a reasonably safe space for him, from which he nonetheless flees once a week, usually to the next-door neighbors', to whom he appeals for protection from the strangers he says have kidnapped and imprisoned him. This is not to mention the daily trials, the small acts of meanness, vindictiveness, the piss and shit left on the bathroom floor, the stale and rotten food hidden under the bed and in the cushions of his easy chair, the sudden insults and rages. He could live another ten years, his doctor has said, he could give up the ghost tomorrow. You didn't sign up for this, you've said to yourself with increasing frequency, neither of you signed up for this.

Madame Painte might be the solution to your dilemma. Yes, the story is likely so much fantasy, but suppose it isn't? Just suppose. Your grandfather wouldn't have to know she was there. You could wait till he's asleep, hide her in his bedroom closet. Didn't the man say Lenard hadn't felt any pain? Plus, how would—how could—such a thing be traced back to you?

The wave of horror that sweeps through you carries the, "No, it isn't," from your mouth before you realize you've said it.

"That's all right," the man says. "Feel free to keep browsing. I'm sure you'll appreciate, I'd like to return the Madame to her proper place."

"Sure," you say, your face burning with shame.

For politeness's sake, you spend a few minutes wandering the shop's narrow aisles while its proprietor carries the figure out to the front step. Once he's behind the counter again, you depart the antique shop at something close to a run. The man nods to you as you pass him; in reply, you lift your left hand in a half-wave.

You can't help yourself: as you hurry up the front walk, you cast a glance over your shoulder at Madame Painte. She smiles her closed-eye smile at you, as if she knows you'll be back.

(For Fiona, and for Kaaron Warren)

CHIVALRY

NEIL GAIMAN

MRS. WHITAKER FOUND the Holy Grail; it was under a fur coat.

Every Thursday afternoon Mrs. Whitaker walked down to the post office to collect her pension, even though her legs were no longer what they were, and on the way back home she would stop in at the Oxfam Shop and buy herself a little something.

The Oxfam Shop sold old clothes, knickknacks, oddments, bits and bobs, and large quantities of old paperbacks, all of them donations: secondhand flotsam, often the house clearances of the dead. All the profits went to charity.

The shop was staffed by volunteers. The volunteer on duty this afternoon was Marie, seventeen, slightly overweight, and dressed in a baggy mauve jumper that looked like she had bought it from the shop.

Marie sat by the till with a copy of Modern Woman magazine, filling out a "Reveal Your Hidden Personality" questionnaire. Every now and then, she'd flip to the back of the magazine and check the relative points assigned to an A), B), or C) answer before making up her mind how she'd respond to the question.

Mrs. Whitaker puttered around the shop.

They still hadn't sold the stuffed cobra, she noted. It had been there for six months now, gathering dust, glass eyes gazing balefully at the clothes racks and the cabinet filled with chipped porcelain and chewed toys.

Mrs. Whitaker patted its head as she went past.

She picked out a couple of Mills & Boon novels from a bookshelf—*Her Thundering Soul* and *Her Turbulent Heart*, a shilling each—and gave careful consideration to the empty bottle of Mateus Rosé with a decorative lampshade on it before deciding she really didn't have anywhere to put it.

She moved a rather threadbare fur coat, which smelled badly of mothballs. Underneath it was a walking stick and a water-stained copy of *Romance and Legend of Chivalry* by A. R. Hope Moncrieff, priced at five pence. Next to the book, on its side, was the Holy Grail. It had a little round paper sticker on the base, and written on it, in felt pen, was the price: 30p. Mrs. Whitaker picked up the dusty silver goblet and appraised it through her thick spectacles.

"This is nice," she called to Marie.

Marie shrugged.

"It'd look nice on the mantelpiece."

Marie shrugged again.

Mrs. Whitaker gave fifty pence to Marie, who gave her ten pence change and a brown paper bag to put the books and the Holy Grail in. Then she went next door to the butcher's and bought herself a nice piece of liver. Then she went home.

The inside of the goblet was thickly coated with a brownish-red dust. Mrs. Whitaker washed it out with great care, then left it to soak for an hour in warm water with a dash of vinegar added.

Then she polished it with metal polish until it gleamed, and she put it on the mantelpiece in her parlor, where it sat between a small soulful china basset hound and a photograph of her late husband, Henry, on the beach at Frinton in 1953.

She had been right: It did look nice.

For dinner that evening she had the liver fried in breadcrumbs with onions. It was very nice.

The next morning was Friday; on alternate Fridays Mrs. Whitaker and Mrs. Greenberg would visit each other. Today it was Mrs. Greenberg's turn to visit Mrs. Whitaker. They sat in the parlor and ate macaroons and drank tea. Mrs. Whitaker took one sugar in her tea, but Mrs. Greenberg took sweetener, which she always carried in her handbag in a small plastic container. "That's nice," said Mrs. Greenberg, pointing to the Grail. "What is it?"

"It's the Holy Grail," said Mrs. Whitaker. "It's the cup that Jesus drunk out of at the Last Supper. Later, at the Crucifixion, it caught His precious blood when the centurion's spear pierced His side."

Mrs. Greenberg sniffed. She was small and Jewish and didn't hold with unsanitary things. "I wouldn't know about that," she said, "but it's very nice. Our Myron got one just like that when he won the swimming tournament, only it's got his name on the side."

"Is he still with that nice girl? The hairdresser?"

"Bernice? Oh yes. They're thinking of getting engaged," said Mrs. Greenberg.

"That's nice," said Mrs. Whitaker. She took another macaroon.

Mrs. Greenberg baked her own macaroons and brought them over every alternate Friday: small sweet light brown biscuits with almonds on top.

They talked about Myron and Bernice, and Mrs.

Whitaker's nephew Ronald (she had had no children), and about their friend Mrs. Perkins who was in hospital with her hip, poor dear.

At midday Mrs. Greenberg went home, and Mrs. Whitaker made herself cheese on toast for lunch, and after lunch Mrs. Whitaker took her pills; the white and the red and two little orange ones.

The doorbell rang.

Mrs. Whitaker answered the door. It was a young man with shoulder-length hair so fair it was almost white, wearing gleaming silver armor, with a white surcoat.

"Hello," he said.

"Hello," said Mrs. Whitaker.

"I'm on a quest," he said.

"That's nice," said Mrs. Whitaker, noncommittally.

"Can I come in?" he asked.

Mrs. Whitaker shook her head. "I'm sorry, I don't think so," she said.

"I'm on a quest for the Holy Grail," the young man said. "Is it here?"

"Have you got any identification?" Mrs. Whitaker asked. She knew that it was unwise to let unidentified strangers into your home when you were elderly and living on your own. Handbags get emptied, and worse than that.

The young man went back down the garden path. His horse, a huge gray charger, big as a shire-horse, its head high and its eyes intelligent, was tethered to Mrs. Whitaker's garden gate. The knight fumbled in the saddlebag and returned with a scroll.

It was signed by Arthur, King of All Britons, and charged all persons of whatever rank or station to know that here was Galaad, Knight of the Table Round, and that he was on a Right High and Noble Quest. There was a drawing of the young man below that. It wasn't a bad likeness.

Mrs. Whitaker nodded. She had been expecting a little card with a photograph on it, but this was far more impressive.

"I suppose you had better come in," she said.

They went into her kitchen. She made Galaad a cup of tea, then she took him into the parlor.

Galaad saw the Grail on her mantelpiece, and dropped to one knee. He put down the teacup carefully on the russet carpet. A shaft of light came through the net curtains and painted his awed face with golden sunlight and turned his hair into a silver halo.

"It is truly the Sangrail," he said, very quietly. He blinked his pale blue eyes three times, very fast, as if he were blinking back tears.

He lowered his head as if in silent prayer.

Galaad stood up again and turned to Mrs. Whitaker. "Gracious lady, keeper of the Holy of Holies, let me now depart this place with the Blessed Chalice, that my journeyings may be ended and my geas fulfilled."

"Sorry?" said Mrs. Whitaker.

Galaad walked over to her and took her old hands in his. "My quest is over," he told her. "The Sangrail is finally within my reach."

Mrs. Whitaker pursed her lips. "Can you pick your teacup and saucer up, please?" she said.

Galaad picked up his teacup apologetically.

"No. I don't think so," said Mrs. Whitaker. "I rather like it there. It's just right, between the dog and the photograph of my Henry."

"Is it gold you need? Is that it? Lady, I can bring you gold . . . "

"No," said Mrs. Whitaker. "I don't want any gold thank *you*. I'm simply not interested."

She ushered Galaad to the front door. "Nice to meet you," she said.

His horse was leaning its head over her garden fence, nibbling her gladioli. Several of the neighborhood children were standing on the pavement, watching it.

Galaad took some sugar lumps from the saddlebag and showed the braver of the children how to feed the horse, their hands held flat. The children giggled. One of the older girls stroked the horse's nose.

Galaad swung himself up onto the horse in one fluid movement. Then the horse and the knight trotted off down Hawthorne Crescent.

Mrs. Whitaker watched them until they were out of sight, then sighed and went back inside.

The weekend was quiet.

On Saturday Mrs. Whitaker took the bus into Maresfield to visit her nephew Ronald, his wife Euphonia, and their daughters, Clarissa and Dillian. She took them a currant cake she had baked herself.

On Sunday morning Mrs. Whitaker went to church. Her local church was St. James the Less, which was a little more "Don't think of this as a church, think of it as a place where like-minded friends hang out and are joyful" than Mrs. Whitaker felt entirely comfortable with, but she liked the vicar, the Reverend Bartholomew, when he wasn't actually playing the guitar.

After the service, she thought about mentioning to him that she had the Holy Grail in her front parlor, but decided against it.

On Monday morning Mrs. Whitaker was working in the back garden. She had a small herb garden she was extremely proud of: dill, vervain, mint, rosemary, thyme, and a wild expanse of parsley. She was down on her knees, wearing thick green gardening gloves, weeding, and picking out slugs and putting them in a plastic bag.

Mrs. Whitaker was very tenderhearted when it came to slugs. She would take them down to the back of her garden, which bordered on the railway line, and throw them over the fence.

She cut some parsley for the salad. There was a cough behind her. Galaad stood there, tall and beautiful, his armor glinting in the morning sun. In his arms he held a long package, wrapped in oiled leather.

"I'm back," he said.

"Hello," said Mrs. Whitaker. She stood up, rather slowly, and took off her gardening gloves. "Well," she said, "now you're here, you might as well make yourself useful."

She gave him the plastic bag full of slugs and told him to tip the slugs out over the back of the fence.

He did.

Then they went into the kitchen.

"Tea? Or lemonade?" she asked.

"Whatever you're having," Galaad said.

Mrs. Whitaker took a jug of her homemade lemonade from the fridge and sent Galaad outside to pick a sprig of mint. She selected two tall glasses. She washed the mint carefully and put a few leaves in each glass, then poured the lemonade.

"Is your horse outside?" she asked.

"Oh yes. His name is Grizzel."

"And you've come a long way, I suppose."

"A very long way."

"I see," said Mrs. Whitaker. She took a blue plastic basin from under the sink and half-filled it with water. Galaad took it out to Grizzel. He waited while the horse drank and brought the empty basin back to Mrs. Whitaker.

"Now," she said, "I suppose you're still after the Grail."

"Aye, still do I seek the Sangrail," he said. He picked up the leather package from the floor, put it down on her tablecloth and unwrapped it. "For it, I offer you this."

It was a sword, its blade almost four feet long. There were words and symbols traced elegantly along the length of the blade. The hilt was worked in silver and gold, and a large jewel was set in the pommel.

"It's very nice," said Mrs. Whitaker, doubtfully.

"This," said Galaad, "is the sword Balmung, forged by Wayland Smith in the dawn times. Its twin is Flamberge. Who wears it is unconquerable in war, and invincible in battle. Who wears it is incapable of a cowardly act or an ignoble one. Set in its pommel is the sardonyx Bircone, which protects its possessor from poison slipped into wine or ale, and from the treachery of friends."

Mrs. Whitaker peered at the sword. "It must be very sharp," she said, after a while.

"It can slice a falling hair in twain. Nay, it could slice a sunbeam," said Galaad proudly.

"Well, then, maybe you ought to put it away," said Mrs. Whitaker.

"Don't you want it?" Galaad seemed disappointed.

"No, thank you," said Mrs. Whitaker. It occurred to her that her late husband, Henry, would have quite liked it. He would have hung it on the wall in his study next to the stuffed carp he had caught in Scotland, and pointed it out to visitors.

Galaad rewrapped the oiled leather around the sword Balmung and tied it up with white cord.

He sat there, disconsolate.

Mrs. Whitaker made him some cream cheese and cucumber sandwiches for the journey back and wrapped them in greaseproof paper. She gave him an apple for Grizzel. He seemed very pleased with both gifts.

She waved them both good-bye.

That afternoon she took the bus down to the hospital to see Mrs. Perkins, who was still in with her hip, poor love. Mrs. Whitaker took her some homemade fruitcake, although she had left out the walnuts from the recipe, because Mrs. Perkins's teeth weren't what they used to be.

She watched a little television that evening, and had an early night.

On Tuesday the postman called. Mrs. Whitaker was up in the boxroom at the top of the house, doing a spot of tidying, and, taking each step slowly and carefully, she didn't make it downstairs in time. The postman had left her a message which said that he'd tried to deliver a packet, but no one was home.

Mrs. Whitaker sighed.

She put the message into her handbag and went down to the post office.

The package was from her niece Shirelle in Sydney, Australia. It contained photographs of her husband, Wallace, and her two daughters. Dixie and Violet, and a conch shell packed in cotton wool.

Mrs. Whitaker had a number of ornamental shells in her bedroom. Her favorite had a view of the Bahamas done on it in enamel. It had been a gift from her sister, Ethel, who had died in 1983.

She put the shell and the photographs in her shopping bag. Then, seeing that she was in the area, she stopped in at the Oxfam Shop on her way home.

"Hullo, Mrs. W.," said Marie.

Mrs. Whitaker stared at her. Marie was wearing lipstick (possibly not the best shade for her, nor particularly expertly applied, but, thought Mrs. Whitaker, that would come with time) and a rather smart skirt. It was a great improvement.

"Oh. Hello, dear," said Mrs. Whitaker.

"There was a man in here last week, asking about that thing you bought. The little metal cup thing. I told him where to find you. You don't mind, do you?"

"No, dear," said Mrs. Whitaker. "He found me."

"He was really dreamy. Really, really dreamy," sighed Marie wistfully. "I could of gone for him."

"And he had a big white horse and all," Marie concluded. She was standing up straighter as well, Mrs. Whitaker noted approvingly.

On the bookshelf Mrs. Whitaker found a new Mills & Boon novel— *Her Majestic Passion*—although she hadn't yet finished the two she had bought on her last visit.

She picked up the copy of *Romance and Legend of Chivalry* and opened it. It smelled musty. *EX LIBRIS FISHER* was neatly handwritten at the top of the first page in red ink.

She put it down where she had found it.

When she got home, Galaad was waiting for her. He was giving the neighborhood children rides on Grizzel's back, up and down the street.

"I'm glad you're here," she said. "I've got some cases that need moving."

She showed him up to the boxroom in the top of the house. He moved all the old suitcases for her, so she could get to the cupboard at the back.

It was very dusty up there.

She kept him up there most of the afternoon, moving things around while she dusted.

Galaad had a cut on his cheek, and he held one arm a little stiffly.

They talked a little while she dusted and tidied. Mrs. Whitaker told him about her late husband, Henry; and how the life insurance had paid the house off; and how she had all these things, but no one really to leave them to, no one but Ronald really and his wife only liked modern things. She told him how she had met Henry during the war, when he was in the ARP and she hadn't closed the kitchen blackout curtains all the way; and about the sixpenny dances they went to in the town; and how they'd gone to London when the war had ended, and she'd had her first drink of wine.

Galaad told Mrs. Whitaker about his mother Elaine, who was flighty and no better than she should have been and something of a witch to boot; and his grandfather, King Pelles, who was well-meaning although at best a little vague; and of his youth in the Castle of Bliant on the Joyous Isle; and his father, whom he knew as "Le Chevalier Mal Fet," who was more or less completely mad, and was in reality Lancelot du Lac, greatest of knights, in disguise and bereft of his wits; and of Galaad's days as a young squire in Camelot.

At five o'clock Mrs. Whitaker surveyed the boxroom and decided that it met with her approval; then she opened the window so the room could air, and they went downstairs to the kitchen, where she put on the kettle.

Galaad sat down at the kitchen table.

He opened the leather purse at his waist and took out a round white stone. It was about the size of a cricket ball.

"My lady," he said, "This is for you, and you give me the Sangrail."

Mrs. Whitaker picked up the stone, which was heavier than it looked, and held it up to the light. It was milkily translucent, and deep inside it flecks of silver glittered and glinted in the late-afternoon sunlight. It was warm to the touch.

Then, as she held it, a strange feeling crept over her: Deep inside she felt stillness and a sort of peace. *Serenity*, that was the word for it; she felt serene.

Reluctantly she put the stone back on the table.

"It's very nice," she said.

"That is the Philosopher's Stone, which our forefather Noah hung in the Ark to give light when there was no light; it can transform base metals into gold; and it has certain other properties," Galaad told her proudly. "And that isn't all. There's more. Here." From the leather bag he took an egg and handed it to her.

It was the size of a goose egg and was a shiny black color, mottled with scarlet and white. When Mrs. Whitaker touched it, the hairs on the back of her neck prickled. Her immediate impression was one of incredible heat and freedom. She heard the crackling of distant fires, and for a fraction of a second she seemed to feel herself far above the world, swooping and diving on wings of flame.

She put the egg down on the table, next to the Philosopher's Stone.

"That is the Egg of the Phoenix," said Galaad. "From far Araby it comes. One day it will hatch out into the Phoenix Bird itself; and when its time comes, the bird will build a nest of flame, lay its egg, and die, to be reborn in flame in a later age of the world."

"I thought that was what it was," said Mrs. Whitaker.

"And, last of all, lady," said Galaad, "I have brought you this."

He drew it from his pouch, and gave it to her. It was an apple, apparently carved from a single ruby, on an amber stem.

A little nervously, she picked it up. It was soft to the touch—deceptively so: Her fingers bruised it, and ruby-colored juice from the apple ran down Mrs. Whitaker's hand.

The kitchen filled—almost imperceptibly, magically—with the smell of summer fruit, of raspberries and peaches and strawberries and red currants. As if from a great way away she heard distant voices raised in song and far music on the air.

"It is one of the apples of the Hesperides," said Galaad, quietly. "One bite from it will heal any illness or wound, no matter how deep; a second bite restores youth and beauty; and a third bite is said to grant eternal life." Mrs. Whitaker licked the sticky juice from her hand. It tasted like fine wine.

There was a moment, then, when it all came back to her—how it was to be young: to have a firm, slim body that would do whatever she wanted it to do; to run down a country lane for the simple unladylike joy of running; to have men smile at her just because she was herself and happy about it.

Mrs. Whitaker looked at Sir Galaad, most comely of all knights, sitting fair and noble in her small kitchen. She caught her breath.

"And that's all I have brought for you," said Galaad. "They weren't easy to get, either."

Mrs. Whitaker put the ruby fruit down on her kitchen table. She looked at the Philosopher's Stone, and the Egg of the Phoenix, and the Apple of Life.

Then she walked into her parlor and looked at the mantelpiece: at the little china basset hound, and the Holy Grail, and the photograph of her late husband Henry, shirtless, smiling and eating an ice cream in black and white, almost forty years away.

She went back into the kitchen. The kettle had begun to whistle. She poured a little steaming water into the teapot, swirled it around, and poured it out. Then she added two spoonfuls of tea and one for the pot and poured in the rest of the water. All this she did in silence.

She turned to Galaad then, and she looked at him.

"Put that apple away," she told Galaad, firmly. "You shouldn't offer things like that to old ladies. It isn't proper."

She paused, then. "But I'll take the other two," she continued, after a moment's thought. "They'll look nice on the mantelpiece. And two for one's fair, or I don't know what is."

Galaad beamed. He put the ruby apple into his leather pouch. Then he went down on one knee, and kissed Mrs. Whitaker's hand.

"Stop that," said Mrs. Whitaker. She poured them both cups of tea, after getting out the very best china, which was only for special occasions.

They sat in silence, drinking their tea.

When they had finished their tea they went into the parlor.

Galaad crossed himself, and picked up the Grail.

Mrs. Whitaker arranged the Egg and the Stone where the Grail had been. The Egg kept tipping on one side, and she propped it up against the little china dog.

"They do look very nice," said Mrs. Whitaker.

"Yes," agreed Galaad. "They look very nice."

"Can I give you anything to eat before you go back?" she asked.

He shook his head.

"Some fruitcake," she said. "You may not think you want any now, but you'll be glad of it in a few hours' time. And you should probably use the facilities. Now, give me that, and I'll wrap it up for you."

She directed him to the small toilet at the end of the

hall, and went into the kitchen, holding the Grail. She had some old Christmas wrapping paper in the pantry, and she wrapped the Grail in it, and tied the package with twine. Then she cut a large slice of fruitcake and put it in a brown paper bag, along with a banana and a slice of processed cheese in silver foil.

Galaad came back from the toilet. She gave him the paper bag, and the Holy Grail. Then she went up on tiptoes and kissed him on the cheek.

"You're a nice boy," she said. "You take care of yourself."

He hugged her, and she shooed him out of the kitchen, and out of the back door, and she shut the door behind him. She poured herself another cup of tea, and cried quietly into a Kleenex, while the sound of hoofbeats echoed down Hawthorne Crescent.

On Wednesday Mrs. Whitaker stayed in all day.

On Thursday she went down to the post office to collect her pension. Then she stopped in at the Oxfam Shop.

The woman on the till was new to her. "Where's Marie?" asked Mrs. Whitaker.

The woman on the till, who had blue-rinsed gray hair and blue spectacles that went up into diamante points, shook her head and shrugged her shoulders. "She went off with a young man," she said. "On a horse. Tch. I ask you. I'm meant to be down in the Heathfield shop this afternoon. I had to get my Johnny to run me up here, while we find someone else."

"Oh," said Mrs. Whitaker. "Well, it's nice that she's found herself a young man."

"Nice for her, maybe," said the lady on the till, "But some of us were meant to be in Heathfield this afternoon."

On a shelf near the back of the shop Mrs. Whitaker

found a tarnished old silver container with a long spout. It had been priced at sixty pence, according to the little paper label stuck to the side. It looked a little like a flattened, elongated teapot.

She picked out a Mills & Boon novel she hadn't read before. It was called *Her Singular Love*. She took the book and the silver container up to the woman on the till.

"Sixty-five pee, dear," said the woman, picking up the silver object, staring at it. "Funny old thing, isn't it? Came in this morning." It had writing carved along the side in blocky old Chinese characters and an elegant arching handle. "Some kind of oil can, I suppose."

"No, it's not an oil can," said Mrs. Whitaker, who knew exactly what it was. "It's a lamp."

There was a small metal finger ring, unornamented, tied to the handle of the lamp with brown twine.

"Actually," said Mrs. Whitaker, "on second thoughts, I think I'll just have the book."

She paid her five pence for the novel, and put the lamp back where she had found it, in the back of the shop. After all, Mrs. Whitaker reflected, as she walked home, it wasn't as if she had anywhere to put it.

FULLY BOARDED

RAMSEY CAMPBELL

THE ROOM AT the Mediterranean Magic apartments was even worse than Warden expected. Both of the mattresses that made up the rudimentary double bed sagged in the middle, and the thin threadbare quilt fell inches short of covering their width. The flex that led to the air-conditioning was frayed where it met the unit, and the plug for the electric kettle was cracked, matching the pair of grubby mugs that stood in the stained metal sink. One door of the flimsy wardrobe slouched on a single hinge, revealing wire hangers entangled on an insecure rail. So many of the discoloured plastic slats of the blind at the floor-length window were warped that it was impossible to shut out all the view of a weedy field where goats roamed around overgrown heaps of rubbish. As for the bathroom, the toilet seat was so misaligned that it resembled a double image, while the shower appeared to be hanging its head in shame, since the screws of the bracket that held it up were losing their grip on a splintered tile. A drooping plastic rail revealed that the shower had once been furnished with a curtain, and there wasn't a towel to be found.

When he made for Reception Warden almost lost his footing on the slippery tiles near the pool, in which the only swimmers were a bedraggled cigarette packet and an empty bag of crisps. Half a dozen guests in swimwear lay on loungers, with a band around one wrist to signify they'd booked full board. They hadn't been among the guests queuing to complain when Warden had checked in. Now Reception was deserted except for the manager, an expansive woman with shoulders even broader than the rest of her. As Warden crossed the pointlessly spacious room, where maps and posters hid some of the shabbiness, her eyes and lips widened in her large face. "Mr Warden," she protested in an accent that had stayed mostly English, "you haven't got your band on."

He could have thought she meant to forestall his grievance with one of her own. "I haven't even unpacked yet," he said. "I just—"

"We can't serve you properly without."

"Why's that?" Warden said like, he thought, an ordinary customer.

"If my people can't see it they won't know you're fully taken care of. It's a token of our hospitality, as well."

"I hadn't thought of it like that."

"They made me a guest in their land and now I'm paying it back."

Warden might have been touched if not for the state of his room. "I don't suppose I'll need your band to get—"

"For everything, and then there can't be any argument." As he wondered who she was saying might start one, she said "You wouldn't want to upset anybody."

"How do you think I'd do that?"

"Someone makes the bands for us. It's a local craft and it helps our economy. Have you got yours with you? I'll show you what I mean."

Warden fished the wristband out of his breast pocket. It had formed a loose knot that he had to disentangle from his fingers. The manager spread it on her palm to display how intricately woven the strands of green material were, in a reiterated pattern Warden thought could be as ancient as it was elaborate. He was peering at it out of politeness, though it hardly compensated for his room, when she said "You'll appreciate it better on."

Before Warden realised what she meant to do she slipped the band onto his right wrist. At once it was so snug that the band might have been designed for him. He felt a hint of moisture that put him oddly in mind of a kiss, and then it was gone. "What is it made of?" he said.

"That's their secret," the manager said and raised her eyes from his wrist. "Was there something else you wanted?"

"There aren't any towels in my room."

"We've had a day of changing rooms. We won't forget you, Mr Warden."

Was she admitting newcomers had demanded to be moved? He meant to insist on that himself, but not until he'd experienced how bad his room might be. He ignored the wristband, which felt slightly tighter, while he asked "So when could I have some?"

"As I say, all my people are occupied just now," she said and turned her back on him. He was struggling to believe he'd been dismissed when she said "You can have mine."

She brought a towel from a room beyond the office behind the counter. It felt damp and was half the size Warden would have expected a bath towel to be. Was her gesture intended to disarm him? "Thank you," he barely said.

"You're welcome. All our guests are." She rested an

unnecessarily maternal gaze on him until he stepped back from the counter. "And do call me Win," she said.

"Win."

"Short for Winifred," she said as if she'd made her name sound too triumphal. "I hope you'll enjoy your stay with us, Mr Warden."

He might have retorted that it was up to her and her staff to make sure he did. He could have taken her comments for disguised appeals, and might something of the kind have prompted the inexplicably positive online reviews of the Mediterranean Magic? He'd already seen enough to justify the hostile ones—"deserves to be bulldozed", "not even fit for dogs", "you'd be better sleeping on the beach" and dozens more from guests who weren't even fully boarded—and the complaints the travel operator had received. "I'll do my best," he told Win and made for his room.

He always did his best on behalf of the customers. While he took pride in investigating wherever the firm sent him, posing as an ordinary holidaymaker or an invisibly average hotel guest, discovering the worst often left him feeling mean, and so did knowing that most of his reports left their subjects unsupported by his firm. It was the owners' fault if they didn't raise their standards, and he was helping the customers who paid his wages, but how many staff might Warden have put out of a job? He had to remember that if they'd attended to their work he mightn't have needed to do his. He might even have been out of a job himself.

He draped the towel over a rickety rail in the bathroom and set about emptying his suitcase. When he tried to open the drawers under the wardrobe the handle of the topmost came off, and the front of the lower drawer creaked outwards before the rest of it staggered free.

Once he'd unpacked he used his phone to photograph all the failings of the apartment, and then he ventured out for dinner.

The restaurant was another of the concrete blocks that made up Mediterranean Magic. Through the holes it had for windows Warden saw an assortment of trestle tables scarcely covered with checked cloths and provided with a variety of seats—benches, folding chairs, even the odd stool. As he followed a family into the restaurant, a man hailed the father. "Aren't you coming out to a taverna, Dick? You're never going in there twice."

The man he'd addressed was just as wilfully bald, but the sun had rendered his scalp pinker. "Tell us about it when you've been, Stan."

"Last night you said you weren't eating here again."

"We can change our minds, can't we? We're getting what we paid for."

The bands on their wrists and their teenage son's weren't quite as prominent as those Stan and his family sported or Warden's own. When the taverna party headed for the road, Dick turned to Warden. "Some people aren't happy till they've found something to moan about."

For a moment Warden felt identified. "You don't think they could have a reason."

"They only got here yesterday and they've been complaining ever since."

"Have you been here longer yourselves?"

"Twice as long as them and we're making the best of it. We think that's what us English do. It's what Win's doing, some people might like to remember."

Having found a plate that wasn't too chipped, Warden surveyed the buffet that occupied a long table: olives, cheeses, oily salads, dips so watery they bordered on colourless, some kind of raisin bread—no, loaves with flies in attendance. One dip displayed a black olive or else a drowned fly, which helped him decide against sampling any of them. Platters of sliced meat kept company with bowls of rice and a plate piled with greasy potatoes, along with soggy salads indistinguishable from those he'd already left alone. He spooned a few lumps of rice out of a bowl and took a slice of each meat, which proved to be not just as unidentifiable as they looked but so timidly spiced that they tasted less than national. A middle-aged couple at the table next to his watched him eat, presumably because he was a newcomer. "Good?" the woman said, if it was a question.

"What do you think?"

"Good," she declared, and her husband said "Just as good."

"As what?" Warden felt he should learn.

"As last night."

"And the one before that," the woman said.

When Warden left quite a portion of his dinner, they stared like disapproving parents at his plate. "I've had what I need," he told them, and might have gone in search of a taverna if he hadn't felt a little sick. He tried to wash away the vague insidious flavours with a gulp of house wine, which only brought them lurching back.

He chewed two chalky indigestion tablets as soon as he was in his room. From the balcony, having managed to decide which of the pair of grubby plastic chairs was less precarious, he watched a sunset gild the goats and set the mounds of refuse in amber until a parched breeze brought a shitty whiff that sent him inside. He felt unusually ready for bed, and made for the bathroom, where the mirror reminded him that he hadn't taken off the wristband. When he tugged at it, the band yielded just a fraction of an inch, not enough to let him slip it off. Had it shrunk in the heat? Since it didn't trouble him, he might as well wear it to bed.

He had to bruise his fingers on the remote control before the air conditioning clattered into action. The metal slats kept up a rattle that ought to have denoted more than the tepid feeble draft they let loose. Warden felt compelled to listen for a pattern in the relentless stutter, but eventually he fell asleep. He dreamed he was stored in a clammy bag, and wakened to find he was— wrapped in the sweaty sheet, at any rate. The room was hotter than it had been on his return. As he groped for the control to rouse the chill, his right arm felt unhelpfully numb. The unit on the wall gave a solitary clatter and died with a sputtering flash.

Had he been lying on the arm? The numbness seemed to dissipate by spreading through him. He fumbled to switch on the light, which showed a thread of smoke hovering above the exposed wires of the unit. The wires had fused together with their rubber sheath, and Warden stared at them until his head began to feel as senseless as his arm had been. Would anyone be at Reception this early? His room had no phone, and he wasn't going to the office just to discover it was unstaffed. Instead he dragged the sodden sheet over himself.

Despite the heat he wakened well after dawn. He managed to use the toilet by aligning the emaciated plastic seat with the pedestal and holding it there with both hands. When he tried to raise the shower head towards him, having persuaded the water at least to hint at warmth, the screws shifted in the wall. He crouched beneath the enervated downpour and then used the towel, which was still damp. At least the wristband wasn't wet by the time he remembered he had it on.

Much of the breakfast buffet looked familiar—dips,

olives, salads, rice. The cold meats could be last night's too, sliced thinner, and the hard sawn loaves weren't new, though the attendant flies might be. Warden left most of the samples he took, earning a dumb rebuke from more than one fellow guest, and went to Reception. "You'll have had a sleep," Win said across the counter.

Warden started framing a retort, but the effort felt as though a band was tightening around if not inside his head. "Was there anything you wanted, Mr Warden?" Win said.

"Yes, air conditioning. Mine died in the night."

"Oh dear, what a pest." As Warden wondered if she could mean him, Win said "I'll have someone put you in a fan."

"Don't you think you'd better get the unit fixed? The wires are bare. It could be dangerous."

"We'll look at it if that's what you want."

Warden hardly thought he needed to confirm this, and it almost made him forget to ask "How does this come off?"

Win gazed in some disappointment at the wrist he was holding up. "You won't want to till you leave, will you? Not when you're all in."

It would give him access to any facilities he needed to investigate. When his stay was over he could cut the wristband off. He retired to the pool, where a hot breeze sent litter for a sluggish swim and wafted a harsh smell of chlorine out of the water. From a lounger he watched a Mediterranean Magic man trudging about in search of abandoned glasses and any other items that weren't too much trouble to retrieve. Warden found the man's somnolent progress close to mesmeric, and wasn't far from sleep by the time the representative of his firm met new guests from several accommodations in the poolside bar. "Hi, everyone. I'm Rhona," she cried.

She was a slight girl adorned with a watch so large that it appeared to cast a shadow on her wrist, not unlike a stain. While identifying the attractions of the island on a map she gestured so vigorously that she might have been miming her job. The customers who booked tours with her weren't fully boarded at Mediterranean Magic. Warden's fellow guests were more concerned about their rooms, along with the food and other drawbacks. As Rhona undertook to have a word and have a word he found her brightness far too studied, not to say repetitive. He would have liked to overhear what she said to Win if his presence mightn't have betrayed his mission. She didn't spend much time in the office, and she was heading for her motor scooter when pink-pated Dick and family arrived at the poolside. Blood was seeping through a large plaster on the teenager's right shin. "Someone's been in the wars," Warden said.

"Used to be," Dick said with a blank stare. "I'm a civvy now."

"No, I mean your son. What happened there?"

"Trev didn't look where he was going," the boy's mother said. "Cut himself on there."

Following her gaze, Warden saw a jagged strip of concrete where tiles should have been at the edge of the pool. He was dismayed to have overlooked the hazard, which clearly wasn't recent. "Does Rhona know about that?" he urged. "You can catch her if you're quick."

"No point in that," Dick said. "Deb here's patched him up."

"Don't you think it ought to be reported? It doesn't look any too clean."

"You've got some eyes if you can see through a plaster. His mother put plenty of disinfectant on." Before Warden could explain he'd meant the concrete, Dick said "You can go and moan if that's your style."

Rhona's scooter departed with a tinny snarl, and Warden gave up. Striving to persuade Dick had left him with a headache like a ring around his brain. It tempted him to snooze beside the pool or in his room, but he ought to stay alert. He went out for a quick tour of the resort in the hope of walking off the tension of the job.

A sandy beach extended for a mile around a bay, though the section closest to Mediterranean Magic was chunky with rubble. Tavernas lined the promenade, and he found more in the winding side streets, where supermarkets and souvenir shops had ousted many of the houses. His roaming only aggravated the tightness in his skull, and he wandered back to the apartments. He was in sight of the block that housed Reception and the staff when he noticed it was opposite a graveyard.

The cemetery was the kind he'd often seen in this part of the world, with many of the graves covered by marble slabs and headed by memorials displaying mementoes behind glass. Candles and lanterns stood on most of the graves, waiting to be lit after dark. Facing the back of the Mediterranean Magic block was a hut composed of wood so old that it resembled a mossy tree. Surely just a strip of moss was protruding under the door, but Warden went to look.

It was one of the wristbands Win used. Though the door had torn the pattern ragged, it was unmistakable. As he walked around the hut, which was windowless, a woman tending a grave met his eyes. She sent him a sign of the cross and murmured a word.

"Sorry?" Though he thought she'd said that, he sounded mindless as an echo. "Sorry for what, sorry?"

Her wary gaze moved from the hut to his wrist. "We need," she muttered and returned to her task.

She must have his economic contribution in mind,

but unlike Win, she was apologising. Warden thought it made sense for the graveyard caretaker to earn a little extra with a traditional craft, and perhaps some version of the bands was sold in the souvenir shops. He returned to his room to find the bed as rumpled as he'd left it, and no sign of a fan. Either the sight or the thought of complaining once again made his head twinge like an unhealed wound. He went back to the poolside bar, where the wristband entitled him to free drinks. The house wines came from boxes that didn't pretend to be Greek, and the barman was the silent sullen fellow he'd previously seen clearing away litter. A greenish tattoo encircled each of his wrists, though Warden couldn't see exactly what the blurred designs were supposed to represent. They could hardly be meant to bring shackles to mind.

Sour though it was, the wine numbed Warden's headache. He dozed on a lounger beneath a tipsy umbrella, jerking awake to discover it was the middle of the afternoon. His room still hadn't been touched. As he marched to Reception he saw he'd abandoned his glass by the lounger. He mustn't turn into an untidy careless guest—he needed to remember he was here on official business—and he took the glass to the bar, where the morose man gave it an unwelcoming blink.

Win's look wasn't too enthusiastic either. "What can we do for you now?"

"When is my room likely to be made up, do you know?"

"We can't do everything at once." She sounded like a parent dealing with an unreasonable child. "We're bringing you a fan," she said as though promising a treat or an indulgence.

"When you do, could I have a proper towel?"

"What do you mean by proper?"

"I don't mean yours wasn't. It was generous of you." Warden's lips felt constricted, along with his brain, and it took him some effort to add "I'd still like the kind you provide for your guests."

"We'll see about it. Was that all?"

Warden was thrown by how unreasonable he was being made to feel. He was a guest, after all, and not just that either. Nevertheless he turned away before mumbling "For now."

As he resumed his place by the pool, having collected another glass of wine from the bar, he saw a woman with a stack of towels making for his block. Shouldn't he feel more annoyed that she was dealing with the rooms so late? All he felt was relief. He drank and dozed and trudged to the room, where the sheet had been yanked more or less smooth on the bed. A single frayed towel drooped on the bathroom rail. At least it was dry, but the floor remained sticky, and there was no fan. The idea of complaining yet again made his head feel clamped, and he opted for dinner instead.

He was sidling along the buffet, which looked entirely too familiar, when he saw Stan and family following him. "Didn't you say you were never coming here again?" Warden said.

"We can change our minds, can't we?" Stan retorted, rubbing his forehead with his wristband, unless the action was the other way around.

"That's exactly what your friend told you," Warden couldn't resist observing.

"Shows we're friends then, doesn't it?"

Though Warden wasn't sure what sense this made, it sounded like a warning. He turned to the buffet, where grease had congealed around the cold cuts, while he suspected the other meats were reheated. He contented himself with salads, and passed Dick's family on his way to a table. The bloodstain on the boy's plaster was a muddy brown. "How is he now?" he felt bound to ask.

"Fine," all three said in chorus, as if they'd practiced the rebuff.

Once Warden saw off some lumps of rice and an assortment of wilted leaves he decided he'd had dinner. He sat on his balcony, wishing he could see the graveyard hut, to determine if its occupant was at work. Leaning out at full stretch let him see a few graves lit by lanterns. He was straining to crane further when the plastic chair twisted out of shape and collapsed under him.

He had to laugh, however ruefully. It was his fault, after all. He would be better off in bed, where he couldn't do any more damage. In the bathroom he was about to scrub his stained wrist until he recognised the wristband. It was scarcely identifiable as one—more like a raised tattoo. Once he was in bed he couldn't feel it at all, and the unawareness seemed to reach within his head, expanding into sleep.

He didn't know how long he'd slept when a crash wakened him. He poked inaccurately at the light switch and staggered about until he located the disaster. The shower holder had fallen off the wall, taking a tile with it to smash. His laugh at this involved very little mirth. It was more of a preamble to the complaint he would make in the morning, though the prospect made his head feel empty and numb.

Now that he was aware of all the heat that had gathered in the room he didn't expect to sleep much, but he'd hardly returned to bed when he no longer knew where he was. Sunlight wakened him, and he remembered the shower. Was it really worth reporting, or should he just leave it for the staff to notice, which they presumably couldn't avoid? He lay in the companionable tangle of the sheet until a surge of anger at his inertia roused him. He wasn't supposed to be here just for himself, and as soon as he was dressed he stalked off to Reception.

Win spoke from the office as he approached the counter. "You'll have your fan today, Mr Warden."

"I hope so, but meanwhile the shower has fallen off the wall."

"You're meant to hold it. That way you won't make the room so wet."

Didn't that seem reasonable? Straining to recall why it shouldn't revived the tight ache in Warden's head. "It smashed a tile, as well," he said.

He thought Win was about to tell him to clear them up until she said "Have your breakfast and I'll look into sending someone."

If she meant him to hear weariness, that was surely how he ought to feel. At the buffet he made do with a glass of orange juice and a ragged chunk of bread that he smeared with liquescent butter. The items tasted only slightly stale, he reassured himself. He lingered over them and then over their remains in the hope of giving someone time to deal with his room. At last he ventured back to find that most of the broken tile had been taken away, and a fan was plugged in near the bed.

The bracket from the shower lay on the toilet cistern. While he showered he tried to avoid spraying the room. The mirror reminded him that he was wearing a wristband, though by now it looked almost as undefined as the image blurred by condensation. Was there something else he ought to remember? Yes, he'd neglected to take his passport with him the last time he'd gone to see Win. Instead of slipping it into his pocket he'd left it on the bedside table. He towelled himself more or less dry and padded into the main room. The passport wasn't by the bed.

He searched all the pockets of every item of clothing in the room, but he hadn't forgotten putting it there, and it was nowhere else in the apartment. He dressed so hastily that he heard a shirt button skitter into the bathroom. As he made for Reception, Dick and family watched him, and so did Stan along with his. Warden heard a not especially stifled laugh, followed by a murmur. "Looks like someone's off to make more trouble."

Win stayed in the office to watch his approach. "I'm sure your fan is on its way," she said.

"It's there." As she conveyed that she wouldn't mind being thanked Warden protested "My passport's gone from the room."

"What a pain. Where do you think you might have left it?"

"I told you, in my room. Someone's taken it. Whoever put the fan in must have."

"I don't think you can say that, Mr Warden. If the door was open, anybody could."

"Then they shouldn't have left the door open. What's going to be done, may I ask?"

"I'll make enquiries. You're with us for a while yet. We'll see you're fixed up."

Warden found her undertaking worse than vague. "Maybe the police should make the enquiries."

"You can have what you ask for, Mr Warden."

He gave that a fierce nod, though it tightened the noose of a headache, which was making it hard to talk. He heard Win pick up the phone and dial, and her side of a conversation in Greek. She leaned out of the office to say "Someone will be coming for you. Don't leave the Magic."

"I'll be by the pool," Warden said and took a glass of wine to the lounger, hoping to regain some calm while he waited for the police. He stayed well clear of the families he felt sure were surreptitiously watching him. In a while he dozed, only to keep waking with a sense that it was dangerous to drift off. He felt close to fancying he was handcuffed by the wristband to the lounger, but was the impression hindering a memory? Recalling that he'd lost his passport threatened to rouse his headache, but was that all he'd lost? No, his identification from the travel firm had been inside the passport. Both the loss and having overlooked it made him feel as if he hardly knew who he was. He needed reassurance, but not where he could be overheard, and he took his phone to his room.

The answer wasn't as swift or as bright as Rhona's welcome meeting had suggested. "Rhona Martin."

"Rhona, it's Douglas Warden at Mediterranean Magic." He sounded as though he was associating himself with the place, which was one reason why he added "I should tell you I'm with the firm."

"The firm."

"Yes, ours. They sent me to report on the accommodation."

After quite a pause Rhona said "Why didn't you tell me?"

"I thought I just did."

It wasn't much of a joke, and it earned him another silence before she said "Are you reporting me, as well?"

"I'm afraid that's part of the job."

"What are you going to say?"

"You must know I can't reveal that. That's how the job's done too."

"Then I don't understand why you've told me as much as you have."

"So that you know who I am in case you have to help me get home. Somebody's stolen my passport."

"Are you sure you haven't just mislaid it?"

"I most certainly am. I've got all my wits about me."

He didn't need her to pause yet again, especially if that was some kind of response. "If it's been stolen," she said at last, "you need the police, not me."

"I'm waiting for them now."

"Then I expect you'll be taken care of. You can let me know if you haven't been," she said and immediately ended the call.

Did she treat all her clients' problems like this or just his? In any case he would be reporting her behaviour. How dull must the girl be if she didn't realise she'd made trouble for herself? Though he shouldn't expect special treatment, it might have helped them both. He'd told Win he would wait by the pool for the police, and he hurried back to the lounger, seeing only fellow guests. "Putting up with it after all," he heard someone mutter.

"Putting up with us," someone murmured lower still.

Warden wasn't going to acknowledge the comments. As he fetched another drink he asked the barman "Have the police been here?"

The man kept any expression to himself, not least with his voice. "No police."

He could hardly be saying they weren't welcome, let alone that they wouldn't come. Warden subsided onto the lounger, raising his head whenever he heard anyone approaching. Before long he forgot this was a reason to move his head. When he woke he felt as though his arm was weighing him down, unless the whole of him was. He didn't need to stir when he was here to enjoy the sun—

no, to talk to the police because it was somehow his job— no, because he'd lost his passport. Prising his leaden eyelids open, he saw it was late afternoon. This sent him off the lounger to stumble to Reception, where Win made a visible bid to look resigned at the sight of him. "Have the police been in touch?" he demanded.

"Why should they?"

That felt like a threat of having his memory stolen. "Because you called them on my behalf," Warden said with all the force he could find.

"They haven't come just yet, if that's what you're asking."

"Do you think someone should remind them?"

"Best not to pester, Mr Warden."

It sounded like more than advice, and he understood it wasn't prudent to antagonise the Greek police. As he returned to the poolside he could have fancied that he was being led by the wrist back to the lounger. Once he'd finished another drink he fell into a doze. He had days before he would need the passport, after all.

An outbreak of shuffling roused him. Guests were heading for the buffet, and he saw Dick's son was limping. Since nobody seemed concerned, Warden was disinclined to comment. "Are you coming for dinner?" someone called.

Though Warden was unsure if he was being addressed, he said "Maybe later."

"Isn't their food good enough for you?" the man said, or someone else did.

Warden's hunger simply felt too remote to need assuaging—certainly not worth the bother of troubling Win yet again, since he would have to let her know he wasn't by the pool. He couldn't even find the energy to go to the bar, which would involve summoning the barman now that he was morosely busy with diners. Warden reverted to dozing until Win's voice to some extent roused him. She was only saying "In future we'll just do full board" and not to him. Could that bring her unanimously favourable reviews? Before he'd grasped the thought he was asleep.

He woke to find he was alone. Even the bar was deserted. It was almost midnight, and he couldn't help shivering with a sense of an imminent chill. When he hurried to Reception he wasn't surprised to find it unstaffed. Knocking on the counter failed to bring anyone out of the office or wherever they were hiding. He craned over the counter and found a pad together with a splintered ballpoint pen. He wrote **I'M IN MY ROOM WARDEN** on the top sheet, which he tore off and left behind the counter. Perhaps just the shaky ballpoint had made it hard to write. He was heading for his room when he realised he'd glimpsed movement in the graveyard.

He sneaked along the side of the staff block and piled up rubble so that he could peer over the wall. At first the view hardly seemed worth the effort—the activity he'd glimpsed had just been the flickering of light on some of the memorials—and then his vision grew used to the intermittent dimness. The door of the hut was open, and the occupant was at work.

The only illumination within the hut came from the lights on the graves. Surely the worker couldn't be as thin as the dim unstable outline made the figure look. It was dressed from head to foot in black, exposing no more than the sketchy arms. From their rapid relentless movement Warden deduced that they were weaving some material. Why should he think of a spider? He tried to think that just the movements suggested the resemblance, until he couldn't avoid noticing too many arms on the table where the figure was at work. Surely the extra limbs were composed of stone and belonged to a memorial. That would explain why they were overgrown with vegetation, strands of which the figure was peeling off with its exceptionally long nails to weave into another wristband.

Warden retreated from the wall so fast that the heap of rubble collapsed with a protracted clatter. He wasn't conscious of taking a breath until he was back in his room. He might have tried to tear the greenish bracelet off his wrist, but it was indistinguishable from his skin. Trying to insert a fingernail beneath it only scratched his wrist until it bled. This failed to dismay him as much as it should, and he tried to recapture his awareness of the situation by phoning Rhona. A voicemail message met him, and he wondered if she was refusing to answer, having recognised his number. Unable to think of a message to leave, he called their firm in England, but that line was recording messages too. "It's Douglas Warden investigating a hotel for you. My passport has been stolen. You may need to help me get home," he pleaded. "Call me back."

He'd done all he could think of to do, and he subsided on the bed. At least the police would be able to find him. Before he managed to decide how much of his plight they could be expected to believe, he was asleep. Did a trace of his thoughts about the police make him dream that he was being handcuffed and led to a cell? Another notion roused him—the possibility that Win had never called the police. His eyes sprang open, letting in more of the dark.

Far too little of the dream had gone away. Both his wrists felt constricted, and so did the room. By the time he finished groping for the light switch he knew it wasn't where it ought to be. The naked bulb fluttered alight, showing him how much the room had shrunk. No, it was

a wholly unfamiliar room, with walls patchily darkened by damp and furniture so meagre it seemed hardly there at all. There was a band on his left wrist now, already growing embedded in the flesh. He lurched to his feet and saw lights dancing in the graveyard beyond the window. The occupant of the hut was still crouched over its spidery work, and Warden was in one of the rooms for the staff. "I don't belong here," he cried, or tried to, but his voice barely left his restricted mouth. "This isn't me."

"It is now," the answer came, and he was reduced to hoping he'd heard Win or even Rhona until the figure in the hut turned slowly but inexorably to face him.

In Amelia's Wake

ERINN L. KEMPER

May 15, 1937. Kenyon Airfield, Lethbridge, Alberta, Canada.

THE FIRST NIGHT of guard duty was quiet for Edward Hammer and his brothers. Or at least nothing happened with Amelia Earhart's plane. The Hammer brothers did a lot of talking, which meant they started out talking and quickly raised their voices to echo in the cavernous hangar. At midnight, even with the bay doors open, it was still hot, adding fuel to their already foul mood.

The air show's organizers hired three of the brothers to guard the plane—Edward, Roy and Frank. Arnie, being deaf, didn't get the job. The regular night guards skulked about the airfield while the Hammer brothers kept an eye on the Earhart plane. Things might have been different if Arnie had been there. His deafness allowed him to turn away from his brother's bickering and focus on more important things. Things you could glimpse if you didn't look too hard in one direction. Things you could feel like a quake in the air.

Edward got them the job. He'd been spending time at

the airfield. The Hammer farm was a few fields down from the landing strip and the back of Edward's neck got sore some days from tracking dusters and passenger planes as they tipped their wings and swooped around. Pa kicked clouds of dust, gazing out over his fields and said those flyboys were just showing off, looking to get themselves killed. Edward knew different. It was an expression of joy. The pilots felt it in their chests, in their lungs, like a bellows stirring a fire they filled, and their joy came shooting out in bursts of elation they scribbled across the pale blue sky.

Only one thing in the world made Edward feel that way. And each time he saw Mata Setter waiting on the highway for the bus to secretarial college, swinging between her crutches like a bell, he had to turn away for fear his brothers would see how his chest swelled, his cheeks flushed, and say something to Pa.

In Pa's mind there was only one curse more terrible than life as a cripple, and that was letting a machine do what a man could do with his own two hands and a little backbone.

"What business does a pretty girl like Miss Earhart have with all this pilot daredevilry?" Roy said. He was the youngest, just turned twenty-one in April, dressed for the rodeo in his tight jeans and dress boots. He'd even polished up his buckle so it flashed as he walked over to the plane. He wore his black Stetson with the owl feather he'd found on the day of Ma's funeral tucked in the band. Ma would have kept the feather for luck. She had been gone a month, but Roy planned to wear that hat and feather all year.

"Not everyone's happy with flying off the back of a horse, kiddo," Frank said to Roy as he ducked under the wing of the plane and ran his hand along the gleaming metal, leaning close to the reflective surface to check his teeth for bits of tobacco. He turned to face his brothers, tipping his tan Stetson back and hooking his thumbs in his suspenders. "Maybe she dreamed about it as a kid. I've had dreams like that, about riding my horse out over the hills, nothing holding us back, the freedom like a wind pushing us on. Sure wouldn't feel so free stuck in this tin can, hurtling through the heavens." He flicked one of the propeller blades and it sounded a bright ping.

"Careful. Don't break anything," Edward said. His brothers stalked about the hangar, the hollow clomps of their cowboy boots echoing up to the ceiling.

"If I can break this machine by touching it, she's better off knowing that now, wouldn't you say?" Frank kicked the tire, but not hard.

"Thing looks like an overgrown trout." Roy sat on a crate and leaned against the wall, taking off his hat and hanging it on his knee. "Wouldn't catch me in one, no way."

Edward admired the airplane's torpedo-smooth hull. The polished metal glowed under rows of lights that dangled from between the trusses that crisscrossed the hangar's ceiling. In the morning, when Amelia Earhart fired up the engines, would this beauty have a deeper voice than the buzzing whine of the crop dusters that usually worked the landing strip? He'd have to convince his brothers to stay on a bit for the demonstration— endure their jibes. That made him nervous, too.

"Wonder who the trouble-maker is?" Frank was talking about the reason the Hammer brothers were guarding the plane. "Jesperson thinks it's that Japanese kid down the way. Complains that the little fellah's cagey. Way too quiet."

"Naw," Roy said. "That kid's just shy. More likely it's those rascals you see fishing down by the Baker Bridge.

Caught them laying stones on the road out by the Hutterite colony, trying to tip one of their wagons. Tampering with farm equipment would be a day at the circus for those boys." He smoothed his hair and put his hat back on, setting it just right. "Or maybe it's something else. Hey Eddie? You see anything at the house, any little critters fooling around with the engines? Some of Ma's wee friends messing with the radio?"

Frank smacked Roy with the newspaper he'd brought. "Don't make fun of Ma." He flapped the pages open, tugged his suspenders up on his shoulders, and cast a stern glance over the paper at Roy. For a moment Edward saw the deep lines of Pa's scowl in his expression.

"I'm not making fun of Ma. Eddie and Arnie used to see them, too."

"We were kids, Roy. And Ma was . . . Ma." Edward shook his head, fed up with the conversation.

He dragged a crate to the other side of the plane from his brothers, turning to look out the hangar's gaping doors at the night sky. It was clear overhead, the air so dry it parched his mouth, and in the distance lightening stuttered across the horizon. Frank and Roy went on bickering, but their voices slipped away. Edward imagined what things looked like from up there, hills and mountains reduced to the size of waves in a lake, lights winking like reflected stars.

Edward was pleased when Arnie—still wearing his grease-stained coveralls—came to pick them up after their shift and his brothers agreed to stay and watch Ms. Earhart fly. A crowd of women pilots were there to cheer her on, as well as newspapermen, oilmen with their pledges of support, folks from town—the applause loud enough that even the roar of the plane's engines couldn't drown it.

On the drive home Edward sat up front. Roy and Frank hauled themselves in the back and slumped against the cab. The truck's engine sputtered in fits when Arnie changed gears. Not at all like the smooth animal roar of Amelia Earhart's plane as it surged down the runway and took to the sky.

Edward rocked in and out of a doze, sunlight flashing warm on his face, until the truck cut over to the side of the road and jerked to a stop on the sloping shoulder. Edward cracked an eye open and watched as Arnie hopped out of the truck, walking stick in one hand, hunting knife in the other, and limped across the road, down into the tangled weeds. Arnie stood for a moment, head prairie-dogging left, right, then lunged and struck with the handle of his stick. He pulled a dead rattler from out of the bush. Its body swung as he sawed off the rattle with his knife, then Arnie chucked the snake across the ditch and it caught in the cattle fence and hung there, oozing blood onto the bone-colored grass.

Back at the truck Arnie fished a lunch box out from under the bench seat, snapped it open, and dropped the fresh rattle atop the others, some so old they'd crumbled to sand in the bottom of the box.

It was that way with Arnie. He'd be going along the dusty roads in the truck, on his horse, even on the Indian motorcycle he'd bought against Pa's instruction, and you'd see his ears twitch, his head sweep to the side like a weather vane. All tensed up, eyes narrow, nostrils wide he'd be on that snake the way Duke, Pa's old hound, took after tom cats. According to the doctors he couldn't hear a thing. But Arnie knew when a snake was near, and every rattler that crossed his path met the same end.

Pa blamed the truck for what happened to Ma. But not Arnie. Arnie blamed the snake.

He had been ten the day of Ma's accident. The other three boys, younger and older, worked the farm while Arnie stayed home and helped with the housework. It was one of those days where the wind came in, cut low along the fields, blasting everything in its path. In winter, the ground all slick with ice, that wind would blow you right off your feet. In summer it hit you like opening the door to a furnace.

On that day, the wind ripped through the row of poplars and the clothesline snapped free. All the fresh washing tumbled across the yard, wild phantoms before a howling gale. Ma and Arnie scurried after the linens. The parched brown grass cracked under Arnie's bare feet. The dust-spiced wind caught funnels of earth and blew them up Arnie's nose until it formed a thick crust in his nostrils. He giggled when one sheet twisted around Ma, hog-tying her ankles so she tripped and fell butt-first into the laundry hamper. She tipped her head back and laughed, mouth open, eyes closed, face painted bright by the sun.

The last pillowcase flapped all the way up to the highway and Ma ran after, dress billowing, straw-blond hair spinning loose of its coil. She peeled the pillowcase off of the thicket and jumped back when she saw the rattler hiding behind, poised to strike. It darted at her, angling up to strike her high on the leg.

She jumped back again. Into the path of Mr. Jesperson's Ford.

Arnie drove out to the field to where his brothers and

father were working, Roy handling the wagon while Frank and Pa slung bales of hay up to Edward. Arnie's tear-red eyes barely cleared the dash of the truck as he hung on to the wheel and stood on the gas pedal, racing ahead of a cloud of dust.

Almost falling out of the truck, he stumbled the last few feet, saying "Ma . . . snake!" over and over again.

"Quiet, boy, you sound like a fool," Pa said, like he did every time Arnie tried to talk. Arnie's brothers caught his meaning and ran around to the bed of the truck where Arnie had hauled up the body of their mother and laid her out as best he could, her being so bent and with that oddly flat spot near where her hair parted.

"A snake didn't do this," Pa said, his fingers gripping the side of the truck so his knuckles turned white. Then he vaulted up beside his wife and wiped at the blood that wound down from the corner of her mouth, which was already drying in the hot wind.

Frank drove to the hospital as fast as the truck would allow. Mr. Jesperson raised his hand when they came to the site of the accident, where his tires had burnt S's into the pavement. He held a cloth to his head, the truck rolled up in the ditch, chassis bent beyond repair. Frank slowed long enough for him to hop in the back.

The doctors fixed Ma to the best of their ability, splints and casts for her broken bones. Called it a miracle she was even alive, but she was never the same. Until the day she died, fifteen years later, in her sleep, she moved slowly, and talked to the shadows—her two little *tomte* she called them—in a flattened out tone, so terrified of even the smallest snake that she wouldn't go outside.

Pa would always blame the truck. *We Hammers don't fit with machines. Never had any luck with them. Best to stay well away.* If Jesperson had been using his horse that day he would have been paying attention, rather than sitting on that padded seat, behind a glass shield, while the *infernal combustion engine* blared in his ears.

But Arnie knew it was the snake, sneaking through the low places, striking the unwary. Taking his poor Ma, and leaving a sad, limping ghost behind.

Edward sipped his tea, the cream and honeyed sweetness doing little to wake him. It was dinnertime, only a few more hours 'til they had to be at the airport.

"I could have slept another eight hours," Roy said and stretched his arms back before scratching his chest. "That roast sure smells good. Hey, Arnie." He signed a few words to his brother and rubbed his belly.

Arnie nodded and turned back to the stove, taking the hot gravy over to strain into Ma's rose china gravy boat. The brothers were staying with Pa at the farm that week while they worked guard duty. The farmhouse rattled with their footsteps as they moved from room to room, trying to keep out of Pa's way. Once they were finished at the airfield, Roy and Frank would be back to the Cassidy Ranch and their cow-hand duties. Arnie would go with them and look after the ranch trucks and the neighbors' farm equipment.

While they were all together Arnie was treating every dinner like Sunday. Same as Ma would have.

Edward had slept most of the day, and woken to the sound of pots clanking and the smell of fresh biscuits and roast. From above him, in the eaves, came the scrape and muttering of pigeons and other attic dwellers, the distant boom of thunder disturbing their rest.

The kitchen had steamed up, the windows a sweating blur. Arnie jostled Edward's chair as he squeezed around the table to pile dirty pots in the sink, nudging the cat back under the stove before someone stepped on her.

"You should have seen that girl, Pa," Frank said. "She climbed up in that big plane in her pilot getup, smiling and waving while everyone popped off pictures. She is something, I'll give you that." He slapped Arnie's shoulder as he arranged the roast in the middle of the table. "And she handled that machine like a pro."

Roy shook his head. "You wouldn't believe the circus there to see her fly. A bunch of other lady pilots showed up. Even saw reporters all the way from Vancouver." He paused. "I think Eddie's in love."

Edward dropped a slice of roast on his plate, glanced up at his brother, and then reached for the gravy.

"He practically chased the damn plane down the runway." Roy continued. "Stood there rubbernecking and grinning like an idiot."

"Won't be no fly boys in this family." Pa shook salt all over his dinner, scowling down into his plate. "Never have been, never will. You got your farming to do, Edward. That's head-to-the-ground work."

Frank gave Edward's shoulder a light punch, but Edward busied himself pouring gravy. His brothers had keen eyes. Couldn't keep anything from this family for long.

"You hear about Old Man Jesperson?" Frank asked. "Saw his tractor sitting in the middle of his field. Did our neighborhood mischief-maker strike again?"

Arnie filled a small bowl with porridge, and poured milk and honey over the top.

"What the hell is that?" Pa slammed his hand on the table. Arnie looked up from where he was standing near the stove, nearly dropping the bowl of porridge. "You throw that out."

Arnie shook his head and placed the steaming bowl on the bit of exposed framing behind the stove that Ma always used as a shelf. He turned to Pa and signed a few quick words. Roy cleared his throat and prepared to translate what Arnie had signed. Pa silenced him with an angry glare.

"You don't throw it out, I will." Pa slapped the table again, but Arnie had turned his head so he couldn't read Pa's lips.

Pa scraped back his chair, his brow creased in anger, and grabbed the bowl. Edward could tell it was hot when Pa sucked in a breath, but he held on, carried it across the room and chucked it hard into the garbage. The ceramic cracked against the side of the bin. He turned and glowered at his sons, smoothing his work shirt down into his jeans.

"She's gone and that foolishness stops now. Feeding imaginary critters—I won't have it."

Pa had teased Ma about her strange superstitions, said they never did the family much good. He knew she was lonely, and these little rituals gave her comfort.

Since she'd died there'd been endless trouble with the truck, which didn't bother Pa, he preferred to go by horse. He didn't use the radio either. When Edward tried to tune in most evenings he found nothing but static, and then not even that. Pa said the damned thing had never worked right, even when Ma was alive. He was right, but you could usually tease out a signal. Enough to listen to a little music or the weekly episode of *Jack Armstrong, The All-American Boy*, as long as Ma wasn't in the room.

Edward wondered if Pa had something to do with it not working. That in his grief, or his guilt, he kept the silence for Ma. Just like he kept Arnie from honoring her rituals. Reminders that brought him pain.

"You boys can live without your gadgets while you're here. And you can certainly do away with that nonsense of your mother's. Now let's eat this food before it gets cold." Pa cut off a dripping chunk of roast and shoved it in his mouth, chewing as he glared from one son to the next.

They ate to the sound of knives scraping and cups thunking on the table. Pa left the room as soon as they'd finished, so he wasn't there to stop Arnie from retrieving the broken pieces of bowl. Arnie washed them and added them to the mound of cracked dishes Ma had piled under the front porch for luck.

It was strange that all three vehicles were acting up.

At least it kept Arnie busy and out of the house, for that he was grateful. After dinner he escaped to the barn to try and get Roy's truck running right before his brothers headed out for the night. He was tired of Pa's scowls and his constant banging on the table or counter, stomping on the floor, just so he could give Arnie some piece of backward wisdom, tell Arnie how he had it all wrong. How spending time learning about machines, fixing them, was unnatural.

Arnie knew Pa would never understand. His brothers all made choices Pa approved of, was proud of. Arnie's deafness was the first wall. When he was a kid and Pa took the boys to town, he'd see it in Pa's eyes. The shame and the guilt when folks realized the skinny jug-eared boy couldn't hear them. And then when Arnie showed such a knack for fixing things, taking them apart to see how they worked, Pa complained endlessly. Men got soft when they depended on machines, soft in the body and in the head. That's what Pa said.

For Arnie it was completely natural. He fired up Roy's truck and took it for a test drive, leaving the farm lights behind in the dusk. The fields spread out grey on either side, long grasses shifting back and forth with the trickling currents of wind.

He concentrated on the vibrations, alert for coughs and sputters that changed the way the truck moved. He could feel an engine hesitate, its labored grind. When things worked perfectly he felt the open-throated surge of the engine, ready to go. It was a lot like riding was for Frank and Roy—the twitch of muscle that told a rider what the horse was up for.

But nothing could compare to a well-tuned engine. Probably like what that Earhart woman felt in her plane. On his Indian motorbike, leaning into the curves that wound up the undulating foothills, the powerful thrum of the engine, vibrations changing speed and intensity as he moved through the gears, the grit of the road coating his teeth. Pure freedom.

He'd get the Indian on the road as soon as he'd chased the problems with the tractor and the farm truck. Roy's truck was an easy enough fix. His brother simply didn't know how to drive it. He set the timing wrong and didn't mind when the engine told him to gear up or down. By the end of the month, the truck would be backfiring so badly the poor cat bolted under the house whenever someone started it, and the chickens clucked and beat their wings in a frantic cloud. Regular as clockwork, Arnie would have to rub the black crust off the valves and adjust the timing until it thrummed.

What was really strange lately was how Arnie found odd little issues each time he folded back the hood. Loose connections, dead battery, burnt plugs. Nothing Roy could have done on his own, and Arnie didn't think it was a vandal. Kids would more likely put a potato in the tailpipe, or take your tractor out for a joyride, leaving figure eights cut in your cornfield.

If Ma was here he knew what she'd say. Sometimes she was pretty convincing. When he was a kid he believed in the *tomte*, felt their vibrations as they wound through the walls on stormy nights, even found the apples Ma said they left for the horses. Until the day he woke early and saw Ma in the yard, heading for the barn, a bushel of apples caught up in her skirt. She walked up on her toes, unsteady but trying to hurry. She kept looking from side to side, wary of snakes coiling up from the long shadows of dawn.

Ridiculous, of course, putting out the porridge, keeping the broken dishes, but when he worked on the trucks he really did feel like he was chasing something. Not a little spark-eating demon. A mechanical or electrical problem, but one that didn't follow the normal rules.

The second night of guard duty was quiet, too. Much the same as the first. Though it started out differently for Edward.

He'd gone early, walked the length of their farm, the Setter farm, then the airstrip as gloom turned to twilight. He stood in front of Miss Earhart's plane, hands in his pockets, wondering what that lift felt like. Was it like riding a bull, when your teeth rattle and your guts drop and then for a moment you just hang there, floating, the clouds whipping by and the sun catching in your eyes, before gravity smacks you down?

"She's a beauty, isn't she?" A soft female voice came from behind.

Edward didn't turn around, afraid if he saw her face he'd lose his tongue. "Sure is, ma'am. You can see a thing like that is built to go right the way around."

"Yes she is. I trust her with my life."

"How does it feel? Flying her up there, skimming the clouds?" Edward's voice cracked with embarrassment. A flush crawled up from his collar.

"Just like you think it would. Free. Light. Powerful. That all is possible."

Edward stole a glance at her then, her gaze far away, already picturing herself in flight.

"Thank you for keeping an eye on her. Just wanted to tuck her in for the night," she said.

They stood for a moment more in silence.

"I'll keep her safe, ma'am." Edward heard steps behind him and turned to watch the tall slim woman in flight gear stride away into the shadows.

"I thank you for that." She turned back and flashed him a wide grin, and then pushed through the service door, and was gone.

From the bay doors out front Roy and Frank came clacking in, their cowboy boots dusted from the road.

"Ho there, Eddie. Hope we're not late. Arnie's got my truck all pulled apart. And the farm truck. We may be walking in the morning, too." Roy settled back on his crate. "Pa's in good form tonight. Frank wanted to head into town and see about why the house's electric keeps cutting out, but Pa said he needed the horses rested for tomorrow, and he'd rather use the old lanterns anyways. Claims the light bulbs bother his eyes. Farm's falling apart, Eddie. Thought you'd be taking better care of things."

"Come on now, Roy." Frank tended to be more understanding. As the oldest son it should have been his place to take over the farm. But he'd had no affinity for farming, preferring to run cattle and ride rodeo. "Arnie will fix things before we go. Even get the tractor going if Pa'll agree to use it."

Edward shook his head. "That battle's lost. We've been using the horses to pull the plow all year."

"I don't know how you do it, Eddie. He's even worse with Ma gone." Roy took off his hat and hung it over his knee. "I'll be glad to be out of there when we're done with this gig."

"Well, it's not like there's much choice. If I quit and come work the Cassidy ranch with you all, we'd have to sell the farm. Then what? Where would Pa go?"

"Don't worry. We'll be fine. Pa'll be fine. He just needs some time to stop missing Ma so much."

Edward couldn't tell them it had been better since Ma died, mostly. Even the fury of Pa's grief was manageable. The reason he'd moved a few years before, out of the house and into the farm-hand quarters out back of the barn, was to get away from her, not Pa. He loved Ma, but after her accident she changed, and over the years it got worse and worse.

She'd have conversations in Danish with herself and with people no one could see. The *tomte*—her little ones.

I know you're hungry, little ones. Ma said, her words slow and thick as she placed the porridge on its shelf. *Eat up, or the cat will. See, Eddie. They're so far from home and they're our family. If we take care of them, they'll take care of us.*

Sometimes she claimed they were the spirits of her grandparents that she'd brought with her from Denmark in a pot of dirt from the family farm. *Oldemoder wants you boys to go out and play now. Enough of that radio racket. That machine is disturbing the air in here. Poor*

Oldemoder can't think. Edward was sure it was Ma who kept breaking the radio, though she blamed *Oldefader*.

Her doctors assured them this was common in cases like hers. But that didn't make it easier. She would laugh with the shadows that huddled in the kitchen, and sometimes when Edward passed by the room he saw those blotches of darkness shake in ripples of glee. If he stopped to get a good look they'd melt back into the corners, perfectly normal shadows cast by stove, cupboard, chair.

Pa said there was no harm in it. Something to help her pass the time.

But when she died he cleaned up most of her tokens, the pot of dirt from the kitchen shelf went into the vegetable patch, along with the feathers she kept in her top drawer. He left her dresses hanging in the closet, however, and some mornings Edward smelled her *eau de toilet* coming through their bedroom window when he fetched eggs to make their breakfast.

"Have you met her? What's she like?" Mata swung between her crutches, kicking stones with her good leg while the other hung stiff in its polished steel cage. Her chin-length hair so feather light it floated around her face, up toward the pale blue sky. "I can't believe you're guarding Amelia Earhart's plane."

Edward was collecting the mail when the bus from secretarial college dropped Mata Setter off on the road at five in the evening. The bus creaked to a stop and as Mata disembarked the other girls leaned out the windows, calling to her in sunny voices, giggling and waving at Edward. He smoothed his hair, hoping it wasn't all pillow-tufted.

"I talked to her last night. She was very polite. Feminine." He blushed. "I mean, of course she's feminine. She's a girl . . . woman."

Mata scowled at him, but a smile lurked behind it. "You think she's pretty?"

"I . . . well of course . . . "

With a bright, throaty laugh Mata swung back and kicked a stone. It bounced off Edward's shoe.

"She's wonderful, I bet," Mata said. "I've heard she's really intelligent. Very kind. Tell me everything she said."

Edward walked with Mata up the drive to her house. Like the Hammer farm, it was flanked by pale rows of poplars, and a narrow porch stretched across the front. He told her about the plane, a custom Lockheed Electra with all the new radio equipment, even a Morse code machine. Everything was fixed and running well, ready for her second try. He described the gap between Amelia Earhart's teeth and the way her nose crinkled, just like Mata's did. How she walked with such long strides and he showed how she held up her hand with the first finger higher than the rest before heading down the runway.

"She's a lucky gal, getting to do what she's doing." Edward sighed.

"There's no luck in it," Mata said. "She got to where she is by a lot of hard work. My dad says you can see it in her chin. Her determination." She looked at the sky, and then pointed with one of her crutches at a crop duster looping around for a landing. "One day I'm going up."

She leaned against his shoulder and they watched the plane drop like a bird of prey. Edward wanted to tell her he'd take her. Together they would skim the clouds, the farmland laid out below with roads cut between.

A door banged. Mr. Setter came out onto the porch, fists on his hips. In the front window the round faces of

Mata's mother and sisters pressed against the rippling glass.

"I'd better go." Mata smiled at him and gave his leg a soft touch with one of her crutches before she turned and crossed the front yard to her porch. She hopped up the steps, kissed her dad's cheek and ducked inside.

Edward and Mr. Setter looked at each other across the yard, then Mr. Setter nodded and went in the house.

That was the moment Edward Hammer's life changed. In an instant he gave up the idea of joining the air force, an idea that had been tickling at him for the past year, since they expanded the airfield and bigger planes had started coming, since Roy and Frank had moved out, leaving him as the only son to take over for Pa and run the family farm.

No. He would stay on the farm. And he would marry Mata Setter.

Arnie could tell by the slow, soft steps which brother had come into the barn. He turned when Edward tapped his shoulder.

"Think you can get it running, Arnie?"

He shrugged. There was something in his brother's face, a new happiness that made Arnie smile.

"What's so funny?" Edward scowled and scratched his head, but the frown was just on the surface. His lips moved as though they wanted to twist back into a grin all on their own.

Arnie's hands moved in a series of quick gestures.

"You can say it, Arnie. You know I'm no good at reading that."

Arnie shook his head and repeated the gestures, this time more slowly.

Edward shrugged. "The lessons are too expensive. I don't have enough, and Pa would never agree to pay. I can just hear him . . . what the hell you want to fool around in the clouds for, boy? That hay ain't gonna bale itself . . . "

Arnie signed again, and made an exaggerated scowl.

"No, it's okay. You keep your money. Besides, I'm saving up for something else." Edward's gaze flashed warm and distant and his neck flushed, the red climbing to his cheeks as he spoke. "I've almost got enough, as long as it doesn't cost much to get this tractor going, and we have a good harvest."

Arnie signed "okay" and bent back to the repair work. He felt Edward's easy steps as he walked out of the barn, off to prepare for guard duty.

One side of the farm truck's hood folded open for him to work on the engine. He'd been over it three times already and decided to have a look under the chassis, see if he could locate a leak, some indication of what the problem was, other than the truck had a tendency to stall, for no reason he could see. He laid his tools in reach and rolled under the truck.

Arnie talked as he worked, not in his head, but out loud. He practiced what the doctor taught him, how to keep his volume low by paying attention to the muscles in his throat. Whispering was hard. At least he hoped he was whispering, talking to the engine, asking it to tell him what was wrong and how to fix it.

He'd already pulled off the oil pan and checked for bits of metal. Now he'd replace the gasket and hope that helped. The truck was losing oil, but not enough to be a major concern. There were only so many options of what could be wrong; he'd eliminated all the obvious. There was gas and spark. No sticking valves, plugs all good.

Everything checked out up top. He'd even checked the gas in the tank in case those local vandals had poured sugar in, but it tasted how it should, like gas.

He rolled farther under the truck, dipped his rag in gasoline and repositioned the lamp. From the corner of his eye he saw a dark shape. It slipped along the crankshaft and up out of sight—too long and thin to be a rat. When Arnie tried to get a better look, it disappeared. He tapped the crankcase with the adjustable wrench, trying to scare the critter out, and realized it was likely just shadows moving around when he adjusted the lamp. The fact that the shape appeared as a slug of liquid darkness, little points of light glinting on its skin as it slipped up into the deeper shadows—just his eyes playing tricks.

He gave the bottom of the engine a good wipe down with the gas-soaked rag and set the gasket and oil pan in place, bolting two corners first. He worked his way around the pan, tightening bolts. A small shadow slithered around in the periphery, but each time he turned his head toward the movement it was gone. So he worked, all the while tracking from the corner of his eye.

A movement near the starter engine.

He rolled farther under the truck, following the shadow. It was quick, slithering up around the side of the starter. Without turning his head, Arnie swung with the wrench, and made contact with something soft. He dropped the wrench, his hand gone numb from a pulse of electricity. He'd probably also hit a couple of exposed wires. The critter fell somewhere behind his head, he could just make it out, writhing on the ground, the lamplight catching on its inky skin. Snake. Not a rattler, but some kind of snake.

The floorboards shifted, alerting Arnie that someone

had entered the barn. He pushed out from under the truck, rolled off of the dolly, and searched the shadows under the truck for the snake. It was gone.

Frank and Roy stood ready for guard duty in a fresh layer of aftershave and boot polish. Roy climbed behind the wheel of his truck, Arnie had already tuned it up for him and everything worked fine now. Roy looked out toward the field, his black hat casting his face in shadow, his jaw clenched and his shoulders riding up high, still angry.

Arnie knew he shouldn't have laughed at his brother. A few days ago, when he bought those new chaps with the fuzzy lamb pelt, Roy had strutted around like king of the rodeo. And earlier in the afternoon, despite the heat, he had worn them to help Palmer Setter check his fence line. The Setters' truck was in the shop, another victim of the strange rash of vandalism. Roy needed sleep to be ready for guard duty, but he clearly couldn't resist the chance to strap on his new chaps and parade past the Setter girls.

When Roy got home, chaps bristling with burrs and spikes of hayseed, Pa said he looked like a lamb that had lost a wrestling match with a badger. Arnie laughed, and he knew that he'd laughed too loud when Roy told him he sounded like a damn donkey. Roy spent the evening on the porch picking the burrs and chucking them into the yard. His refusal to look at Arnie meant Arnie could only read their lips, but he couldn't say much of anything to the family. Roy was the only one of the Hammer men who was any good at sign language and since Pa couldn't read much, Arnie didn't like to bring out a pen and paper.

"Hey Arnie, Roy's truck good to go?" Frank looked tired, dark circles blackened his eyes so they were hard to see under the rim of his hat.

Arnie nodded. Movement along the barn floor, seeping out from behind the farm truck, he turned to look. Nothing there. Frank tapped his shoulder and he turned back to read his brother's lips.

" . . . take Pa to the bank tomorrow, see about getting a loan for a new tractor if you can't get that one fixed. We could at least keep it for parts."

There again, a shadow sliding toward the underside of Roy's truck. Not wriggling like a snake, more inching along like a worm, and vibrating in weird shuddering twitches. When he looked directly at it, it disappeared.

Arnie signed a message to Frank, but his older brother shook his head in confusion and waved as he climbed into the passenger seat. Roy wouldn't look at him when he stomped on the floor and clapped his hands.

"Roy, Frank, there's something strange . . . " Arnie's throat opened wide, the words came with easy force. He was talking too loud, he felt it.

Roy's face twisted in disgust, so much like Pa. "You sound like a dummy, Arnie." Roy slammed the truck into drive and drove off in a blast of exhaust.

The last night of guard duty was coming to an end, and Edward was glad. Roy had been in a foul mood the whole night and spent most of his time patrolling the other hangars, convinced he'd catch that little Japanese kid sneaking around in the dark. Frank and Edward sat side-by-side on empty crates, looking at Amelia Earhart's plane.

"I can't imagine all that time up there in the sky, going all the way around. You'd have no control. Why would you want to?" Frank chewed tobacco, said working his jaw kept him alert.

Edward shrugged. "It's like those explorers. They went out in boats, people said they were crazy, but they needed to see it . . . the world. Understand the mystery. Maybe it's like that?"

"Figure life's mysterious enough. Watching the sunrise out there herding cattle; coyotes howling at the moon; the way a woman's smile can make you feel weak and strong all at the same time—that's enough mystery for me." Frank leaned back against the hangar wall and closed his eyes.

Edward looked at his brother, his face lined by the sun, his hair slipping back under the band of his tan Stetson.

"I'm going to ask Mata Setter to marry me." He spoke the words quickly, pushed them out before he lost his nerve.

Frank nodded without opening his eyes. "That's good, Eddie."

They sat side by side, listening for the scuff of Roy's cowboy boots as he paced around the airfield. When the sun began pinking the horizon, the first of the ground crew arrived, the signal that their final shift was done.

Roy came swaggering back and threw his keys to Frank. "You're driving, big brother. I can't even see I'm so tired."

"I'm going to stay a bit," Edward said. He wanted to watch Amelia Earhart's departure. Next time he saw Mata he'd tell her all the details, and then he'd ask her if she wanted to go for some ice cream.

Roy's eyes flashed with anger. "What's with you, Eddie, and this airplane foolishness? You're never going to be a fly boy—you don't have the smarts or the money. You see what it takes with this crazy girl . . . flying around the goddam country begging money off bankers and oilmen. You need more charm than you got. Better looks, too."

"Come on, Roy, let's get home." Frank turned the key in the ignition and the engine made a slow grinding sound.

"Damn truck." Roy kicked the quarter panel twice, the truck rocked from side to side on its springs . . . and fired up with a shotgun blast.

From where Edward stood he thought he saw something drop from under the truck, behind the front wheel. It shivered like a leaf on a windy day, then moved forward as though a gust of a breeze compelled it, pulled by a force that was irresistible. But when he tried for a better look the blot of darkness had blown away.

Roy spat on the ground, then climbed into the bed of the truck and stretched out, crossing his ankles and tipping his black Stetson over his eyes. With a wave and a smile in the rearview mirror, Frank pulled out of the hangar and drove for home.

The truck hitched and blew a halo of white smoke that slowly dissolved in the still air.

Edward wanted to warn the ground crew, though he wasn't sure what to tell them. He explained to one of the workers that something may have gotten in to the plane. When the man asked him what, he said it could have been a snake, he wasn't sure. The man scratched his jaw and adjusted his coveralls, the name Alvin stitched on the pocket.

"We'll be doing a complete check, pal. Always do. If a snake got in, we'll find it, not that a snake could get in. Plane's put together pretty tight." Alvin squinted as he studied Edward's face. "Fell asleep on the job, did ya? Had a bad dream? Or are you boys causing trouble?"

"No, sir. Just being careful."

Alvin walked Edward out of the hangar. "We got work to do, pal. You go get some sleep."

He patted Edward on the back and gave a little push.

Edward stopped at the edge of the airfield to wait for the takeoff. Thunderheads built up on the horizon, dark pillars of cloud on the edge of an otherwise clear day.

Amelia Earhart's plane rose up into view, the morning sun catching on its steely skin. It lifted higher and higher, a feather caught in a puff of wind that drew it up to the heavens. Edward's heart thrummed with the beauty of it, the wonder. The plane, a mere speck, flashed like a cold spark against the rose-tinted blue sky and then was gone.

The sun had long burned the blush of dawn from the sky when Edward arrived at the entrance to the farm. He looked down the road and saw Mata there, waving her crutch in the air like some featherless wing, waiting for him, and for a time he forgot his worries.

She was waiting for him.

July 5th, 1937.

Edward heard about the search for Amelia Earhart the day after Frank and Roy's funeral.

They held off on Frank's service a few days while Roy lay in a coma in the hospital. Roy lingered, fading bit by bit, then passed in the early morning three days after the accident. The brothers were buried the same day to spare the expense of two funerals.

Edward and Mata parked near the airfield to watch the planes, as they did when they both had an afternoon free. The air above the landing strip rippled with heat. The prairie spread out flat, and beyond the purple waves of the foothills. They had taken Mr. Setter's buggy since Pa's truck wasn't working and Roy's truck was still wrapped around the oak tree at Dead Man's Bend. Arnie swore that the truck had been working fine when his brothers took it out, but he'd said the same about his motorcycle.

Edward rubbed sleep grit from his eye. He'd gotten up early to get a jump on chores. Sleep didn't come easy, anyway, and when it did come, dark hungry shadows slithered into each of his dreams. At breakfast he prepared an extra serving of porridge and placed it on the shelf behind the stove, next to a jar containing soil from Frank and Roy's graves. Mata laughed when he told her about the porridge, and when they snuck offerings of apples to the horses, but she understood.

Mr. Setter had resisted Edward and Mata's courtship, suspicious of a man who would choose a cripple over a woman with two good legs. But it was clear, in the gentle way Edward helped her up into the buggy, in Mata's bright laughter and shy smile, that this was love. Edward's love buffed Mata's beauty to a shine, and Mr. Setter wouldn't stand in their way.

Today Mata's expression was solemn. She pulled a newspaper out from under the seat and placed it on Edward's lap. Her eyes were red-rimmed from crying. Edward had assumed it was because of his brothers and his father, but the way her breathing hitched now and new tears started, he knew there was more. Something he'd been dreading.

"What is it?" He turned the paper over and read the headline. He couldn't breathe.

Amelia Earhart Missing in South Pacific.

"She can't be gone. Not her." Mata's hand slipped into his. "She probably had some trouble and had to land somewhere. They say her radio was acting up."

Edward's heart pounded in his chest.

Arnie had asked him on the day of the funeral if he'd seen anything that last night of guard duty. He'd waited in his hospital bed until a nurse took Pa to the washroom. Whispered it in his strange, slurring voice so Pa wouldn't hear. Edward said no.

How could he explain to Arnie about the strange shivering thing he'd seen plop down from under Roy's truck? The worm-like shadow he thought he saw inching up the wheel strut of the Earhart plane, drawn to the gleaming hulk of the plane like filings to a magnet. Only one of the little devils. The other waiting back at the farm for its wayward mate who would never return. How when he blinked, the creature flickered and was gone.

"She's probably just a little lost," Edward said to Mata without conviction.

"Her husband says he won't give up. He'll keep looking even if they call off the search." Mata wiped her eyes and leaned against his shoulder. "He'll find her."

Edward folded the newspaper and looked down at Mata's hand, at her long, graceful fingers. He hoped she'd accept his mother's ring. It wasn't going to be easy, running the farm and looking after Pa and Arnie. Not the most romantic future for a woman with her spirit. A woman who dreamed of flight. But she was strong, practical, determined. And she didn't believe life dealt you anything resembling luck, good or bad.

Arnie learned about the search for Amelia Earhart from the nurse who came to adjust his hospital bed. Pa lay in the bed next to his, head turned away from Arnie as he slept.

It was the news of Pa's stroke that had sent Roy and Frank hurtling down the road in their truck. When word of his father, and his brothers' accident, reached Arnie, he jumped on his Indian motorcycle and raced to the hospital.

There was a strange pull when the bike took the corners, but Arnie ignored it. At the 'T' junction by the water tower he hit the brake. The bike kept surging forward, down the ditch at full speed, and up the other side into the cattle fence.

In the hospital, Pa woke up.

Arnie wanted to tell him the news of Amelia Earhart's disappearance. He could feel his hands twitch, forming words his Pa would never have understood, but only the left hand moved. His right arm ended in a bandaged stump. Arnie opened his mouth to speak, to say something about his grief, their losses. To tell Pa he'd been right. The Hammers didn't fit with machines at all. But he stopped, knowing it would only upset Pa to hear his son's voice.

Pa's mouth pulled down on one side, skin slack, eyes bright with anger, fear, and loss. Just like the creature that haunted the darkness when Arnie closed his eyes. A bubble of spit rose from between Pa's lips and burst. Doctors claimed frustration was common is cases like his, but he would be able to speak again if he practiced, though likely with some impediment. They also claimed Arnie would be able to walk again, and learn how to write with his left hand. Arnie was tired of the doctors' claims.

He closed his eyes, but didn't sleep. If he slept he'd have the nightmare, or was it a memory? It was hard to tell . . .

He opened his eyes to the sun—blazing down, nearly blinding him—and a burning pain in his hand. He tried to move his crushed fingers, tried to curl them into a fist. The whole hand had blackened and swelled as it filled with blood. The motorbike pinned his legs to the ground and the cattle fence twisted around him, tearing clothing and pieces of flesh. The air was thick with the smell of gas.

He opened his mouth and called for help, his throat caught on the words and he ended up coughing.

A movement beside his head. Long, serpent-like, sun reflecting on the dark scales of its hide. He knew if he turned to look, it would disappear, so he let his gaze go soft. Let what was in front of him blur.

There. The creature. *Tomte.*

A shudder contracted its flesh as it writhed in slow undulations. Right across the middle was flat, and in places the skin split so Arnie could see its insides. Flickering sparks of stolen electric impulse lit up the creature's innards. It had one eye, blood-red, and it stared at Arnie, unblinking, accusing. Arnie could feel its anguish vibrating in the air—at the loss of its other, its mate who had slipped into a shining steel machine and flew away, stripping the one left behind of everything but emptiness and rage.

Despite its injuries, the creature slithered toward him in shuddering contractions. Arnie studied the organs— or nerves or veins—that sent cold bursts of light along the rift in its oil black skin. An ignition that failed to catch.

He waited until the creature was close enough, then reached out with his good hand. A shock of static burst through him when he touched it. The creature made a low buzzing hum he could feel right up his arm and into his chest. His fingers, so deft at fixing things, sank into the shivering wet mess, located a strand, thin as a number fourteen wire. His fingers numbed as the creature sent small charges of electricity into him, but he followed the

strand to where it fastened to the whole—rooted behind the creature's glaring red eye.

With one quick movement Arnie pinched and twisted, severing the strand from the whole. As the creature's writhing slowed, the sparks extinguished, one by one, until finally it burnt out, leaving nothing but a dusty black husk.

A WARE THAT WILL NOT KEEP

JOHN F.D. TAFF

Clay lies still, but blood's a rover
Breath's a ware that will not keep.
Reveillé
A.E. Housman

PHIL STOPPED ON the sidewalk in front of the modest brick bungalow, inhaled the air the house seemed to exhale. Inside, atop a bed so big it made him look like a child, his Grandpa Lev lay dying. The old man's death seeped through the pores of the structure, rolled over the lawn like a miasma, hung in a heavy cloud over the roof as if the structure respired with the same labored, gray exhalations his grandfather breathed.

Grandpa Lev had cancer, which had started in his lungs but had quickly burrowed into his bone marrow. Perhaps a year to live, he was told; a painful year. There had been tears all around, but none from Grandpa Lev. Phil had seen simple acceptance in his grandfather's demeanor, but something else, too, something deep; as smooth and familiar as a worry stone rubbed in cracked hands for many years. Something Phil was sure no one else saw.

Grandpa Lev was a Polish Jew of the old-school

persuasion, whose alumni included Lot and Job, the ones who accepted all God threw at them and more with a weary *meh* and a determination to press on.

So Phil knew that look.

It was *acceptance.*

The old man's face held the look of someone who had just been told to finally pay the bill . . . a large bill that had been hanging unpaid for some time accruing interest. It was the face of someone who accepted that, but who was also rueful of the price.

Phil knew that his grandfather would tell him what that price was here, *today.*

Shivering, he walked to the porch, used a key to let himself in.

Inside, his grandfather's possessions looked dull, drained of color, objects in a sepia-toned picture. It was as if they, too, were slowly dying, fading.

Phil turned toward the glow of late afternoon light that slanted down the narrow staircase, warm with golds and oranges and delicate greens. The light played on the dozens of framed photos that hung on both sides of these walls, giving a fitful life to the dead. Relatives that had come to this country, many of them, *most* of them on a wave of shock and pain and death that continued to resonate in their family, in their country . . . in their *faith.*

Phil climbed the steps slowly, feeling the weight of their scrutiny.

Grandpa Lev's room was a strange combination of Old World and high-tech. Dark, heavy wood furniture sat cheek-and-jowl by exotic medical equipment, beeping devices on poles, blinking boxes squatting atop his grandmother's linen chest. Tubes and wires ran across the floor, met at the bed.

The old man caught sight of his grandson over the shoulder of the nurse, who was adjusting a line from one of the hanging bags of fluids, down to where it entered, by needle, the back of his grandfather's heavily veined hand.

A smile broke out on his grandfather's face, bright enough to push away the denser shadows hanging over the bed.

"So, my grandson finally comes," he said in a broken voice. "It only took my dying to get him here."

Phil went to the bed a little quicker than he'd intended, fell into his grandfather's arms like a little boy. He buried his head in the old man's neck, closed his mouth, bit his lips, willed himself not to cry. He inhaled the scent of his grandfather, that familiar mixture of tobacco and aftershave that Phil had found soothing as a child.

Now, it was tinged with age, a kind of old man mustiness with something sour and sweetly off-putting underlying the forcibly neutral odors of the medicines that permeated the room.

Grandpa Lev gave him one more squeeze, kissed his cheek. The old man put a shaking hand to his grandson's other cheek, patted it gently. Phil cleared his throat, pulled away to stand beside the bed.

"My grandson," Lev said, tears glistening in his eyes. "I told you he'd come today, didn't I?"

The caretaker nodded, stepped toward the door. Phil and his grandfather listened to her footfalls on the steps, heard the front door open, close, the deadbolt set.

Lev patted the edge of the bed. "Come, sit. I have a story to tell you while I still have breath."

Phil sat carefully so as not to disturb any of the wires or tubes snaking across its length and into his grandfather. "Why don't you let me close the oxygen tent? It'd be easier for you to talk."

"Bah," Lev said, settling back onto the pillow. "My lungs have little life left. Why waste it on false breath?"

He cut his eyes at his grandson, took a deep, deep breath as if to make a point.

Phil could hear it rattle in the dry corrugations of his grandfather's lungs.

Lev pressed tissue against his chapped lips. Specks of red soaked into the tissue before his grandfather tossed it into a wastebasket near the bed, already filled with identical pink-stained clumps.

"So, what is it you called me here to tell me?" Phil asked.

Lev sighed, closed his eyes.

"The only person I ever told this was your grandmother, who took it with her when she left."

"Then why not just let it go?"

"Telling you *is* letting go. After, there's something you must do. If you love me."

Phil took the old man's hand.

Lev settled his head onto the pillow, licked his blood-flecked lips.

"I've never spoken much about 1945, no? There's a reason for that far beyond the reason that should have been enough . . . "

Spring of 1945 was cold in southwest Poland. The sky was a dense, compact gray as low as a ceiling, pressing down on the land with great weight, reverberating like a struck gong from all the violence transpiring beneath it.

I was 14 years old, not much thinner than I am now. I was dark-haired, dark-eyed, with a manic energy that my flesh could not contain.

Three months earlier, my family and I had been hauled away by the Germans, hauled away along with our entire village in the middle of a cold, moonless dark. In the commotion, I was separated from them—my parents, my two younger brothers, my baby sister—herded first onto a covered truck with dozens of other men and boys, all stunned into silence. From there, we were loaded into boxcars, perhaps a hundred to a car, taken all night to a camp.

I wasn't sure exactly where my family was or, for that matter, where I was. Poland still? Germany? Austria? The name of the camp was on the rough wooden sign over the gate I had passed through, in a language I didn't speak. I know it *wasn't* one of the bigger, more notorious camps—Buchenwald, Auschwitz, Treblinka.

I was processed into this camp along with what seemed to be only men—from my age all the way up to . . . well, my age *now*. I was taken in with a group of about fifty others, stripped naked, hosed down by the guards, given a scratchy uniform of grey wool with the Star of David sewn roughly on its breast. My head was shaved, my wrist tattooed with a number. I was fed a sparse, rushed meal of boiled potatoes and a stale heel of bread, then led into a long, low wooden building that was filled from end to end with bunks stacked to the ceiling three-high.

The place smelled of new wood and sawdust, of dirty bodies and unwashed feet. As bad as it smelled inside, it was better than the smell outside—the flat odor of mud and the bitter reek of ashes coming from a building at the center of camp.

I was assigned a bunk at the very top. I clambered up there and fell into a deep sleep where my dreams brought no comfort.

Immediately upon waking the next morning, I started thinking about *escape*.

The guards roused us roughly. There was a short speech from the commandant, concerning the schedule; wake, eat, work, eat, sleep. We were lined up, and guards went back and forth, pulling the old men out, leading them away to the mysterious building with the four huge chimneys. The rest of us were separated into groups and led away to our jobs—building new bunkhouses, digging drainage or latrine ditches, chopping wood or cleaning.

Me and a couple of boys my age were led to the back of the building that belched grey smoke. Down an incline was a narrow alley with a series of brick stalls filled with ash. Wheelbarrows leaned against the wall next to a dozen makeshift shovels. The enclosed space was so hot it took our breath away. Ash and cinders, still glowing red, swirled in the air.

Our job was to shovel ash into the wheelbarrows, take the laden barrows back up the incline to the low series of structures that looked like horse stables. We were to offload the ash there, return and refill the wheelbarrows and repeat the circuit.

We stared at the guard for a second, unsure of what to do.

"*Schnell!*" he shouted.

There was a flurry as we rushed to the barrows, grabbed shovels, clambered to the stalls and began shoveling frantically. In seconds, the air became opaque, filled my lungs with the choking remains of whatever had been burned.

Those first few weeks were a blur of shoveling, hefting the barrows of ashes out to the building, emptying them, returning, filling, emptying. There was a small meal of potatoes and bread in the morning before work, a slightly bigger meal of potatoes, milk and bread after work, then to bed.

Even for someone young and full of energy, the work was exhausting. At the end of the day, my arms and legs ached, my back throbbed, my stomach growled for more food. My nights were thick with sleep, sleep so profound, so deep that dreams seldom reached me, even though I desperately wanted them. Where were my father and mother, my brothers and sister? How were they? Did they miss me? Did they dream about me?

There were rumors of what was going on, what the Nazis were really doing. But I comforted myself with thoughts of escape, of breaking free from the camp and running, perhaps returning home, perhaps striking off to find my family. I said nothing to anyone those first few weeks, but the desire, the *need* to escape, to stand up in some way to what was happening to me, to us, burned so bright that it consumed more of my energy than even the shoveling.

I'd often get screamed at for going too near the gate or the perimeter fence, for playing with the windows in the bunkhouse, for snooping around the big building with the furnace . . . whose purpose had become chillingly clear. I was even shot at several times for straying where I wasn't supposed to be.

The guards took these actions casually, almost off-handedly. They seemed pre-occupied by other thoughts.

It was rumored the Americans were coming, the Soviets were coming. That the war was nearly over and soon Berlin would be in flames, if it wasn't already.

Someone did notice, though, a rabbi. He occupied the bed at the bottom of my rack, but I'd never spoken to him, other than to mumble an "Excuse me" as I climbed down for breakfast or up to sleep. I certainly didn't know he was keeping an eye on me.

As I climbed to my bunk one evening, the rabbi put his hand on my ankle, gave it a tug.

I looked down, surprised.

"If you're thinking of escaping, you maybe shouldn't be so obvious."

I came down to the ground, my face burning.

"How do you know what I'm thinking, rabbi?"

"You wear it like a fine suit of clothes and you don't think it noticeable when the rest of us are dressed so shabbily?" he asked, pulling at his woolen shirt and raising one hoary eyebrow.

The old man took my hand, patted it, smiled.

"Give up this madness before *they* notice. If you try to run, if you try to squeeze through the fence or dig your way out, you will die. They will shoot you inside the fence or another soldier will shoot you outside."

I remember feeling real, boiling anger for the first time at an adult, much less a rabbi.

I pulled my hand from his. "Rabbi, is it better to sit here and wait for them to burn us?"

God help me, the rabbi's smile grew broader, but still gentle.

"What you see as *acceptance*, I see as *acceptance*, too . . . in a different way."

Those words *didn't* fill me with anger. I was already too full with that to hold any more.

Rather, they filled me with *contempt* . . . for him, for all the other broken men and boys I saw shuffling across the rough floor, collapsing into their beds.

For they agreed with him, and in some way I only vaguely grasped, they were complicit with *them*, knowingly or not.

I tried to see in them what the rabbi had seen in me, the burning to escape, to avoid the end that everyone in the camp would come to . . . *knew* that they would come to.

I saw nothing.

No spirit. All broken. All accepting.

All pathetic.

I twisted away, clambered to the top of the bunks.

I lay there fuming until my body, apathetic to the anger that seethed within it, banked the fire with sleep.

I dreamt that night I lay in bed in our family home, peaceful, happy.

Then, the commotion started, the yelling, the rumble of the tanks, the chatter of gunfire.

My father herded us into the main part of the house.

Lights flashed, people screamed.

A shadow fell over the front window, and the door was kicked in.

Shapes poured in, gun bolts clacked, and a hush fell over my huddled family.

Another shadow fell over the front window, pushed through the stone wall of the house.

The soldiers who turned to face it were swept aside, flung into the darkness.

I could hear their bones breaking, the reverberating clang as their helmets struck stone.

The shape loomed in the darkness.

My father uttered one word, thick with terrified hope. *Golem*.

"A golem?" the rabbi said as he dunked his bread into a slurry of potatoes and water. "You dreamt of this and now you want to make one of your own? Fancy yourself a *Judah Loew ben Bezalel*?"

I flushed in anger and embarrassment.

"And this golem . . . what would you have it do?"

I considered this for a moment. "Kill them. Tear up the camp, allow us to escape."

"To where? All around is war. All around, the Germans are doing this." He spread his hands slowly so as not to attract attention.

"Isn't it at least worth trying, rabbi?" I blurted, leaning across the table. "What can it hurt?"

The rabbi sat for a second appraising me, a thin gruel of potatoes running into his beard. He didn't say anything for a few moments, and I know . . . I know now that he was thinking of how to humor me, to give me something to do. Something to occupy my time until they came to cart me off to the furnaces and some other scrawny kid would shovel my ashes into the barrow and carry it up the hill.

He broke the silence with a small shrug of his shrunken shoulders.

"Build a golem then. What can it hurt?"

I scanned his deeply lined face for signs that he was patronizing me, which, of course, he was.

"I'll need a *shem*."

He finished his bread. "Tonight, after dinner, I'll give you the *shem* you need. Until then, you should eat. Building a golem will require all of your strength."

Nodding in agreement, I crammed the food into my mouth.

Ash. And mud.

I had a surfeit of both.

What is clay if not ash and mud?

My golem would be built of the ash of my people, the mud of our prison.

And he would be the stronger for both.

I started putting some of both aside in the narrow confines of the pit behind the furnaces. As hot as it was, it was also damp most of the time. Rainwater ran down the incline and pooled there, and the ground was usually a slurry of mud and ash.

In the shadows, I spent spare moments mixing, shaping, creating the form of a man stretched atop the ground.

The other boys watched with narrow, fretful eyes, knowing that the guards would shoot me if they saw what I was doing . . . but they seldom came. It was uncomfortably hot, difficult to breathe. Normally, they stayed above ground, smoking their cigarettes and chatting.

It didn't take long to build, and a few days without rain ensured that the clay hardened—*cured*, I guess—in the awful heat of the furnaces. It lay still on the ground, fused to it, as if it had emerged directly from the earth.

I had made it huge, about eight feet tall, with broad shoulders, legs like tree trunks, arms capable of dealing tremendous punishment. Its eyes were deep, empty craters and its mouth was open, ready to accept the *shem* the rabbi had promised.

He gave it to me willingly, a little too willingly I thought even then.

We were back in the bunkhouse after dinner. As before, he grabbed my ankle as I went to bed.

When I descended, he pressed a small folded piece of paper into my hand.

I opened my palm, and the paper unfolded. I could see writing on it, Hebrew.

"A piece of the Torah, rabbi?"

He nodded solemnly, pointed at a word scrawled across the printed text in a thin, spikey script.

Emet.

Truth.

"Put this into your golem, and he will obey," he said. "Or so the story goes."

I stared at the scrap of paper, said nothing.

"When he has done your bidding, remove the *shem*, cross the 'e' from *emet*, put it back. He will return to clay."

Met

Dead.

I closed my hand onto the paper.

"Thank you, rabbi."

I climbed to my bunk and fell asleep.

All that night, my fist never uncurled from the paper.

At breakfast the next day, I didn't see the rabbi in his usual place at the table. That concerned me momentarily as I shoveled my food in. Only momentarily, I'm ashamed to say. I was anxious to get to the pit, to bring my golem to life.

I supposed . . . *knew* what had happened to him, where he'd been taken.

But I could feel the piece of paper in my pocket, feel its heat through the rough wool trousers, goading me on.

At the entrance to the pit, the guards stopped me, and my heart galloped in my chest.

"You're early," he said, twisting my shirt in his fist. "Anxious to begin the day? Shoveling out what remains of your friends?"

The soldier tightened his grip on my shirt, yanked me off my feet and threw me to the muddy ground. I stayed there, letting the gritty water cool my forehead, my cheeks.

A boot kicked my stomach, just enough to drive the wind from me.

"Up! Up and get to work, if you're so anxious!"

I fought to catch my breath, to say something, but instead just smiled . . . *smiled*.

Like a fool.

I suppose they thought I was, for they started laughing.

And I was a fool.

I went down the incline, and the heat from the furnace brought the stain of blood back to my face.

The other boys weren't here yet, so I strode directly to the farthest end, knelt by my golem.

His mud skin was dry, cracking in places. I put my palm to his chest, felt the cold, stone-like swell of it.

My other hand fished the paper from my pocket, slipped it into the dark, strict rectangle of his mouth.

What is there to say?

The golem came to life, of course.

I don't mean "of course" because that is what I expected.

I mean "of course" because if he hadn't, we wouldn't be here today chatting about it.

As I knelt beside him, there was a crackling, soft at first, then louder; like slivers of glass snapping.

Another sound, this one a low, terrible moaning.

He bent at the waist, sat up. The dried mud that held him to the earth broke, shattered as he rose.

I still had my palm against his chest, and now I could feel the moaning vibrate through his huge form, reverberate through the clay. I could feel the slow, deep respiration as the creature took in air . . . *breathed*!

After a moment, I noticed that he breathed in time with me. His massive chest rose and fell with mine, as if I breathed through him.

I fell backwards, sprawled to the hot, damp ground, scrabbled away as he rose to his feet.

His lumpen head, imperfectly crafted by the hands of a child working in the dark, turned to me.

There was something in the hollow depressions of his eyes, something that didn't precisely glow, but pulsed with a flat, nacreous light.

"Command me," he said, his voice strange, deeply grating.

I tried to make sounds for a moment. My throat seemed closed with heat and the dust of his rising.

"Kill everyone against me. Help me escape. Don't let me die."

He said nothing, simply inclined his head.

He stepped over me, strode past me, went up the incline.

As he stood outlined against the wan, grey sky, I leapt to my feet, chased after him.

I was halfway up when I heard the chatter of machine guns.

Emerging from the heat of the pit, I stumbled to a halt.

The golem towered above four guards. His fists were huge, as big as their helmeted heads.

They were falling back, disbelief stark on their faces.

The golem swung on them, and one of his enormous fists struck the guard that had thrown me to the ground.

His fist kept moving as if it hadn't connected, arcing high in the air, and my elation gave way to disappointment.

What if even a golem couldn't get me out of here?

Then I saw it, the soldier's head and part of a shoulder, flying through the air on the same trajectory as the fist, tumbling awkwardly, trailing gore.

God help me, I *cheered* . . . a wordless shout of wonderment and exhilaration.

Still the machine guns spat bullets, but they did no damage.

The golem plowed into the remaining soldiers, literally tore them apart.

The noise from the guns had barely faded when more soldiers poured in, shouting at it, barking orders.

Gunfire erupted again, wild, everywhere, spattering the dirt around me. I threw an arm up to shield my head, crouched and ran to the side of the furnace building.

The golem shredded these soldiers, too, making no effort to protect himself from their bullets. I could see his great, brown arms rising, dropping.

Soldiers fell to the ground and were stamped on.

Soldiers flew through the air to land with wet, sickening thuds.

The creature plodded to the commandant's headquarters. More Germans appeared, were killed. The men in the watchtowers fired, but couldn't stop him.

As I watched, he walked into the headquarters, right through a wall. There was a terrific splintering of wood, screams, more gunfire.

My fellow prisoners had begun to take notice. In the trenches, in the latrines, from the lines lurching to the furnace, the men stopped to watch. Even though they didn't know what was happening, they knew it wasn't good for the Germans.

A ragged cheer went up, much like my own earlier, as the golem burst from the commandant's office. The figure he held over his head was cursing, screaming.

The commandant.

The golem tightened his grip on the wriggling man, brought him down hard and fast to break his body across one stony knee. A spray of viscera burst in the air, and the golem dropped both halves absently.

A few soldiers still fired at him, but he remained still. He was covered in blood, shining from it.

He seemed to look at me with those terrible, dark eyes, then turned to the crowd that had gathered, the other prisoners.

After a moment, he lurched into motion, headed toward them.

The prisoners, knowing the legend, thought he was coming to accept their gratitude.

Dear God . . . dear God.

I leaned against the side of the building for support as he waded into them with the same silent deliberateness he had shown with the Germans.

The hoarse cheers turned to screams.

"No!" I pushed from the building, raced to him.

Men ran, fell in the mud, crawled away from the golem.

He slapped at them, punched, stomped them into the mud where they lay.

I skidded to a halt, punched at the pillar of one thigh.

"Stop!" I yelled. "I command it. Golem, stop!"

He turned on me, one enormous clod of a fist raised to smash whatever this annoyance was.

When his dull eyes fell on me, though, he stopped, cocked his head like a dog trying to understand its master.

"What are you doing?" I shouted, not afraid that it would hurt me.

As screams echoed in my ears, the golem bent to me.

"Kill everyone against me. Help me escape. Don't let me die," he rumbled, then rose to his full height and strode after the fleeing.

I stood there, slack-jawed. I wanted to scream, to explain what I'd meant, to make him understand that these men weren't the ones against me.

But I knew, even then I knew, and this understanding spread within me like dark ink in water.

I slumped to the cold, wet ground and wept.

I could feel my shirt and trousers grow damp as the wool leeched up the muddied, bloodied waters.

I watched him shuffle away, dispatching slow moving, half-dead men struggling to flee.

I watched for a long time, believed I had to. Believed I *owed* it to them all.

At some point, a building caught fire, probably an untended stove.

The fire took quickly, jumped from one wooden structure to the next.

When I looked up again, it was twilight. I saw shadows on the ground, cast by the dozens of fires engulfing the camp.

There were no screams. No gunfire. No moaning or pleading.

Just the roar of flames.

I looked up, saw that he stood over me, silent, unmoving.

I closed my eyes, held my breath.

I have held it ever since.

Grandpa Lev lay back on the bed, a deep sigh rattling through his body.

Phil held his hand, didn't know what to say.

"That morning, we simply walked away. *Escaped*."

Lev laughed at that word, and it was bitter and sharp and anything but humorous.

"*We?*"

Lev turned to his grandson. "The golem and I. He wouldn't leave my side. I tried . . . Lord, I tried. But he followed me . . . always found me. I ran all the way here, to America. And he found me even here."

"Grandpa . . . "

"No, no," Lev said. "This isn't where you ask me if I'm making this up. Not where you think I'm crazy. This is where you do that thing for me . . . if you love me."

Phil looked hard at his grandfather. "You know I love you, but . . . "

"I'm trying to die . . . but I *can't*. He won't *let* me. I asked him to kill me, hundreds of times over the years, and he wouldn't."

"You asked *it* . . . this golem . . . to kill you?"

"That's the part of the story you disbelieve?" Lev asked, and this time he cracked a small smile. "Of course I did. How to live with the self-loathing that had birthed him? The cost of my escape? The shame? Didn't you listen?"

"Grandpa, I listened, but . . . "

"It wasn't just that. That was my first mistake, not choosing my words correctly. Because in the end, the golem's breath was mine. More so his heart was mine, my poor, injured, foolish boy's heart. Even I didn't understand what was in it. My hatred of the men in the camp for not *wanting* to escape . . . not *trying*. How could I understand? It was a blight within me. And I passed it to the golem."

Phil frowned, searched for words.

Finally, "You said the *first* mistake."

"Such a smart one," he said, patting Phil's cheek. "That's why I need your help."

Phil never knew that his grandparents' house had a basement. Certainly, he'd never been in it, never seen anyone go into it or emerge from it.

It was simply a locked door in the kitchen, one that he'd dismissed long ago as the door to a closet or storage room of some sort.

It wasn't out of bounds or forbidden, it was simply never addressed. That kept it safe over the years from everything but the occasional curious jiggle of its knob, first from Lev's children, then his grandchildren. Never addressed, never forbidden, it simply disappeared in the house.

Now, Phil stood before it holding a shining, newly cut key.

Feeling a little silly, he slipped the key into the door lock, turned it.

It turned easily, obviously well lubricated and maintained over the previous seven decades.

He drew the door open onto a set of stairs that led into darkness smelling of damp and gritty concrete.

Phil flipped a small switch, and weak light illuminated the steps.

He descended into a vast empty space filled with cobwebs and shadows. And that smell . . . damp earth, concrete . . . no . . . mud.

It was *mud*.

The darkness in the farthest corner of the space congealed, moved.

Phil stepped back to the stairs, put a reality-affirming hand on the bannister.

The basement was not low-ceilinged, but the shadow could not rise to its full height. Its shoulders bent and its head bowed as if in obeisance.

"You are of the blood," came the voice. "Will you release me?"

Phil licked his lips, swallowed in an attempt to work up enough spit to talk.

"Release?"

The thing shambled forward with the sound of rock scraping rock.

"My job is done, yet the maker will not release me. He would have me kill him as payment for my release. This I cannot do. It violates his command."

Phil tried to make sense of this, tried to assign a rational explanation for what he was seeing, hearing.

"Come out," he said.

The golem crept forward until he bumped into a hanging incandescent bulb. The wavering light showed his form, massive, brown. His limbs were thick and rumpled like a bed sheet. His chest was broad, corrugated. His head was a misshapen clay oval, with deep eyes and the stark line of a mouth.

Phil thought he could see the curl, just the slightest curl of paper in that mouth.

"Release me."

Though the voice was rough and nearly monotone, Phil could hear ages of grief and loneliness in it. Had his grandfather kept him down here all this time, alone, coming down at intervals to ask it to kill him?

Coming back upstairs and locking the door when each denied the other's release?

Phil's head, his heart reeled at this.

Each of these things, the creator and his creation, alone in this house, sick with what they'd done so many years ago, the terrible mistake they'd made.

But neither able to let go.

Neither able to rest, to die.

"I don't know what . . . how . . . "

"The *shem*," he rumbled.

What was it the rabbi had told his grandfather?

Cross out the "e" in *emet*.

Make it *met*.

Dead.

"Are you sure?" Phil asked.

"Yes," he said, almost pleaded. "Release me."

Phil let loose of the bannister, walked to the crouched figure.

As much to steady himself as to prove its reality, Phil touched the golem's massive chest.

He could feel the labored breathing through the clay, the air that rasped in and out of the thing.

Just like his grandfather's breathing.

Tears squeezed from Phil's eyes.

The golem knelt, rested his hands on the floor, lifted his head.

His face was solemnly blank, weary.

The swaying light showed the curl of paper in the opening of his mouth.

Phil leaned into the golem, braced against his slowly respiring chest.

Gently, he reached into that mouth, drew out the small slip of paper, unfolded it.

The paper was brittle, yellowed, the ink faded, but he

could still make out the Hebrew printing, the looping script of what the rabbi had penned over it.

Phil fumbled a pen from his pocket.

He held the paper and pen, looked around for something to write upon.

Shrugging, he settled the slip of paper on the golem's shoulders, crossed out the "e."

The creature raised its head slightly.

"Release. Release us both."

Phil slid the paper into the slot that was its mouth.

Though there was no movement, no light or sound, there was a change in the atmosphere in the cellar. It was as if a switch had been flipped.

Phil, still braced against its chest, pushed away. There was a brittle crackling, and his hand broke through the hardened clay, turned it to dust.

The golem split into two, its top half sliding to the floor, shattering.

The rest of it squatted there, silent and immobile.

Phil stepped through the debris, found the paper, took it from the dust.

It unfurled in his hand, and he read the word there.

Met.

Just then, he heard a sound . . . faint, coming from upstairs.

A high-pitched, steady beep.

Phil raised his head, stared at the basement ceiling as if he could see through the dusty rafters and into his grandfather's room upstairs. He thought of the golem's last words.

Release us.

And what his grandfather had said.

After, there's something you must do. If you love me.

He knew his grandfather, knew he hadn't sent him down here just to release the golem.

He could have done that years ago.

Phil stared at the word on the paper, sighed.

The second mistake.

Don't let me die.

He folded the *shem* back into his palm, turned to the steps.

There was sadness, but no fear anymore, only . . . *acceptance.*

Phil did love his grandfather, and he'd corrected that second mistake.

Finally.

EARL PRUITT'S SMOKER

PATRICK FREIVALD

"**E**ARL PRUITT DIED."

Jamie Schwaeble froze, forkful of hash browns halfway to her mouth, ears pricked to catch the rest of the old man's pronouncement. A mainstay at church each Sunday, Pruitt and his wife had kept to themselves despite generous annual donations to the congregation.

"His wife found him last evening, next to some of those hives of his."

"Was he allergic?" His companion, the square-jawed man who worked the counter at the auto parts store, darted his blue eyes at Jamie, from her face to her chest and back up. She turned away, flushing, and buttoned the top of her blouse to hide the glimpse of white T-shirt beneath.

"No," the older man continued. "Been stung a million times and never had a problem. Must have been his heart, or his brain."

"At his age? Could have been anything."

Their conversation wandered from the weather to plans for Vacation Bible School but came back to Pruitt, and the auction his widow planned to make up for their lack of life insurance.

Goosebumps shot up Jamie's arms, a tingle of excitement she shared with, she was sure, a hundred other people. The reclusive old beekeeper never let anyone on his property, a fenced-off farm on the far edge of town that boasted who knew how many bee hives scattered around the barns and outbuildings just visible from the road. The thought of getting a taste of what he kept inside, maybe even picking up a little something, brought a flush of heat to her cheeks.

Pastor Carr would have something to say about such feelings, as he did about any feelings that didn't keep a soul on the narrow, straight path to Heaven. She'd trembled under the weight of his words, one with the hundreds of sinners to bow down at his church each Sunday, and if he were here he'd see the excitement on her face and ask her, and she'd tell him, and he'd admonish her for her sinful desires. She turned back to her food, grateful for her corner booth where the old men and young men couldn't tempt her with their knowing looks and their lustful smiles. She wanted those smiles, and the promises behind them, and knew that wanting them was as wrong at twenty-two as it had been at fourteen.

She paid her bill and fled home to her lonely single-wide, all she could afford on a retail salary but enough to escape the stifling attentions of her stepfather and his son.

Guilt knotted her insides, twisted and pulled at her conscience the rest of the week, castigating her for her weaknesses. But the next week, she drove to Pruitt's farm, through the main gate and onto the parcel of lawn now dedicated to parking. Her turtleneck and loose-fitting jeans hid her body from leering eyes, so she hoped the Lord would forgive her a touch of eyeshadow, a tiny rose of blush. Pastor Carr had called beekeeping a vocation suitable for a young woman who had not yet found a husband, a holy calling as old as the New Covenant itself.

Hundreds of people milled around, most of them old bearded beekeepers in denim and fraying flannel. License plates on their vehicles said everything from Georgia to Montana to Maine, but they talked like neighbors as they surveyed the equipment, slapping their hands with battered, wrinkled checkbooks. Some had brought flatbed trucks and forklifts in anticipation of going home with something worth the trip, while others spoke of U-Hauls should the need arise. She hovered around them, another group she could join but never quite become a part of.

Jamie had read of the dangers of used woodware, most especially the specter of American Foulbrood destroying her girls and every honeybee colony within flying distance, so she avoided even the so-called "nuc boxes"—half-sized chipboard containers built to hold starter colonies. Cost and practicality kept her from bidding on the larger equipment—centrifugal extractors, chain uncappers, and other esoteric machines of great use to large commercial operations but far too much for a clerk with one hobby colony she'd owned for less than a season. Even if she could have afforded them a lack of time and space prevented her from considering the live colonies, grouped as they were in five-pallet blocks, four hives on each, each lot starting at two thousand dollars.

She stopped cold, frozen in place by a table heaped with Pruitt's personal equipment. A dozen beekeeping books, including a first edition Richard Taylor with a reserve of $100, hive tools and other widgets and bobbins piled into musty cardboard boxes held together with little more than duct tape and hope. She fingered through several of the books, interesting for their historical perspective but of little use in the age of varroa mites, GMO crops, and neonicotinoid pesticides; she'd have bought them all if she'd had the money.

Someone cleared their throat, drawing Jamie's gaze.

Mrs. Pruitt sat off to the side as strangers poked through her late husband's things, modestly dressed in a New York Giants sweatshirt, faded jeans, and dusty brown cowboy boots. Her white hair shone almost blue under the summer sun, and webs of old, dark blood crackled under her papery, liver-spotted skin. The childless widow wore a tight-lipped, mirthless smile, a mask of propriety against the lonely cruelty of a life ended, a seventy-three-year marriage that wouldn't see seventy-four. The ancient woman watched for a while, then retired behind the hard wood of her farmhouse door to let her lawyer and the auctioneer handle the rest.

Jamie rummaged, and an electric thrill jolted up her spine at the ancient hive smoker buried beneath a pile of comb-cutting equipment. Just smaller than a coffee can, the weathered tin sported a small dent near the bottom, but otherwise appeared to be in good shape. Several layers of metal reinforced the crimp holding the cylindrical body in place. In lieu of rivets, hot-bent pegs held the polished wood handle and supple leather bellows to the fire chamber, a soot-crusted cylinder that smelled faintly of pine sap and char. The wire cage around the fire chamber had black flecks around the soldered joinings, but held firm when she tapped it with a finger. A single Phillips-head screw held the perforated metal an inch above the air chamber, the only nod to post-1920 technology, an unwelcome stainless-steel concession to the ravages of time and entropy.

It hummed in her hands, a beautiful example of late-nineteenth century metalwork, solid and practical like the country folk it had been built to serve. She entertained the possibly that Moses Quinby himself may have made it hundreds of miles to the east in the Hudson Valley, a personal tool for personal use before his invention spread across the world.

She searched for a maker's mark, and found none.

Jamie glanced around to see if anyone else had noticed, then stuffed the smoker back under the junk in the box and joined the crowd waiting to bid on each lot. The auctioneer started small to milk the most he could out of the cheaper items. She passed on the initial lots, but perked up at the first of the cardboard boxes. Bidding started at two dollars. Her heart leaped into her throat when she took it for nine.

She rushed home with her prize, not quite able to outrun a twinge of guilt at the score.

Dumping the comb-cutting equipment onto the picnic table, she scooped up the smoker. With a little dryer lint for kindling and a few twigs, she pumped the bellows until a rich gray puff launched from the nozzle, then popped it open and added a handful of small twigs. It shut with a satisfying snap, the fit still perfect after so many years. She went back to pump it a few more times while dressing in her crisp white bee suit and mesh veil, until a heavy white cloud rose over her home.

A trail of wood smoke followed her to her single colony. An earthy mélange like cloves and allspice mingled with the sharp tang of the smoldering twigs, a heady mixture reminiscent of fresh cookies baking on a cool spring day. She breathed it in, held it, savored the faint burn in her lungs, the warm, homey taste on her tongue. She'd always loved the smell of smoke, another tally Pastor Carr put against her soul.

Worker bees took off from the landing board at twenty miles an hour and came back heavy with nectar, or with their legs laden with pollen in bright forsythia yellow and pale jasmine violet. A few guard bees peered at her from the long, narrow slit of the bottom entrance, and a few more from the hole drilled halfway up the top super. Vigilant, watchful, but not yet hostile. She sent a light whisper of smoke to the hole, scattering them, then leaned down and doused the entrance with a heavy trio of puffs.

The billowing cloud surrounded her, a hundred times more intense. A hot rush enveloped her like the dark throes of the Passion, and her vision blurred. The world became indistinct, her body light as a feather under the warmth of the summer sun. Head swimming, she put a hand out to steady herself on the hive's metal outer cover, and it vanished in the smoke.

The acrid tang of burning wood gave way to the warm beeswax scents of vanilla and honey and a million summer flowers, intermingled with the chemical communication of tens of thousands of honeybees. A gasp escaped her lips, the noise drowned by the hum of countless wings. A myriad of insects made into one glorious whole, Jamie rose up, out of the garden, her consciousness expanding with the whirling storm of pheromones to where the drones darted and raced in their ceaseless quest to end their lives in a coital explosion with a virgin queen. Everywhere at once, she flitted from blossom to blossom, sucking up sweet nectar into her honey stomachs, or stuffing precious pollen into the baskets on her legs. She foraged water to cool the hive, extending her proboscises to lap dew from fallen leaves on the forest floor or the drips from the leaky sprinklers in the vegetable garden next door.

In the hive she raised larvae, feeding nectar and pollen and just the right amount of royal jelly to make them strong enough to serve the hive but keep them forever juveniles so that they might never challenge the queen. She dragged the dead out the front entrance, larvae or workers who succumbed to the constant threats of bacteria, viruses, poison, mites. She built comb, reaching down to countless abdomens to pull from the glands there, white wax as pure as snow and not yet stained by the tracks of her million feet. She fed and groomed the queen as she lay the next generation of workers, the nexus and life's blood of a superorganism that despite what humans called her she did not rule, as much a slave to the pheromone cloud as the least of her daughters.

Following the sun, she soared out and away from the hive, laughing in pure joy at the speed and grace of her new neurons, her ultraviolet-seeing eyes and delicate, hypersensitive olfactory antennae. A field of buckwheat drew much of her attention, but she suppressed it to the back of her distributed mind to gaze with fascination at the panoply of flowers scattered around the village. On Lake Street, she drew pollen from bright purple Russian sage while a bevy of boys taunted a little girl out on her pink bicycle. In the supermarket parking lot she flitted between spirea while Jim Hanks loaded canned goods from his pockets into the driver's seat of his rusty farm truck. Behind the church she pulled paralytic nectar from a rhododendron, and caught her breath at a naked man writhing on the couch with a middle-aged blonde in red lingerie.

She knew those hands, firm but gentle as they gripped the pulpit, now buried in the deepest of perversions. She knew that black hair, short but unkempt, as a man of God had no need for frivolous vanities. She knew those lips, spewing filth where on Sundays they spoke of abstinence and righteousness.

She tried to flit closer, to catch a glimpse of her face.

But the foragers darted among the flowers, drinking deep of the sweet, tingling liquid, and ignored her commands, her requests, her desires. Another fleeting pass by the window showed her a flash of gold—a wedding ring. Blonde, athletic but not too young, married; it could have been anyone.

Carr's Sunday voice thundered through her, each pronouncement a condemnation of sin and temptation, the "natural urges" sent by Lucifer to bring man to the level of dogs and then cast them out of the House Eternal to wallow in the cold and darkness outside of God's grace. His baritone had terrified her through her whole life, the promise of eternal damnation a weight on her soul as she tried dating, an ever-present judgment that thrust her into a gibbering panic the first and only time a boy had unbuttoned the top of her blouse, the Valentine's Dance six years earlier. His righteous fire consumed her in guilt when she touched herself, the only hands she'd ever felt.

Frustration bubbled as the foragers retreated, flowing back in waves to the colony as the sun went down. Her world closed in as the last of the field bees crawled inside, joining their brethren in quarters so cramped she couldn't move without brushing legs, body, or wings against her sisters. The foragers took no breaks, but instead fanned nectar to pull out the water and convert it to honey for the long cruel winter, filling the colony with an all-consuming buzz while the nurse bees fed and cared for the larvae as they had all day. Finally a part of something she understood, even so, claustrophobia crushed Jamie's chest, buried her under infinite bodies, too close, far too close, a smothering darkness from which she might never escape. She struggled against the confinement, reaching desperately toward something, anything.

Gasping, Jamie bolted upright, eyes wide to take in the light of the quarter moon illuminating the small yard behind her trailer. Sucking in sweet air, she gulped down the taste of the night. Her body weighed her down, unable to fly, to spread itself throughout the town and become one with the bounties offered there. The sense of choking confinement shuddered through her, squeezed her throat shut, ravaged her bones and organs with utter desperation.

The iron grip softened and her eyes focused on a lump in the grass. Earl Pruitt's smoker lay on its side next to the hive. Omnipresent crickets overwhelmed the buzz from the colony, joined by the high-pitched peeping of frogs from the unkempt pond across the street. Snatching up the smoker, she popped the lid to reveal nothing but cold ash.

It smudged her fingers, made them slippery. Holding it to her nose through her veil, she breathed in deep and smelled only char—no exotic spice, no wax or vanilla, only the harsh incense of dark, pagan sacraments.

A desperate loneliness squeezed her heart. Her whole life she'd wanted something, something less stifling, some way to escape, something more to belong to. A taste of that smothering freedom had left her mouth dry in desperate anticipation to feel it again. Scrambling, she found enough small sticks and dried grass to fill the fire chamber, sparked a flame with her lighter, and pumped the bellows to build up a thick cloud of shimmering phantoms that glistened in the moonlight. She blasted the entrance, and the buzz lowered to a dull thrumming . . . but otherwise nothing happened.

She frowned, tried again, sucking smoke into her lungs as she did so.

Choking, chest burning, she rolled away from the cloud of guard bees that spilled from the entrance. They latched on to her bee suit, searching for a gap or thin spot to bury their stingers and die in defense of the hive, but found none. Stumbling to her feet, she walked toward the house, gently puffing smoke at the few guards that clung to her in order to maximize their deterrence, until at last they detached and fled home. Several bounced off her veil in a final warning before disappearing back toward the hive.

She stripped outside and left the suit on the railing in case of unseen stragglers caught in the folds, and hung the smoker on a plant hanger where it wouldn't cause a fire. Exhaustion dragged at her heels as she stumbled into the tiny kitchen, chewed numbly on a dinner she barely tasted, and crashed in bed. The clock glared an angry three a.m. Work started at seven.

She shuffled through the day, stocking clothes and bedding between helping customers. A blonde surveyed king sheets, middle-aged, a wedding ring on her finger. Jamie tried to remember if her hair had been that flaxen, if the calves beneath her knee-length skirt matched those wrapped around the preacher's thrusting backside. Would Carr's lover shop at the mall? Would Jamie recognize her if she did? Would Satan find her here, or find the preacher at his dalliances?

She couldn't be sure, and the dozen middle-aged blondes she met through the day all could have been smiling with the secret knowledge of their carnal dalliances.

After work Jamie bustled home with an armload of groceries, gulped down a lukewarm TV dinner, and ducked out onto the stoop.

Earl Pruitt's smoker hung where she'd left it, the lone steel screw a shining beacon in the late afternoon sun. A curious worker bee hovered next to her gloves and hive tool, perhaps intrigued by the lingering signature of honey left behind in the ultraviolet spectrum. Her hands shook as she fired up the smoker, pumped the bellows to create a thick white cloud; it took three tries to zip up her suit, another two to secure her veil.

The hive rumbled as she approached, a sound her human brain interpreted as chaos, in reality the concerted dance of thousands of creatures dedicated to a singular, collective goal: survive the snows until dandelions bloom.

A whisper of smoke drifted across her vision, sweet ginger mingled with rich myrrh and charred pine. She blasted the entrance, and exploded outward into the fading day.

Jackson Bard screamed at his cowed wife next to their barbecue, a gold cross tangled in the thick hair springing from his white T-shirt. Light from the necklace sparkled off of a row of purple coneflowers, and the hemispheres atop the ring of purple gave a rich harvest of high-sugar nectar. Ankle-high chicory lined the roadside, low in nectar but loaded with pollen the same bright blue as its flowers that dotted the dirt shoulder next to Dave Cullen, handcuffed on his knees between his Camry and a police car, a half-empty bottle of ten-dollar whiskey spilled out at his feet. The alcohol and smoky resins drew her interest, but only for a brief moment. Late-season Dutch clover spotted the park lawn where Kylee Jones slapped the boy groping at her jeans next to a spilled picnic basket, each flower a bounty of sweet juice and bright white pollen.

She poured malice toward the boy who wouldn't take "No" for an answer, and envy erupted at Kylee for being young and attractive and charming and everything that Jamie couldn't seem to be. The young woman yelped and slapped at her neck.

Jamie cried out as she pulled away from the stinger embedded in the girl's skin, her guts tearing free in a streak of gelatinous goo to leave behind the venom sac, dismembered muscles still pumping venom into the wound.

A rush of pleasure brought her back to the coneflowers. Another three of her sisters died driving Bard from his wife and his meal, sending him stumbling for the safety of the indoors. She laughed, somehow without lungs or voice; the hive didn't mourn the loss, any more than a person mourns the hair or fingernails they discard on any given day.

The buckwheat distracted her, and she lost herself for a while in the snowy blossoms and the dark nectar, almost black with a taste like sweetened oatmeal. Regaining herself, she roamed the town from plant to plant, riding the cloud to the giant pink flowers of the rhododendron behind the church rectory, where the view into Pastor Carr's private sanctum should have found him preparing for the Saturday sermon the next day.

He sat at his desk, in full view of the highest bees, writing free-hand on loose leaf paper. Next to his pad sat a tangle as pink as the flowers, the thong's lace edge giving way to thin fabric meant for seduction, not practicality. He stroked it with a finger now and then, eyes closed, before going back to his work.

This man had denied her even thoughts of pleasure with his weekly promises of damnation and hellfire, all while he indulged his depravities at a whim, defiling another's marriage and his own vows for a taste sweeter than honey.

Her wrath meant nothing to the bees; behind the closed window he may as well have not existed. Snarling in frustration, she let her mind escape to the flowers, let it pull back into the hive with the setting sun, let it settle in turn to the business of evaporation and brood-rearing. As she came to on the ground, human once more, she grinned.

He'd be outside tomorrow. He had to drive to church.

Jamie slept in on Saturday, waking without the alarm at nine-fifty-two. She showered and ate lunch, bologna and American cheese on white bread, then read a little. With church at five, the pastor wouldn't leave his house until four. That gave her a few hours to clean house and do laundry, chores she'd neglected in favor of riding the cloud.

Sweaty, exhausted, but satisfied, she fired up the smoker and approached the hive at ten minutes to four. A puff, and she joined the swarm, consciousness spreading out over the town to find her target.

Carr's Forrester wasn't in the driveway. Up, up she rode, into the whirling storm of drones and virgin queens, casting her gaze downward. He wasn't at church. Frantic, she scoured the streets, jumping from hedge to shrub to garden plot, until at last she found his dark green Forrester skulking in the shadows of a linden tree on Ringwood Circle.

She waited in the comfortable hum of the branches until Carr came outside. A peek through the doorway dashed her hopes of catching him in further depravity; a frail old woman held his hand as he left, letting go only when another step would have dragged her outside. Jamie wondered what she'd think of the panties he probably had in his pocket as he jingled his keys on the way to his car.

Fueled by Jamie's rage, her sisters rushed him, seeking out unprotected areas on his neck, face, and hands. She gritted her teeth as her guts came out, again and again, each sting a divine rebuke and a holy sacrifice that filled the air with the dense, banana-like scent of alarm pheromone.

Screaming and slapping at the already-dead bodies, he flung open the door and dove inside. Breathing hard, he stared wide-eyed out the window, apparently not knowing enough to scrape out the stingers before they could inject their full load of venom. She followed as he peeled away, his scowling face red with pain and anger. He sped, racing toward home or church at twenty over the limit, but not near enough to outrun the pheromone cloud that enveloped the town from her backyard.

A hollow filled her stomach, pulled and stretched like taffy, oozed as the stinger came out. One of her sisters had stayed behind, trapped in the preacher's clothes, violent and aggressive because of the scents her dying sisters had erupted all over his body. His car swerved as her body crushed between his hand and temple.

Jamie heard the crunch, and the cry, and the shrieks. From high in the air she saw the red streak stretching twenty feet behind and under Carr's vehicle, over the sidewalk and onto the lawn. Children gaped, horrified, at the mangled bicycle half-pinned under the Forrester's front grill.

She fled, up and away, riding the cloud to the buckwheat field, to the simplicity of sweet nectar and wholesome pollen, to a world where humans meant nothing and cars didn't crush little boys.

But when she woke, she cried, her sobs tearing out of her chest in the middle of the night, drowned by the symphony of crickets.

She went to the funeral, where a guest preacher presided, gently speaking of the evils of drink and speeding, and the power of compassion and forgiveness, and of a divine plan beyond our comprehension. He couldn't know that there had been no plan, only the petty envy of a sinful woman.

They shunned her, though from aggrieved apathy rather than malice. Surrounded by the people she'd called her own, she wallowed in the emptiness of their company. No one asked how she knew the boy, or why his death would bring her to such tears. No one pointed fingers, no one accused her. No one paid her any attention aside from the occasional curious glance.

No one except Mrs. Pruitt, who had as little place at the funeral as Jamie. Mrs. Pruitt stared at her through the service, and the internment, her rheumy blue eyes pinpoints of dark knowledge stabbing into Jamie's soul. She said nothing, though, only hobbled to her car to let a young man Jamie didn't know drive her home.

After, Jamie wept on her stoop, the world a blur of tears. Tires crunched on the gravel, drawing her gaze. An ancient minivan pulled into the driveway, "Pruitt's Bee Services" emblazoned on the side in fading yellow paint. The young man hopped out of the driver's seat, came around, and opened the passenger's side to let Mrs. Pruitt down, both still somber in their funeral attire.

She held his arm all the way up the walk, but when they reached the steps she stood tall and held out a gnarled hand.

"Give her back, dear. She doesn't belong to you."

Jamie scowled. "I bought it."

"She isn't *meant* for you, and I didn't come to argue. So stop dillydallying and give me the smoker."

The young man put sun-weathered fists on his hips,

not quite relaxed, not quite threatening. He might have weighed two hundred pounds, far too much of it lean muscle, and his scowl could break rocks.

Jamie reached under the step, pulled out the smoker, and froze, unable to let go. The farm boy snatched it from her grip and passed it to the old woman. Mrs. Pruitt sighed, eyelids fluttering, as she clutched it to her chest, lips upturned in a rapturous smile.

"You know what it can do?" Jamie asked.

Without opening her eyes her lips turned down into a vicious snarl. "If you can't let it go it consumes you, and you die."

"Jesus," Jaime said.

"You have no idea, back before mites, before all the poisons. Today is a pale shadow of the past. We'd drift away for hours, Earl and I, sometimes for days, let the world crumble around us. That first winter was so, so hard. The second almost killed us." Her eyes snapped open, bored into Jamie, pupils reflecting nothing, not even the sunlight. "It took a long time to come back, to get used to human living again. Earl never did quite get the gist of it, God rest him. She's not something to give up lightly."

Jamie swallowed. "I get it. Even with . . . with everything that happened, everything that's wrong, I still want to do it again."

Mrs. Pruitt patted her hand, dry and firm, an unwelcome intrusion to her space and her body. "And you would, too, if I'd let you keep it. No matter how much you tell yourself that young boy died because you played with something you shouldn't, that you wouldn't do it again, you would. Nobody's that strong, dear. You'd do it, knowing more terrible things would happen, and you'd feel bad and you'd do it again. And again." The old woman rolled the smoker around in her hands, face softening into almost fondness. "My husband's jealous mistress. She's been a thorn in my side a long time, and caused me more grief than is right. I tried to pull him away, one last time, and she killed him. Took his love and his faith and buried it under dry sod. But the farm isn't the same without her."

"Then why did you sell it—her?"

Pruitt grunted. "I didn't."

"You did. It was in—"

She stopped Jamie with an upraised hand, far too fast for her age. Her eyes crinkled as she smiled, but no light touched them. "Dearie, have you ever plugged up a hive to move it?"

Jamie swallowed, nodded. "Once, when I brought my first nuc home."

"And what did the bees do when you trapped them?"

"They tried to get out. Boiled out of a hole until I found and taped it up. Clawed at the screen. Stung the s . . . stuffing out of me when I got them home, too. I've never seen them so mad."

"That's right." Pruitt passed the smoker to her companion. "Like some people, honeybees don't like to be contained, and like some people, they seek to hurt those that contained them. I've kept her cooped up since Earl passed, and planned to do so until I join him. I guess she has other ideas."

"You can't destroy her."

Pruitt clucked her tongue. "Of course not."

"Then what? I mean, you're what, ninety-three?"

"Ninety-six." A hint of a smirk touched her lips. "Had a few years on Earl. I don't have much time, God willing, but I'll keep her from causing too much trouble from here out. It's best you don't know the details."

"But I need—"

"No. You want. And whatever it is you want, get it. Sell your home. Move to the city. Find yourself a man or a woman or a passion. But don't come back to the farm. It won't end well if you do."

Jamie sighed, stood, and tried not to stare in longing at the metal in the young man's hands.

"So that's it, then."

"That's it."

Mrs. Pruitt allowed Jamie to help her down the walk and into the van while the young man started the motor. A honeybee lay upside-down on her dashboard, unmoving, desiccated by the midday sun. She swept it out onto the road with her hand, said goodbye, and faced forward. Jamie closed the door and stepped back.

They drove out of sight. Moments later the dead bee quivered, stood, and took to the air, racing after her queen.

As a Guest at the Telekinetic Tea Party

STEPHANIE M. WYTOVICH

Mismatched outfits drenched in earl grey design,
the ladies stretch their legs,
their platform heels dusted with tea cakes
against a heralded cry for the haberdashery
as rogue buttons line the floor.

Move down! Move down!

They each float to new spots,
their honey-soaked spoons dripping nectar
on their plates,
such beehive gossip
against poison clouds and milk.

The clock strikes thirteen
inside strawberry hookah rings,
laughter and lullabies paint blueberry scones
on flying saucers,
their girlish whispers slathered in apricot jam,
sprinkled with pecans and preserves.

No room! No room!

They pin their hair back with shards of bone,
as soft curls frame their heart-shaped faces,
their fingernails tapping on both table and tea pot.

Uniformed in madness, they hold hands in sisterhood,
the women all a flutter on cushions stuffed
with soaked butterfly wings,
bodies rising, minds expanding,
their dresses swishing, dancing in the air.

Move down! No ROOM!

They crack their necks
remove their matcha-stained ribbons,
the scent of burning around them,
a boiling high-pitched hiss
amongst a table stained with tarot and tears.

They open their weeping eyes to blood,
Sip the sacred tea as their heart beats slow,
each girl rising, never to stop,
forever a sleeping witch in the sky.

HAZELNUTS AND YUMMY MUMMIES

LUCY A. SNYDER

I WAS AT the edge of the SowenCon Author Alley in the main vendor hall when the drugs began to take hold. A guy in a black Batman tee shirt was frowning down at my books, clearly not liking what he saw. I'd nailed a smile to my face as I chatted about the plot of my first novel, but I knew I wasn't connecting because his scowl deepened and deepened but he wasn't walking away so I started babbling about the plot of the rest of the series while thinking, *Oh god, why did I agree to do this?*

You agreed to this because they offered you a free hotel room and you have to stay busy this weekend, my Inner Responsible Adult replied. *On Halloween, you have to stay busy. You* have *to, or you will think too many thoughts and end up in the bin again.*

Keeping busy was good. But I wasn't any kind of plausible saleswoman. Nobody was going to hire me to pitch jewelry or juicers. I became a writer in the first pea-picking place because I could only seem to gather my thoughts on paper; I constantly found myself tongue-tied whenever I had to meet new people. So why in the name of sweet candy corn was I working a table trying to talk up books I'd written precisely because I could never reliably form complete sentences except with a keyboard? Couldn't I have chosen to stay busy doing something less painful, like competing in ghost pepper eating contests? Nude sandpaper surfing? Milking angry sharks?

In my mind, I heard my dead mother's voice: "Life is a grand comedy, dear; just do your best."

I suddenly felt too hot despite the chilly diesel-stinky October draft from the loading dock in back and my head felt floaty and puffy like a party balloon. And I wasn't even sure what words were coming out of my mouth. *Something something* action *something* adventure *something* award-winning *something*. Batfan's face scrunched up more and more, getting impossibly wrinkled, and his nose squinched and flattened and inverted, his eyes shrunk tiny, black and beady and suddenly I was looking up at the head of an actual bat. A brown bat like the ones that roosted under the overpass near my mom's house back in Missouri. Except fifty times as huge, because brown bats are itty-bitty and the Batfan had a noggin the size of a cantaloupe.

I trailed off, gaping at him. *What. The. Actual. Fuck.* And then wondered: *Did I say that out loud?*

The bat gave me a weird, suspicious look and walked away without a screech.

Elaine, the SowenCon author liaison, came hurrying up, her tall pointy witch hat askew, her glittery blue satin dress swirling and glowing like galaxies. Her whole outfit seemed to have turned into a portal to another dimension. I felt as though I might fall right into it.

"Miss Bowen?" she said, and by her expression it wasn't the first time she'd tried to get my attention. A halo of stardust seemed to float around her face.

"Yes?" I replied. My tongue felt too big in my mouth. It felt huge as a tuna, and it might wriggle free and go swimming across the sea-green carpet. I'd have to chase it down in the gaming room, tackle it near the Munchkin tournament. The idea of that made me laugh out loud.

"Did you eat one of the black raspberry cookies?" Elaine was frowning, looking worried. Her face was getting wrinkled up. I wondered if she was going to turn into a bat, too.

She'd been by a half-hour before with a big basket of homemade Halloween cookies for all the guest authors and artists. A whole spread of tiny frosted tombstones, snickerdoodle ghosts, gingerbread cats. And black cookies, each decorated with a single blue candy eye. I have blue eyes, and after three hours of sitting at my table, the thought of devouring my own flesh had started to appeal to me. So I took two, and gave one to my friend Heather, who'd come with me to the convention to help schlep books and maintain my sanity.

"Did you eat one of the black cookies?" Elaine repeated.

I nodded slowly. "It was tasty. But the frosting was a little bitter."

"Oh no." She leaned in over by books. "Listen. I meant to give you a treat, but you got a trick by mistake. You've just consumed a fairly large dose of a hallucinogen. Those black cookies were for our ritual tonight, but our initiate got the batches mixed up."

Elaine's eyes were swirling, glittering, dark as a black pearl ring my mom used to own. It was always her favorite. She lost it in the ocean the same day she got her first diagnosis.

"My mom died five years ago today," I blurted out. "She had two kinds of cancer and ehrlichiosis and cryptosporidium and it all killed her. It was like watching Boromir get shot with those black arrows. She never did *anything* halfway, not even dying."

"I'm . . . I'm really sorry to hear that. But the hallucinogen—"

"On Halloween we're supposed to remember the dead," I said. "But how can I not remember my mom dying? How could I ever *not* think about that? So she could have died any other day and I'd still remember. Dying on Halloween was just . . . overkill. But hey, that's Mom! Never do things halfway."

"I'm truly sorry about your mother, but *listen!*" Elaine was speaking very slowly and clearly, as if she were addressing a learning disabled child. "The hallucinogen is going to give you visions. It might last five or six hours."

I had a moment of rational clarity: "I take antidepressants. There's a bunch of stuff I'm not supposed to take with them. Is the cookie going to make me sick?"

"I don't think so." She sounded profoundly uncertain, and her voice echoed as if she were in a large cavern. "Many of us in the coven are also on antidepressants and nobody's had a problem. But you do need to drink a lot of water. I'm going to call someone to take you back to your hotel room and keep an eye on you. I'll get someone else to watch your table for the rest of the day. Everything will be fine."

"I have a panel on zombie poetry in an hour," I said, watching tiny stardust pixies dance around her hat.

"Don't worry about the panel—"

"But I have to warn them." I gazed up at her, suddenly realizing it was not merely another convention panel but a very important personal mission. "I have to warn them all that when you write poetry, you are letting the brain eaters into your mind. You are letting them into your mind!"

"Listen, don't worry about the brain eaters. Just come around the table take my hand and we'll get you back to your room and get you some blankets and water, and—"

"VICTORIAAAA!"

Heather was zooming down the carpeted aisle full-speed on her electric, candy apple red mobility scooter. Startled con-goers were dodging right and left to get out of her way. She'd had surgery on both feet four weeks earlier and while she'd been okayed to walk short distances, the vastness of the convention center was just too much.

Her eyes were hugely dilated, and she had a sweaty look of determination I seldom saw outside end game rounds of Iron Dragon. In her free arm, she clutched a brand-new skateboard decorated with the colorful unicorn logo of one of the role-playing game companies that was sponsoring the convention. As far as I knew, she didn't skateboard and certainly wasn't in any condition to do it now. Had she bought it? Won it? *Stolen* it? Was this Grand Theft Skateboard?

She plunked it down on the floor beside my table as though she were throwing a gauntlet. "Victoria! The Ghost of Trick-or-Treat needs us!"

"It does?"

"Yes! Come with me if you want to save The Great Pumpkin!" Her words rang with irresistible authority. I was needed. Summoned. *Destined.*

"I don't think—" Elaine began. Nervous purple fairies orbited her head.

"OK!" I jumped up and stared down at the skateboard, which was undulating slightly, like a cat that was about to hork up a hairball. "What now?"

"Get upon this flatfish steed and grab the back of my Harley!"

I was sure that the skateboard might vomit all over my shoes, but a good soldier in the Halloween army honors the call of duty. I stepped on the wobbly board and grasped the back of the scooter's seat. The black vinyl bubbled up between my fingers and hissed at me, but I held fast.

"Oh, Miss Bowen, no—"

"To infinity!" Heather punched the scooter into high gear.

We zoomed past the laughing liquid racks of vendors' books and games, faster and faster, the colors streaking and boiling with sparks as we approached light speed. And then with a blast of outer space cold, we were in the Haunter's Hall where cartoon ghosts whooshed above the bloated foam animatronic zombies and shrieking funhouse mansion-fronts. Heather's speeding wheels kicked up a storm of autumn leaves that made me sneeze from the smell of wood smoke and pumpkin spice. The leaves swirled up around us in a rattling vortex of reds and oranges and browns, their brittle serrated edges lashing my face and arms, and I let go of the scooter to shield my eyes—

—the skateboard squirted out from beneath my feet and my arms windmilled as I fell forward through empty darkness—

—and I face-planted onto someone's frosty lawn, the air whoofing out of my lungs.

"Clumsy," a man above me said. "A princess shouldn't be clumsy."

I pushed myself up onto my knees. My arms were tiny, and I was wearing a pink princess outfit made from cheap satin and stiff crinoline with stars made from glue and silver and pink glitter. The dress was loose. I'd outgrown this costume when I was five or six, and my mom gave it to Goodwill.

I looked up at the man, whose face was obscured by mist. The only thing I could see clearly was the Budweiser longneck in a blue coozie in his right hand.

"Papa?" I asked uncertainly. Mom had burned all his photos after he left us when I was five, and all I could really remember about him was the beer he always seemed to have. But before he decided fatherhood and marriage weren't for him, he had taken me trick-or-treating when Mom was attending night classes after her waitressing shifts to become a computer operator. It was possibly the least he could do. But he did it.

"Well, get up, Whoopsy-Daisy, and let's get you some candy." My father held out his free hand, helped me to my feet, and picked dead leaves off my dress.

Decades later, during an online search, I learned that he died in a drunk driving accident in Mexico about two years after he left us. If Mom knew about that, she never let on. She'd been so furious and hurt that not only did she destroy all evidence of his existence in the house, she changed both our last names back to her maiden name. Alex Ronson had given me nothing that lasted except some DNA and a couple of hazy memories.

If he'd sobered up, he might have called or written me. He might have come back and tried to be a father. A lot of things could have happened, but of course they didn't. The brief article I found just listed his expiration date and the cause; it didn't say if he'd died instantly in his smashed fast car or if he'd lingered in pain in the hospital as my mother had.

"Did it hurt?" I asked him.

"Did what hurt?" he grunted as he led me up the

sidewalk of our old neighborhood toward Mrs. Robinson's house. She always had the best candies for trick-or-treaters: full-sized Kit-Kats and peanut butter cups and Almond Joys.

"When you died," I said. "Did it hurt?"

"No, it didn't hurt at all."

His voice had changed. I looked up, and saw the man was now my mom's boyfriend Joe Moreno. He looked the same as he had when he was thirty or so: angular face softened by his gentle brown eyes, his thick black hair parted down the middle and feathered back like it was still 1988. He worked as an ER nurse. He met my mom when I was seven, and they stayed together until he suffered a massive heart attack in the hospital parking lot and died.

He took a long drag from his Lucky Strike and puffed smoke rings into the chilly autumn air. "Well, that's a little lie. It was the worst crushing cramp in my chest you can imagine, but my knees buckled and I fell and cracked my head on a concrete parking block. Knocked me clean out, and I didn't feel anything after that. They found me quick and brought me back into the ER; it took me maybe a half hour to die while they were working hard on me. They busted nearly every rib and I didn't feel it. As deaths go, mine was totally ironic, but I got off easy pain-wise."

"I'm sorry," I said, gripping his warm hand more tightly. "You were only forty-five, and it wasn't fair."

"Don't be sorry. I got to help a lot of people at the hospital. Save little kids. I got to be *worthy*. And I had a good life with Donna, and after a while I thought of you as my own daughter. Even if I always told you to call me Joe. I did my best to be a good dad, but I never figured I had the right to claim to be your father unless Donna and me got married, and we didn't."

I blinked, surprised at the regret in his voice. "I thought you never wanted to?"

Another, longer drag, and more smoke rings. The smell of his tobacco in the air made my heart ache at how much I'd missed his calm, steady strength in my life the past thirteen years. He was the perfect balance to my mom's passionate volatility and he'd mediated plenty of arguments between her and me. Without him around, not much could stop Hurricane Donna. I loved my mom and I knew she loved me, but when I had the chance to move across the country for a job, I took it. And, later, I lay awake at night wondering if my absence meant she hadn't gone to the doctor when she needed to.

"I thought about marriage plenty," Joe said, "but things were good the way they were, you know? Marriage changes things; it's like a mutation. Sometimes your relationship gets superpowers, but sometimes it goes malignant. I didn't want to risk the good thing we had. And neither did your mom, not after the ways your dad changed."

If Joe had lived, he might have spotted signs of Mom's cancer earlier when it was still treatable. He would have been able to go with her to appointments and advocate for better care.

If he'd lived, maybe they'd both still be alive.

"You were always good to us," I told him. "I'll never forget that."

Joe smiled around his cigarette. "That's the best thing an old ghost like me can hope for."

I felt myself grow bigger as he led me to Mrs. Robinson's house. By the time we reached the front door, I was adult-sized again and my princess dress was gone, replaced by my usual outfit of jeans and a black tee shirt. Joe pulled open the screen door so I could knock.

After two raps, the door swung inward, but it wasn't Mrs. Robinson's living room. It was the cluttered den in my mom's sister Catherine's split-level in Maine. The smells of warm apple cider and popcorn wafted from the kitchen. My aunt's six-year-old twins Noah and Natalie had dressed up as pirates and were shrieking with glee and chasing each other around the room with foam cutlasses.

I hadn't seen Catherine since my mom's funeral; the twins were still in diapers, and she'd left them at home with her husband. She only stayed for the funeral and reception. Seven hours at the most, and then she was back in the air. I'd only seen her kids in photos and videos on Facebook, but they looked like a real handful for a couple of forty-somethings. Somewhere I read that older mother's kids inherited weakened mitochondria, but Noah and Natalie seemed to have enough energy to power an entire city.

"I'm not taking you trick-or-treating if you don't calm down and put on your coats!" Catherine yelled.

I tried to take a step forward into the house, but found myself blocked by an invisible wall.

"Just as well," I muttered. "They don't know me anyhow."

"They *could* know you," Joe said. "You could be there right now."

I shook my head. "She didn't have much time for me before Mom died, and later . . . well, she acted all weird after I tried to kill myself. Acted like . . . like the crazy would rub off on her or something. Facebook's as close as she wants me, I guess."

"She did say to visit any time."

"Yeah, but . . . come on, she didn't mean that. She was just trying to be polite."

"She can't know that you even want to visit if you don't try. And your cousins won't remember you if they never get to see you."

"It's too hard." I stared down at my black Chuck Taylors, still dusted with purple and silver glitter from the princess dress. "I can't put myself out there and have her reject me again. I just can't."

The light dimmed. I looked up, and realized that Joe and I were standing in a cramped efficiency apartment between a drab brown couch and a flatscreen TV tuned to a cheesy 50s horror movie. The room stank of spilled beer, garbage, and unwashed laundry. A sallow-eyed woman in a blue bathrobe was sitting on the couch, blankly staring past us at the screen; she didn't seem to know we were there. Her face was bloated, and so it took me a second to realize that the woman was *me*. A broken-down me 15 or 20 years in the future, fifty pounds heavier with an alcoholic's reddened skin. This was surely what giving up looked like.

"Well, shit," I whispered.

The coffee table in front of her was cluttered with empty bottles of Budweiser and cheap whiskey along with crumpled Taco Bell and Halloween candy wrappers. She pushed through the mess until she found a mostly-full bottle of Wild Turkey and a bottle of Tylenol. The sad woman started tossing back the painkillers by the handful, washing them down with the whiskey.

"Fuck, no, stop!" I stepped toward her, but the invisible wall blocked me again.

"She'll be dead in days," Joe said. "I saw my share of people who decided to commit suicide like this. It's effective, cheap, and an awful way to die. The alcohol and acetaminophen turns your liver to dog food. There's no help for it except an emergency transplant, and almost nobody can get that. Not without money, and . . . well. Doesn't look like there's much of that around here."

I pressed the heels of my hands against my eyes. "Shit."

When I dropped my hands, Joe and I were standing in a darkened hospital corridor. It seemed familiar, but I couldn't quite place it. Hospitals all look pretty much the same. The walls were decorated with cardboard Halloween witches, pumpkins, and black cats. Most of the rooms were dark and their doors closed, but the light was on in one open room toward the end of the hall.

"I'm sorry you didn't get any trick-or-treat goodies." Joe reached into the pocket of his windbreaker and pulled out a colorful package of candy. "Here you go."

I took the proffered pack. The cartoon ancient Egyptian on the wrapper gripped a blue Tropical Fruit Punch mummy that looked more like a board he was going to use to surf some dunes. "Yummy Mummies? Really?"

Joe shrugged and grinned. "Hey, I'm stuck in 1988, what did you expect?"

His grin faded and he nodded toward the lighted room. "You should go see her now."

My stomach churned. "Is . . . is Mom in there?"

"She is."

"I . . . I can't." I shook my head. I couldn't go back to that night. It was my worst failure. I *couldn't*.

"Vicky, I can't make you. But you know what happens if you don't try. The guilt will keep eating you from the inside out."

"Okay." I took a deep breath. "Okay."

I tucked the pack of Yummy Mummies into my back pocket and slowly walked down the hall to my mom's room. My dread increased with every step. I'd had nightmares about this nearly every week for the past five years, and now I had to face her.

She lay mute and too sick to move in the bed just as I remembered her. And the smell—the hospital antiseptic overlaying the stink of diarrhea and vomit made me want to gag. The veins in her arms had collapsed and she'd gone into kidney failure, so they had stuck a quiver of painful-looking needles into the pulsing vessels in her neck to hook her up to various IV tubes. One was for saline, another for an antiparasitic drug, and the rest for dialysis. The surgical tape over the needles hadn't held properly and blood had slowly seeped out in a sticky, uncomfortable-looking pool spreading across the hollows of her collarbones and down her cleavage. Futile silver bags hung on the IV tree above her.

And I—the five-years-younger version of me—sat in the chair beside her. Staring at her with a dazed expression. Just staring and watching her die.

"C'mon," I begged myself. "Get up and call a nurse to come sponge her off. *Get up.*"

But I couldn't hear myself and just kept sitting and staring. I know what I was thinking. The nurses during the day had buzzed around my mother with impatient efficiency and I'd just tried to stay out of their way. At night, I hadn't been able to shift to realizing that now nobody else was checking on her and I needed to do something. But I felt like a bystander, an observer. I felt helpless in the face of all those needles and tubes and malignant cells I couldn't stop. It never occurred to me that the extra bit of discomfort my mother was suffering was something I *could* stop.

The whole point of my flying a thousand miles to stay with my mother in the hospital was to try to provide some comfort during what turned out to be her final days. I'd gotten a portable player with her favorite Dead Can Dance and The Incredible String Band CDs. I'd read to her from *To Kill a Mockingbird*, her favorite book. But the one thing I could have really done to make things better was the one thing I was too stupid to do.

A few hours later, the morning nurse would come in and declare, "Well, if it were my mother, *I'd* have called someone in to clean her up!"

And then, shamefaced and embarrassed, I'd go home to try to sleep.

And then my mother would die while I was gone. While nobody was looking. While nobody was there to hold her hand.

The nurse's words would take root in my memory and grow, tainting every other memory they touched. They were loud in my head when I swallowed the bottle of tranquilizers. And they never went away even after the few post-hospital therapy sessions my insurance grudgingly covered. They would never, ever go away, condemnation and proof that I had failed my mom.

"Vicky." My mother sat up in bed and was giving me a stern look.

My heart jumped when I realized that she saw me. I felt pierced by her amber eyes. "Yes?"

"The blood was a little uncomfortable, yes. But my intestines were being torn apart by microbes and cancer. My kidneys were rotting inside my body. A little itch on my neck just didn't matter, you know? Stop beating yourself up over it. That's an order, okay?"

"Yes, ma'am."

She beckoned me closer and held out her bone-thin arms for a hug. The invisible wall didn't block me this time. I sat down on the bed beside her and held her close. As I breathed in the familiar scents of her perfume and hair spray, I was overwhelmed at the enormity of what I'd lost when she died, and I began to weep.

"I'm so sorry you died alone," I sobbed. "I'm so, so sorry. I wanted to be there for you."

"But you were!" My mother gently pushed me back and wiped the tears off my face with her thumbs like she had when I was little. "I heard the music, I heard you read. I knew you were there. I wasn't even conscious when I died. It was like slipping from sleep into . . . more sleep. It wasn't scary. You didn't fail me."

She turned to the hospital tray beside her bed and picked up three small brown nuts beside her insulated plastic water jug.

"Hold out your hand," she said.

I did as she asked, and she dropped the nuts onto my palm.

"What are these?"

"Hazelnuts," she replied. "For wisdom, healing, and maybe a little inspiration for those books of yours."

"Thank you." I tucked them into the left front pocket of my jeans.

"Have a happy Halloween." My mother gave me a gentle push, and I tumbled backward off the bed into darkness.

I came to in the bed in my hotel room. The room was dark except for a head-splitting band of light under the blackout curtain. My head ached, and my mouth felt fuzzy. I still wore my convention clothes. Heather was snoring away in the other bed.

"Ugh." I moaned like a zombie.

"Oh, thank goodness you're awake!" Elaine said. I

heard her get up from the desk chair and walk to the bed. "You need to drink water; here's an Aquafina."

I took a tentative sip from the bottle she stuck close to my face. The water was cool and delicious, so I took a longer draw.

"We looked all over for you," Elaine said. "Nicole found you in the convention center basement—how you got down there, we'll never know! She says you were hugging a steam pipe. You're lucky you didn't get burned!"

"Lucky. Yeah. I gotta go pee."

"Let me help you—"

"Nah, I got this."

I rolled out of the bed and staggered toward the toilet. Heather's sleep-frowsy head rose from the sheets.

"Hey, I saved the Great Pumpkin," she slurred at me.

"Good job!" I locked the bathroom door behind me in case Elaine decided I needed assistance. To be fair, she was probably panicking that I was going to sue her and the convention for feeding me illicit drugs. I went to the toilet and unzipped my glitter-smeared jeans and heard something fall out of my back pocket onto the floor.

It was a package of Lik-a-Stik Yummy Mummies.

I pulled my jeans back up and reached into my left front pocket. My fingered encountered something round and hard: the three hazelnuts. I took them out and stared at them for several minutes, rolling them around on my palm with the tip of my finger. One for healing, one for wisdom, and one for inspiration. One for me, one for Mom, and one for Joe. One for my past, one for my present, and one for my future.

Elaine rapped gently on the door. "Are you okay in there?"

"Yes, I'm fine," I replied.

And realized that, for a change, I actually was.

UNDEFINABLE
WONDERS

THE SHINY FRUIT OF OUR TOMORROWS

BRIAN HODGE

HOW TO HOP a train without getting yourself clubbed, caught, or killed, that was the first thing you learned when hard luck set you to riding the rails. It was the first thing Owen taught the green ones when he spotted them, the scared ones who kept their eyes on the other riders instead of on the train, hoping to learn on the run.

It was the first thing he'd taught Carole, outside of Joliet, while waiting for a westbound to Davenport. He'd taught her how to hop a freight before he knew her name. Taught her how before he'd even known she was a she, and not some fresh-faced boy, lost inside men's clothes with her hair pincurled up under a newsboy's cap. She picked it up quick and now she was the one keeping the keener eye out for the green ones.

It was all about timing. And location. In the train yard, while the locomotive was idling, taking on coal or water or new cars, that was no good. The bulls lurked along the tracks there, on patrol. The mean ones carried clubs. The meaner ones carried shotguns.

No, you had to wait until the train was chugging along on its way again. You picked your hiding spot on the outskirts of the train yard, or past the platform, and laid low. From up behind the throttle, the engineer might not see a thing, just the two shiny rails and open ground. Then it was like a flock of birds lifting off all at once, men springing up from the sloping sides of embankments, or from behind trees and bushes, or slipping out from between idle cars on the next tracks over.

Then you ran. You ran like the devil was after you, because he sure enough was. The devil worked for the Southern Pacific and the L&N and the rest, and there wasn't anything he hated more than someone catching a free ride out of town on one of his trains. Even if the train wasn't his at all and never would be, because it was owned by some rich man a thousand miles away.

Do it proper, with a spot of luck, and you got to the train before the bulls could stop you. You matched your speed with the train and closed in from the side and kept your eyes on what mattered.

"Never watch the wheels," Owen would tell the first-timers. With some folks, those rolling steel circles had the power to hypnotize. "Wherever you keep your eyes on, that's where you're apt to end up."

The key was to focus on the handhold you'd picked out. The grab-iron on a boxcar, the ladder up one end of a hopper. Get close, grab on, and grab high, that was the ticket. The tricky part was knowing, feeling, when to let the train take over. You needed strong arms and a good grip for that. You pulled yourself clear of the ground and let the train sweep you up and away, and from there all that was left was to get yourself secure for the ride. It was the best reason for traveling light, nothing more in your bindle or bedroll than you needed to weigh you down.

On the morning he and Carole left Kansas City, with the sun barely on the rise, there were twenty-odd of them scrambling for whatever they could latch onto, when Owen saw it go bad for two of them on the next cars ahead.

"Them old boys ain't gonna make it," he said.

One fella who didn't move entirely sober went clomping along trying to dive into the open doorway of a boxcar. He hit the edge with his chest and went down holding his ribs, and didn't seem to notice someone inside flailing to grab him. Another fella with scraggly gray hair waited too long to pull, and wound up hanging on as the train got to rolling faster than he could keep up. It dragged him another fifty feet before his hands gave and he dropped away.

It was a miserable thing to witness even when they didn't slip under the wheels. Owen looked down as their own car rolled past, helpless to help. He'd spend the rest of the morning trying to shake the despondent look in their eyes as they watched him glide above, both men banged up and sprawled in the dirt and rocks and clinkers. Waiting for the bulls to stomp in if bad luck was running double today, to beat a few more knots on their heads and leave their pockets empty.

He didn't look back. He helped whoever he could, but he'd stopped looking back more than a year ago. Looking back never showed you anything you wanted to see.

"The one looked as drunk as my daddy used to get," Carole said over the rising chug of the engine and clatter of the wheels. "The other one, he was older than either of my granddads ever got to be. Poor old soul."

From their grimy perch between the cars, Owen stared down past the rust-brown couplings, saw the ties begin to blur. No bull could catch them now.

"High or low?"

"High," she said. "Feels like it's fixing to be a pretty day."

"High it is." Owen went first, the gentlemanly thing to do, because while most folks out here weren't looking to hurt anybody else, you still never knew who might be waiting on the top of the next boxcar. If he was the type to see a girl poke her head over the top of the ladder and decide God had finally answered a prayer and so he'd better get a move on it before God changed his mind.

This car, there was just one fella sitting in the middle of the roof, and he didn't look to care much about them either way. Hard to say which the man had gone more days between: decent meals or close shaves. They came over the front edge and crawled along the center planks, picked their spot and gave the man his space. They settled into the rhythm of the rails, same as a dozen others making their way atop the cars ahead and behind. They swayed this way, then that way, as Kansas City fell behind and the endless flatlands unfurled ahead.

"How far is Salinas from here?" Carole said.

Owen gave it some thought before saying he didn't know, to make it look like he might.

"I couldn't say, exactly. I never rid straight through to California. Lots of stops. A lot of fruit to pick." Strawberries in Florida, peaches in Georgia, apples in Washington, hops in Oregon, and bunches more in between. "It's a long ways off."

"You think it'll still be there by the time we get there?"

"Salinas? I don't expect Salinas is going anywhere."

Carole gave him a scowl, playful like, the way she did when he was joshing her but sounded serious. "You know what I mean."

He feared he did. Wherever a hobo jungle sprang up,

they tried to keep it far enough away from the train yards and depots that the bulls wouldn't take overly much offense to it, but there were no guarantees. A bunch of bulls might gang up and charge in to bust heads and smash everything to pieces and send whoever could still run on their way, for no better reason than because they could and it was fun.

But Salinas?

"What can I tell you? If it's there, it's there," Owen said, then tried harder to sound cheery. "Maybe there's a few things that even a railroad bull could find it in him to hold sacred."

They rode a good portion of the day and stopped in Hays. You got off the trains the same as you got on: quick and watchful. The new bulls weren't going to be any nicer than the old ones. If you were careless enough to climb down next to a man waiting to swing a club, that only made his day and ruined yours.

But they came down fast and got away clean, feeling grimy from the ride and the high heat of the September afternoon. They followed a fella who said he knew to a jungle where they could bed down for the night and get some grub. It wasn't much of a place even by jungle standards, but there was shade from the brush and a few trees, and not much dust blowing through. It would do for a night.

After they had their bearings, they set off for town. There wasn't anything edible left in their bindles, and Owen wasn't going to gamble that if they didn't contribute to the night's mulligan they'd get a share regardless, other than what they might lick from the empty pot.

It was too late in the day to hit the shops and see if they could stock shelves for a few hours, so they went for the neighborhoods instead, where even a leaky roof over your head was better than none. They walked along the streets, eyes down to watch the curbs, until he pointed out a chalk curlicue that was faded but hadn't yet washed away.

"Here we go," he said, then whispered a thank-you to the sky, in hopes it might land on the head of the hobo who'd left the mark, to tell whoever came along next, and knew what to look for, that there was a kind lady who lived here, a soft touch.

They went around to the back porch, because they weren't made for front doors. His knock was answered by a stout woman with a cross around her neck. Owen asked if she had any chores that needed doing, payable in whatever vegetables or such she might have to spare. She looked him up and down, and probably found him able-bodied enough, then looked at Carole, then beyond her to the sky, where the sun was low and golden, and said, "How about we save the chores for next time," and just like that, they had a cabbage and two carrots plus a boiled egg each for the morning.

Back out on the street, he took a nub of chalk from his pocket and freshened up the mark.

"She'd've put you to work if it hadn't been for me," Carole said.

"And I would've been fine with that, too."

"I can work just as hard as you, you know."

"Harder, probably. Save it for them melons in Colorado, if you want."

"Is that the real reason you took up with me? It goes easier on you at people's doors?"

"Or how about I enjoy your company? Couldn't just be that, could it?"

Carole scuffed along in the ankle-high, lace-up boots she'd snitched from her biggest little brother when her father threw her out. "What kind of company is that, exactly? Because you're not sweet on me, that much is plain."

"I never thought you'd have me."

"I'm not saying I would, either, just so you know."

"Then what is it we're arguing about again? Because I can't tell."

She scuffed along awhile longer, then one hand strayed up to her cheeks, one side then the other. "It won't last, is what I'm getting at. Out in these parts, this dry air, all the dust, the coal smoke . . . I'm not going to have a face these women look at and feel sorry for much longer. I'm going to look as hard as any of the men. So in case you're thinking of trading me in for a younger one as soon as you find one, you just be man enough to let me know. Don't sneak off in the middle of the night and leave me waking up alone in someplace I never heard of."

"Nobody's sneaking off and nobody's getting traded in." A younger one? She was just eighteen herself, for cripes' sake. Then he backed up to what she'd said before the trading part. "You think I look hard already?"

"Are you joking? You've got a face that looks like it could drive railroad spikes." She laughed and gave his shoulder a shove, and things were okay again, and he felt relieved. Because it was the same with Carole as it was with his mother and his aunts and the teachers he remembered, and just about every other woman he'd known. You never realized things weren't okay until they were so not okay you could hardly think how to fix them.

Back at the jungle, Owen used his knife to chop up the

cabbage and carrots, a contribution to the mulligan that the others were happy to see. But what really got everyone going was the fare a couple colored fellas wearing shapeless fedoras had just brought in. One had a fistful of wild onions, and the other had honest to God meat, a squirrel he'd clipped out of a tree with a slingshot.

As the stew cooked down and the sun set as red as a splattered tomato, it was the same as any other hobo jungle. Owen had never seen more colorless places in his life. If there were shacks made of scrap wood, they were paintless and gray. It was nearly always all men, as hardscrabble as the earth, and the older they got the grayer they looked, too. They'd been wearing the same clothes so long the sun had bleached them to a uniform hue, blending into the dust before they darkened again with grime.

Everybody dipped cans of mulligan from the pot and tried not to burn their fingers. Carole sat close as they waited for someone to get around to asking what they were to each other.

Once the pot was empty, stories were all they had left to share, nothing else to do but sit around the fire and trade, maybe see who had the worst one. The longer anyone was out here riding the rails, the tougher it got to think of there being a year to it. It was hard times, was all. Or, as Owen had heard one would-be vaudevillian back east put it, "nineteen-hundred-and-thirty-shit-outta-luck."

One fella's lament was that he wanted to go to New York City, because he'd heard there was work there, and if there wasn't, there were no better docks to ship out from to some better place in the world. Zanzibar—maybe there. He didn't know where it was, but he loved the sound of the name. *Zanzibar*.

"Then what are you doing in Kansas getting off a westbound train?" somebody asked.

Too afraid to go to New York, the man said, because he figured he'd be more likely to end up in jail than with a job. The first thing he'd probably do when he got to town would be to find out where Wall Street was, then go whale the tar out of the first man in a ritzy suit he saw, for getting them in this fix. Then drag him upstairs a few floors and throw him out a window, and maybe he'd hit somebody else who deserved it, too.

"So here you sit," another fella said. "Afraid to move anywhere but the wrong direction."

The Zanzibar-man cackled. "Pretty much."

The longer the evening went on, the sorrier Owen got to feeling for the colored fellas. He knew their names now, Leo and Micah, and that they were from Louisiana, but nothing else. They sat farther back from the fire than the others, heads down over their cans of stew even though they'd added to it as good as or better than most.

"What about you?" Owen said.

The pair of them looked at each other, then Micah, the one who'd brought the squirrel, said, like it was just another day, "Spent near two weeks lost in a swamp this summer. There was more of me when I went in, but the skeeters got the rest."

Now this was a story Owen wanted to hear.

"Got inside this boxcar back home. Couple hours later, old man in there with me wakes up, he's looking at me real keen-eyed. He's already been where we're going, just got turned around the day before. So he already knows that in the next town up ahead they're hunting for someone looks too much like me. Same old thing, say he been messing with a white woman. Well, the old man and me both know how that goes. One black neck stretches as good as the next, and they ain't too particular long as they get to string somebody up. If I ain't the one that done it, I done *something*."

Around the fire, it wasn't hard to tell apart the fellas who were already looking at Micah with fresh suspicions, like squirrel or not, maybe he wasn't one of the good ones after all.

"Old man waits for the train to slow down as it goes around a bend, then he hustles me to the door to jump me off that car. Ain't nothing but swamp out there, I tell him. Old man just laughs, says I can take my chances with the snakes or with the rope. So I picked the snakes."

He looked down at his can of stew like it had something to tell him.

"*And* the skeeters. And the gators," Micah laughed, then turned somber. "That old man saved my life. If I'd got in another boxcar, or if he'd kept on sleeping, or if he hadn't got hisself turned around in the first place . . . "

"You'd be four inches taller with a wobbly head," Leo said. "And I wouldn't have to listen to you telling this every night."

"I tell it to figure it out for myself. Ain't never had a turn of luck like that before in my life. Makes me scared I might've done used up all the good luck I got."

"I think luck is more like love," Carole piped up with. "It may come and go, but you don't use it up if it's real, and on the worst days of your life, it's what's there for you when nothing else is."

Micah puzzled on that, then broke into a smile. "Well, if you can still say that out here, then maybe there's something to it."

It came soon after that, curiosity getting the better of someone, the way it always did. "The two of you married, is that what you are?"

"Brother and sister," Owen said, like always. It was easier that way, apt to keep Carole safer from someone sniffing too close while not setting up expectations to act in a way they couldn't if he'd said yup, been married most of a year now.

The answer was good enough for some but he knew what the rest were thinking, as long as they had decent eyes. Owen, he was a Riley, and rawboned Wisconsin hayseed. He looked every inch of it, too, from his big clomping feet to the unruly shock of blond hair piling up from his head. Carole, though, was a Delaporte from Joliet, with a heart-shaped face and kewpie doll eyes and that thick black hair pinned up under her cap most of the time, but when she let it loose, lord have mercy, that was a sight to behold.

Every time he saw it, he wondered what it would be like to touch. But Carole wouldn't have him, and he wasn't asking, not yet anyway, because if a fella expected to pursue an arrangement like that, he had to have prospects, something better than one more day of dust and wind and picking fruit.

So here they sat, pretending and waiting, because somebody always had to bring it up: "For brother and sister, you two don't look anything alike."

"Neither did our mothers," Carole said, which wasn't even a lie, but shut them up just the same.

Later, once it was pure dark out, and the owls hooted and the bats chased the bugs drawn to the flames, Carole asked if anyone had been to Salinas recently. Or if they might have heard of what was supposed to be there. Nobody had. When she told them what she'd heard last week, around a fire just like this, in Georgia, they seemed uncertain what to make of it.

Yes, it would be grand if such a thing existed, but it

surely didn't, because why should it, and even if it did, what would it be doing at a hobo jungle in Salinas, California?

A stringy fella with a smirk for a face waved it off. "Sounds like nigger talk to me."

Leo straightened with a scowl. "Then you won't fall off your seat from me saying it sounds like something I heard about when I was a bitty boy. Place I grew up, there was a hoodoo woman they said had a smoky-looking mirror that showed her things. Only difference is, she was the only one it showed anything to. Didn't nobody else know how to look, I suppose. Or could be she was the only one the mirror liked."

"What'd I tell you? Nigger talk."

"Maybe so, peckerwood. You look more like a chicken guts man yourself, so I can see how you might have a problem telling fortunes with a mirror."

For a minute it looked like there was going to be a fight, but nobody really wanted one, and soon enough everybody simmered down and moved along. No reason to do the bulls' work for them.

Carole seemed to take heart in it, somebody believing her, but she hadn't been out here long enough. Owen figured he knew the real trouble. Whatever there was or wasn't in Salinas, it was foolish to hope on such things, because hope was what broke hearts the quickest.

Owen was up with the dawn and whistling with the songbirds. At one end of the encampment was the nearest thing to a bathroom—not for relieving yourself, you did that farther along, but for spiffing up. An oval mirror with a busted handle hung by a string from a scrawny cottonwood, head height. On the ground below, a crate served as a table for a scummy cake of shaving soap and a razor. No blade, but if you had your own, you were good, and he did. He carried it in his wallet, kept it sharp by whetting it on stones along the rails and stropping it on the leather of his belt. He splashed water from a bottle and lathered up and started with his neck.

"Never saw a man take that much pleasure in a shave out where birds could shit on him." It was Micah.

"Keeps me civilized. You stop caring about a good shave, you let go of pride." Owen tilted his head for another view in the mirror and cruised along the edge of his jaw. "I may be dressed like a bum, might smell like one too, but that don't mean I got to think like a bum."

Micah scruffed at the wool on his own face, maybe a week since he'd scraped it off. "I can take it or leave it. What I miss out here, talk about civilizing, I miss a piano."

Owen locked eyes with Micah's reflection and cocked a brow. "You play?"

"If I know one Scott Joplin tune, I bet I know fifty, and that's just getting warmed up."

Now his cheeks. "I'll have to hear you play sometime, then."

"You point out the ivories, I'll do the rest." Micah scruffed at the dirt like he had something else to say but had to dig it up first. "I'm hoping you might even get a chance, too. Wondering if you'd much mind if me and Leo was to keep company with you to Salinas. What Miss Carole was talking about last night, Leo, he sets store by it. Not sure if I do, but Leo's stuck on it now, and if it's true, if that place shows you what she say it does, that could make things some easier on us, too."

Owen flicked away a foamy wad of lather and whiskers, then started under his nose. "If Carole's okay with it, then I am too."

"We don't gotta ride on the same cars or nothing, just didn't want you thinking you's being followed, that's all."

"No, ride where you want, it don't matter." He nicked himself at the corner of his nose and hissed. "What's so important about it to Leo?"

"Just trying to make finding work easier if we can. Leo, he heard there used to be black cowboys out west, maybe still is, thought we could give that a try. Cows don't care about no color but the red of the branding iron. Might help knowing ahead if we got a future in it, though."

Owen caught his reflection again. "Have you ever even rid a horse?"

"Not so much legal, but yeah, I done it. Didn't fall off drunk, figure I'll do even better sober."

"Okay, then." Owen had to laugh, but it didn't come out as happy-sounding as he thought it might. "There's gotta be a ranch foreman somewhere who appreciates that kind of attitude. Maybe Salinas can help you find him. Yep. Who knows?"

Micah eyed him a moment, turning squinty. "You do wanna go, don't you? I thought last night you did, but you don't much sound like it."

Owen started mopping the suds from his face with a rag. "It means the world to Carole, so I want to get her there. But me . . . if all I'm doing is riding, I ain't working, and if I ain't working, I ain't sending money home. I'm a fruit tramp 'cause I choose to be. There's nothing for me back in Wisconsin. My ma, she's got the consumption. They got her bedded up in the sanatorium in Waukesha County. My pop, he used to have a job putting sheet steel in a press. The machine'd come down and stamp it into a cookpot. Until it took his right hand halfway to his elbow. That was it for him. He always said he was only ever any good for picking things up and putting them down again, but nobody wants a hired hand who's just got the one. So it's all on me, wherever I can find it."

Micah made a groan of sympathy. "Should've told that story last night, you'd've maybe won that last bit of squirrel."

"But Carole, she's—"

Owen stopped himself before he could go further. Cripes, he nearly let it slip. It was too early, and he needed coffee to get him going, and nobody had any. He just had yesterday's boiled egg to look forward to. Better than an empty belly, but there was no kick to it.

"She not really your sister, is she," Micah said.

"You got no call to say that. You don't know nothing about us, neither one."

"Well, I know a man don't look at his sister the way you do her unless he got a sickness in the soul, and you don't seem the type."

Owen shook his head, furious as a wet dog. "I don't look at her. Like hell I do." Then he shot a glance back to make sure Carole wasn't hearing any of this, and nobody else, either. "Do I?"

Micah juggled his hands up and down. "Maybe not so's most would notice."

"Then what in hell are you doing noticing?"

"Ain't nothing but seeing what most folks overlook. Just used to reading white faces, is all. Can't help it. Where I come from, that makes a big difference in how your day goes."

Owen had to laugh again, even less happy-sounding than before. Found out by a colored piano player cowboy with no cows and no piano. Didn't that beat all.

"It's your business. Ain't gonna say nothing to nobody. Just thought I could save you the trouble of pretending. That can be hard to keep up." Micah took a step away, then turned back. "Sounded like you was gonna tell me something about Miss Carole before you bit it off. You still wanna get that off your chest?"

He did. And didn't. But might as well. "Like I told you, I got a purpose out here. I got reasons for putting up with this. It ain't like that for Carole. Her pop threw her out for no more cause than he said she made one too many mouths to feed. Kept both her brothers cause they'd be pulling their own weight soon enough, the way he saw it, but Carole, he told her to scram and never come back."

Micah shook his head at the evil of it, looking at the ground.

"So this Salinas business, it's all she's got. She just wants to know there's a path forward that don't end up with her on her back all day, if you get my drift. Just one look at it, to know it's there . . . that'd do her a world of good."

Micah nodded. "Amen. A thing like that, you can hang onto it for a long time. Take it from somebody who knows hanging."

The world was always changing around them, but some parts stayed the same no matter where they were. There was always another train and a need to catch it. Always another hateful man trying to keep you from jumping on, and another one wherever it stopped, itching to punish you for jumping off.

There was always another town with another shopkeeper ready to put you to work for a few hours, claiming an empty till at the end of the day with an apology that wouldn't fool a deaf man. *Sorry, buddy. Wish I could do better. But here's a couple brown apples for you. You look like you'd be glad to have them.*

There was always another cop ready to beat you into the dirt for being down already. Always another house with a chalk mark on the curb, and somebody inside willing to share something worth keeping, and send you off with the wonder of it all renewed—that just when you thought it was the devil's world through and through, you caught a little glimpse of God.

The four of them sweated across the plains of western Kansas with the taste of grit in their mouths. They shivered in the snowy passes through the Rocky Mountains, sweltered down the western slopes and over the high desert on the other side. Mile by mile, they ate the smoke and the dust; they huddled together for warmth; they coughed and spat and heaved. Past Utah, past Nevada, through the parched inhospitable lowlands of eastern California, they began to despair of ever seeing anything green again, until the fertile valleys down the middle restored hope that it wasn't all shades of brown.

When they got to Salinas, Owen was farther west than he had ever been. He'd worked the valley, but never been to the town. His nose found a new smell in the air, clean and crisp—the scent of the ocean blowing in from a few miles away on a kiss of cool breezes. Even Micah and Leo, no strangers to damp air, said it was nothing like the heavy, dank smell of Louisiana wetlands.

After they jumped off the train past the west side of town, it didn't take much asking to get pointed the right way. A mile's walk to the north at most. Now that they were here, Carole was as scared as he'd seen her that they were too late. That while the site may still have been there, their destination would be gone, smashed the day before by men with clubs who couldn't abide its presence, despising the very idea of it, something that gave without taking and asked for nothing in return.

The camp was tucked alongside a shallow creek and a friendly grove of spindly trees—the most populous hobo jungle he'd come across, enough folks milling around that it needed three cookfires. They had tents made of tarps, and even did laundry here, clothes scrubbed in the creek, then draped on ropes stretched between trees to dry. A few of the older men looked thoroughly at home, jungle buzzards who'd found their way here and lost their reasons to move along.

"You come for the mirror tree?" one of them asked. Bald and browned by the sun, bony within overalls, he took stock of them—Owen and Carole, Micah and Leo, dirty-faced and rumpled and weary.

"What makes you ask that?" Owen said. "We just got here."

He shifted on a rickety cot like his joints ached. "You've got a look I've seen before. All four of you."

"What kind of look is that?"

"Like you're hungry and don't know if you're getting fed or not."

Carole took a step forward, one hand wrapped in the other. "But we can? We still can?"

"That's up to the tree." He swiveled with a grimace to point further to the north. "That way. Give it time, though. Don't rush it. Treat it like a horse you don't want to spook. Let the place get used to you first."

It was the finest moment of Owen's life, the feeling sinking deep—no, they were *not* too late. He rejoiced in the relief on Carole's face, and her smile, dear sweet Jesus, the brilliant giddy smile on her, just this side of tears, like she'd dropped a weight she'd been dragging since Georgia. He could've danced. Could've asked her to join him and twirled her until they fell down dizzy, then jumped up and done it all over again.

But he never danced.

"Seems to work best early and late, too," the jungle buzzard said. "Mornings and evenings, when the sun sits low. Couldn't tell you why."

"I could," Leo whispered from behind. "When the worlds is in-between. Yeah."

Right now the sun was high but it wasn't cruel. With plenty daylight left to burn, it seemed a sin to sit around when there was a town nearby and work to hunt for. His pockets weren't going to fill up by sitting on his ass. But this place wasn't going to get to know him if he wasn't here, either. It made for a long afternoon . . .

Then next thing he knew Carole was shaking him awake and the sun was in a whole new place in the sky, and the clouds blazed with pink and orange underbellies.

"It's time, sleepyhead," Carole said.

He could only blink as the setting sun made a halo of her hair. He had no idea when he'd curled up on his bedroll and sleep had taken him. He hadn't even dreamed.

"I don't know how you could grab yourself a siesta." She sounded envious. "All I could do was pace up and down and look out for the bulls."

"It's okay," he said. "Let's get to it."

Nothing would do but that Carole go first. Micah and Leo agreed. They hung back while she went ahead, losing sight of her as she moved away through the trees. How long was it supposed to take? He didn't know. As long as it took.

And why, even though this was supposed to be a good thing, did it feel like waiting for someone to die?

Five minutes? About that. When she came back, Carole walked slower than usual, and unsure, like her feet weren't quite touching the ground and she had to watch the earth for every step. Owen started to ask how it went, but she stopped him without even a glance his way, raising a palm to him, and glided on by to go sit by herself.

"Your turn," Micah said. Both he and Leo seemed to defer to him for, what, no better reason than the grubby white of his skin? Like it was his right when he hadn't earned a thing? He didn't like the feel of that, either.

"Why don't you go on. I ain't ready yet."

Leo, then. Leo had been ready since Kansas.

Micah watched him leave. "Little earlier, I asked that old man where it come from. Near as he knows, it was just some big old mirror, used to be fancy, that somebody hauled in from the town dump. Got it all this way, then they dropped it."

"That don't sound very charmed."

"No, sure don't. But, I tell you, sometimes it's the sweetest music that comes out of the most busted-down-looking pianos. No sense to it."

"I gave up looking for sense a long time ago." Owen cocked his head. "Something I was thinking on earlier. They probably got all the pianos you could want up in San Francisco. Something to look for at the tree, anyhow. In case nothing comes of the cowboying."

Micah mused it over. "Know soon enough, won't I?"

"If you're lucky."

Micah stuttered a choppy laugh. "Now you sunk it."

As the air cooled and the sky grew deeper and richer, Leo drifted past with a bewildered little smile on his face, trudging for the flicker and crackle of the cookfires. Micah went for his turn, and when he came back Owen knew better than to ask.

By now he understood why it felt earlier like waiting for someone to die. Hopes died the same as people, hard and gasping, and when it was their time to go, there was nothing you could do for them. He had hopes. He just didn't know if they were worth anything. As long as he didn't, they could still feel like they were kicking.

He cursed himself for a coward, then marched off to find out.

He didn't know what he'd expected. Something grander, though, than this. At first glance, it looked like no more than what it was: shards of a shattered mirror, dangling from branches and brush. But instead of one or two, for shaving and combing your hair, they numbered over twenty.

Someone had taken every piece big enough to salvage, irregular shapes and skewed triangles, wrapped them corner-to-corner with wire to make frames, then suspended them with twine. They hung within easy reach, some at head level, the rest a bit higher or lower, like the low-hanging fruit you hoped to find at the end of a long, sweaty day in the orchards.

At first when Owen looked into one, all he saw reflected was himself, staring back with yearning too great to bear. Then he reached out and set them moving, and the breezes helped. Some spun around to show him their backs, nothing to see. Others caught the slanting rays of the sun to set in motion a dazzling dance of light spots.

It was when shards spun around to face each other just right, their reflections locking and seeming to open up tunnels between, that he saw it was true, all true. But there was not just one path before him, he realized. They were as numerous as the thin and supple branches of the tree.

Pick one. Just pick one.

He saw himself at the bedside of his mother, soothing her brow with a damp cloth as she hacked her tubercular cough, and if he read her red-flecked lips right, she called him a good son.

Pick another.

He saw himself in the clearing of a pine forest beneath a vast blue sky, in the company of several young joes like himself. None of them he recognized, but they all looked content as they wielded shovels and saws and hammers.

He saw himself miserable and alone with crack-lined cheeks and hair going gray, gazing hollow-eyed across desolate plains from atop a boxcar clattering along rails that could've led anywhere.

For a moment that nearly stopped his heart, he saw himself little different than he was this moment, writhing on ground littered with rocks and coal, both hands clutched at his throat as he tried to hold in the blood. As quickly as the vision appeared, it twirled away, but when he clawed to get it back—*where, when, how?*—it was already lost to him, irretrievable.

He saw himself in a jungle, a real one, thick and close, beside a concrete bunker with flames curling up out of a narrow horizontal port. He wore a helmet and fatigues, and was running forward with a rifle, to shove its bayonet through the belly of a half-burned man with slanted eyes. The sight shook him even more than the notion of ending up with his throat cut.

The languid mirrors spun and flashed, revealing scenarios good and bad. Some might have fit together, but they all couldn't have lain along the same road. He had to get off the rails, though. That was the main thing. Get off the rails, keep away from the jungles. Despite their warnings, he still began to wish he'd never stepped up and set the mirrors in motion. Some sights repelled him, but none lured him, made him want to go there . . .

Until, with a slowing spin that let him watch with a lingering joy that made it seem truer than the rest, one pair of mirrors at last showed him the only thing he'd hoped to see. There was a future with Carole in it, far from the dust and desperation. He looked heavier, but not bad, it just meant they'd been getting enough to eat. Maybe it was an apartment, or maybe a house, but either way they had a roof and a radio, and it looked like he had a job, because why else would he have a lunch pail? Yet for all he appeared to possess, none of it mattered as much as what he saw in Carole's eyes, when he knew he had her love and trust and respect.

This one. I pick this one.

And it did him a world of good.

Around the fire that night, they ate beans, simmered with salt pork and onions and molasses, a feast. Over their tin plates he smiled at Carole, and she smiled back. He thought of the jungle buzzard warning them not to rush it, to not spook anything, and figured the old man knew a trick or two.

The respectful approach would be to let her sleep on it before asking Carole what she saw.

He rose ahead of the dawn, before the songbirds found their voices. He'd never opened his eyes on a day he was more eager to see begin. The ground wanted him off it, and his bedroll urged him out. Owen was up a good ten minutes before he realized Carole was gone.

At first bewildered, then frightened, then dumbfounded, he searched. In vain, he searched. She wasn't waiting by the cold ashes of the cookfires, wasn't at the mirror tree. She never came hiking back from the outhouse, and her cap and bindle were nowhere to be found. Carole was gone, and despite the rising light of daybreak, she had taken the sun with her.

The same could be said of Micah.

When he roused Leo, all he got was the same bleary-eyed confusion he himself had felt when Carole had roused him the afternoon before.

"Ain't nothing I can tell you but sorry," Leo muttered. "Micah never said nothing to me."

By ones and twos, the people of the encampment arose, and though he was still among them, he no longer felt *of* them. If they spoke to him, he didn't hear a word. He ate a breakfast of cornmeal mush, but had no recollection of its taste. When he looked at faces, at trees, at log seats and the earth underfoot, everything was a mocking blur that dimmed and reeled around him.

All he could see clearly were the rails to the north. He had pointed them in that direction himself, toward San Francisco and pianos.

Owen cursed himself for a fool and began putting together his bindle.

He should let it go, he knew that. If Carole had seen a future he'd never guessed at, and Micah too, and they'd made their choice to seek it, then he should let it go.

But that was the cruelty of the mirror tree, wrapped within its wonder. It showed destinations, but not how to get there. It revealed endpoints without connecting the steps and missteps of the path.

He should let them go.

Instead, he followed. Along a rugged path of steel rails and creosote-blackened ties, littered with rocks and coal, he followed.

Somewhere up ahead, amid the tangle of tomorrows,

was a future with her in it. Somewhere in between, there was another where his throat spilled everything he had.

Today, he could live with finding either.

The Wakeful

KRISTI DEMEESTER

"**H**OW LONG UNTIL there's nothing there anymore. In the ground?" Edith looks up at me and blinks. The sun is too bright. A white, indifferent star. She covers her eyes but doesn't look away.

"Things don't disappear when we plant them. They just change. Into something else."

She nods, all solemn, serious eyes and lips pressed tight. She looks over her shoulder, her eyes passing over the small garden beds the fourth graders planted in the courtyard this past Monday, and mumbles something. "Disappeared," I think she says, but I can't be sure.

The other children have gone home for the day, their parents pulling through the car pick up line in their cross overs and their mini-vans, and now it's only Edith and me sitting on the old bench in front of the gymnasium. Her feet scrape against the pavement, her black shoes scuffing, and I want to grab her shoulders and shake her and yell at her to stop it, but I keep my hands folded in my lap and focus on how my head feels like it's filled with air. Everything swollen and tight.

It's the third time this week Edith's mother has been late. I've thought about calling to remind her of the school's policy, but Cameron thinks it isn't necessary. Not yet.

"Cut the woman some slack, Charlotte. It's not as if she's done this before. Could just be a tough week," he said when I brought it up.

But now, sitting next to Edith with the sun slipping away in a fury of pink and purple, I envision what I'll say to Edith's mother when she finally arrives. She can't leave her child here so late. If she can't pick her up at a normal time, she could enroll her in after school care or have a friend or a relative pick her up. It isn't my responsibility to sit and wait.

"She won't be much longer, Ms. Pratchett. She's almost finished," Edith says and pats my hand. Her skin is fever-hot and sticky despite the chill of early October, and I shift away from her. Slow. Casual. So she won't see it as a rejection. That's what they said in all of my education courses. To never let children think you are put off by them or made uncomfortable by their presence.

Edith glances again at the garden beds, and it's almost like she shivers, like the air has shifted into something it's not, and then she's hopping off the bench and gathering her backpack.

"Good night, Ms. Pratchett," she says. Before I can move, she slides into the dark car that's appeared in front of us.

"Good night," I say because it's what I'm supposed to say.

I sit on the bench until the dark drops around me heavy as a cloak. I dare myself to turn around and look at that freshly turned earth, but I can't.

I'm too afraid.

"It's been a few days. Not a big deal. I don't understand why you're getting so worked up over this." Cameron stands next to the bed, his pants still unzipped, his dress shirt still piled on the floor. Wrinkling. He won't like that.

"It's just weird. That's all."

He sighs and rests his hand against my thigh, but it's an absentminded touch. Light. Airy. Nothing to tie him here to this bed. There's another bed, across town, with another woman, her wakeful eyes trained on the ceiling as she traces the shadows with her fingertips, the taste of something bitter on her tongue.

Cameron pauses, his eyes crinkling at the corners as he smiles, and I resist the urge to draw him back, to press my teeth to his throat and take the smell of his skin into my mouth.

He's never stayed. Never. Tonight is no different.

"It'll probably be back to normal next week," he says and bends to drop a dry kiss against my cheek. His lips are chapped; the memory of them against my thighs still burning like the blood threading under my skin. "See you tomorrow," he says, and then he's gone.

I listen for the soft click of the front door and wait until I can't hear the gentle hum of his car before forcing myself out of these sheets that still hold his smell. I'll have to wash them. If I don't, I'll spend the rest of the night caught up in the tangle of everything I cannot have.

After I know Cameron isn't coming back, I creep through the apartment, turning off the lamps one by one until my own hands are pale shadows swooping through the dark.

I don't sleep.

Edith isn't at school for the next two days. I should call and ask if she's all right and offer to send home the work she's missed, but I don't. The other children don't seem to notice she's gone, and I avoid looking at her empty desk.

I see Cameron at lunch, and I smile, but he looks the other way, and I spend the period picking at the salad I packed before throwing it in the trash.

That afternoon, I sit on the bench and watch the children climbing into their parents' cars. Some of the moms wave as they pass by, and I lift my hand and bare my teeth in a smile. Everything a learned routine. A pattern.

The air still smells of earth and water. Of bright green things growing in the dark. The other teachers nod as they pass me, their faces masks of happiness, and I wait for everything to be quiet. Empty.

When everyone has gone home, I walk through the little garden, my feet pressing against the dirt, my fingers trailing through sprouted things, but there's nothing here. Nothing strange.

"Disappeared," I say, and the word lies heavy and damp in my mouth.

I drive home and wait for Cameron to call. He doesn't.

I try to sleep but the room is hot. The dark a looming palpable thing that expands and contracts.

I think of Edith's face as she watched the garden, her question about how long it takes for the things buried there to disappear. I spend the night drifting in and out of nightmares. Each time I wake, I can taste hard grit between my teeth.

At four a.m., I get up and shower, but no matter how hard I scrub, I can still feel the dirt on my skin.

Cameron's left a note for me in my mailbox. His handwriting loops over the scrap of paper: the number 7 with a heart scrawled around it. His initials at the bottom. I fold the note into tinier and tinier squares and hide it in the center of my palm. I think about putting the paper on my tongue, of swallowing down all those sharp, hard edges. Maybe it will bloom into something else. Something like love.

Edith is back in class. She spends the day watching the window, her eyes faraway and dreamy. I stumble through the day's lessons, end too early so the kids start to get restless despite my telling them they should use the extra time to do their homework quietly.

Edith is already on the bench when I come out to the pick-up area, and she scoots to the far corner. I stay at the opposite end of the line, but one by one, the children disappear until, again, it's only Edith and me, alone in the falling night.

"I was sick," she says. I can't pretend I haven't heard her.

"I'm sorry to hear that." I keep the distance between us, and Edith twitches, an almost imperceptible movement. Insect like.

She falls quiet again, and we wait, the minutes stretching on and on into something I can't find the end of.

"How much longer?" I say because I can't bear this suffocating quiet.

"She's not finished yet."

"Who's not finished yet? Is your mother on her way?

She can't be late like this all of the time." My voice pitches higher, and my hands are shaking.

"It's not time yet. To disappear," Edith says, and again, her body seems to vibrate, her skin a pale smear against the bench, but then everything goes still, and she hops off the bench. "I'll show you."

She kicks off her shoes, leaves them next to the bench, and walks barefoot into the little garden.

"Come and see," she says, and I don't want to follow her into that damp, green space, but my legs are moving and then I'm standing with her in the dirt.

"Here," she says and points to the ground, but there's nothing to see.

"Edith, where's your mother?"

She doesn't answer.

I wake up to the sound of someone knocking. It's soft. Insistent.

"Charlotte?" Cameron's voice. Cameron at the door. Knocking. Asking to come in.

I roll over, and my body feels light. Incorporeal. My mouth tastes foul. The fecund, stale flavor of something dead. I push myself onto my elbows and glance at the clock. Seven-fifteen. Cameron. His note told me he'd be here at seven.

Swinging my legs over the edge of the bed, I pitch forward, my knees burning against the carpet. "Hold on," I say, but my voice is paper-thin and scrapes out from my throat. Cameron didn't hear.

When I open the door, he rushes forward, his hands grasping my shoulders, my forearms, and he's flushed, his cheeks and forehead burning scarlet.

"What the fuck, Charlotte? I've been standing out

there for ten minutes. You don't come to the door. You don't answer your phone. I mean, Jesus Christ, I thought you were hurt or dead. *Jesus.*"

"No."

"No? That's all you can say? What happened to you? Are you okay?"

"I'm fine. Fell asleep. That's all," I say, but I don't remember coming here. Don't remember anything past this afternoon. Past Edith.

"I didn't want to freak your neighbors out, but I was getting ready to break your door down if you didn't answer."

I nod and move to the kitchen and grab a glass from the dishwasher. Turn on the tap and fill the glass and then drain it. Fill it again. Water dribbles down my chin and neck. I don't bother to wipe it away.

He moves behind me, his breath falling hot on my neck, and presses himself to me, and he's already hard, and all I can taste despite the water on my tongue is dirt.

"Don't," I say, turning, and he frowns, his eyes unreadable in the dim light.

"Seriously?"

I try to think of something to say, some lighthearted dishonesty that will keep him standing in this spot, but there's no amount of water that will loosen the words he wants to hear.

"Are you sick or something?" I shake my head, and he steps forward and places his hand against my forehead. "You're warm. Let's get you back to bed. Probably just a cold. Nothing to worry about. Poor lamb."

"I can do it. You should go. Don't want to carry it home to your family."

He clenches his hands into fists, and I bare my teeth. "Goodbye, Cameron."

If he says anything else, I don't hear because I move out of the kitchen, away from him, from the intangible thing I built there, and go back to my bedroom.

I lie down. I sleep.

I notice the spot while I'm in the shower the next morning. On my left hip, a small, raised bump turned bright red. It doesn't itch, but I put some cortisone cream on it anyway. Cover it with a bandage. Probably a spider bite. Or a mosquito.

At school Cameron passes me in the hallway, but I look in the other direction, smile at the children as they file past.

Edith is already in her seat when I unlock the classroom door. She lifts her head and blinks as I switch on the overhead lights.

"Good morning, Ms. Pratchett." Her voice is sing song. Too childish for a girl of twelve.

"Edith, did someone let you in? A janitor? Or another teacher?"

"No," she says.

"How did you get in here?"

"Did you go out into the garden last night, Ms. Pratchett? Did you dig a hole way, way down? Did you peek?"

I set down my bag, my coffee, and close the door behind me. "Edith, you have to stop this. There's nothing in the garden, okay? Just plants and dirt."

She untucks her shirt and lifts it so her right hip is exposed. "See? I have one, too. A spot. Like yours."

My hands go cold. "Put your shirt down this instant," I say, but the room feels small, and my breath comes in shallow bursts, and Edith smiles and does what I've asked.

The door bangs open behind me, four other students chattering among themselves, and I move to my desk and try not to look at Edith.

Underneath the bandage, the spot itches.

"Trade with me. Just for the rest of the week. I'll pick up whatever duty you want. Lunch. Morning. Doesn't matter. I'll do next week, too." Kathryn looks back at me with overwrought sympathy.

"So sorry, love. I can't. Trey has tennis right after the last bell, and if we're late again, Coach Sellman swore she'd kick him off the team. You understand."

"Sure. Of course," I say.

Kathryn pats me on the arm. "Chin up, Charlotte. Only two more days to the weekend, yeah?"

I scrub my hands over my face. "Yeah. Thanks anyway, Kathryn."

She smiles and turns back to her lunch, and I try to force myself to eat my sandwich, but each bite is dry as sawdust. I wait for the bell to ring, and then stuff what's left into the trashcan.

The rest of the afternoon passes in a blurred rush of seconds, and when the final bell rings, I clap my hands over my ears. The students don't even notice as they rush out the door. I close my eyes and tip my head back and wait for the ringing to stop. When I look up again, even Edith isn't in her desk.

I know where it is she's gone.

But she isn't on the bench. She's already in the garden, crouched down, her face streaked with dirt, her fingers tracing dark patterns over her arms. No one else seems to notice what it is she's doing. The other children mill past her, but they don't stop to stare.

Invisible, I think, but I can see her skin, her hair. Solid. Real.

I sit on the bench and listen to the sounds of her hands scrabbling through dirt and her teeth opening and closing. Around us, the sky tumbles down into shadow; the other children long gone.

"Your mother isn't coming, is she?"

"But she's here. She's finally finished."

I don't go and look. Close my ears to the sound of the ground cracking open as something crawls to the surface.

Cameron calls four times, the message light on the machine blinking deep red, and I go searching through the kitchen cabinets for the bottle of bourbon I always keep behind the rice and oatmeal and other bland things that add up to my life.

Ten fingers later, and my body feels loose, like every muscle has come untethered. My phone rings again, and the machine picks up. Cameron's voice coming through the speaker all tinny and hollow in its anger and pitched just above a whisper. His wife sleeping somewhere above him while he calls the co-worker he's been fucking for three months to tell her he wasn't the one who'd wanted this. It had always been her. She threw herself at *him,* remember? The back-to-school faculty dinner at Rosaria's where she'd had too much red wine and pulled him into the little hallway that led to the restrooms.

I tug the phone out of the wall, my fingers smarting from the force, and fold myself onto the floor. The shadows on the wall shift and come apart, strange devils wound into a dervish, and I lift my glass in a mock toast and laugh.

How easy, how quiet to disappear inside whatever it is that's come awake. The mother. Her naked body climbing to the surface, reborn and emerging into the sunlight. Not disappeared but something else altogether. Our bodies like so much dust. Beautiful.

I'm not sure when it is I put on my shoes, but I'm running, and my muscles burn and burn underneath thin skin, and I pull my shirt over my head, and the moon shines silver overhead. The spot on my hip is bigger now. A deep bruise.

I tip my head back. I scream.

Edith isn't at school the next day, but I knew she wouldn't be. The void space where she should be seems to breathe and shift. Even when the children are at recess, the wide room gaping and empty, her seat still seems occupied. I run my hands over the polished wood of her desk, but there's nothing there to feel. No vibration, so sensation of something solid or tingling along the backs of my hands. I hover there, letting my fingers tremble through the air. I don't hear the classroom door open and close.

"We need to talk." Cameron's voice. The edge in it razor sharp.

I turn, and he's standing behind the door, his back pressed against the wall so if someone were to pass by and peek through the window, they wouldn't see him.

"You shouldn't be here," I say and turn back to Edith's desk.

"What the hell is going on with you, Charlotte?"

"Nothing."

"It's not nothing. You've been acting crazy since last week. And *this*?" He gestures toward me, toward the desk. "What are you doing in here?"

"Nothing. You should go."

"Charlotte," he says and takes a step forward, realizes he might be seen, and shrinks back against the wall like some insect caught in the light. "Listen. It doesn't have to be like this."

"Doesn't it?" I let my hands drift across the desk's surface slow and dreamlike, trace my name and Edith's name across the wood.

I don't look back at him, at the things I've buried and ignored. "Please go, Cameron."

"You're a real bitch, you know that?" he says, and the door closes behind him.

Something damp brushes against my fingers.

"Edith," I say.

The bell rings.

I wait for all the children to go home. They shout to each other with Friday afternoon glee, and I smile at them from my place on the bench.

Cameron watches from across the parking lot, his face blank, but then he leaves, and I wonder how many pieces of myself have died at his feet.

For a long time, I've called it love. Told myself it's what I wanted.

Only when it's completely dark do I stand and make my way to the garden. I lie down in the dirt. Close my eyes. "Please," I say because I want to disappear, too.

"It isn't like that, Ms. Pratchett," Edith says, but she isn't there when I open my eyes.

"You said she was finished. You said it was time."

Edith doesn't respond, and I lift my shirt, pass my fingers over the swollen, tender skin. "It isn't a bruise is it, Edith. It's something else."

"Yes," she says. Her invisible fingers press against me, and I cry out in pain.

Edith goes silent, and I watch the sky, the clouds low and a lighter shade of night.

I fall asleep there, tucked among the quiet, growing things, and in the morning, nothing has changed.

I don't go home. I spend the day crouched down, my hands scrabbling through the dirt, my teeth closing around any wriggling creature I find. The thing under my skin stretches, and I watch it move, rub my hands over the hard mound it has created for itself.

All of these things I've buried. All of these things I've wanted dead and rotten. "Disappeared," I whisper.

When the time comes, I'll put this squirming thing inside of me in the dirt, and it will bloom. Become something else.

Something beautiful.

KNITTER

CHRISTOPHER COAKE

IMAGINE A SMALL village, in a world not unlike, yet not too much like, your own.

To the west of the village lies a thick deciduous wood, carpeting the foothills of a high mountain range. To its east, past a wide, dark river, stretches a vast grassy plain. The village is located at a bend where the river, having tumbled down from the mountains, grows deep and calm. A few hundred souls live here, in small houses built from logs and sod. To these people, what lies on the other side of the mountains, on the far edge of the plain, is largely a mystery (I can tell you: They wouldn't want to know). Though these people visit other villages, most accessible by horse-drawn cart or barge, they live the bulk of their lives confined to this place, its possibilities, its memories. A few days' journey downriver, where the water empties into an ocean, is a city, but while the villagers might find an excuse to visit, few ever aspire to live there.

Imagine this place: A cluster of small houses with canted roofs, upon which grow wigs of rippling yellow prairie grass. Insinuating afternoon winds blow down from the mountains, scented by ice and evergreen. An old tree stands in the center of the village, lightning-struck and agonized, older, it is said, than gods (the villagers believe in gods, but I can tell you they do not exist). The skies above are depthless and vast.

At night you would be astonished by the number of visible stars, though their strange patterns, the colorful galactic clouds aglow between them, would fill you with unease.

Would you find these people strange? Yes.

But not *too* strange. The villagers are more or less like the people you see around you. Their skin is smooth and honey-colored; they wear their hair long and braided; their eyes are dark and deep. Their teeth, yes, are a little sharper than yours. These people tear meat from the bones of animals, but they also bake sweets and warm breads. They play instruments and sing bawdy songs. They read books. They dream; they marry and have families; they aspire.

For the most part, they fear what you do.

They fear drought, and barter with their gods for rain and snow. They fear funnel clouds writhing down from towering thunderheads to touch the plains. They fear pain in the joint, in the root of the tooth. Tumors and blights. Loneliness. Murder. Unrequited love. Shame.

And you must know this, too. They fear monsters.

Imagine: In deep holes under the river live fish with long, snakelike bodies and wide unhingeable jaws; they have seized splashing children and mothers doing wash. Above the high peaks wheel cruel, featherless birds the size of kites. Squat, scaled things roam in prides far across the plains. In the heart of the forest, wings rasping like saws, live wasps the size of birds, the sting of which—it is said—can silver a woman's hair.

Here is a secret I will share with you: In a hollow at

the center of the world, coiled into a tight ball the size of a moon, sleeps a dragon. No one who lives on this world suspects. Its presence has no bearing on anything else I will tell you, but you must know of it nevertheless. You must live with the knowing. If someday the dragon wakes, this world will end. It has never woken before, but I can tell you it dreams.

Every monster dreams. Every monster imagines, aspires.

For instance, the dragon was probably put there—who knows why?—by a knitter.

Knitters: This is the name given to the most fearsome of the monsters of this world. What else could such beings be named? When they are visible to the naked eye—which is almost never, and for reasons no one understands—they are terrifying. They are shaped like people, but are taller, thinner; their skin is hairless and bone-white; they have spindly, unsettling, many-jointed arms; those arms end in sharp points, and these constantly stab and darn the air, like the needles with which a granny knits a scarf. They have heads on long necks: featureless, yet attentive, turning this way and that.

They knit and unknit the world, and this is terrifying to behold.

I will tell you now about a man and woman of this village. Their tale is a sad one; you must know this at the outset, though its ending might yet surprise you.

The man, when he was a boy only ten years old, saw a knitter. Many people—the happy, blessed ones—live their entire lives never beholding such a horror. Our boy, however, was not so lucky.

This occurred when he was away from the village, near the river, on a cool afternoon in the early autumn. He was alone. He wandered, throwing stones, daydreaming of the future, of his life as a man. He aspired. He dreamed, of happiness, of a wife, of children. If he did not know the particulars of such a life, no matter; he walked along, happily untroubled, guessing.

And then, in the dimming light, he saw it at the edge of his vision—where knitters are said to reside, flashes of omen and unease—but when our boy whipped around, this knitter remained in view. The boy's skin prickled. The knitter loomed only a short distance away, pale and busy, half-hidden behind a tall, old tree, its arms dipping and fishing at nothing. The knitter seemed to look at the boy; it cocked its head.

Then its needles darned the air on either side of the trunk, and seemed to *catch*, and the trunk of the tree shuddered, as though seen through a heat-ripple, and then the knitter crossed its arms, and the world on either side of the tree—there is no other way to put this—*folded over*, and then the tree was gone, and the knitter too.

The boy was a boy, as prone to curiosity as fear. He hurried to the place the knitter had been, where the tree—a tree the boy had touched, and into the sturdy boughs of which he had climbed—had been rooted.

It was not only gone; it had never been. It left behind no stump, no fallen leaves, no turned-over earth. The ground was undisturbed, thickly-covered by grass and bush, the soil beneath firm and dry to the touch.

Only then, *then*, did the boy begin to understand the doom that had befallen him. He ran, weeping, for home. He did not dare look back; he was sure, if he did, that he would see the knitter, looming, ready to unmake him too.

This is what knitters do. They make, and they unmake.

Most of the time no one in this world can know exactly what a knitter has created, what one has stolen. Knitters work in secret, the world changing at their whim, no one the wiser; the changes they make, you see, extend beyond the world of flesh and blood and stone and wood, and into *time*. If a knitter takes a tree, it removes that tree not only from the world as it is, but also from the memories of those who knew it. If it makes a tree, then the tree has *always* been—along with all the times the tree has been seen, touched, climbed.

But sometimes—who knows why?—this making, this unmaking, is not wholly perfect. This is the way of this world. Its people must live with the knowing.

As a villager walks along the riverbank, for instance, past a large sunbleached stone, he might grow puzzled, and the world might seem . . . not right. *Changed*. And if he puts his hands on the old stone, the one he's seen every day of his life, the stone might seem to him, for half a moment, alien, superimposed over a landscape where he is sure—sure—nothing ought to be.

Elsewhere a woman might look out her window, upon the figure of her beloved husband working in the yard, and—for a harrowing moment—think, *I have no husband*, I have *never* had a husband, and yet *there he is*, chopping wood, his shirt tied around his head to catch his sweat, stopping to smile and wave.

Is he real, or did a knitter *make* him real?

The villagers joke, when they trip upon a shoe: *A knitter set it there.*

They joke, upon losing a key: *A knitter took it, gods know where.*

Why must this world be so cruel, so strange? *If you find a knitter, ask it.* This is what they say.

Let's return to our boy, running home, terrified.

He'd seen a knitter. And this knitter had done the most terrible thing of which its kind is capable: It took away part of the world, but it left a witness.

Left a *memory*, living, in the boy's mind.

To be so afflicted, the boy knew—all the people of this world know, and now so do you—is to be cursed. Not with ill fortune (no matter what happens to our boy); no; this curse is the peculiar burden of nonexistent things. What is one to do with a memory of an unmade tree? Without soil in which to root itself, the tree might now grow wild and tangled within the mind, might bear poison fruit, might draw down unexpected lightning.

The boy had to live with this: This dream, this loss, this grief.

Along the way, without realizing it, he ran past the knitter (see it, cocking its sightless head?).

The knitter jabbed the air, threaded and cut.

A young girl stood where no young girl had stood before.

She ran home to her mother, in the house next door to the boy's. Her mother greeted her, embraced her; then she stared after her as the girl went to her bedroom and picked up a wooden doll and sat, smiling, on the floor beside a sniffing, tail-thumping dog. Her daughter. Her beloved daughter. The daughter for whom she'd always yearned. The puppy for which the daughter had clamored and begged, now grown. All was well. Yes. The mother's heart swelled with love.

The boy entered his home next door. His heart pounded, but he could say nothing to his mother. Her terror at his tale, his curse, would be too great to bear.

He wondered if, tomorrow, he should tell the little girl—his best friend!—what he had seen. He went to sleep thinking of what he might say. The undeniable pleasure he would find in her belief.

This is how the village lives: on and on, loving, fearing, made and unmade, the years knit one into the next.

The years pass. The girl grows into a woman; the boy grows into a man.

They remain the closest of friends—they have cared for one another (their parents assure them of this) since they were toddling babes. They share their secrets; they make one another laugh. When they are old enough, they share kisses. Dreams. Aspirations.

They fall in love. Or perhaps it is more truthful to say their love only deepens as it must. To the surprise of no one, least of all the knitter, they are, in their eighteenth year, betrothed.

Look at our boy, now grown into a good man, brawny and big. He cares about the welfare of others; he loves and is loved. He is not a leader—he's too dreamy, too much a jokester, for that—but he is a fine craftsman; he works with wood, builds and repairs boats, as his father does. He can wrestle, brawl, but the woman loves him for his secret sweetness, his inherent stillness and peace.

Look at our girl, grown now into a good woman, curved and lithe. She is smart, sly. She teases everyone, but never cruelly; she never minds being teased. She learns and betters her parents' craft: how to brew beer from the grains of the fields. They send jugs of it in carts to the neighboring villages and to the city; this makes them wealthy. She daydreams too much, her parents say, but the man loves her daydreams; she returns from them bettered, cheered. She longs to see the ocean, with him.

When they are in their nineteenth year, the man and the woman wed. On the morning of their wedding they hold hands and offer a salute to the rising sun and—after a long day of revelry and games, during which time their hands never part—they bid farewell to the sun as it sets. Then they walk, swaying with drink, to their home: a house the man has spent the last year building, one the woman has, by tradition, up until now been forbidden to enter.

But one night, weeks ago, when the outer walls and roof of the house were complete, the woman waited until her family slept and sneaked away into the cool night. She took with her a candle, one she lit only when she had crept, her heart thumping, inside the house. In the dark she passed a knitter and did not know it. It drew its needles close to its chest and watched her from a corner of the parlor as she beheld, with fear and awe, the place she would love and live and make children. She was pleased, then. Pleased with the house; pleased with the man for making it so well. She could feel his love in the walls, in the complicated joins of the wood, everything sanded smooth.

She thought of the children she would raise. The making of them—here, in the bedroom, in a wide feather bed. For a moment, standing above the place the bed would be, she was ashamed of herself. She should have waited, seen it new, drunk and exhausted from dancing, wearing nothing but a bride's good fortune.

But, she assured herself, perhaps it was better to know. She could live, and love, with the knowing.

The knitter loomed behind her, and bumps rose on her arms and calves; she brushed them down. The knitter reached out a needle and touched its point to the end of a single strand of her hair. The woman blew out her candle and crept home to her bed.

The next night she found the man at sunset, alone by the riverbank. She put a finger to his lips. Kissed him. Pulled him down to the ground and, for the first time, urged him into her. He gasped, which she liked. They rolled in the dirt and grass and laughed, and she felt none of the pain the old women had promised. She felt a great deal of pleasure. So many lies had been told to her; she was sure she would never tell them to her daughter. She was sure they would one day make a daughter.

After their wedding the husband and wife take a barge downriver and stay for the first time in the city. They hold hands as they walk the streets and canals. They eat honeycakes sold from wheeled carts. They observe wrestling matches and magicians pulling coins from empty palms and mouths and ears. They see an old woman swallow fire. They wear blue ribbons around their wrists, which signal to all who meet them that they are newlyweds, and not to be robbed. They are given many free sweets, and old men bless the woman's belly. They carry money gifted to them by their families, and with it they purchase a room in an inn overlooking the ocean. Here, on the second night of their stay, listening to the intoxicating crash of the waves, they conceive a child.

Do knitters live in the city? Who do you suppose built such a place? The palaces, the cathedrals, the catacombs where the knitters, in the dark, add to and subtract from the piled skulls and bones?

On the third day of our couple's visit, they are handed a square of peppermint by a kindly woman from the rounded doorway of her candy shop; after she does so a knitter rises behind her and the woman is thereafter gone, but our couple does not see this, does not see how the neighborhood children drift inside her shop, curious, when she does not close up at dusk. The children know before anyone else what has happened, because the knitter has allowed them, for a time, to remember the woman, who sometimes gave them treats and sometimes beat them, as stormy and unpredictable as the goddess of the seas. Her absence fills them with terror—the knitter could be anywhere! It could still be here (it is)! And yet they steal her candies and her chocolate and her pots still half-full with butter frosting. The next day the building that contained her shop is gone, and all the children but one remember nothing.

(Look at that child, sobbing, watching the waves beat the shore. She will grow old, carrying a perfect candy store within her, and the memory of a woman no one else knows. She must always carry this story, ended without resolution, and she is cursed, cursed, cursed.

She grows up to become a poet, mocked and reviled.

Why must she suffer so?

Find a knitter and ask it, child.)

The couple returns to their village. The woman knows, already, that she is pregnant.

She does not tell her husband, or her mother. Truth be told, she hoped conception would take longer. Even though she wants a child, sometimes longs for a child, she has never before felt so serene as now: her girlhood safely packed into a trunk and stored in memory, her motherhood hovering like a distant cloud above her future. She is, now, in the cooling autumn afternoons, simply a woman, a wife; these are the new rooms through which she walks, and she finds them absorbing and pleasingly strange.

One night, in the seaside inn, she dared to imagine herself as barren. She thrilled at the thought, and, guilty and flushed, pulled her husband to her. What harm would come from imagining such a thing in the private and humid dark? Who was there to hear?

Only the knitters and gods, goes the old saying, and only one such creature shared the room with her and her husband.

The man, though, is eager for a baby. A son. Yes, a daughter, too—he would like many children, as many as his wife will bear him, and in the meantime he certainly likes the making of them. He is religious, through and through; he is a good man, but not prone to questioning any of the laws and customs to which he is beholden. Why would he? They work, by and large, to his benefit. For this reason most of all he wants a son, a boy with whom to share in his good fortune, a boy to whom he may teach his craft and cede the riches of the world. Sometimes, when he has finished filling his wife, and she sleeps soft beside him, he presses his cheek to her belly and thinks, hurry now. The rest of his life, fatherhood, cannot come quickly enough.

When the the wife and husband walk past them, hand in hand, the people of the village say: It is as if they were made for one another.

Well.

People say: They are lucky.

Are they? You've seen the knitter. The way it has kept them close. Know that as the years pass it remains with them, unseen. Know that it continues to visit them—not only in moments of joy, but in the moments of loss and regret and doubt that sometimes come upon both wife and husband from, seemingly, nowhere: the sudden irrational moments of fear that befall them (as they befall all of us), the moments in which they are sure, sure, that their life has changed, passed them irrevocably by, when their backs were turned.

The thought that comes upon each of them, from time to time:

I have lost something. Something precious to me. But I cannot remember what it is.

The world blooms and fades, blooms and fades.

Much is made; much is lost.

I must tell you something more.

One afternoon, ten years and some months after their marriage and trip to the city by the sea, the man and the woman return from a picnic together on the shores of the river, just before sunset. This is springtime; the air is warming but not warm. They are dressed in jackets and boots. They are still in love, despite, after all this time, remaining childless.

The fact of it saddens both of them, in different ways. To be childless is to be unlucky. The people of the village do not know how to speak to the childless. When the woman mentions her troubles, offhandedly, to her friends, all of them mothers, she feels grief in their silences. Pity. She grows angry at them—but in those evenings, after, she makes sure to draw her husband close, to try, yet again.

She still loves him, more fiercely now than ever. Know this. Even when her blood comes, she thinks, I am not unlucky. Not with this man, this life.

The man feels the grief even more deeply than he lets on. It staggers him, sometimes. For a long while he struggled, as the years passed and his wife's belly remained flat, to remember his happiness. A man is judged, in this place, by the children he can make, by the strength of his sons and the beauty of his daughters. Nevertheless, he loves his wife, her quiet courage and cheer; he has always enjoyed time spent with her alone. He turns his energies to his boats, and becomes renowned along a hundred miles' worth of river towns for the splendor and sturdiness of his barges. He and his wife grow more and more wealthy. Over the years he builds extra rooms onto their home, but this is only to pass the time. No children come to fill the spaces he has made.

But if the sadness ever threatens to overwhelm him, he has only to look at his wife, and behold her persistent happiness in the face of their fate. He has only to see her pleasure in him. He is humbled, but as the years pass he comes to understand: He is not unlucky. Not with this woman beside him, not with this life. He could lead a childless life with no one else.

After their picnic, they make love, in the same spot they chose that first time, when they were children. They like to revisit it, now and again. In the silence afterwards he rebraids her hair and they gossip, her warm back pressed against his knees. She falls silent as the stars begin to glow through the deep blue dusk, and husband and wife are purely and simply happy, wordless, full.

They have been given a gift.

Know this. Live with the knowing.

As they walk along the dirt path home, however, they are stopped by a merchant selling metalware out of a wagon drawn by snorting mules. He is coming from the city, visiting villages upriver. They have not seen him in over a year, but he is known to them.

What luck, he exclaims, that he has seen them! They are his favorite customers, and they will have first pick of his wares! The wife selects a new pot; the husband a hammer and chisel. The merchant rubs his beard, happy and fat.

Then, when they have finished, he says, Ah! Wait!

He digs in his bag and then hands them a small toy: a rearing horse, crafted from black iron. Then he produces a small iron star hanging from a necklace of fine blue silk, with a blue glass bead suspended in its center

Here, he says. Please take this stallion, for your strong, handsome son. And this charm for your lovely little girl. Lovely like her mother, yes!

The couple do not take these gifts. The merchant has mistaken them for another couple, and they do not wish to insult him, or admit their own sadness. The merchant will be appalled at his mistake, when he realizes. They wait for this to happen.

Please, the merchant says.

The husband clears his throat and says, Perhaps you have mistaken us for someone else.

The merchant straightens, pulls back his gifts. An understanding dawns on his face, and it is horrible to behold his shock and fear.

Of course, he says. You must forgive me.

The merchant takes a copper teakettle from a hook and hands it to the woman without meeting her eyes: You must accept this. It is my apology, and it is not enough.

He is formal, now, which unsettles them further.

The woman takes the teakettle, lowers her chin in thanks. Then the merchant whips the mules and rattles away, muttering. The husband turns and sees him make a sign against evil, then hunch his shoulders against the growing dark.

Perhaps that is when they first begin to know.

Nevertheless, the man says, when they are home: It was only a mistake.

A mistake, the wife agrees.

This is a plausible explanation. The merchant travels for a living. He meets many, many villagers; he meets many children. He is an old man, and old men's memories are fragile things—mats woven, as the saying goes, of dry grass.

And yet the woman wonders. She cannot help but wonder. She can see the house's two extra rooms, the ones the husband built some years ago for their guests and her weaving and books. She stands in their dark doorways and can almost hear, from inside, the cries and laughter of children. She feels a pull at her breasts.

In the kitchen the man stares at the teakettle, turns it in his hands. He thinks of the emptiness in his life, the terrible loss he cannot help but apply to it. He remembers, for the first time in a long while, the knitter of his boyhood, unmaking the tree.

It cannot be.

Yet, in the middle of that night, the woman wakes, crying, from a terrible dream. A dream of a girl, a boy, their round faces and runny noses. A dream of the smell of their skin, milk and sweat and sugar and sage.

Why? she asks her husband, who rubs her back.

I don't know, he says.

Why can't we remember?

The man tells her the truth: We would die of sadness.

They rise from bed. The woman draws a shawl around

her shoulders. She walks with a candle from room to room, the floorboards cold beneath her feet. The man follows. The woman kneels in a room stacked high with books, all the frivolous lies and stories that have filled her childless hours.

Which one of them lived in here? she asks, and the husband knows she is not addressing him.

It's as though she can see the knitter in the corner, its head cocked, watching.

What were their names? the woman asks. At least let me remember their names.

I've known, the man says. He, too, is addressing the dark. I've always known you would take something else.

He kneels beside his wife, holds her shoulders. The shudders that wrack her are new to him; she has always been the brave one. They fill him with terror, and then he shakes too.

Take us, the woman says to the dark. Take us to them.

The man holds her and bows his head.

The knitter regards them, their kneeling forms, their tender scalps. Can it hear their voices? Feel their terror, their agonies, their grief that has no name?

It extends a needle, then the other. The points make infinitesimal adjustments. It makes and unmakes. Its motions are slow, considerate. They might, if someone were to witness them, be mistaken for acts of love.

Then the husband and wife are slumbering in bed, holding tightly to one another. They dream of nothing, want for nothing.

In the morning they will wake and remember nothing of the merchant. They will remember, rather, their lazy lovemaking by the river. A beautiful evening, one that has somehow—for reasons to which they cannot put words—become sweeter in the intervening hours. A night like few living people ever experience. A treasure.

A dog sleeps on the foot of the bed. The dog is new; it has been made. Its mind is filled with love and awe for the woman and the man. It would kill to protect them. For them it would fight the dragon at the heart of the world.

It kicks its paws as it dreams.

For a time the knitter watches them sleep.

Then it lopes slowly from room to room within the house the man and woman have made. In the kitchen it causes to vanish three sweet rolls, a head of garlic, a speck of dust. In the parlor it removes a section of string from the wife's oud, then a mouse, crouched and trembling. By the fireplace it takes the head of a single match.

Then it returns to the bedroom, where it crouches for a long time, still, waiting, before jabbing out and seizing an evil spirit, a small chittering vapor only a knitter could perceive.

I can tell you this: The spirit, the size of a lock of hair, would have, the next day, burrowed into the sleeping woman's breast, where it would have then caused the tissue to warp and fester.

Does the knitter feel anything, as it unmakes the spirit—begging for its life, its screams like the whistling of a teakettle?

Does the knitter feel anything, later that night, when it rises behind the metal merchant, half-slumbering near the coals of a fire, and causes him, and his cart, and the heat of the fire, to vanish?

Did it feel anything a year before, almost to the night,

when it loomed up, invisible, behind a young girl and her brother as they waded in the shallows of the river? When it caught the stuff of the world around its needles, on either side of the children? When it pulled them with it back into the endless dark velvet of the Unmade?

You must know: The children felt nothing.

You must know: they lived short, happy lives.

You must understand: A short, happy life is a great gift.

You might ask: Does a knitter cause one thing to vanish in order to summon another? Does the making of a dog require the unmaking of a mouse? What is the cost of an unmade spirit?

One child? Two?

I can tell you this: Had the children remained, they would have outlived their parents. They would have married and had families of their own. And they would have come, in their middle years, to live in a time of war. This will be difficult for you to hear, but it is true. A distant nation's army will swarm, many years hence, across the great plains, a terrible, ravaging wave. This will happen.

Both children would be slain. Before that they would suffer. It is better you do not know how.

(Know, too: This war will last a decade. It will end when one of the generals reads a poem, written by a long-dead madwoman from the city. He will recite its words to himself as he rides his horse through a field strewn with bodies. The words will live sweetly on his tongue, like candy in the mouth of a child.)

This all would have happened.

The parents can never know it. They are better for the lack.

Do knitters obey laws, balance scales?

If you find one, ask.

The next day the woman wakes. She feeds the dog, then releases him to hunt joyously in the woods. She makes tea with her kettle (she looks at it for a long moment, her mind fuzzy, trying to remember where she obtained it) and watches her husband sleep. The house is strange, still, yet somehow charged with magic, portent. She is surprised—as she always is—by the depth and force of her happiness. She remembers the night she woke beside her new husband in the seaside inn. How she wished for the world to remain exactly as it was. How she was content.

She thinks exactly what the husband does, when he wakes to the touch of her lips upon his brow:

I am happy in this life. I am lucky.

You expect a lesson, don't you?

A reason? An explanation? A different ending?

What makes you think I can provide such things? I am both more and less than what you suppose, and I can tell you: So are you.

What a horrifying tale, you say. A world of pain and questions, of monsters. A man and a woman, made and unmade; their children, made and unmade. So much sorrow and joy, and none of it exactly true. And here it ends, like *this*? Why tell it at all?

You say: These people deserve better. *I* deserve better.

What arrogance.

To believe this, you see, you must imagine yourself better than the knitter that made this village, this world, these people, the knitter that tucked and twined and cut these threads. You must believe yourself above such

concerns and manipulations, free of all complicity. You must believe you are not a dreaming monster, at the whims of which others must dance.

And yet: You are dreaming, and you will soon wake.

You will turn a page; you will fold another world across this one, and this village, this story, all its people, the man and the woman, will cease to be, unmade.

You will carry them with you only in memory, as a curse. They will live in you, and you will tend them, or forget them, as you will. You must live with the knowing.

I made them for you. *With* you. And in you, now, they will dwell.

Yet still you want an answer? Some meaning you might grasp?

Very well:

Find me, and you may ask.

THROUGH GRAVEL

SARAH READ

WE TWISTED OUR bent backs and held our flowers up through the fine-grit gravel and soggy cigarette filters—up through the gaps and the spaces where things don't fit together anymore, and we waited.

Beth came to us that spring, in her red cardigan, reaching down for the buttercup sprouting from the crack in the sidewalk. She pinched the stem, as delicate as her own little fingers, and she was gone before her guardian could turn to see why she had stopped. She slipped through the cracks of the busy world above, and was ours. The first child of the new spring. The first child in more than eight years.

In the dark of the understreets, by the light of the grates and drains overhead, she smiled nervously as we marveled at her small digits, at how the dimples in her knuckles were fading into lily-slim fingers, at how straight her spine had grown without the weight of the city pressing down from above. At the gap in her smile.

Many of us had gaps in our smiles that year—but none so fresh as hers. Our arthritic fingers grasped at her shining hair. Youth was a balm to eyes even as weak as ours.

We huddled in excited half-formed factions for the meeting where one of us would be blessed with her guardianship. When the hour came and the name was drawn—and it was mine, Aemon—I confess, I wept.

I had never dreamed that when I stooped to my own small flower in the pavement years ago that I would be given a new life. One far from the paths of those I'd lost aboveground.

A new child. My heart filled with love for her—filled the holes in the spaces where things don't fit together.

I stumbled through the custom of her adoption. It had been so long since I'd seen it done. I wrapped her in my parka and handed her a tarp, freshly patched, washed and folded. It would become her room, and annex to my home—our home. I gave her a trowel—my better one, with the smooth handle and less rust. I sprinkled her brow with water from the Last Drain.

Though it was Chev that had drawn my name, he was the one to protest. As soon as the ritual was complete, he stood; his reverence for the old customs the only thing that had kept him in his seat till then.

"Are you sure you're up to this, Aemon? You are old in years but young to our kind. Perhaps the child should be placed with someone younger and with more experience in our ways." He meant himself, of course. He'd been here since he was a tiny thing, born to the understreets to a Kindred mother long since washed away. But he still had youth in him. His hair still grew the color of shadows.

"I am no stranger to raising children, Chev."

"Yes. I recall. I believe it is relevant for us to inquire as to the nature of your daughter's death?"

Gasps echoed off the high stone walls of the meeting chamber. Chev raised his hands. "This is a rare moment where I feel a discussion of his life before coming to us as Kindred is not only prudent but necessary."

I thought of not answering. This was a violation of my rights. As far as the Kindred are concerned, no one has a life before their life underground. Our lives start with the appreciation of small flowers, from the time we notice a spot of brightness and pause to take it in. When the city forgets us and we slip through the cracks, we are born again beneath the streets.

But Beth looked scared. Her cheeks, rosy with chill a moment before, had gone white. I couldn't have that. For her sake, I let the fight fall from my shoulders.

"It was a car accident. My wife and daughter were driving home from the ballet. A drunk driver struck them. They both died."

I felt Beth's small hand then, inside my own. It was already taking on the cold of the underground, but it warmed me better than any sun that I remembered.

Chev's gambit had worked against him, and the Kindred shot him troubled glances as they crept away into their tunnels, to their tarp homes to cultivate their small patches of flowers. In hope of catching a Beth of their own.

Beth clutched her tarp to her chest, her red sweater darkening in the damp air of the tunnels.

"I'm sorry about your daughter." Her pupils stretched wide in the darkness, searching for scraps of light. Soon they would learn to fix open into the black stare of the Kindred, able to pull in the light from a storm drain three tunnels down.

I squeezed her small hand. "You're my daughter, now. And the only one in all the understreets."

She was silent, then. I thought it was out of shyness. But knowing her now, I believe she was thinking. Planning.

"Why doesn't anyone else have children?" Beth crumbled compost over the delicate buttercup sprouts that lined the old brick wall.

"Most of us are very old. Only the very old and the very young stop for small flowers anymore. And the young these days are older than the young that used to be. There are too many cares on their shoulders to bother with a small bit of brightness underfoot." I looked at how her arms bent to her task—willowy and lean. "And you are very old or very young, for a newborn."

I could hear her thinking in the way that she breathed. Slow and shallow, like a rush of fresh air might interrupt her train of thought. Though the air isn't fresh. Not down here and not up there.

"Do you miss your mother, Beth?" I shouldn't have asked it. I should have done as Kindred do and pretended she'd never had one. That the canal through which she was born was a drain—her caul the tender leaves of sidewalk weeds.

"I never knew her. I don't miss the nuns. They never let us play in the dirt." She ran her fingers through the black soil at the base of an unfurling sprout.

It's not uncommon for a Kindred. It's easier to slip through the cracks when no one is looking.

"Are you bored, Beth? Are you lonely?"

"No." She plucked at a mushroom sprouting from ancient grout and popped it in her mouth. "But maybe a little. Or maybe just worried."

I paused in my digging and fixed my black eyes on her. "Worry leaves no room for small flowers." It's what Belle had told me once, when I was newborn to the understreets, before the sun had faded from my skin and my collar sprouted lichen.

"But I'm worried *about* the Kindred, Aemon."

"No need for that, child. We left our worries aboveground."

"But if there are no other children, who will there be when the elders are gone?"

"No one, love."

"But who will tend the flowers?"

"No one. Might be that's an end for small flowers in the city above. Or might be that they never needed tending. Might be that the tunnels will fill with streams of wild buttercups."

She smiled through the dark and I saw her eyes were as black as mine. But then her smile wilted and her pupils shrank to pinpricks—her eyes wide discs of blue.

"I'll be alone, then. When all of you are gone. That can't happen," she said, and jabbed her trowel into the offal piled under a drain.

Toes tapped like the incessant drip of water, echoed through the meeting chamber as we waited. Beth balanced along an old train rail, dragging her toes through the grit, oblivious to the empty seat that held the elders rapt.

Roz never came.

The agenda was cast aside in favor of organizing a search. Chev knew where her tarp was, but none knew her fishing spot—her crack in the sidewalk where she held her flower, hopes high.

"Her knees have ague," Dane said, "It won't be far from her tarp."

No maps are allowed in the understreets, but any

Kindred worth his muck can follow the glowing fissures in the street overhead. It's the branching vascular system of our world.

Dane found Roz in a bright beam of light pouring from the hole where a slab of sidewalk had fallen in and crushed her. Her fragile frame curled in at jointed angles, like a dry spider. She held a fistful of buttercups—one still pinched in her outstretched fingers. The flowers drank in the light and glowed with it.

We squeezed our eyes against the glare, wrapped strips of black cloth across them, and felt our way toward her. She had to be moved before the sunwalkers found her—before their light-kissed faces peered curiously through the hole, now a window to our world.

There was a rustling and crunch of gravel.

"Aemon, what should we do with her flowers?" A small voice echoed from somewhere in front of me. I peered at her from beneath my cloth. She stared at Roz's fallen form, her face pinched in a familiar kind of pain. Her childhood had faded from her in that moment—her shoulders squared and fists clenched.

"Beth, get away from there! The street here isn't stable. Put your blindfold on and stand back."

"I don't need a blindfold, Aemon, the light doesn't hurt after a minute or two." She kneeled and took Roz's hand in her own.

Chev's deep voice came from the left, "Obey your father, child. If you would be Kindred, your eyes must be attuned to the dark. Light poisons them. Shun it."

"The light isn't poison. Our flowers need it—so we need it. We need *more* of it," Beth said.

Heavy footfalls fell beside me. I ripped off my blindfold.

Chev had removed his as well, and he sprinted to

Beth, grabbed her ear, and dragged her from Roz's sunbeam. My eyes burned in the light. Chev swung her by the ear into my arms. He narrowed his black eyes to see, and glowered. "Your duty is to raise her as Kindred. If you fail in this duty, you will be banished. I'll raise her myself. Properly."

Beth clutched at the redness of her ear peeking from between her curls.

Dane stood from where he'd cleared the concrete from Roz's crushed form. Raw pinkness bubbled up from where she had folded. "You can't banish a Kindred, Chev. And even if you could, you shouldn't. We need every Kindred who comes to us."

"If you could see her eyes right now, Dane, you'd know she isn't one of us."

Beth's eyes were as wide and blue as the sky. Sunlight danced across their shining surfaces. My own eyes had stopped burning, and I stared in wonder at the way the concrete dust sparkled in the beam of light.

"Change takes time," Dane said. He hefted Roz into his arms. "I only hope we've got *enough* time." He walked into the tunnel, heading for the Last Drain, the final resting spot of all Kindred.

Beth handed me a bouquet of Roz's buttercups. She grinned. Light glinted off her snaggletooth smile. "Your eyes are green," she said.

Roz's tarp was patched, washed and folded, and handed to Chev at the next meeting, ready to be given to the next child, whenever one might come to us.

Beth sat in Roz's empty chair. Chev overlooked it, though his brow lowered at the breach in decorum. There were now more chairs than elders.

Chev stood with his fists clenched in his coat pockets. "We are here to discuss new openings found to the street above. Has anyone witnessed promising new fishing grounds?"

No one answered. Beth toyed with a strand of yarn that had unraveled from the cuff of her cardigan. Her black eyes roved over the circle of elders. "Have you checked at the new museum?" She flinched as all eyes turned to her. I reached for her hand.

"What museum, child?" Belle asked.

"There's a new children's learning center, up on Wilson Stree—"

"We do not name streets here," Chev bellowed, his voice frothing into a white cloud in front of his mouth.

Beth stared at him. The soft lines of her face hardened. "In the far west sector, there is a new children's museum. They have a large parking lot, and a playground. The concrete is fresh. It may crack when it settles."

Dane stood. "I have no new fissures to report in the far west sector. But I will check there often in the next few weeks." He nodded his thanks to Beth.

"Have you tried—" Beth's voice trailed off as Chev hissed at her further interruption. She lowered her eyes.

I squeezed her small, cold hand.

Belle stood. "I would like to hear what the child has to say."

Beth slid off the end of her chair, shoes tapping against the damp brick. "Have you tried making a crack?" she asked. "Splitting a small hole in a spot where you know our flowers might be seen?"

Chev made a sound like a drain. "If finding small flowers were so easy, those that found them would not be Kindred," he said. "The Kindred are drawn to them because they are looking for something—and only in that moment understand that they have found it. It is a rare person who stops for small flowers."

"But what if it isn't? What if Kindred are not rare at all? What if they're just in the wrong place?"

Chev's voice rose and echoed through the tunnels. "A Kindred still looking for their flower is not yet ready for the understreets. This meeting is over." He stalked from the chamber, vanishing into the tunnel that led to his tarp.

The other elders remained in their seats, looking at Beth.

"We don't have many tools," Dane said.

Beth held her trowel out, small fingers curled around the worn handle; its blade flashing in light so faint that even our gaping pupils strained.

Beth slipped the edge of her trowel into the seam where the rough under-grit of road met the smooth sidewalk near a drain, where the road had been opened before and worked soft. She twisted and pushed, digging away at loosened slag until a small seam of light opened and grew across her knuckles. She pushed the metal in farther. The plane of pavement shifted.

Beth's dark hair was showered with grey dust that sparkled in the light from the new fissure. She turned to me and smiled. I traded a flower for her trowel, and she raised it into the daylight. We breathed the fine dust that hung in the air.

Laughter and joyful shouting spilled through the beam of light. Within moments, the flower was pinched. The world blurred, as it always did at the birth of a Kindred. A deep scrape, as if all the streets of the city above were sliding over the tunnels, sounded in my ears. Like the world pulling apart and then falling back together.

Beth tumbled to the tunnel floor, a fair young boy in her arms. His hair was so bright it stung my eyes. He smiled at Beth, and wrapped his chubby arms around her neck.

Trowels chimed like small bells against the rough rock overhead. All through the tunnels, they made music, and seams of light opened across the understreets. So much light that new flowers bloomed—ones we hadn't seen since our sunwalker days. Our faces pinched, adjusting to the new brightness in our world. Our black eyes began to shrink back into a multitude of color.

"I wonder what color Chev's eyes are?" Beth dug at a sooty spot overhead. A small rush of dirt dusted her hair. She coughed and scrambled back as a chunk of concrete fell at her feet and shattered. The sounds of a busy street tumbled down through the new hole.

"I don't think we'll ever know, darling. I don't think he's coming back. And if he does—be kind to him. He doesn't even remember the sun." I collected the fistful of flowers that the bright boy—Beth had named him Bracken—harvested from our small patch.

He never spoke a word, but smiled and followed Beth everywhere. His feet were bare and unflinching against the cold tunnel floor and his golden hair soon took on the texture of seaweed.

In Chev's absence, the Kindred's gapped smiles twinkled in falling bars of sunlight. The old adoption rituals were abandoned. Every elder now had a child—some two—and laughter sounded in the underground for the first time in living memory. There were now more children than tarps. The future of our line was secure.

A sound like a siren wailed through the tunnels. Kindred crawled from under tarps, blinking in the light. As the sound fell and then rose again, I realized it was a child. Crying. I raced around corners, down tunnels, now unfamiliar in their sunlit map, until I found the source of the cries.

Belle held a young girl in her arms, fresh from the streets above. The girl pushed at Belle's face, her eyes wide with fear.

Belle looked to me, bewildered, her brows raised, raining concrete dust across her cheek. "What do I do? Why is it crying?"

Chev stepped out of the tunnel behind her. His face had grown gaunter, his eyes even blacker than before, as if he'd sheltered someplace deep, away from our growing light. "Because it isn't Kindred. That's a sunwalker child you've pulled down. Your greedy opening of the streets is contaminating our world."

Belle looked in horror at the child, and dropped it. It scrambled away from her, backed to the wall, and reached up for the light from the hole Belle had dug. A woman was screaming in the street above, and the child screamed in answer.

Beth ran up behind me, her face pale, her hand clamped around Bracken's fist.

"Go home, you two," I said. "Let us handle this."

The commotion aboveground intensified. The roaring screech of power tools sounded from the drain grate nearby. The understreets concussed with the assault of a jackhammer.

"They're coming," Chev said. "Leave the child and run. Its kind will claim it soon. Hide—or you're finished. We all are."

Beth lifted Bracken's feet from the ground and clutched him to her chest as she splashed down the tunnel. I limped after them.

"Pack the tarps," I called to the disappearing bob of her curls.

The Kindred packed their homes on their backs and vanished into the network of tunnels as the sunwalkers broke through to reclaim their stolen child. Dust rained all along the cracks we'd made—our unnatural breaches widened under the stress of the city's machines.

Beth, Bracken, Chev, Belle, and I huddled in an enclave, listening to their frantic mission. A loud crack echoed from the tunnel. It traveled, ripping along the underground network. The air filled with dust. A roar like a wrecking train followed. And then all went black with soot, then as bright as day.

The stone all around us seemed to roar, the bricks at our backs throbbing with the vibrations of the world coming undone. Tides of dust rolled past our enclave, chased by light strong enough to throw our shadows against the walls.

The city had fallen. The understreets were now the settling ground for the rubble of that which had rested above our heads. Small tracts of tunnel remained, clogged with debris.

Chev rubbed at his eyes and gasped as the pure sunlight raked at his pale face. Beth reached up and took his face in her hands. His breathing slowed. His eyelids split and peeled back to reveal nothing but a field of white shot through with bulging red capillaries. The red spread through the sclera like a stain. His pupils had contracted to nothing, sealed, shut off from the light forever. Beth's hands flinched back.

"You see what you've done, child? That's an end to us all. The sun has risen on the understreets, and the time of the Kindred is over."

I pulled Beth and Bracken behind me. Belle reached out and stroked Chev's cheek. "What do we do now?" she asked.

Chev choked on another wave of dirt blowing through our small section of tunnel. He grasped Belle's hands to his cheeks and a tremor slipped into his voice. "We do what we have always done. We follow the tunnels. Whatever is left of them."

"But where?" Belle asked. In the light, her bulging white knuckles writhed like compost grubs.

"To the only place left—the last place, the Last Drain."

Chev shoved Beth in the small of her back. She stumbled through the knee-deep water toward the metal grate. "You're the expert with a shovel, child. Now, dig."

I grasped Chev's wrist and squeezed till he let out a grunt. "Touch her again, and I'll send the rest of you where your pupils have gone." Rage made me young again. But Chev pulled away from me and spat into the reeking water.

Belle held Bracken out of the water and stroked his damp curls. "Enough, the both of you. You wear my nerves worse than the sirens."

The crooning alarms hadn't quit since the dust had settled. The city above had rushed to the aid of its fallen streets. Crumbled houses wedged like barricades along our ancient pathways. Dane's tunnel was gone. He and his three children were somewhere beneath the ruin of a home that had had green curtains and white walls.

Chev flinched with every strike as Beth's trowel chimed against the cement that encased the bars blocking the opening of the Last Drain. Her brow furrowed in concentration. "I don't understand . . ."

"Don't understand what, love?" I watched as her breathing turned slow and shallow again.

"If this is where you take the Kindred when they die, why isn't there space already? How do they get through?"

Belle looked to me and shook her head.

Chev nodded to the grate. "You'll find out soon enough, child. Sooner, the faster you dig."

With the bar pulled free, we squeezed through the gap, the water at our feet flowing in a current that pulled us toward the space beyond.

"There," Chev said. "We have passed through the Drain. All the Kindred are dead, now."

Beth's fingers scuttled up the side of my coat, gripping their way to my elbow. "Aemon?" She swept her foot across the unseen floor of the drain tunnel. "What are we standing on?"

The floor rolled beneath us, shifting like a landslide.

"Your ancestors," Chev said. "Or my ancestors." He reached into the dark and pulled a skull from the slick water. "I'm not certain they'd accept you as their own. Not after what you've done." He held the stone face up to Beth's. "Look into their black eyes and apologize, girl, so they may let us pass safely over their graves."

"Enough, Chev!" Belle took the skull from him. She kissed its brow and lowered it back into the water. "What do they care anymore?"

We stumbled over the rolling bones of our ancestors till the drain's pull grew heavy and its current pressed us against another grate. Beth hammered at the concrete while Bracken pulled, leveraging his tiny weight against the bars. When their arms grew tired, Belle and I took over. And when we wearied, Chev took the trowel from us and drove it into the crumbling rock.

"It seems there are drains beyond the Last Drain," Beth said, rubbing the ache in her elbow.

Chev paused, running his fingers through the water.

"There are whole worlds outside of what you know, aren't there?" she pressed. "This isn't the end at all."

The water beyond the grate ran clearer, the floor smooth brick interrupted with rusted train tracks. Numbered doors dotted the walls at intervals. Chev eyed them suspiciously, as if they would burst open and pour forth an army of angry sunwalkers.

The water grew lower and lower, disappearing through invisible cracks, till it ran in isolated rivulets. Beth's cardigan trailed loose strings into it like trolling lines from a fishing vessel. The tunnel echoed with gurgling—the sound of water falling. Belle had begun to squint and I realized that the tunnel was growing lighter.

The floor sloped to a low dip where the last water trickled into a grated drain. Chev stopped.

He crouched over the drain and pressed his face against its darkness. "Here is our path," he said.

No one responded.

"Give me the trowel." He held a gnarled hand out to Beth. She handed him the tool and stepped back.

"Daylight bathes the understreets. We must go under again. Under-under. The Kindred belong beneath it all, where *rare* flowers grow." He threw himself against the bricks, driving the trowel between them.

"Or maybe . . . " Beth looked over her shoulder at the growing glow at the end of the tunnel. Her eyes flashed a small sliver of blue. "Maybe we should keep going."

Chev tossed a loose brick over his shoulder into the shrinking puddle behind them.

"We could teach them, up above. Show them. We don't love small flowers any less for being in the light. *That's* what makes us Kindred." Beth moved toward Chev.

Chev panted and heaved at another brick. The edge of the grate showed through the old grout like an exposed ribcage. He laughed with what little air he could draw, but his smile faltered.

"Maybe you're right, child," he said.

Belle and I looked to each other. She pulled Bracken close.

"You were right about the Last Drain, after all." The fight had gone out of his voice.

"What about it?" Beth took a step closer to Chev, her toes edging up to where he lifted the groaning metal from the stones.

"That wasn't the Last Drain." He swung his legs into the dark hole. He handed the trowel back to Beth. "This is."

He vanished into the dark, falling with the water that spilled over its edge, its droplets glowing like bright eyes in the rising glow from the end of the tunnel. We never heard him land.

At the end of the tunnel, the metal of Beth's trowel flashed like fire against the crumbling rock. When she paused, we saw our faces in it, pale and veined, pinched against the sting of pure daylight. Bracken reached

through the bars and grasped at the tall grasses that grew up against the opening. I lay my palm against the bricks, the end of the understreets, and said a quiet goodbye to my home.

When we broke through into the stiff grass, we sank into it, burying our faces from the sun, and slept.

We woke as the sun dipped behind a distant hill, relieving our eyes from its sting. We were curled in a ditch—our tunnel set into the side of a hill that overlooked the fallen city. Clouds of dust rose from its ruin, glowing in places where flames shot from tears rent in gas lines and electric hubs. Between us and its endless light, the hill stretched, full of flowers. Blue, like Beth's eyes. Curling leaves green, like mine.

Bracken ran into the field, hopping over and around the flowering clusters, lowering his face to the bright blooms.

We waded onto the hillside. Perfume rose around us and masked the dank funk of the compost and tunnel water.

"Can we live here? Can we make a living like this?" Belle clutched her hands to her chest. Tears traced pale tracks across her dusty face.

"I suppose we'll try." I reached for her hands and pulled them away from her heart, folding them into my own.

Beth called after Bracken. He danced away down the hill toward a tall rose. He cartwheeled around it, a breathless singsong of joy tumbling up the hill back to us. Beth ran toward him. "Bracken—" Her voice strained, the last syllable of his name a wail.

He righted himself and reached for the tall stem. The peach bloom bobbed, orange in the light from the setting sun. He wrapped his small fist around the barbed stem and cried out from the sting of its thorns. The hill seemed to roll beneath our feet as if the earth had turned to water. Bracken vanished.

Beth screamed.

Belle and I ran to her, long grasses catching at our feet. Beth had fallen, sobbing into a patch of blue flowers. I pushed her hair back from her face, cupped her cheeks in my hands.

"Shh, Beth, shh."

She wailed like a sunwalker.

Belle wrapped Beth in her shawl. "That boy goes where he's meant to. He's a new kind of Kindred. He knows tunnels, and cities, and fields. He pulled at the tallest flower—and someone, somewhere, knows that makes him special. Might be it's Chev, in the under-under, building a new world. And when we're ready, he'll hold a flower for us, child. Don't cry."

Beth rolled out of her embrace and ran her fingers through the grass, pinching each flower she came to, pulling at it, ripping it from the ground and moving on to the next. She carved a barren path in the hillside.

Belle and I sat in the blue flowers and watched her trail lengthen in the stretching dark.

"She won't find it that way." Belle brushed torn petals from her shawl and wrapped it back around her shoulders.

"She'll realize that soon."

"But will she realize it before she pulls out all the roots?"

"No. Not her." My heart ached for her, but I smiled. "That one breaks worlds."

"Then how will we find the lad?"

"He'll be at the other end of whatever flowers are strong enough to grow back."

HIRAETH

RICHARD THOMAS

DOWN THE RIVER from the struggling village, a tiny farmhouse sat at the edge of a massive forest, shrouded in the shadows of oak, pine, and flowering dogwood. There wasn't much on this farm, the land hard and difficult to till, but it's all they had. They grew potatoes, the tubers somehow able to survive, the father a scowling presence in all of his height and bluster; the mother always in another room, busy with anything else; the boy forever expanding the hole that grew inside his chest.

Today the boy would go to town, a cart filled with the misshapen crop, a bent donkey pulling him forward. The father stood with his arms crossed, as he often did, lips moving, a litany of curses whispering into the air. His overalls were stained, the long-sleeved thermal shirt underneath torn in several places, stretched over his biceps, his fingernails grimy with soil. The mother wrung her hands, and then wiped them on her apron, her own incantations tumbled into the ear of the exhausted farmer. Sometimes it worked, and sometimes it didn't. To confront him head-on would be unwise.

"Be safe, son," she shouted, waving, as the boy sat

down in the wagon, ready to go, to be anywhere but here. "No stopping along the way," she grimaced.

He smiled, turning his head and waved back. He knew she meant well. And he knew what she meant.

"Be smart, boy, get the full value this time, no bartering for trinkets we don't need to stave off winter."

"Yes, father."

"What does that mean, exactly?" the man asked. A familiar rote that he had taught the boy was what he referenced.

"Oil and coin and coal will suffice, canned fruits and vegetables are also nice."

The mother beamed, as the father stared, waiting.

"Go on," he said.

The blue sky clouded over, a few drops of rain pitting the dusty road.

"Toys and games and cards bore fast, barter only for goods that you know will last."

The father nodded. "Go on, looks like rain."

The boy sighed, cracked the reins, and moved ahead, toward the town. He scratched at his flannel shirt, his faded jeans cuffed, dark boots placed on the footrest. The hole in his chest grew, and the young man took a deep breath. Over the hill and down the road a hedge of thorny bushes held a glistening array of golden fruit. The boy vowed that today he would take one, no matter the cost.

Finally away from the glare and sharp tongue of his father, the whispering ghost of his frail mother, and the endless rows of festering potatoes, Jimmy cracked his neck, shrugged his shoulders, and took in the land around him. A fire burned in the woods to his right, a single wisp of smoke slipping up into the sky. Hunters, most likely. The land was filled with roaming packs of albino wolves, their pink eyes and tongues the last thing most wandering villagers saw before they were torn limb from limb. Often when he stopped for a piss, stepping to the edge of the forest, he would spy an array of bones, with teeth marks running across them—rodents and rabbits, antelope and deer, even bison and elk at times. Now and then, femurs, ribs, and skulls that could only have come from men.

Cresting the hill, the threat of rain still looming, a cool breeze pushed across the land, the scent of pine and cedar filling the air, paired with the musky scent of something sweet starting to rot. And at the base of the road, just before the creek and the trembling bridge, the Gilly bushes sat in all their glory.

There were many myths and stories told across the land—the albino wolves, which Jimmy had never seen, just one of them.

There were Garuda that lurked at the edge of the cliffs to the east, sulking in their caves, diving down to snatch up fish, and wayward children, from the drying lakes. It is said that the Garuda had the body, arms, and legs of a man, but the wings, head, and talons of an eagle. Jimmy didn't believe in them, the boy at the market where he was headed today always waving a giant yellow feather, or two, holding up eggs as large as his head. Ostrich, was what Jimmy thought; that was what he told himself when the nights grew long and empty.

There were stories about bunyip lurking in the swamps down south, bulbous eyes fixed to the front of an elongated head—some versions with a long, forked tongue, others with yellowing fangs—webbed feet capped by sharp claws, a tail sometimes mentioned with thin, piercing spikes. When the boy and his father went fishing several months ago—a constant stream of curses, scowls, and insults filling the air—the oddly shaped object they found by the water wasn't a saber-tooth, merely petrified wood. That's what his father said.

And there had always been talk of witches in their midst—tales of pale flesh encircling fires under the light of a waning moon; cauldrons bubbling over with exotic spices, herbs and exotic animal flesh; markings on doors, and hushed spells conjured in the darkness of the local pubs, for a fee. But Jimmy didn't believe it. Not really. Not much.

Maybe a little. Maybe now.

He lifted his shirt and ran his long fingers over his bony chest, slipping them gently over the edge of the hole that ran all the way through him. His hands trembled as he poked and prodded, a knot settling into his gut.

Jimmy paused the wagon, the donkey eager to drink from the stream. He released the beast from its harness, and stepped toward the bramble of thorny bushes, his eyes darting back and forth, searching for travelers, and wandering townspeople. The bushes were off limits, and had been, for as long as James could remember.

It was forbidden.

The dark vines and branches were nearly black, with veins of chartreuse running through the stalks and leaves. They were ugly—and in fact, might have been mistaken for dead if it weren't for two things—the handful of red berries that dotted the bushes, poisonous if eaten, a rash erupting on your skin from their juice; and the startling gleam of the golden fruit that rested in the center of each bush. The Gilly fruit was somewhere between an apple and a pear, not quite round, lumpy with dull orange leaves at the stem. The inside, it had been said, was a garish striping of purple and white, the core a rotten brown, its pulp juicy and sweet.

Jimmy stared at the fruit, eager to take one. He only had two choices—keep his sleeves rolled down and possibly tear them, incurring the eventual wrath of his parents, or push them up and risk the thorns slicing at his skin.

He rolled up his sleeves and went to work.

Knowing he didn't have much time—for surely another farmer would be along soon, this road well-travelled, the main artery back and forth to the market. Standing close to the prickly bush, he slowly inserted his right arm, reaching for the fruit. If only he could grab it—the flavor, the sweetness, the rumors of its healing properties, the talk of its nourishing meat. The key was to stay balanced, his left hand cocked on his hip, to offset his outstretched arm. Slowly he extended, a long thorn sliding along his wrist, nipping at the flesh, a line of blood drawn up from his skin. He kept going. Bending his arm at the elbow, he turned his head so he could lean his shoulder closer, the branches constricting around his forearm, the space and gap lessening.

"Dammit," he cursed.

The donkey brayed, backing away from the water, and the spikes grazed his arm as he shifted, losing his balance, a wagon in the distance coming closer. He pulled his arm out quickly, cutting and piercing his skin in the process.

"Damn stupid animal," he yelled at the donkey. "I see them coming already."

His arm stung, blood dotting the skin, a gouge across his wrist, shimmering and wet. The wagon approached.

Jimmy walked casually toward the donkey leading it back to the cart as it slowed and stopped.

"Everything okay, son?" a voice asked.

Jimmy nodded, pretending to struggle with the animal, eyes turned down.

"Just fine, thank you. Animal needed a quick drink, but he didn't want to come back to the wagon."

The man nodded, eying the boy. He was in a wagon of his own, the back empty but for a few smashed or rotten pumpkins, his overalls and shirt an echo of the boy's father, the straw hat on top the only embellishment.

"We're off to the market . . . potatoes," Jimmy said, nodding at the back of the wagon, strapping the donkey back into the harness.

"Ayup," the farmer said.

When the boy looked up, the man's gaze was on him.

"Might want to take care of that arm," the man said. "Won't help your business none when you get to town." The farmer cracked his whip, the dappled mare snorting, pulling them forward.

The boy looked down, the blood running to his fingertips, dripping into the dirt. With a weary sigh he walked down to the creek to wash off his arm, a small supply of bandages and cloth tucked into the back of his jeans pocket.

The market was a success—potatoes sold, all manner of coin, oil, and coal taken in return. A few jars of strawberry jam for his mother, which he knew would please her. Peaches, as well. Even a hand-rolled cigarillo for his father, which might go either way—a hand to the back of his head, or a grunt and a nod. But Jimmy didn't care. Nobody noticed the bandages poking out from under his sleeve, or if they did, they didn't comment. This sale was a ritual Jimmy performed several times during the harvest, and for once, it went off without a hitch.

He had one stop left before he went back home, the bakery for a loaf of fresh bread. He hoped that Suki was working today, her long black hair and emerald eyes as much of an attraction as the market, and the store. More so, even. He could smell the bread from here; the decadence.

Tying the donkey to a post out front, he went inside, the handful of coins jangling in his pocket. The bell over the door rang as he stepped inside, his heart pounding in his chest. She stood behind the counter, flour dusting her hands, as she rolled out the dough. He could hardly even see the rows of muffins, donuts, rolls, pretzels, bread, and pastries behind her, she was so radiant. Her eyes raised up to him, a smile spreading across her face.

"James, how good to see you." She was the only one that called him that. For a moment, the ache dissipated, and he almost felt whole.

"Hello, Suki. I've come for some baked goods. Do you have any loaves of French bread left?"

Suki wiped her hands on the apron, pushing up the sleeves of her light blue blouse. Her pale skin glowed faintly in the heat of the bakery, cheeks rosy, a forehead dotted with sweat. Mimicking her motion, his own skin flushing, he pushed up his sleeves, as well. He stood watching her as she pulled a loaf out from under the counter.

"Last one, just for you."

She eyed his arm and her smile lessened, and he followed her gaze, remembering now.

"Just some scratches from gathering kindling earlier today," he stuttered, pushing his sleeves back down. She handed him the loaf and he placed a coin in her outstretched hand.

"Be careful," she whispered. "It is forbidden."

"Ah, I don't know what you mean, Suki. Kindling, I said . . . "

"Your fingertips," she said, nodding her head in his direction.

He looked down and they were purple, easing into black.

"Oh my God, this never . . . " he stopped, eyes to her.

The bakery was suddenly too warm, and his stomach lurched.

Suki ran to the front door, flipped the sign to closed, and glanced out the window. The streets were quiet, most everyone gone home already, the market empty. She'd stayed open late just for him.

"Come here," she said, taking him by his left hand, leading him into the back.

Jimmy followed her into the dark room, the sun setting now, the last of the dying light slipping in through the open back door. The ovens were oppressive, even as they cooled down, the coals a shimmering glow.

"What are you doing?" he asked.

"Quickly, or you'll lose your fingers, maybe your hand, or arm."

Jimmy quieted, as she pushed him down onto a stool.

"Sit. Be still."

She went to the shelves, searching for something, pulling glass bottles and brown envelopes down, tinctures in various colors, a mortar and pestle, and a handful of wild greens out of a vase. She eyed him once, pursing her lips, as she poured powder, then a few drops of amber liquid into the bowl, adding a handful of flowers, and seeds. She crushed them all into a paste, dipped her finger into it, tasted it and then took the potion to him.

"What's this?" he asked.

She didn't speak, only lifted his hand, the fingertips now black, the thumbnail falling to the floor, where it broke into tiny pieces.

Jimmy stared on in horror.

Suki took his hand in hers and rubbed the mixture over his skin, the blackness fading instantly, as her own pale flesh started to darken.

"Your hands," he said.

"It will fade. I have gloves. I'm done today. It will be normal tomorrow."

His own hands tingled, her body close to him, perspiration on her upper lip, eyes wide, as she rubbed, and rubbed, and rubbed.

"Leave it alone," she said. "It's not worth it. It's actually kind of sour."

He stared at her, uncertain how to answer.

Suki turned her right arm over, one little scar running from her elbow to her thumb. It was faint, the thin white line barely visible, even up this close.

"I knew less then than I do now. This is a reminder to me. Some places you just don't want to go."

They looked down and his hand was back to normal, minus the one nail. Her hands were ashen, the pale gone slightly gray.

"It'll be fine, honest," she said. "But you should go."

Suki leaned over and kissed Jimmy on the lips. Nothing much mattered after that.

Or so he thought. Standing by the wagon, as the lights clicked off inside, Suki headed the other direction, no need for rumors, no need to spur on talk of their involvement. The village had a mean streak; it liked to see beauty undone. It would remain a secret for now. One of many.

The boy stood by the wagon, staring at the donkey, the beast looking away from him, as if in shame.

The cart was empty.

Jimmy's hand went to the necklace around his neck, a simple bauble that Suki had given him, to ward off evil spirits, she had said. To protect him. The leather strap ran through a rough silver coin, a hole drilled through it. On one side there was a griffin stamped into the tarnished metal, the back held an eye in the center of a pentagram.

He hoped it worked.

It was a long ride home, back down the dirt road, the night settling in around him, a movement in the woods that seemed alive. He was late. Stars slipped up into the sky, a harvest moon glowing red in the darkness, the sickness and rage slipping over his flesh. He knew what was coming, and he cursed the town for its petty greed.

The money in his pocket and the loaf of bread, they might save his life.

Or they might not.

He pushed the cart on anyway, headed home, the smattering of glowing fruit to his left mocking him as he rode over the bridge and up the hill to the farm. The coal, the oil, the strawberry jam for his mother, the peaches, and the peace offering smoke for his father.

All gone.

When he stopped in front of the house, his parents were outside before he could even put the donkey away, his mother's eyes gleaming with hope and promise, eager to see what he'd brought back. He walked to the barn and back, and by then her face had slipped into terror, worry for her only son's safety. And something else he's never seen before, a panic that she didn't wear very well. He handed her the loaf of bread, and turned to his father, who boiled with rage. Jimmy poured the coins into his hand, and looked him in the eye.

"I was robbed . . . "

And everything went black.

It took two weeks to recover—broken ribs, broken nose, bruises up and down his arm. He couldn't walk, the bandage undone in the melee, blood staining his sheets, his mother finally stepping in, crying, bawling, as he lay in the dirt twitching. He was no good to them hurt. In fact, they had to work twice as hard now to harvest what was still in the ground, the boy unable to help.

Not one for foresight, the father.

Jimmy couldn't breathe until they left for the market again.

"There might still be strawberry jam," he told his mother. "Peaches, too," he said, tears running down his face.

His mother was stone cold. Not because she didn't love him, but because he had put all of their lives at risk, nearly half of their harvest lost to his moment at the bakery. Neither of his parents blamed the thieves. It was his fault, from start to finish.

"Mother . . . " he began.

She placed a hand on his. She was tired, circles under her eyes, blisters weeping on her hands, lacking the strength to guide the plow, even with the donkey. Muffled noises had continuously slipped from their bedroom in configurations he tried not to imagine.

"I'll look. No need for *all* of us to suffer this winter," she said, a small smile creeping over her face. "I'll start on new blankets as soon as my hands heal. And you'll chop half the forest down before the snow settles in. We don't die on my watch," she said.

She slipped out the front door, and Jimmy heard the whip crack, and they left. For the first time in a fortnight the tension was gone. He lifted his shirt to look at his ribs, and the hole in his chest glared back at him. As wide as he was, all the way through. They didn't see it, his mother or father. They never had.

When he opened his eyes, Suki was sitting at the end of his bed.

"What are you doing here," he said, sitting up, groaning in pain, and then collapsing back down, his face gone pale.

"Shhhhhhh," she said. "Quiet. I knew your parents would come to town today. I'm home sick. Don't tell anyone."

He smiled.

"I don't have much time. I had to make sure you were alive. I heard what happened. The people of this town, their cruelty knows no end."

She placed her hand on his chest, running her thumb over the coin necklace, and then pulled her hand away.

"What?"

"Lift your shirt."

"What? No, Suki . . . what are you doing?"

She pulled his shirt up and gasped.

"My God, what have they done to you," she said.

"Broken ribs, I'll be okay."

"No, the other thing. This," she said, placing her hands gently on his stomach, "the hole. This can't stand."

Suki leapt up and went to a bag she had placed at the foot of the bed. She looked at him, paused for a moment, and then carried it back over.

She pulled out a ball of yarn, as large as a watermelon.

How it fit into her tiny bag, Jimmy didn't know. She began to unwind it, laying out the different colors. She tied them together, whispering into the strands.

"Red is for love, for passion and fire, the flesh of your body, the children you'll sire. Blue is for water, the substance of life, for tears shed in laughter, for husband and wife. Green is prosperity, growth for your soul, let flower and fauna help make you whole. Yellow is sunlight, may it shine down in glory, golden ripe harvest, a fairy tale story."

She continued, tying one piece of yarn to another, every color in her bag. When she was done, she raised up his t-shirt and placed the ball in the hole, where it fit snugly, a wince rippling through his face.

Suki leaned over and kissed him, her hands on his shoulders, as the hole started to shrink, her skin a heady perfume of butter, cinnamon, and a hint of vanilla, her tongue in his mouth sparking emotions for which he had no name.

Their secret would remain that way, his trips to the village hard to come by, but he was a creative boy. He put quite the dent in the forest, clearing trees, and fallen branches, piling up wood as high as the house. When his father finally told him to stop, Jimmy asked if he might keep going—sell some of the lumber to help offset their loss. The old man rubbed his grizzled jaw, and nodded his head in a reluctant acceptance.

In time, Jimmy would take the timber to the village, again and again, selling it cheap to those with no woodland of their own, but hearths still in need of warmth. Winter was looming, and the coal was long gone, the oil a distant memory, the oak and hawthorn a welcome gleam of hope.

He would visit Suki when the wagon was empty, sneaking off to the very woods that helped provide his newfound sustenance. They would couple in the darkness, the very blanket his mother made him underneath them, her scent a heady wonder Jimmy would cling to in the long empty nights back at home.

One night as he was leaving, he found a jar of strawberry jam on the end of the wagon. Two jars of peaches sat next to it.

Suki was not without her own imperfections—her hands on his waist as she wrapped her legs around his back, their bare skin glimmering in the moonlight. Her fingers slipped to the edge of the hole, caressing the scarred flesh, as he grew larger inside her, a glossy friction between them, his damage something she was drawn to, in measured doses.

In the afterglow, as the stars danced around them, she penned lines of poetry, one strip of paper at a time, conjuring images of gods and goddesses, whispering incantations and ancient fables. The paper was gently slipped into her watering mouth, wadded together into a sticky ball, and then placed gently in the shrinking void, not much larger than her fist.

Soon, the trips to the bakery were on foot, no more chores to be done, the biting cold of the season around them never enough to keep him away, his parents unwilling to support his infatuation, no time for such intimacies in their home. As the world grew dark around them, the glow of fire filled the windows of the village, logs burning gently in stove and fireplace alike. Jimmy stood in front of the bakery and stared for a moment at Suki, her belly swollen, her face alight as she hummed under her breath, the baked goods around her a golden wonder.

Jimmy went inside.

At the edge of the sprawling city a young man sat on the edge of his mattress, running a thumb over the scars on his left wrist, the itch inside his rib cage convincing him that the quickest path to a solution was not outside, or above, but within. The healing of his flesh held such sweet promise, the release of his own sabotage a heady relief. In his lap, a black cat purred, her emerald gaze quieted, the soft fur under his hand a calming presence. She had not moved in hours. Outside, the golden orb shone through the open blinds, the translucent drapes pulled back to reveal cars, buses, and children walking home from school, laughter spilling from their lips. There was a chill in the air, winter looming, a sharpness and bite to the wind. On the oak dresser a vanilla candle had melted down to a puddle of solidifying wax, no longer needed, surrendered to the night. James fingered the coin that rested on his chest, his heart stammering, the leather strap running around his neck, a hint of cinnamon in the air.

James heard a knock at the apartment door, and in his mind's eye, he saw another young man—not quite as skinny, not quite as pale—eager to come in, and sit with him, to palaver, deep into the darkness as the night expanded with sparkling stars.

ACKNOWLEDGEMENTS

To my wife, Jessica, and my children (Rocco, Evangeline, Luca and Francesca): Thank you for giving me the time and support I needed to bring this dream into being.

To the authors and artists: Thank you for taking a chance on another one of my ideas. Your work breathed life into this book in ways I couldn't have anticipated.

To the artists who helped inspire this anthology's concept and execution (including, but not limited to, Guillermo del Toro, Pee-Wee Herman, Rod Serling, Tim Burton, David Lynch, David Bowie, Tom Waits and Jim Henson): Thank you for filling my brain up with your dreams, visions and nightmares. Thank you for showing me that strangeness often signals beauty and that stories don't have to be just one thing—that darkness and light can coexist and enhance each other's depth. Thank you for your fearless individuality and for setting an example for the rest of us to aspire toward. You've scarred me for life in the most wondrous and productive ways.

To Joe Mynhardt at Crystal Lake Publishing: Thank you for making this book's production possible and for hustling hard on my behalf.

To the readers: Thank you, forever and always. Thank you.

THE END?

Not quite . . .

Have you read editor Doug Murano's *Gutted* anthology:

Gutted: Beautiful Horror Stories—an anthology of dark fiction that explores the beauty at the very heart of darkness. Featuring horror's most celebrated voices: Clive Barker, Neil Gaiman, Ramsey Campbell, Paul Tremblay, John F.D. Taff, Lisa Mannetti, Damien Angelica Walters, Josh Malerman, Christopher Coake, Mercedes M. Yardley, Brian Kirk, Stephanie M. Wytovich, Amanda Gowin, Richard Thomas, Maria Alexander, and Kevin Lucia.

Or dive into more Tales from the Darkest Depths:

Whispered Echoes by Paul F. Olson—Journey through the Heart of Terror in this eerie short story collection. Listen. They are calling to you. Do you hear them? They are the whispered echoes of your darkest fears.

Twice Upon an Apocalypse—Lovecraftian Fairy Tales—From the darkest depths of Grimm and Anderson come the immortal mash-ups with the creations of HP Lovecraft. These aren't your mother's fairy tales.

The Third Twin—A Dark Psychological Thriller by Darren Speegle—Some things should never be bred . . . Amid tribulation, death, madness, and institutionalization, a father fights against a scientist's bloody bid to breed a theoretical third twin.

Embers: A Collection of Dark Fiction—These short speculative stories are the smoldering remains of a fire, the fiery bits meant to ignite the mind with slow-burning imagery and haunting details. These are the slow burning embers of Cain's soul.

Aletheia: A Supernatural Thriller by J.S. Breukelaar—A tale of that most human of monsters—memory—Aletheia is part ghost story, part love story, a novel about the damage done, and the damage yet to come. About terror itself. Not only for what lies ahead, but also for what we think we have left behind.

Beatrice Beecham's Cryptic Crypt by Dave Jeffery—The fate of the world rests in the hands of four dysfunctional teenagers and a bunch of oddball adults. What could possibly go wrong?

Visions of the Mutant Rain Forest—the solo and collaborative stories and poems of Robert Frazier and Bruce Boston's exploration of the Mutant Rain Forest.

The Final Reconciliation by Todd Keisling—Thirty years ago, a progressive rock band called The Yellow Kings began recording what would become their first and final album. Titled "The Final Reconciliation," the album was expected to usher in a new renaissance of heavy metal, but it was shelved following a tragic concert that left all but one dead. It's the survivor shares the shocking truth.

Where the Dead Go to Die by Mark Allan Gunnells and Aaron Dries—Post-infection Chicago. Christmas. There are monsters in this world. And they used to be us. Now it's time to euthanize to survive in a hospice where Emily, a woman haunted by her past, only wants to do her job and be the best mother possible. But it won't be long before that snow-speckled ground will be salted by blood.

The Final Cut by Jasper Bark—Follow the misfortunes of two indie filmmakers in their quest to fund their breakthrough movie by borrowing money from one dangerous underground figure in order to buy a large quantity of cocaine from a different but equally dangerous underground figure. They will learn that while some stories capture the imagination, others will be the death of you.

Blackwater Val by William Gorman—a Supernatural Suspense Thriller/Horror/Coming of age novel: A widower, traveling with his dead wife's ashes and his six-year-old psychic daughter Katie in tow, returns to his haunted birthplace to execute his dead wife's final wish. But something isn't quite right in the Val.

Tribulations by Richard Thomas—In the third short story collection by Richard Thomas, *Tribulations*, these stories cover a wide range of dark fiction—from fantasy, science fiction and horror, to magical realism, neo-noir, and transgressive fiction. The common thread that weaves these tragic tales together is suffering and sorrow, and the ways we emerge from such heartbreak stronger, more appreciative of what we have left—a spark of hope enough to guide us though the valley of death.

Wind Chill by Patrick Rutigliano—What if you were held captive by your own family? Emma Rawlins has spent the last year a prisoner. The months following her mother's death dragged her father into a paranoid spiral of conspiracy theories and doomsday premonitions. But there is a force far colder than the freezing drifts. Ancient, ravenous, it knows no mercy. And it's already had a taste . . .

Eidolon Avenue: The First Feast by Jonathan Winn— where the secretly guilty go to die. All thrown into their own private hell as every cruel choice, every deadly mistake, every drop of spilled blood is remembered, resurrected and relived to feed the ancient evil that lives on Eidolon Avenue.

Flowers in a Dumpster by Mark Allan Gunnells—The world is full of beauty and mystery. In these 17 tales, Gunnells will take you on a journey through landscapes of light and darkness, rapture and agony, hope and fear. Let Gunnells guide you through these landscapes where magnificence and decay co-exist side by side. Come pick a bouquet from these Flowers in a Dumpster.

The Dark at the End of the Tunnel by Taylor Grant— Offered for the first time in a collected format, this selection features ten gripping and darkly imaginative stories by Taylor Grant, a Bram Stoker Award® nominated author and rising star in the suspense and horror genres. Grant exposes the terrors that hide beneath the surface of our ordinary world, behind people's masks of normalcy, and lurking in the shadows at the farthest reaches of the universe.

Little Dead Red by Mercedes M. Yardley—The Wolf is roaming the city, and he must be stopped. In this modern day retelling of Little Red Riding Hood, the wolf takes to the city streets to capture his prey, but the hunter is close behind him. With Grim Marie on the prowl, the hunter becomes the hunted.

Through a Mirror, Darkly by Kevin Lucia—Are there truths within the books we read? What if the book delves into the lives of the very town you live in? People you know? Or thought you knew. These are the questions a bookstore owner face when a mysterious book shows up.

If you've ever thought of becoming an author, we'd also like to recommend these non-fiction titles:

Horror 101: The Way Forward—A comprehensive overview of the Horror fiction genre and career opportunities available to established and aspiring authors, including Jack Ketchum, Graham Masterton, Edward Lee, Lisa Morton, Ellen Datlow, Ramsey Campbell, and many more.

Horror 201: The Silver Scream Vol.1 and *Vol.2*—A must read for anyone interested in the horror film industry. Includes interviews and essays by Wes Craven, John Carpenter, George A. Romero, Mick Garris, and dozens more. Now available in a special paperback edition.

Modern Mythmakers: 35 interviews with Horror and Science Fiction Writers and Filmmakers by Michael McCarty—Ever wanted to hang out with legends like Ray Bradbury, Richard Matheson, and Dean Koontz? *Modern Mythmakers* is your chance to hear fun anecdotes and career advice from authors and filmmakers like Forrest J. Ackerman, Ray Bradbury, Ramsey Campbell, John Carpenter, Dan Curtis, Elvira,

Neil Gaiman, Mick Garris, Laurell K. Hamilton, Jack Ketchum, Dean Koontz, Graham Masterton, Richard Matheson, John Russo, William F. Nolan, John Saul, Peter Straub, and many more.

Writers On Writing: An Author's Guide—Your favorite authors share their secrets in the ultimate guide to becoming and being an author. *Writers On Writing* is an eBook series with original 'On Writing' essays by writing professionals.

Or check out other Crystal Lake Publishing books for more Tales from the Darkest Depths.

ABOUT THE EDITOR

Doug Murano lives somewhere between Mount Rushmore and the mighty Missouri River. He is the Bram Stoker Award®-nominated co-editor of the best-selling, critically acclaimed horror anthologies, *Gutted: Beautiful Horror Stories* and *Shadows Over Main Street*.

He is an Active Member of the Horror Writers Association, and was the organization's promotions and social media coordinator from 2013-15. He is a co-recipient of the HWA's Richard Laymon President's Award for Service. Follow @muranofiction on Twitter.

ABOUT THE AUTHORS

Josh Malerman

Josh Malerman is the author of *Bird Box*, *Black Mad Wheel*, *Goblin*, and *Unbury Carol*. He's also one of the singer/songwriters for the band The High Strung. He lives in Ferndale, Michigan with his best friend/soul mate Allison Laakko.

Lisa Morton

Lisa Morton is a screenwriter, author of non-fiction books, award-winning prose writer, and Halloween expert. Her work was described by the American Library Association's Readers' Advisory Guide to Horror as "consistently dark, unsettling, and frightening," and Famous Monsters called her "one of the best writers in dark fiction today."

A rare Southern California native, Lisa's career as a professional writer began in 1988 with the horror-fantasy feature film "Meet the Hollowheads" (aka "Life On the Edge"), on which she also served as associate producer. For the Disney Channel's 1992 "Adventures in Dinosaur City," she served as screenwriter, associate producer, songwriter, and miniatures coordinator. Other screenplay credits include the feature films "Tornado Warning," "Blood Angels," "Blue Demon," and "The Glass Trap"; in addition, she wrote numerous episodes of the children's television series "Sky Dancers," "Dragon Flyz," "Vanpires," and "Toontown Kids." For stage she has written and co-produced the acclaimed horror one-acts "Spirits of the Season," "Sane Reaction," and "The Territorial Imperative," and has adapted and directed Philip K. Dick's "Radio Free Albemuth" and Theodore Sturgeon's "The Graveyard Reader." Her full-length science fiction comedy "Trashers" was an L.A. Weekly "Recommended" pick.

She has written more than 100 short stories, including the Bram Stoker Award-winning "Tested" (from *Cemetery Dance* magazine). In early 2010 her first novel *The Castle of Los Angeles* was published to critical acclaim, and was awarded the Bram Stoker Award for First Novel. Her novellas include *The Lucid Dreaming*, The *Samhanach*, *Hell Manor*, *Smog*, *Summer's End*, and *By Insanity of Reason* (co-authored with John R. Little). She also wrote the novels *Malediction* (nominated for the Bram Stoker Award for Best Novel), *Netherworld*, and *Zombie Apocalypse: Washington Deceased*. Her works have been translated into eight languages.

As a Halloween expert, Lisa wrote the definitive reference book T*he Halloween Encyclopedia* (now in a second edition), and the multiple award-winning *Trick or Treat: A History of Halloween*. She has spoken about the holiday in *The Wall Street Journal* and *The Boston Globe*, on the BBC and The History Channel, on the supplements for the Blu Ray release of the feature film *Trick 'R Treat*, and at the Utah Humanities Book Festival. She supplied a section on Halloween candy for *The Oxford Companion to Sugar and Sweets*, wrote the Halloween chapter for *The Art of Horror*, and served as consultant on U.S. Postal's first official Halloween stamps.

Her other non-fiction books include *The Cinema of Tsui Hark* (the first comprehensive study of the influential Hong Kong filmmaker), the award-winning *Witch Hunts: A Graphic History of the Burning Times* (co-authored with Rocky Wood, illustrated by Greg Chapman), and *Ghosts: A Haunted History*.

She currently serves as president of the Horror Writers Association, and is also an Active member of Mystery Writers of America, International Thriller Writers, and Sisters in Crime.

Lisa lives in North Hills, California, and can be found online at http://www.lisamorton.com.

Brian Kirk

Brian Kirk is an author of dark thrillers and psychological suspense. His debut novel, *We Are Monsters*, was nominated for a Bram Stoker Award® for Superior Achievement in a First Novel, and optioned for film development by Executive Producer Jason Shuman. His short fiction has been published in many notable magazines and anthologies, most recently *Gutted: Beautiful Horror Stories* alongside multiple New York Times bestselling authors.

Feel free to connect with him at www.briankirkfiction.com or on Twitter @Brian_Kirk. Don't worry, he only kills his characters.

Hal Bodner

Hal Bodner is a multiple Bram Stoker Award nominee, known for his best-selling gay vampire novel, *Bite Club* and the lupine sequel, *The Trouble With Hairy*. He tells people he was born in East Philadelphia because so few people know where Cherry Hill, New Jersey is located. The first person ever saw was the doctor who delivered him, C. Everett Koop, the future US Surgeon General. Thus, from birth Hal was ironically destined to become a heavy smoker—a habit he greatly misses.

He moved to West Hollywood in the 1980s and has

rarely left the city limits since. In fact, he is so WeHo-centric that he cannot find his way around Beverly Hills—the next town over. In a burst of over-optimism, he bought a six-bedroom mansion in Highland Park, a supposedly up-and-coming area of East Los Angeles. After three years of watching the street gangs doing drug deals in his back yard, he fled back to WeHo.

During his sojourn in East L.A., he was protected from the harm because of his habit of chasing his escaped pet peacock down Figueroa Boulevard at night, dressed in his fluffy bathrobe and fuzzy Cthulhu slippers while yelling "Apollo! Apollo! Come back!" None of the gang members would shoot him; they were laughing too hard.

His various professions have included stints as an entertainment lawyer, a scheduler for a 976 sex telephone line, a theater reviewer and the personal assistant to a television star. For several years, he owned Heavy Petting, a pet boutique where movie stars bought gold-plated water dishes and designer wardrobes for their Chihuahuas.

In the erotic paranormal romance genre—which he refers to as "supernatural smut"—he is best known for having written *In Flesh and Stone* and *For Love of the Dead*. His comic gay super hero trilogy will hopefully debut shortly with *Fabulous in Tights* to be followed by *A Study in Spandex*. With *Browne & Brownie: The Case of the Purloined Prince*, the first novel in a trilogy featuring a gay detective and his side-kick, the "madam" of an escort agency, Hal is busily turning classic noir fiction upside down and tinting it with a health splash of lavender.

Hal married a man roughly half his age who had no idea that Liza Minnelli and Judy Garland were related. In consequence, he has discovered that the use of hair dye is rarely an adequate substitute for Viagra.

Clive Barker

A visionary, fantasist, poet and painter, Clive Barker has expanded the reaches of human imagination as a novelist, director, screenwriter and dramatist. An inveterate seeker who traverses between myriad styles with ease, Barker has left his indelible artistic mark on a range of projects that reflect his creative grasp of contemporary media—from familiar literary terrain to the progressive vision of his Seraphim production company. His 1998 "Gods and Monsters," which he executive produced, garnered three Academy Award nominations and an Oscar for Best Adapted Screenplay. The following year, Barker joined the ranks of such illustrious authors as Gabriel Garcia Marquez, Annie Dillard and Aldous Huxley when his collection of literary works was inducted into the Perennial line at HarperCollins, who then published *The Essential Clive Barker*, a 700-page anthology with an introduction by Armistead Maupin.

Barker began his odyssey in the London theatre, scripting original plays for his group The Dog Company, including "The History of the Devil," "Frankenstein in Love" and "Crazyface." Soon, Barker began publishing his *The Books of Blood* short fiction collections; but it was his debut novel, *The Damnation Game* that widened his already growing international audience.

Barker shifted gears in 1987 when he directed "Hellraiser," based on his novella *The Hellbound Heart*, which became a veritable cult classic spawning a slew of sequels, several lines of comic books, and an array of merchandising. In 1990, he adapted and directed "Nightbreed" from his short story "Cabal." Two years later, Barker executive produced the housing-project story "Candyman," as well as the 1995 sequel, "Candyman 2: Farewell to the Flesh." Also that year, he directed Scott Bakula and Famke Janssen in the noir-esque detective tale, "Lord of Illusions."

Barker's literary works include such best-selling fantasies as *Weaveworld*, *Imajica*, and *Everville*, the children's novel *The Thief of Always*, *Sacrament*, *Galilee* and *Coldheart Canyon*. The first of his quintet of children's books, *Abarat*, was published in October 2002 to resounding critical acclaim, followed by *Abarat II: Days of Magic, Nights of War* and *Arabat III: Absolute Midnight*; Barker is currently completing the fourth in the series. As an artist, Barker frequently turns to the canvas to fuel his imagination with hugely successful exhibitions across America. His neo-expressionist paintings have been showcased in two large format books, *Clive Barker, Illustrator, volumes I & II*.

In 2012 Barker was given a Lifetime Achievement Award from the Horror Writer's Association, for his outstanding contribution to the genre.

Stephanie M. Wytovich

Stephanie M. Wytovich is an American poet, novelist, and essayist. Her work has been showcased in numerous anthologies such as *Gutted: Beautiful Horror Stories*, *Shadows Over Main Street: An Anthology of Small-Town Lovecraftian Terror*, and *The Best Horror of the Year, Volume 8* (edited by Ellen Datlow).

Wytovich is the Poetry Editor for Raw Dog Screaming Press, an adjunct at Western Connecticut State University, and a book reviewer for *Nameless Magazine*. She is a member of the Science Fiction Poetry Association, an active member of the Horror Writers Association, and a graduate of Seton Hill University's MFA program for Writing Popular Fiction. Her Bram Stoker Award®-winning poetry collections, *Hysteria: A Collection of Madness*, *Mourning Jewelry*, *An Exorcism of Angels*, and *Brothel* earned a home with Raw Dog Screaming Press, and her debut novel, *The Eighth*, is published with Dark Regions Press.

Her next poetry collection, *Sheet Music to My Acoustic Nightmare*, is scheduled to be released October 2017 from Raw Dog Screaming Press, and her short story collection, *Inside the Skin Bouquet* is set for a late 2017 release from Dark Fuse.

Follow Wytovich at http://www.stephaniewytovich.com/ and on twitter @JustAfterSunset.

John Langan

John Langan is the author of two novels, *The Fisherman* and *House of Windows*, and two collections of stories, *The Wide, Carnivorous Sky and Other Monstrous Geographies* and *Mr. Gaunt and Other Uneasy Encounters*. With Paul Tremblay, he co-edited *Creatures: Thirty Years of Monsters*. He is one of the founders of the Shirley Jackson Awards, for which he served as a juror during their first three years. Currently, he reviews horror and dark fantasy for Locus magazine. Forthcoming is a new collection of stories, *Sefira and Other Betrayals*. He lives in New York's Hudson Valley with his wife and younger son.

Neil Gaiman

Neil Gaiman makes things up and writes them down. Which takes us from comics (like *Sandman*) to novels (like *Anansi Boys* and *America Gods*) to short stories (some are collected in *Smoke and Mirrors*) and to occasionally movies (like Dave McKean's "Mirrormask" or the "Neverwhwere" TV series, or my own short film "A Short Film about John Bolton").

In his spare time he reads and sleeps and eats and tries to keep the blog at www.neilgaiman.com more or less up to date.

Ramsey Campbell

The Oxford Companion to English Literature describes Ramsey Campbell as "Britain's most respected living horror writer." He has been given more awards than any other writer in the field, including the Grand Master Award of the World Horror Convention, the Lifetime Achievement Award of the Horror Writers Association, the Living Legend Award of the International Horror Guild and the World Fantasy Lifetime Achievement Award. In 2015 he was made an Honorary Fellow of Liverpool John Moores University for outstanding services to literature. Among his novels are *The Face That Must Die, Incarnate, Midnight Sun, The Count of Eleven, Silent Children, The Darkest Part of the Woods, The Overnight, Secret Story, The Grin of the Dark, Thieving Fear, Creatures of the Pool, The Seven Days of Cain, Ghosts Know, The Kind Folk, Think Yourself Lucky* and *Thirteen Days by Sunset Beach*. He is presently working on a trilogy, *The Three Births of Daoloth*—the first volume, *The Searching Dead*, was published in 2016, and *Born to the Dark* is forthcoming. *Needing Ghosts, The Last Revelation of Gla'aki, The Pretence* and *The Booking* are novellas. His collections include *Waking Nightmares, Alone with the Horrors, Ghosts and Grisly Things, Told by the Dead, Just Behind You* and *Holes for Faces*, and his non-fiction is collected as *Ramsey Campbell, Probably. Limericks of the Alarming and Phantasmal* are what they sound like. His novels *The Nameless* and *Pact of the Fathers* have been filmed in Spain. He is the President of the Society of Fantastic Films.

Ramsey Campbell lives on Merseyside with his wife Jenny. His pleasures include classical music, good food and wine, and whatever's in that pipe. His web site is at www.ramseycampbell.com.

Erinn L. Kemper

Erinn L. Kemper lives on the Caribbean coast in Costa Rica where she writes, runs with her dog on the beach, and drinks ridiculous amounts of coffee, at least until happy hour. Erinn has sold stories to *Cemetery Dance* magazine, *Dark Discoveries* and *Black Static*, and appears in various anthologies including *You, Human, Shadows Over Main Street Volume 2*, and *Chiral Mad 3*. Visit her website at erinnkemper.com for updates and sloth sightings.

John F.D. Taff

John F.D. Taff has more than 90 short stories and four novels in print, including *The Bell Witch*. *Little Deaths* was named the best horror fiction collection of 2012 by HorrorTalk. His collection of novellas, *The End in All Beginnings*, was published by Grey Matter Press in 2014. Jack Ketchum called it "the best novella collection I've read in years," and it was a finalist for a Bram Stoker Award® for Superior Achievement in a Fiction Collection. His work has appeared recently in *Gutted: Beautiful Horror Stories*, the five-author novella collection *I Can Taste the Blood*, and in a freestanding novella *The Desolated Orchard* out from Cutting Block Books. *Recent sales have been to Let Us In, Vol. 1, Garden of Fiends and* Shadows Over Main Street 2. Learn more about him at johnfdtaff.com or follow him on Twitter @johnfdtaff and Instagram at johnfdtaff.

Patrick Freivald

Patrick Freivald is a four-time Bram Stoker Award®-nominated author, high school teacher (physics, robotics, American Sign Language), and beekeeper. He lives in Western New York with his beautiful wife, two birds, two dogs, too many cats, and several million stinging insects. A member of the HWA and ITW, he's always had a soft spot for slavering monsters of all kinds.

He is the author of the zombie teen novels *Twice Shy* and *Special Dead*, serial killer thriller *Blood List* (with his twin brother Phil), the kickass action-fantasy Matt Rowley novels (*Jade Sky*, *Black Tide*, and *Jade Gods*), a growing legion of short stories, and the *Jade Sky* graphic novella (with Joe McKinney) in *Dark Discoveries* magazine. There will be more.

Lucy A. Snyder

Lucy A. Snyder is a five-time Bram Stoker Award®-winning author of ten books and about 100 published short stories. Her writing has been translated into French, Russian, Italian, Czech, and Japanese editions and has appeared in publications such as *Asimov's Science Fiction*, *Apex Magazine*, *Nightmare Magazine*, *Pseudopod*, *Strange Horizons*, and *Best Horror of the Year*. She lives in Ohio and is faculty in Seton Hill University's MFA program in Writing Popular Fiction. You can learn more about her at www.lucysnyder.com and you can follow her on Twitter at @LucyASnyder.

Brian Hodge

Brian Hodge is one of those people who always has to be making something. So far, he's made eleven novels, over 125 shorter works, and five full-length collections.

Recent and upcoming titles include his latest novel, *Dawn of Heresies*; *I'll Bring You the Birds From Out of the Sky*, a novella of cosmic horror with folk art illustrations; and his next collection, *The Immaculate Void*, coming in early 2018. Two recent Lovecraftian novelettes have been optioned for feature film and a TV series.

He lives in Colorado, where he also likes to make music and photographs; loves everything about organic gardening except the thieving squirrels; and trains in Krav Maga and kickboxing, which are of no use at all against the squirrels.

Connect through his web site (www.brianhodge.net), Twitter (@BHodgeAuthor), or Facebook (www.facebook.com/brianhodgewriter).

Kristi DeMeester

Kristi DeMeester received her M. A. in Creative Writing from Kennesaw State University in 2011. Since then her work has appeared or is forthcoming in publications such as *Black Static*, *The Dark*, *Year's Best Weird Fiction* Volumes 1 and 3, and several others. Her debut novel, *Beneath*, was published by Word Horde in spring 2017. In her spare time, she alternates between telling people how to pronounce her last name and how to spell her first. Find her online at www.kristidemeester.com.

Christopher Coake

Christopher Coake is the author of the novel *You Came Back* (2012) and the story collection *We're in Trouble* (2005), which won the PEN/Robert Bingham Fellowship for a first work of fiction. In 2007 he was named one of Granta's Best Young American Novelists. His short fiction has been anthologized in *Best American Mystery Stories 2004* and *The Best American Noir of the Century*, *Gutted: Beautiful Horror Stories*, and published in journals such as *Granta*, *The Southern Review*, *The Gettysburg Review*, *Five Points*, and *The Journal*. A native of Indiana, Coake received an MA from Miami University of Ohio and an MFA from Ohio State University. He is an Associate Professor of English at the University of Nevada, Reno, where he directs the new MFA program in creative writing.

Sarah Read

Sarah Read is a dark fiction writer and freelance editor recently relocated from the foothills of Colorado to the frozen north of Wisconsin. Her short stories can be found in *Gamut*, *Black Static*, and other places, and in various anthologies including Exigencies and Suspended in Dusk. She also writes numerous articles about crocheting and fountain pens. She is the editor in chief at *Pantheon Magazine* and a member of the Horror Writer's Association. When she's not staring into the abyss, she knits. You can find her online on Instagram or Twitter @inkwellmonster or on her site at www.inkwellmonster.wordpress.com.

Richard Thomas

Richard Thomas is the award-winning author of seven books—*Disintegration* and *Breaker* (Random House Alibi), *Transubstantiate*, *Staring Into the Abyss*, *Herniated Roots*, *Tribulations*, and *The Soul Standard* (Dzanc Books). His over 100 stories in print include *Cemetery Dance*, *PANK*, *storySouth*, *Gargoyle*, *Weird Fiction Review*, *Midwestern Gothic*, *Arcadia*, *Qualia Nous*, *Chiral Mad 2* and *3*, and *Shivers VI*. He is also the editor of four anthologies: *The New Black* and the Shirley Jackson-nominated *Exigencies* (Dark House Press), *The Lineup: 20 Provocative Women Writers* (Black Lawrence Press) and the Bram Stoker Award®-nominated *Burnt Tongues* (Medallion Press) with Chuck Palahniuk. In his spare time he writes for *LitReactor* and is editor-in-chief at *Gamut Magazine*. For more information visit www.whatdoesnotkillme.com or contact Paula Munier at Talcott Notch.

ABOUT THE ARTISTS

Cover Artist: John Coulthart
John Coulthart is a British graphic artist, illustrator, author and designer who has produced book covers and illustrations, CD covers and posters. He is also the author of the critically acclaimed Lovecraft-inspired book *The Haunter of the Dark: And Other Grotesque Visions*, which contains a collaboration with Alan Moore entitled *The Great Old Ones* that is unique to this book and also has an introduction by Alan Moore). He was nominated for a British Fantasy Award, for Best Artist, in 2005. In 2012 he won the Artist of the Year award at the World Fantasy Awards. www.johncoulthart.com

Story Illustrations: Luke Spooner
Luke Spooner currently lives and works in the South of England. Having graduated from the University of Portsmouth with a first class degree he is now a full time illustrator working under two aliases; "Carrion House" for his darker work and "Hoodwink House" for his work aimed at a younger audience. He believes that the job of putting someone else's words into a visual form, to accompany and support their text, is a massive responsibility as well as being something he truly treasures. www.carrionhouse.com

Hi, readers. It makes our day to know you reached the end of our book. Thank you so much. This is why we do what we do every single day.

Whether you found the book good or great, we'd love to hear what you thought. Please take a moment to leave a review on Amazon, Goodreads, or anywhere else readers visit. Reviews go a long way to helping a book sell, and will help us to continue publishing quality books.

Thank you again for taking the time to journey with Crystal Lake Publishing.

We are also on . . .

Website
http://www.crystallakepub.com/

Books
http://www.crystallakepub.com/book-table/

Blog
http://www.crystallakepub.com/blog-2/

Newsletter
http://eepurl.com/xfuKP

Instagram
https://www.instagram.com/crystal_lake_publishing/

Patreon
https://www.patreon.com/CLP

YouTube
https://www.youtube.com/c/CrystalLakePublishing

Twitter
https://twitter.com/crystallakepub

Facebook page
https://www.facebook.com/Crystallakepublishing/

Google+
https://plus.google.com/u/1/107478350897139952572

Pinterest
https://za.pinterest.com/crystallakepub/

Tumblr
https://www.tumblr.com/blog/crystal-lake-publishing

We'd love to hear from you.